INDIRECT OBJECTS

Joe Lehrer Mystery #2

David Allen Edmonds

Indirect Objects is a work of fiction. Characters, events, places and dialogue are products of my imagination or are used fictitiously. Any similarities to actual events, places or persons, living or dead, is a coincidence.

Published by Snowbelt Publishing, Ltd.
Medina, OH

ISBN-13: 978-0-9985466-3-6
ISBN-10: 0-9985466-3-1

Cover design: Julie Bayer, State by Design
Editing: Jeff Gabel
Proofing: Sue Sayers; Amy Davis

To my grandchildren,

Benny,

Nick,

Finley,

Emma,

Hazel,

Blake,

and

Kellen:

May you

love books

and

diagraming sentences.

ACKNOWLEDGEMENTS AND THANKS

I am grateful and indebted to all those who helped bring *Indirect Objects* to life. I couldn't have done it without them.

Jeff Gabel, Sue Sayers, Amy Davis and Julie Bayer for their assistance in creating the book.

Peter Danczszak, Paul Kubis, Paula Lynn, Dori Stewart and the MCWC, The-All-Ladies-Except-For-Me Book Club and the Medina Men's Book Club for their reading and commentary.

Jean Lee, Bob Stowe, John Bruening, D.M. Pulley, Ken Schneck, Mindy McGinnis for their inspiration.

Hajni Blasko, Josh Grant, Courtney Davis, Judi Terrell Linden and local Indie Bookstores for their promotion of my work.

And Marie Mirro Edmonds for a lifetime of love.

DEFINITION OF
INDIRECT OBJECT

An indirect object tells *to* or *for whom* the action of the verb, however welcome or unwanted, is committed:

I gave *the gadfly* a piece of my mind.

I sent *Satchmo* a billet-doux.

The mannequin gave *the baby vampire* her phone number and returned to her window alone.

The Deluxe Transitive Vampire: The Ultimate Handbook of Grammar for the Innocent, the Eager, and the Doomed by Karen Elizabeth Gordon, 1993, Pantheon Books.

CHAPTER ONE

With a minimum of cursing and finger pointing, four men managed to find their way through the warren of twisting streets that comprised the Deer Woods Creek development.

Filya poked the young man driving the Corolla, and he pulled into a dark space between the feeble decorative streetlights. He set the binoculars against his face and peered at the house across the street. "Now we sit and wait."

Vadil beside him screwed a suppressor onto his weapon. "I hate waiting."

Filya adjusted the field glasses. The streets were bare, but several inches of snow covered the yards. The house was built like every other one on the block, two stories, wide front porches, two car garages. If they were different colors, the darkness hid it. "Me too, but at least we should wait for a target, shouldn't we?"

The driver pointed over the steering wheel. "Someone's coming." The kid was green and raw, a *shestyorka*. Filya would have to keep his eye on him.

A dark colored sedan stopped at the corner, turned right onto Hill Valley Drive and pulled into the driveway of the house across the street. They watched a man look to the left and right before climbing the steps onto the porch. He knocked once — Filya and his crew watched closely — and the door opened.

"No lights. Inside or out." This from Iosif in the front seat next to the newbie.

Filya noticed the time. "Nothing in his hands."

Several minutes later, the man exited the house, now carrying a small package. It looked to be wrapped in brown paper, but the four men in the car couldn't tell. As the car pulled out of the drive and made the left onto Stag Thicket Trace, another car was pulling into the driveway.

The scene was repeated several more times as the men watched from the shadows. "How much longer do we wait?" Vadil's knee was jumping up and down.

Filya leaned toward him. "Looks like the traffic is slowing down. You want to take a closer look?"

The big man tensed. "Da."

"Thought you would. Take Iosif and see what's going on inside. Looks like no one's home in the house to the right."

They were dressed in black, and easily blended into the shadows of the trees behind the houses. Filya glanced at his watch again. No traffic at the house, no cars passing by. The driver flinched as the rear door opened and Iosif dropped into the seat beside Filya.

"Didn't see you coming."

"Da. That's the point."

Filya would have slapped the insolence from the man's face, but his father had been the team leader, the *avtoritet*, before Filya. "What did you see?"

"Pill making machine in the basement," Iosif said.

"Two machines, *avtoritet*." Vadil twisted his head past the head restraint. "Mixing in the big room upstairs. Making pills downstairs."

"Doors?"

"Front porch, one on the deck in the back, one on the side of the garage," Vadil said.

"Did you see any money?"

"Kitchen. Upstairs in back. A big table. Woman sitting there counting." Iosif spoke quickly as if planning on keeping it.

Filya frowned. He wasn't expecting money. It would be a shame to leave it, but they had their orders. "How many people?"

"Six, no five."

Filya looked to the front seat. "Six," Vadil said.

"Stuff we can use?"

"Good size stones and branches from a dead tree."

Filya nodded. "Let's go."

Iosif carefully shut the trunk and followed Filya and Vadil around the darkened house next to their target. Each carried a dark duffel. The three men crept through the backyard to the access door of the garage. Iosif pointed to the row of soccer ball sized rocks lining the flower bed. Vadil picked one up and placed it in front of the door. Filya wedged a tree branch under the knob, and the three of them added more stones. At the leader's gesture, they silently moved around the back of the house.

The driver wiped the sweat from his hands several times as he watched the dashboard clock count off four minutes, then carefully pulled the car across the street into the driveway. He spun his head at the sound of a car backfiring in the distance, took a breath to calm himself, and walked up the four steps.

Filya motioned Vadil to stop at the edge of the deck. Iosif and he took up positions at basement windows on either side. All three readied their weapons and removed cylindrical objects from the bags. Filya held up a hand and listened.

The driver pinned the storm door with his shoulder and pulled the Glock from behind his back. The guard opened the front door, saw the gun barrel fluttering in front of him and lunged for it. The gun fired as the guard twisted to the side and drove his shoulder into the shooter. The driver stumbled back onto the porch and pushed the guard's hands away. The Glock fired again, tearing off the guard's index finger, embedding itself in the driver's foot. Both men staggered back. The guard held his bleeding hand against his chest; the driver looked dumbly at his foot. When the pain registered, the driver raised the pistol and fired. The guard raised his eyes and didn't move. The driver fired again, then a fourth time and finally the guard dropped onto the floor of the foyer. The driver stood over him and fired twice more. He stopped, panting, and looked to his flaming foot. He didn't know why it hurt so much.

Filya heard the shots and dropped his arm. Filya and Iosif slammed boulders through the basement windows, jammed their MP5s through the holes, and fired. Men scrambled for cover as the muzzles flashed and lead ricocheted wildly through the basement.

Vadil shattered the sliding door with another stone and followed the broken glass with a spray of bullets. A woman died at the counting table in the kitchen as bullets careened across the great room.

The three stopped firing and lit the fuses on their bombs. Iosef and Filya tossed theirs into the basement, Iosef aimed at the double-sided fireplace in the great room. As the Molotov cocktails whumped into fiery life, the men ran around the house.

Filya reached the front porch first and fired a burst over the driver's body into the house. Iosef appeared and together they dragged the wounded driver off the porch. Vadil kept his weapon facing the house. Flames burst from windows on the first floor and into the darkened backyard from the basement. No one was following them, no one was escaping.

They loaded the kid into the back seat, and Filya slid behind the wheel. He slowly backed into the street. Vadil leaned out the passenger window, his weapon still scanning the front yard. Another explosion sent sparks and flames into the black night sky.

Filya turned onto Stag Thicket Trace. Lights flashed on in one house, then another. He kept the car at twenty-five and wound his way past Joe Lehrer's house

5

and out of the development.

"And in conclusion, for all that he has done for the children of Stradford, I am pleased and honored to present one of the PTA Educator of the Year Awards to Mr. Joseph Lehrer." Madelaine Saylor stepped away from the podium and began applauding.

The irony that the PTA met on the stage of the school auditorium was not lost on Joe. For all the sanctity in her voice, this event was a show. Mrs. Saylor and her committee were giving the audience what they wanted. People moved to Stradford for the safe streets, big houses, green space and good schools. They left the crime, poverty, pollution and bad schools in Cleveland. She was showing the audience that everything was fine in Stradford.

A year ago, less than that, Joe would have extended the irony to include the kids in the drama club. On this same stage they pretended to be other people with other values. They played to an audience, just like their elders. They weren't lying, of course, they were reading lines and wearing costumes. They were in a play.

He took a long, slow breath. Politicians proclaiming from a stage. Kids acting on a stage. Now it was his turn to act his part: the Avenging Angel of Stradford.

The applause reached his ears, and he was surprised at his reaction. He wiped a hand quickly across his eyes and squeezed Lexan's shoulder. Her eyes bright, she mouthed 'I love you,' as he stood up.

Bob grabbed his hand as he maneuvered in the

narrow space between the seats. "You deserve it, man." Joe returned the handshake and stepped into the aisle. Bob's expression startled him. Normally he was carefree, disarmingly so. Tonight he was different. Joe held his eye, nodded, then walked carefully down the incline toward the stage.

Both sides of the aisle were lined with people standing and clapping for Joe. He held his smile in place and shook several hands. Some of the women in the audience were wiping their eyes, too.

He pretended to stumble on the first step leading to the stage, caught himself, and made a comic bow. The crowd oohed, then rewarded him with another wave of applause. He took the plaque from Mrs. Saylor, pecked her on the cheek, and moved to the microphone.

"I am overwhelmed," he said. "Overwhelmed by your kindness in giving me this award, and thankful that I didn't fall down and make a complete ass out of myself." The crowd laughed in appreciation of his act.

"The thing is," he said calmly and clearly, "the thing is, I know I am not the best teacher in this building tonight, let alone the whole school district. I can see many outstanding educators in just the first couple rows of the auditorium." He nodded to his fellow language teachers, Nancy and Roberta. He pointed at Zimmerman and wondered fleetingly if this was his first ever appearance at a PTA function. "I applaud them." He began clapping and most of the audience joined in.

"Educating our community's children can be subjective, to say the least. I am proud enough to have been nominated, let alone having my name on this plaque along with all the other great teachers who have been honored over the years."

Another wave of applause. He noticed more of his colleagues, and gave them a grin or a jab with his finger. Several members of the Board of Education were present; they returned his smiles with tight, restrained faces. Business Director Mel Radburn's expression was almost hateful.

"I am especially pleased to be honored tonight along with our Mayor, Kimberly Hellauer Horvath," Joe continued. "She couldn't be with us tonight – pressing governmental business, I'm sure – but she wanted me to extend her thanks to you as well. I'm glad to be the face before you, but it was the Mayor who delivered the money for The Shattered Glass Ceiling Program. It literally wouldn't have gotten off the ground without her help and support." No applause this time, just a nervous rustle passing through the audience.

Bob leaned over to Lexan. "It also wouldn't have been necessary either," he whispered. Lexan shushed him. He shrugged. "Just saying."

"You could say that a program to empower young women should not be needed in our community in this day and age." Joe continued speaking his lines. "Sadly, this isn't always the case, so I am indebted, as we all are, to the Mayor."

This time the audience hesitated, and applauded after he prompted them. There were those who knew the real story and those who didn't. The few who knew Joe had blackmailed the Mayor into providing counselling services for the high school girls she had used as prostitutes, and the many who saw her as a role-model. Joe stayed in character and clapped along, but the voice in his head kept reminding him that it was not that simple. It had broken his heart when he realized that some of the girls involved weren't victims at all, but willing participants. He refused to think about how many. In any case, he reminded himself, they could all benefit from the counselling.

The Mayor had taken the scales from his eyes and shown him that there was no difference between Cleveland and the suburbs. Evil was everywhere. She had abused teenage girls to make money and extend her influence. He had managed to stop the prostitution ring, but his decision to blackmail her haunted him. He was playing her game.

He continued clapping and smiling at the audience. This was now his game.

Nancy said to Roberta, "Our boy does love the limelight, doesn't he."

"And a crowd. Joe loves a crowd," Bert returned. "But he deserves it, he really does."

"OK," Joe was saying as the crowd quieted. "I'd better keep this moving along. There are many more people to thank. My colleagues and friends, Bob McCauley, Lexan Warner, Fr. Gerald Hastings, the Board of Education, the High School Principal, Gale Stevens. Couldn't have done this without their support. Most of all, thank you to the PTA!" Joe waved as he left the stage.

Bob said, "Longest speech in PTA history or what?"

"He did it with a smile." Lexan sheltered her mouth with her hand. "Knowing most of it was bullshit, and thanking the bitch who was responsible."

"He could be a politician." Bob grinned at her.

She returned his smile without any warmth. "Great. He can lie with a smile on his face."

The face in the window winked back at Joe Lehrer as he stood with his hand on the sash lock. He ignored the dark hollow surrounding the other eye and nodded, satisfied. I got this, he thought. The reflected face agreed.

Joe moved to the next window, examined it, and walked through the kitchen to the door leading to the garage. Its lock was weak, a cheap one that came with the house. He slid the chain into the slide and checked the handle again. He knew the garage door was down and secure.

The windows in his office were locked, but the door leading to the deck was a concern. He opened the door and rolled it closed several times, satisfied only when he heard the heavy click. He secured the metal rod in the bottom track with his foot.

Joe made this circuit of his house every night before going upstairs to sleep, before he could go upstairs to sleep. It was unlikely that Kim or her cronies would attack him in his home again, because they knew what his retaliation would be. But the routine was a comfort.

The windows in the living room were rarely opened, especially in winter, but he inspected them anyway. As he pulled aside the last curtain it glowed red, then blue, then red again. Another police car raced by, the second or third he'd heard. He let the curtain fall and opened the front door. More sirens in the distance. A yellow-green EMS van sped past. He was re-locking the storm door when he heard her voice.

"Can't a girl get some sleep around here?" Lexan stood at the top of the stairs. "You having a party, or what?"

She held a hand on her hip, wearing the t-shirt and boxers she considered pajamas. Her voice was light, belying what Joe knew to be true.

"And you weren't invited." When she pushed her lips into a pout, he said, "But hey, I wasn't either."

"Get on up here, you," she said and disappeared into the bedroom.

"Be up in a sec." He looked up at the empty hallway for a moment, then checked the door lock again. He could still hear sirens in the distance, but the street looked to be at peace again. It was always peaceful in this development. Almost always, he thought. Someone at school tomorrow would know what it was about. They always did.

The rug in the foyer had slid out of place, revealing the discolored tiles it was supposed to hide. His eyes flashed to the wall where Lexan's head had left a trail of blood when she slid unconscious to the floor. It had been re-painted and didn't show, but his eyes knew the exact spot, like a bloodhound sensed a spoor.

Maybe the tiles weren't discolored, but his eyes knew where the blood had pooled, where Weigel had died, where Chelsea had killed him. The three of them were united in a dark spot on the floor of his foyer.

Weigel had killed Joe's wife and Chelsea's sister on Kim's orders. In that way of thinking, he had deserved to die. Joe had kept the girl from blame by saying he fired the shots, not her. He had not been charged, and she had returned to school instead of going to juvenile detention. But Joe knew he should have killed Weigel himself.

He shook the thought from his mind. Now he owned a gun. He'd never wanted one, but had to protect himself and those he cared about. St. Michael carried a sword; he kept a Colt 1911 on the shelf of his closet. Sometimes in the glove box of his car. He hated Kimberly for forcing him to change. He hated himself for changing.

Joe was halfway up the stairs when another siren screamed into the night. He crouched to see through the narrow windows flanking the front door. Bands of red light spun across the snow-covered yard reaching for him.

Inside the bedroom, Lexan lay curled on her side. Joe was obsessed with protecting the house; it was their way of dealing with the death of Joe's wife, and the danger they faced from Kimberly. Joe had gloried in his award tonight and enjoyed the power he held over the mayor. But they both knew power was temporary. The mayor was still a threat to them.

Joe protected Lexan, as the Archangel protected the Church, and she comforted him. He patrolled the perimeter, and she held him close when the nightmares came. He had his routine; she had hers. Now she could hear Joe coming to her. A smile curled her lips and pushed aside her doubts. At least with Joe beside her, she felt safe.

CHAPTER TWO

Detective Elmer Kramer watched the fire fighters attack the blaze through the smudged windows of his patrol car. A couple of uniforms held back a line of gawkers, but were watching the fire as well. The windows in his cruiser would normally be cleaner, but the call had gotten him out of bed. Besides, it was cold outside, and he knew they wouldn't let him into the house until it was safe. He rubbed his eyes open and tried to relax.

Chief Callahan had just shut down the hoses pouring water through the windows, and it looked like they were preparing to enter the two-story house through the front door. Kramer racked his brain for anything he knew about this address, or this street, or even the development, but nothing popped. Vandalism didn't make sense in this neighborhood. Arson, maybe. He looked at the tracks leading through the snow and hoped the fire fighters hadn't obliterated evidence. Callahan waved to him, and he got out of the car.

"Looks like we can enter the premises now, Buddy," the Chief said, his voice clear in the cold night air. "I'd tell you to be careful, but you know the drill."

Kramer looked up at the tall, broad shouldered man and extended his hand. "Chief Callahan. Yeah, I might have done this once or twice." He lifted a hand at Grabowski holding the hose. "Just not in this neighborhood."

Callahan furrowed his brows. "Probably an accident."

"Anybody inside?"

"Don't know until we take a look. Open it up."

Kennedy, one of the patrolmen, joined Grabowski as they punched in what remained of the front door with an axe and stepped out of the way for the officers. It had been a nice house in a nice neighborhood, but now it was a black, smoking ruin. The firefighter took two steps into the hallway and held out his arm, barring the others from following. "Too dangerous," he said and faced them.

Kramer looked past him and saw the living room and most of the first floor were simply not there. Instead, a yawning hole where water dripped down into the basement. He caught a glimpse at the other side, maybe the dining room, before the firefighters pushed him out of the house.

"Get back, the rest of the roof could cave in," the Chief ordered. "Way back."

"I gotta see what happened," Kramer said.

"Not now you don't."

"Can we walk around the back? Is it gonna blow up?"

Callahan shook his head. "The fire's out. We turned off the gas line. Just stay away from it." He turned to Grabowski as the policemen moved around the side of the house.

"Coulda been a bomb, Chief," one of the firemen said. Grabowski nodded.

Callahan's face was tightly closed. "Won't know till the county boys show up."

"Think anybody's in there?"

The Chief turned to Grabowski. "I don't think anybody could survive that blast."

"Coulda been a gas leak," the fireman said.

The Chief was about to respond, when he turned to the sound of Kramer's voice.

"You guys go around the back of the house?" the Detective called as he jogged through the snow toward them. "Pour water in the back windows?"

"Of course."

"You see any footprints, tracks in the snow?" Kennedy pointed his hand toward the basement windows.

Grabowski shook his head no. "Didn't notice. Couldn't get too close to the house. Flames were too bright."

"What are you getting at, Detective?" Callahan looked at him directly.

Kramer waved them to follow as he walked quickly to the rear of the house. He squatted and pointed at the trail of steps through the snow. He looked up and said,

"Did you guys get this close to the basement window? Are these your tracks?"

Grabowski looked down, then turned back to Lt. Kramer. "No, we stopped over there. That's where me and Charlie held the hose. You can see the trail back to the hydrant."

"Then who made these?" Kramer asked. "And the ones on the other side of the deck? That's what I want to know."

"I'm trying to determine where the fire started." Callahan frowned. "The damage appears to be spread equally around the whole first floor."

"Maybe the footprints—" Kramer's thoughts were stopped by another siren. "My Boss is here," he said instead and trotted to the curb where a Stradford Police cruiser was opening its doors.

"Our new chief of police," Kennedy said and followed the lieutenant.

"So, Chief, what did Lt. Kramer mean," Grabowski asked, "about the tracks and the windows?"

Callahan pursed his lips. "It means it was a gas leak" The big man slapped his gloves against his leg. "That's what it means."

Grabowski looked up at the Chief. "I don't get it."

"It means the cause of this fire is what they say it is." He looked closely at the younger man. "It means we keep our mouths shut."

Joe carried his lunch tray up the short staircase and crossed the hall to the Faculty Lounge. Mel Reynolds had cornered him for several minutes near the cafeteria, and now the halls were relatively clear. As he pulled the handle, he wondered again why the Lounge door opened out like a classroom instead of in like an office. "Anyone know why Mel is lurking around today?"

Instead of answering, Bob McCauley was standing and clapping. "Now entering the room from the Marvel Universe of Super Heroes, the Educator of the Year, Mr. Joe Lehrer!"

"Co-educator," Joe laughed and stuck a pose. "You gotta admit I look pretty good in spandex." He set his tray between Lexan and Roberta, across from Bob and Nancy.

"Grilled cheese and tomato soup again?" Nancy raised an eyebrow.

"A classic," Joe said and dipped the sandwich into the soup.

At another table, Terri Dieken slammed the lid of her iPad and called, "Well, Mr. Super-Hero, are you gonna do something about this week's schedule, or not?"

Lexan shot her a look. Bob giggled. "Yeah, Joe, are you?"

Joe smiled at him. "Not today, Terri, we'll just have to muddle through."

She muttered something that sounded like "I thought the Educator of the Year could do everything." Beside him Lexan tensed, but Joe didn't take the bait.

Bob answered for him. "They're state tests, Terri. We have to administer them when the state says."

The state of Ohio mandated that five tests be given to all high school sophomores the third week in March, each on a separate day. Stradford had decided to accommodate the necessary time by shortening different classes each day.

"But my morning class is seventeen minutes longer than my afternoon. I'll get too far ahead."

"Or behind," Bob said under his breath.

Joe turned to Terri. "It'll all work out by the end of the week."

"No, it won't. Next week we'll be taking kids out of classes for make-ups. How do we plan for that?" Dieken mumbled something else, and Joe turned back to his table.

"They're year-end tests and we're not even through the third quarter," Nancy Turner said, wiping a napkin carefully across her lips.

Roberta shook her head. "That's true, but that's not the worst thing. These tests are not about learning, they're about prestige." She narrowed her eyes and looked across the table at Joe. "They're about prestige and money."

"Popularity, I call it," Bob said. "Too many kids are being home-schooled, taking their state funding money with them."

"Wait," Lexan said. "If they get home-schooled, the district loses money?"

"We do," Joe said. "We lose a lot of money to home schooling and private schools. But we still have to maintain our buildings and teach our curriculum."

"We have to be popular so we can compete," Bob said. "We need to convince the parents to keep their kids here."

"I still don't get it." Lexan looked around the table. "If we do well on the State tests, two things happen." Nancy held up her fingers. "One, we get bragging rights. A good State Report Card means Stradford can say we are 'Excellent With Distinction'."

"And two, the State is giving out bonuses. The higher our kids grade out, the more cash the school gets back." She nodded her head. "Like I said, it's not about teaching and learning, it's about money. Prestige or popularity, whatever, the bottom line is cash."

Joe looked at the congealed remains of his soup in the Styrofoam bowl and the crumbs of the sandwich scattered across his tray. He didn't want to bring up another danger. He had heard that the Board was planning on linking teacher pay to the test results; their salaries would depend on how well the kids scored on the tests. Instead he bussed his tray and left. At least he had started the day in a good mood.

When the bell ended the period, the table was mostly empty. As Lexan stood up, Roberta put her hand on her arm. "Is he OK?" she asked. "Really?"

Lexan sat back down. "What do you mean?"

"I've known Joe forever," she said. "We started the same year. Bob did too."

Lexan wondered where this was going. "I need to get to my class."

"I do too." Roberta tapped her tray with a plastic fork. "He just seems different. More intense maybe."

"That's a good word for it," the younger woman said. "He's not used to being the one with the power."

Roberta looked closely. "It must be hard on you."

Lexan picked up her lunch tray. "It's fine," she said. "We're fine."

CHAPTER THREE

Alfred Hellauer felt the warm sun on his shoulders and let out a happy sigh. This was what it was all about: why he had labored, why he had suffered through the dark winters, and why he had put up with all the bullshit. He opened his eyes to see his wife sitting across the pool with her book, and Karl gazing through the lanai at the boat dock beyond. He sighed again and stretched. What he didn't understand was why his best friend wasn't as happy.

"Karl, goddammit, you're pacing again like a big cat, back and forth."

Karl didn't turn around, but Alfred noticed the neck muscles bunching beneath his collar-length white hair. "Can't you just relax?"

Karl put both hands on the screen of the lanai. "In a word, no. No, Alfie, I cannot relax."

Uschi shot her husband a look, and Alfie saw it but spoke anyway. "It's the most beautiful place in the world, we have all the money we need, and you can't be bothered to enjoy a minute of it."

Karl spun around. "You think I don't want to enjoy it? You think I don't like Naples? What, you think I don't want to be with you two?" Karl's face had reddened and the pace of his words quickened.

Alfie sat up on the chaise and raised a hand. "I don't want to get into this again."

Across the pool his wife clicked her tongue and dropped her eyes to her book. "I just think you should be happy."

Karl took a step forward, hesitated, and dropped his hands to his sides. "I know, I know."

"You've worked hard, Karl. You've done the heavy lifting for me and for my family. All this," he opened his arms, "is your reward. Hell, it seems like you don't want to even be here."

Uschi nodded behind her book but didn't raise her eyes.

Karl shook his head but remained silent.

Alfie looked from one to the other and said, "The first time we had this conversation, I suggested the three B's." He paused hoping his friend or his wife would laugh. They didn't, but he held up his hand anyway and counted, "Booze, Babes and Blow. But nothing makes you happy. Actually, it's starting to piss me off, Karl."

Karl loosened his hands by shaking them, and slumped onto a strapped patio chair. "I can't help it," he said.

"Sure you can Karl, you—"

"—No! No I can't! I can't sit down here in this, this paradise, this paradise that feels like a cage, and do nothing! I can't do it!"

Uschi closed her book and cocked her head at her husband.

He looked away from her and said, softly, controlling his voice, "Did something happen?"

"Yeah, something happened." Karl's words burst out louder than he'd intended. "And damn, I saw it coming. I saw it coming and couldn't do anything about it because I'm 1200 miles away!"

Alfred furrowed his brows. "We lose anybody?"

"Half dozen runners. A chemist." Karl waved away the question. "Replaceable. That's not the problem."

"Kimberly," Uschi said.

Karl couldn't look her in the eye, but said, "No, as usual, your—"

"That's enough," Alfie barked. He jabbed a finger at Karl. "My sister is not the issue. Your attitude is the issue."

Karl put his large hands on his knees and focused on Alfie. "My attitude is an issue, I grant you. Your sister, however, is the root cause of the problem."

Alfie stood up quickly, balling his hands as he did.

Karl waited a beat then stood as well. "It's not going to come to this," he said over his shoulder to Uschi, keeping his eyes on Alfie. "I'll leave."

"No, you're staying here, Karl. I promised Kimberly she could run things. I promised her I was out of it."

"Pardon me, Boss, but if she ran things, we wouldn't be having this conversation. All she's doing is playing Mayor. It's a game to her. She's letting everything we built in Stradford fall apart."

Alfie looked to his wife, then back. "I gave Kim my word."

"You promised you'd give her space. I was there. You didn't promise I would stand by and let her screw everything up." Karl walked to the lanai and faced the screen. "You need to decide which is more important, the city you organized or your sister."

Alfie's eyes flickered from the pool water to the canal outside, the sky, the sun. "You must be exaggerating. I'm sure everything is fine. I spoke to her just a couple days ago." He nodded hopefully.

"I'm sure she said everything is fine in Stradford," Karl said. "But somebody firebombed one of the distribution centers last night. Did she mention that?"

Alfred saw the look on his wife's face. "No, she didn't."

"Or mention we lost both product and money?"

"How could that be? We never keep them in the same place."

Karl glared at him. "No, we never did. Your sister—"

Alfie's head spun from Uschi to Karl. "That must be a mistake."

Karl kept his gaze on the boat bobbing in the canal outside the lanai. "No mistake."

The former mayor slumped down onto a chair. On the surface of the pool his wife's face twisted and deformed as the breeze disturbed the water. "Give her time."

Oskar Brummelberger had put it off long enough. It was a job he didn't want to do, but one he had to. It meant protecting the love he had for his daughter, but it also meant accepting that she was dead.

He looked out the scratched window of the old Terex 7231 and engaged the loader. He leaned forward as the vehicle hefted the frame of a wrecked Buick, then rocked back as the weight settled. He put it in gear and rumbled away.

Even with the added weight the front-end loader nimbly worked its way between and around the mounds of junk in Brummelberger's Salvage yard. Oskar dropped the rusted frame in an open spot in front of the sagging white barn that housed his office and 'the good stuff' his daughter used to call it.

"Maybe this'll keep the new bastards quiet," he muttered out loud, and sped back for another load, this time from the side of the barn near his house. "City Beautification my ass." The bastards in Stradford City Hall had changed, but they were still bastards. Oskar had helped them, but still they kicked him around, belittled him, put him down.

The fat man paused to adjust his heavy work gloves. Threatening me with eviction if I don't clean up my property, he thought. My property. Three generations we been here. Now they call it an eyesore. His breath clouded the cab. He selected a door-less refrigerator from the pile, worked it into the bucket and returned to the yard in front of the barn.

She loved this loader, Laurel Ann did. Named it T-Rex. Learned to drive on it. Found paint on eBay to match. Oskar grinned as the loader bounced over the rutted path. He looked at the patches of Lawson's Terex Green #06D still on the bucket, the patches that were not orange with rust. He negotiated around a stack of bed springs, and two dilapidated food trucks that looked to be linked together like cars in a train.

The only difference was the old bastards had Karl. The new bastards didn't have anyone like him, anyone to keep things in order. Think they can do everything themselves. Worrying about the wrong stuff. Letting things get out of hand. Maybe it's because they're women, he thought. I don't miss Karl; he's the guy that kept me in my place. But the ladies could use the white-haired asshole.

The spot where Laurel Ann died grabbed him as he neared it. He slammed on the brakes. T-Rex jerked sharply before the refrigerator stopped swinging. He could see the darkened earth through the thin layer of snow. The grass and earth were still black from the fire that had consumed his daughter. He wiped furiously at the fogged-up windshield.

Oskar knew that Peter Weigel had killed his daughter. Karl had promised that he could kill the man, but that stupid teacher had let the girl do it. Slowly and reverently he reversed the loader and held its cargo above the exact spot. He ran his bare hand across his face for the moisture hiding in the fat of his cheeks. "Laurel Ann, this is your place." His voice caught and he had to start again. "The bastards will never see it." He pushed the lever forward and settled the refrigerator onto the others covering the burned and sacred ground.

I'll make it so no one ever finds this place, he thought. He and T-Rex worked the pile of refrigerators into a neater heap that covered every inch of the burn. Oskar slowly backed the loader away and turned off the engine. It occurred to him that with Weigel dead and Karl gone, the only one left was the teacher.

CHAPTER FOUR

It had been impossible for Joe to get any work done in his office. Either people were telling him what they wanted in the next contract (free lunch had been the most popular but far from the stupidest) or suggesting ways he could rid them of their enemies. Radburn had been the consensus choice. It was not how Joe imagined he would spend his time as St. Michael the Archangel.

The Faculty Lounge had been quieter than his office, and Joe had been able to catch up on his grading. The bell rang as he logged the last quiz grade into his laptop. He sat back and tried to ease the knot from his shoulder. It was a lunch period now and the noise in the hallway was finding its way in.

A plastic tray loaded with salad and soup in

matching styro bowls slid into view. "Gene, I didn't know this was your lunch period."

The pudgy, balding social studies chairman, Gene Phillips, dropped onto the chair next to him. "It's not. It's departmental planning."

"What can I do for you?" Gene was also the president of the Association. Joe hoped he had something for him that would vent his anger about Kimberly.

"Thanks for asking." He grinned shortly. "We'll be back in negotiations soon, as you know. The one-year contract we agreed to expires in the summer."

The door burst open. Bob, Roberta and Nancy filled in Joe's table; the women sat down and Bob left to wash his hands. Zimmerman and Terri Dieken took seats at the table next to them.

When Gene had tasted the soup and looked up, Joe said, "I figured you wanted to talk to me about negotiations. Do you want me on the team?"

"Of course he wants you on the team, Joe," Terri said to Zimmerman in a stage whisper. "You're the resident super-hero."

"You don't have to be on the team. You can help us other ways." Gene furrowed his forehead. "Could you kind of get a lay of the land?"

Joe glanced at Terri expecting a comment.

Gene continued. "After the strike I'd like negotiations to go smoothly."

Joe dropped his voice. "You worried about them linking our salaries to test results?"

The Association President nodded. "At the moment that would kill us."

"I'll see what I can do."

"Why do we have to pay you dues, Gene?" Terri snarled from the other table. "Why do we even have an Association with him around?"

"You don't pay the dues to me, Terri," Gene said calmly. He rarely spoke in any tone other than calmly. "It's your Association."

Zimmerman laid a hand on her arm. She snatched it back. "Fine, you guys play your little games, but explain to me why I have prostitutes in my classes. Why, huh?"

"School policy," Gene began.

"Bullshit! You two run everything, and you let hookers sit in my classes, every day! Why don't you do something about that?"

The school had allowed several of the girls who had been involved in the prostitution ring to graduate a semester early, as they were seniors with enough credits. It was also a sign to the community that everything was normal. Other girls were allowed to stay in school if they participated in the counselling program. A dozen or so were doing that. Several had dropped out.

"Now I hear," Terri stood and picked up her tray, "they're being allowed to walk for Commencement. They sell their bodies and get a diploma!"

"Terri, you know—"

"Save it, super star." She slammed her chair into the table and stormed out.

Joe looked around the Lounge. Terri's outburst, probably shared by others, added to the malaise of State Test Week: the shortened periods, inverted class times, constant PA interruptions and exhausted kids. The reprieve of spring break was still weeks away. He was glad Gene had given him a task to focus on.

A heavy hand smashed open the door to the Lounge. Heads popped up, eyes focused, and Roberta screamed. Bob stood in the doorway holding a length of paper towel from his head to the floor. "I got the bastard!" He cringed at the word and quickly pulled the door shut.

"What the hell is the matter with you?" Zimmerman rasped.

Bob bounded to his table and thrust a handful of coarse brown paper at him. "Look, look at this!"

Zimmerman turned back to his plate of nuggets and fries.

"Come on, Zim, paper towels. A long, long roll of paper towels!"

Gene said slowly, "Beats using newspaper."

Bob looked at him excitedly. "Yes, it does, I mean, sure, but that's not my point. Joe, Joey boy, you got to help me here."

Joe winked at Roberta and speared the one tomato in his salad. "You finally beat the machine."

Bob raised both hands to the ceiling, the now-crumpled towel dangling from one. "Yes! I finally beat the machine."

Joe began slow clapping. Roberta joined in, then Nancy and Gene. Zimmerman ate a tater tot and grunted.

Bob was slowly rotating like a demented lighthouse. "I know it's not Educator of the Year, but I did it!"

Joe furrowed his brow. A shot at me. Funny, but a shot.

"Some of you may not know the whole story," Bob was saying.

"Or give a crap," Zimmerman muttered.

Bob put a hand on his shoulder. "Peace, my son."

Zimmerman tried to hold back but burst out laughing. "You are such a piece of work, McCauley."

"OK, so you probably know the story, but for those of you who don't, especially the ladies present, I will elucidate."

"You don't know what that means," Nancy said.

"Hey, I went to a private college, I know stuff."

Joe looked around the Lounge. Faces were smiling, voices lighter.

"---so I'm waving my hands in front of the dispenser, you know, that little plastic window---"

"---with the little hand!"

"That's right, Bert, got those in the ladies' room, too, huh?"

She poked Nancy and nodded. Bob continued, "So I'm waving and waving at the little hand and does anything come out? Huh? My hands are dripping and nothing! Not one blessed sheet."

"You're not sincere, McCauley, that's your problem."

Joe watched his friend nearly double over with laughter.

"That's not it, Nancy, I'm too sincere! I'm too open and caring and, I'm too empathetical to live in a world of machines."

"Empathetic." Nancy sniffed, but her lips turned up in a small smile.

"Whatever. So. I'm standing in front of the black plastic Terminator, begging, pleading for a towel and finally just hauled off and smacked the sucker. Bam! Right in the side of its head!"

"That's where you got the big roll in your hand?"

"No, Bert. It gave me nothing. *Nichts, nada.* I dried my hands on my pants." Bob pawed the floor with the toe of his shoe. The room quieted. "My good khakis. Left big dark spots."

Bob waited for every eye. He lifted his head and his face brightened. "That was last week. Today I waved once, one little time, and it nearly drowned me in paper towels. Yes! I win!"

He raised his fist full of brown paper in triumph and raced to the door. "I gotta tell Gale." He turned back to the laughing faces. "Then I'm writing a letter to the paper towel gods." He flung the towel over his shoulder like a scarf and marched from the room.

The bell rang as the door thumped behind him. They cleaned their trays and returned to class, their moods lightened like a change in the weather. The clouds over the Faculty Lounge driven away by the storm that was Bob McCauley.

Joe was looking forward to teaching a class. So much so that the cacophony of high-pitched adolescent voices and banging locker doors, and the press of halls filled with too many people and too many odors didn't bother him at all. He slid through, around and between kids, clusters of kids, and several adults on his way to his classroom with a smile on his face and happy words for those he knew. The smile and the words were in contrast to the way the morning had gone and the way he felt.

He had been disappointed and hurt to discover that having power didn't feel like he thought it would. It brought him criticism and in Terri's case, jealousy. Did the other angels hate St. Michael? He smiled at himself as he unlocked the classroom door; at least he had the comfort of teaching.

Fifteen minutes later, Joe's mood had improved as he'd hoped. He wiped the homework sentences off the whiteboard and stepped to the front of the class. The preliminary work had gone well, and he was ready to present the new material.

"Chuck, you have a question?"

"Why can't we keep doing pronouns, Herr? I was getting good at those."

Joe assumed the lumpy sophomore was referring to substituting pronouns for nouns. "We did those last semester. They were on the final exam."

"Man, I aced that sucker," he said and reached from his desk to slap TJ Teeple's outstretched palm.

"You did, Chuck, and TJ, and most all of you. You guys worked hard and got really good grades. I'm proud of you," Lehrer said and clapped his hands.

Looking around the room Chuck said, "So why can't we do some more? Then we could keep getting good grades."

More applause, and Joe laughed without thinking. "We'd be masters of the pronoun universe, right? All A's. A's for everybody!" Now everyone was talking at once, Jodi, Chelsea, even Ketul. Joe nodded at Irwin's raised hand.

"But Herr," the young man said as Joe motioned for quiet. "Herr, we'd never be able to do anything except that one grammar skill. How could we communicate?"

The class let out a collective groan. Joe smiled. "Irwin does have a point."

"He always gets A's. Every class," Chuck said. "This is the first time I ever got a B in German."

"You deserved it, and we do use pronouns every day," Joe said. "We can use those same skills, but there are other skills to master."

He moved back to the front of the room. "It's time for a simile, folks."

"Is that a vocab word, Herr?" TJ held his pen and opened his notebook.

"It's English, and I bet it's come up in English class. Anybody?"

"It's a comparison," Jodi said.

"He's going to tell us that learning German grammar is like something else," Chelsea added.

"Man," Chuck said. "The kids in this class are so smart."

"They are, Charles, and so are you." Joe glanced at the attentive young faces. "Yes, Chelsea, I'm going to tell you guys that learning in this class is like playing baseball." He reached onto his desk for a Nerf ball and tossed it up in the air as he spoke.

"I play football, Herr."

Joe tossed him the ball. "Sure, but you played T-ball when you were little, right?"

Chuck unfurled his arms, caught the ball and

tossed it back.

"I bet most of you did, right?"

Jodi dropped the ball when Joe threw it to her, then grabbed it from the floor and threw it over his head. "OK, well, maybe not all of you."

He retrieved the ball and continued tossing it up and catching it as he spoke. "So, what is the verb here? We always start with a verb, like when we were doing pronouns. What am I doing?"

"Throwing."

"Tossing."

"Heaving." The class laughed at that. "Maybe the ball needs to be a little heavier for that, TJ. But we agree that it's an action verb, right? You can see the action, can't you."

"*Werfen,* Herr."

"Probably the only German word we know for 'throw,' Irwin. Good job.

"OK, we found the verb. What is the next thing we ask ourselves?" Joe scanned their faces. "The next grammatical question. Come on."

"Who," Jodi shouted. "'Who' is doing the action!"

"Chill out, girl," TJ laughed.

Joe laughed as well. "And in grammar land, 'who' is called the--?"

"Subject, Herr, 'who' is the subject."

Joe's mind flashed to Abbot and Costello's 'Who's on first' routine but knew the kids were too young to get it. "In this case, the subject is 'I.' I am tossing the ball, or from your perspective, the Herr is throwing the ball, right?"

Several nodded, a couple jotted notes, and he went on. "OK, we got the do-er of the action, the subject, but what else is going on? What about the ball?" The ball rose into the air and dropped into his hand. "Is the ball doing anything? What does the ball have to do with the verb?"

"Ooh, ooh! I know!" Jodi nearly fell out of her seat. "The ball is the object!"

"Close," Joe said.

"Direct! The direct object!" Jodi yelled.

"Great," Joe said and nodded to the girl. "So, we have a verb, a subject doing the verb and a direct object receiving the action of the verb. Right?" He looked around and saw several nods. "Yeah, we did this with the pronouns, right? The subject pronouns had different forms than the direct objects, didn't they? Chuck?"

"What? Yeah, they were like I and me. *Ich* and *mich.*"

"Yes, terrific, young man, really good. They have different functions in the sentence, they have different cases, so they have different forms."

He tossed the ball up, "I'm the subject." The ball rose and fell back into his hand. "The ball is the direct object." He paused, then tossed the ball to TJ. "What's he got to do with the action? He's not the subject. He's not the direct object, but he benefits from the action, right? He gets the ball."

Joe caught the ball from TJ and tossed it to Chelsea. "What does she have to do with the action? She's not throwing it, she's not being thrown, but she receives the ball. What is she?"

Chelsea said something but the clanging of the bell

drowned her out. Books closed, pens returned to pockets, backpacks filled. Chelsea tossed the ball back to him as she stood up.

"Now, what am I?" Joe said. "I got the ball from Chelsea." He looked at the clock and cursed under his breath; the state tests had shortened the class period. He watched his class leave the room. "We'll give this another chance tomorrow," he muttered to himself.

Joe saw the balding back of Fr. Jerry Hastings' head as the priest picked up his order from the barista. When he turned around, Joe smiled and waved him over. His longtime friend had helped him navigate the death of his wife.

"Long time no see."

Joe waited for his friend's smile. Instead, the priest set his coffee on the table and carefully folded his black overcoat before settling in the booth.

Joe looked at his hands. "I guess it has been a while."

"You still working the program?"

"Program? It's not like I'm an alcoholic."

Hastings stared at him over the coffee cup. "Kinda."

Joe looked at the line of people waiting to place their orders. "I'm fine."

"Fine as in healthy, or fine as in leave me the hell alone?"

Joe sighed. He had been hoping for a pick-me-up from the priest, the good cop. Instead the bad cop was glaring at him across the table. "Closer to healthy."

Hastings nodded.

"What? This isn't a session, it's a coffee shop."

His friend pried off the plastic lid and peered into the paper cup. "No, you're all healed, all better." He raised his eyes. "That's what you said the last time I saw you."

Joe tried to remember how long ago that was. "I've got a lot going on."

"Even St. Michael the Archangel relaxes every now and then."

"I can't." Joe sipped his latte. "One thing runs right into the next."

Hastings nodded.

Joe's voice sped up as he set down his cup. "No, really. It's going well. I got the money to rehabilitate the girls. I mean, we, we got the money for the girls. To help the girls. Thank you for that by the way. However we did that." He lifted his eyes to the priest's. "That's good, right?"

"Uh-huh."

"Chelsea's not in jail or juvie." Joe lifted the cup and wiped the spill with a paper napkin.

The priest took another sip.

"I'm not angry at God or blaming him or any of that."

"Uh-huh."

"And the levy passed, so no strike. That's all good."

Hastings let out a breath.

Joe's voice raced out of control. "And, Lexie? Fine. We're fitting in well together. Things are great. We're, uh, committed. Yeah, that's good too."

Fr. Jerry waited a bit. "The m-word?"

"Close to that. Working on it. Yeah, OK."

"Talking about marriage or thinking about it?"

The priest was relentless. The teacher looked at him for a second then checked the table top again. "Thinking about it. Nothing definite."

Hastings raised an eyebrow.

Joe snatched his cup from the table and stood up. He didn't need this from him. Not now.

Hastings raised the palm of his hand. "You're trying to do this alone, Joe. You can't do alone. We both know that." When his friend finally met his eyes, he said. "I'm not talking about marriage."

"It's not that you can't help me." Joe sat back down "If I get you more involved, you're going to get hurt."

Hastings opened his mouth; Joe waved it closed. "I can handle this myself. I'm already in neck deep."

"You get to be the hero." Hastings stared directly at Joe. "That's what you're saying."

"OK, if that's how you see it." Joe shrugged. "But I take care of the bad guys, and you and Lex are safe."

"And Bob, and Chelsea, and the girls, and Stradford and the high school. You know, saving the world is harder than it looks." The priest smiled briefly and opened his palms. "Just saying."

"You're never just saying, Jerry." My whole life is gray, he thought, and all the man sees is black and white. Like his clothing. The priest set down his cup and nodded. "OK, Joe."

"I'm fine. Like I said." Joe stood up and walked away from his friend.

CHAPTER FIVE

As Detective Buddy Kramer waited for the meeting to begin, he tried to list things about his new boss that didn't irritate, disgust or piss him off. At the moment the list was very short, the only possible item being Mangione didn't smell bad.

At that moment the new Chief of Police burst past him into the room and the others sprang to their feet. Kramer followed them, slowly, mentally editing his list. Smells like a whorehouse.

The second worst thing about the new Chief was his appearance. It looked to Kramer as if city council had asked for a typical Italian, and Central Casting had produced one. Glossy hair, no part, shiny suit, white shirt with some kind of pattern in it and, he nearly choked, Dago boots. By god, the man is wearing pointy, narrow, little half-boots. Would it kill him to wear the uniform?

Garrett Mangione stood at the head of the long table with his fingers splayed like tiny white spiders. Yes, Kramer thought, he's a little man with a little man's complex. The Chief nodded and the others dropped into their seats, this time Kramer with them. And a little man's temper, too.

"Gentleman," Mangione said quietly, "we are here for the post-incident report on the fire on, let me see." He shuffled through the pages in the folder in front of him. "Here it is, the fire on Stag Thicket Trace."

Kramer thought the voice was straight out of the Godfather movies, calm, slow and disarming. He looked to his right as Callahan raised his hand.

Mangione slowly rotated toward the Fire Chief. "A question?"

"Sorry to interrupt, sir, but the house was, is, on Hill Valley Drive."

The police chief stared at Callahan until the man reddened, then dropped his eyes to the file and said, "Yes, Hill Valley, at the intersection —" he looked at the fireman — "of Stag Thicket Trace. Is that correct?"

Callahan mumbled something Kramer couldn't hear. Kramer felt like he was watching a car ignore the warning lights and start across the train tracks.

"Well, is that what you wanted to say?" Mangione's eyes now bore into the big man's face.

"Just, just wanted everything to be correct," Callahan managed. "Uh, sir." Next to him Grabowski turned away, embarrassed; the others avoided looking at him.

The police chief waited until everyone was sure

who was in charge, then nodded. "Thank you. It's good to pay attention to detail."

"Now then, wadda we got? Fire of suspicious origin, five, no six dead. Any ID's on the bodies, Detective?"

"No, sir," Kramer said. "Still waiting for lab results, but no papers on them. No chance of fingerprints because of the intensity of the fire. One female, we do know that."

"No lab results yet?" Mangione frowned and jotted a note. "I'll see to that."

He returned his attention to Callahan. "Your findings?"

The Fire Chief began to redden again, then gathered his notes and said, "We have not received the full report from the county Arson Unit—"

"Arson Unit? You contacted the Arson Unit?"

This time Callahan held his ground. "Standard operating procedure in fires of this nature."

"It might have been standard before, but now that I am the Safety Director as well as the Chief of Police, those decisions go through me."

Callahan looked at Grabowski who shook his head no. "We were unaware of the change."

"Now you are." Mangione drummed his thumb on the table. "How can we call them off?"

"Call them off? Who?"

"The county arson idiots, who do you think? We don't want them telling us what's happening in our town." He screwed his close-set eyes tight. "Why did you contact them in the first place?"

"The evidence. It looks to us like arson, at the least

undetermined, or suspicious origin. Thought we could use their expertise."

"Evidence? What kind of evidence?"

"Point of origin was our first thought. There isn't one place the fire started, but several, concurrently. That and the intensity. It burned hot. Hotter than you'd normally find in a house fire." Callahan looked away from Mangione and nodded at Kramer.

"Well, Detective."

Kramer pulled his chair closer to the table and sat up straight. "I can't speak to the heat, that's their business, but I found tracks to three different windows."

"Tracks? What tracks?"

"In the snow. Sign of footprints in the snow."

"They were making snow-angels or what?" Mangione looked around the table for a laugh.

"Good one, Chief," Kramer said without smiling. "The tracks support the fire department's theory of multiple origins. The windows were broken as well, and incendiary devices could have been thrown in."

"Of course the windows were broken; there was an explosion for chrissakes." Mangione shook his head. "There were firemen all over the scene, they could have made the tracks."

"I checked that, sir. The fire fighters kept to the front of the house. The windows were on the back and sides. Most of the glass in them was blown in, not out. They were broken before the explosion."

"Flimsy, weak, not thought out." Mangione erased the details with a wave. "Not up to Stradford standards." He looked around the table as if sniffing out a bad odor.

"Frankly, gentlemen, I expected more."

When none of them spoke, he continued. "Worst of all, by contacting county, without authorization, you've opened us up to criticism. Criticism and scorn. After all this community has been through."

"Chief," Callahan said. "We asked for their help. That's all we did."

"We wanted to get it right, sir," Ptl. Kennedy added.

Mangione froze him with a stare. "What were you even doing at the fire scene, Patrolman?"

"Just helping, sir."

The Chief of Police held his stare. "Are you asking for a transfer?"

"No, not at all, I—"

"That can be arranged." He watched the young man squirm. "For now, just do your job. Your own job."

He returned his focus to Callahan. "I'll explain it to you, in simple terms." Kramer watched Mangione's performance, the sad head shake, the resigned voice. The man could put on a show.

"It was a gas leak. Leaks in several places. That explains your 'multiple origins' dilemma. Witnesses have told us they heard a loud boom, no, several loud booms. Definitely explosions. As for the heat, we know how hot natural gas burns."

"So that's it?" Callahan asked.

"Gas leak." Mangione closed the file.

"Who were the victims?" Kramer asked without thinking.

"Homeowners." Turning to Callahan, Mangione

said, "Do you want to tell the county to butt out, or shall I."

Callahan paused, then said in a clear voice, "No, sir, I think you better handle that."

Mangione stood up. "Well then, we're done here." He looked around the table. "I hope we have learned a lesson today, a valuable lesson about the chain of command." His gaze paused at Kramer, then Kennedy and ended at Callahan. "Dismissed."

Kramer remained at the table after the others filed out. He caught Kennedy's eye and nodded; he'd speak to the kid later. The detective knew that Mangione had been hired to calm things down after his predecessor's participation in the prostitution ring had come to light. Maybe it was right for the new chief to be so concerned about public perception.

But maybe something else was going on here. If a thorough investigation led to arson and the new chief cracked the case, wouldn't that restore confidence and give his career a boost? Why wouldn't he want to do that? Or at least investigate it enough to see if anything was there. If he even understood the difference between window glass blowing in or out.

Maybe Mangione was just doing what he'd been told, like the previous puppet. Karl's gone, Alfie's gone. Who would be giving him orders? Kimmy probably doesn't know anything about it. That Holmgren woman?

Kramer slapped his palm on the table top. It would have been so much easier if they'd given him the job instead of Mangione.

* * *

Joe envied Bob's schedule and his office. The constant pattern of bells rigidly commanded Joe's activities: what he did, where he did it and when he did it were all decreed by the bells. Bob, on the other hand, could set his daily schedule as he wished. Not totally, but for the most part and Joe wished he could as well. Even during non-test weeks the bells often cut a period short when he and his students needed more time, while Bob could extend a student conference as he needed.

Bob's office was a sanctuary from the teeming halls, noisy department pods and crowded classrooms. To be able to work with one student at a time in the peace and quiet of a private office was something Joe could only do while tutoring. He sighed as he knocked on Bob's door.

"Hey, stranger." Bob smiled and pointed to a chair.

"Been awhile."

"You superstars have it rough." Bob smiled faintly beneath his Tom Selleck moustache and ruddy Irish cheeks.

"Everybody wants a piece of me."

Bob reached across the desk and tapped Tiger Woods' Bobblehead. "We need you on this opioid thing."

Joe looked from Tiger shaking his head to Payne Stewart pumping his fist on the poster behind his friend's head. "I know. I'm sorry."

"Forget about it. Water under a dam."

"How does that work? Water flowing under the dam?"

Bob thought a second, then laughed. "Doesn't make sense, does it?"

Somehow that broke the tension. Joe settled into the chair. "So the reason I'm here is to admit I've been an arrogant asshole who sucked up all the credit and shared nothing with my best friend."

"Now you're talking, son." Bob settled his loafers onto the desk calendar. "What can I do for you?"

"You can start by getting rid of those hideous socks. Really? Green and purple paisley?"

"You got no taste. Grammar maybe, but you got no taste."

Joe laughed. "No, OK, I'm here to thank you for that speech in the Lounge about the paper towels."

"What about it? It really happened. Almost all of it."

Joe held up his hand. "You know what I mean. We were sitting there like deflated balloons. You perked us up."

"Just told a story, that's all."

"We both know that's bullshit."

"Wait, wait a minute." Bob slid an envelope across the desk.

Joe picked it up. "Got a cute little red flower on it."

"Like the flower on the side of the towel dispenser."

"No, you actually sent a letter to the paper towel guys?"

Bob snatched back the letter. "And they answered it. See, you're not the only one around here who can get stuff done."

"My hero." Joe shot him a salute.

Bob leaned his arms onto the desk. "There's more,

a lot more."

Joe grabbed his phone and stood up.

"I knew I'd seen that carnation somewhere--"

Joe turned his body away and waved his hand for him to stop. "I'll be right there. OK, bye."

Bob sighed. "Back to work, Archangel."

"What? Yeah, Gotta go." Joe tapped his knuckles on the desk. "Talk later. Promise."

Bob watched him leave and slumped back into his chair. "Sure you will." He knew he would have to follow the lead by himself. Just like last time.

CHAPTER SIX

Gale Stevens didn't like Mel Radburn. At the least he didn't appreciate the man's brusque and belittling style. He was beholden to the man, he used the man's influence and he'd succeeded him as high school principal, but he didn't like bullies, and Mel Radburn was a bully.

Radburn's bulky form now dominated the wing-backed chair, and his piggy eyes peered at him over the rim of his black-framed glasses. "Like what you've done to the office."

Stevens could hear the implied 'my' in the man's unctuous words. He couldn't let it go. "You had it so perfectly decorated, Mel, that I really didn't have to do much."

"True." Radburn glanced from the paperweight on the desk to the digital clock on the bookcase behind Stevens. The younger man could feel the intensity of his stare and fought to control the shiver running up his spine. "What brings you here today?"

The Business Manager waited several seconds before transferring his gaze to the Principal's face. "You got a freeloader in your building. Not pulling his oar with the rest of us."

Stevens took his time responding and kept his face blank as he scanned his mind for whom Radburn meant. He considered saying that it wasn't his school any more, but nodded instead. "Can't pay anybody who's just going along for the ride."

Radburn's mouth grimaced in what he would term a smile. "That's how I taught you."

Stevens' mind continued to spin. Now, he knew, the man would put him on the spot until he named the under-performing teacher. It was a test. If he guessed wrong, he would put a target on the back of some other faculty member. "It makes everyone else have to work harder," he said.

The larger man slapped the arm of his chair. "That's right. Exactly right."

Stevens ran his hand through his thinning hair, hoping to cover his unease as he stalled. "Basically, it's a matter of fairness."

"It is at that." Radburn congratulated himself again for having trained his replacement so well.

Three names occurred to the Principal. He and the Director of Curriculum were working with them, and two were in fact making progress. The third employee wasn't. He looked up as his office door opened.

"Speaker for the faculty meeting is here, boss--oh,

sorry. I didn't know--"

"Be with you in a minute, Mr. McCauley." Stevens stood up quickly.

Bob dropped the paper towel in the secretary's office behind him and extended his other hand. "Good to see you, sir."

Radburn levered himself out of the chair. "A pleasure."

Bob squinted his face in concentration. "Some budgetary crisis brings you back, or are you here for the faculty meeting?"

Radburn's face rotated from the question to his successor.

Stevens looked away from the eyes boring into his and took Bob's elbow. "Not your concern, now is it, Mr. McCauley?"

Radburn shook his head as the two exited the office. He wondered not for the first time if the man had enough spine for the job.

Joe readjusted his back in one of the uncomfortable chairs they used in the Choral room. In other years they had used the Auditorium for Faculty Meetings but found it too large, especially when teachers sat as far away from the stage as they could. He had to admit the size of this room was better. According to the choir teacher Keith Boswell, the chairs were specially designed to promote good posture and airflow, but they forced Joe to lean forward at a funny angle. He glanced at the slide the speaker was referring to on the white board in front. Maybe it wasn't the chair that was irritating him today.

"So then, in order of potency, from the weakest common opioid to the strongest, we have Tylenol with codeine, Vicodin, Percocet, and lastly, Oxycodone."

Bob's thinking was that if you have to attend the boring meetings, you might as well get your money's worth, and he'd persuaded Joe and Lexan to join him in the front row by telling them he knew the speaker. Joe did as well. Now a BCI Agent from Cleveland, Doug Canfield had played basketball and tennis for Bob. He was not particularly tall, but thickly put together. Joe knew him to be at least 25, but he looked younger, except for his eyes. The skin around them was furrowed and below them discolored.

"These are common pain-relieving drugs. I'll bet most of you have one of these in your medicine chests right now." His voice was sharp, his pacing staccato. "Maybe they're current. Maybe you kept some from an old prescription. That's a problem."

Canfield stepped out of the projector light. "Anybody here have a medicine cabinet that locks? Anyone?" He pointed out a few hands. "Good for you. Wish there were more."

He gestured to the list on the screen. "They can stay in your bathroom and alleviate your pain. Or they can make their way to a neighbor's house and who knows what happens to them."

Several hands raised at that, and Lexan nudged Joe with her elbow. He wrapped his arms around his chest. Probably the new Quaalude or Roofie or marijuana or alcohol or blood-born-pathogen or whatever it was the community wanted the school to protect their children from this time. We can't do everything, he thought.

"Listen, this is interesting," she whispered, her gray eyes intense beneath her bobbing yellow curls. "They take pills prescribed for other people or pills laced with something else. They don't even know what they're taking."

Bob slumped forward, his elbows on his knees. "And it can kill them."

"The latest thing to worry about," Joe muttered, but Lex was looking past him at Bob and didn't respond.

Joe didn't want to get involved in things he couldn't control, problems he couldn't solve. Sure, he was horrified at how easy it was for kids to get drugs, and he was angry that so much money was being made from them. But if he stopped and thought about this latest version, the 'opioid epidemic,' he would lose his focus. He couldn't afford to lose his focus. If he did, the things he could control, the problems he could solve, would crush the kids, Lexan and the teachers he worked to protect.

It's not that he didn't think the problems and dangers were real. Kids were dying all over the country, especially in Ohio and West Virginia. But he didn't have any leverage, and he had learned not to go into battle unprepared and weak, like he had before.

No, he could prevent the mayor of Stradford from hurting more kids. He could do that and he could help the Association, but that was all he was able to do.

From the other side Bob jabbed him. "Gangs, Joe, it's gangs in the 'Ford." He returned his attention to Agent

Canfield.

"Great, the 'Ford is the 'Hood."

"No, Joe, listen to him." Bob shook his head.

Canfield capped his marker and laid it next to his laptop. "The house fire, or explosion, last week. I'm sure you've heard about it?"

Bob raised his hand. "Heard it was a gas leak, right?"

Canfield furrowed his forehead. "Probably. That's the initial finding. But what we have to consider is the violence that surrounds drug dealing." He stepped closer to the teachers.

"Gas leak in the Deer Woods Creek neighborhood or not, I don't know. I do know, where there's money involved violence usually follows." He looked up. "I grew up here, Stradford isn't the ghetto, but we need to be vigilant, because sooner or later there will be violence where there is drug dealing."

Joe looked around the room. Stevens and Radburn bracketed the door, their arms crossed. A couple idiots in the back were chatting, but faculty meetings were rarely this attentive.

The Agent scowled. "Lesson two? If one gang is making money, you can be sure another gang has taken notice."

Roberta raised her hand. "We aren't the ghetto, Officer, like you said. Why are there drugs here in Stradford? I thought this was a nice place."

"Look, I hate to say this, but drugs aren't only an inner-city problem, and drug abuse is not new to Stradford." Canfield looked down at his feet, then up.

"But there is a new twist. The heavy drugs are still being sold in what you would call bad neighborhoods. Cleveland, Lorain, Youngstown. But now heroin, cocaine and oxycodone are being sold right here in the 'Ford." The Choir Room fell silent.

"Opioids are often over-prescribed for pain. They're effective, and many people end up not using their full script and sometimes those extra pills are abused. Remember the locks on the medicine cabinets?

"Other people enjoy the high and use the whole prescription, maybe even re-fill it, and the thing of it is, no one can predict who's susceptible to addiction and who isn't." Canfield drew his eyes slowly from face to face. "Those who get hooked, get really hooked, and when they run out--" The Agent shook his head.

"If they can't get any more Oxy, the dealers sell them Heroin or Fentanyl, maybe a mix, and that leads to death. A very high high I am told, but death more often than not."

The faculty buzzed as if jolted by an electric shock. Canfield let them, then raised a hand and they stilled. "There are two reasons for stopping the drug traffic. People die from the drugs themselves, and people kill for the money that comes from drugs. That's why I'm here."

Canfield flipped off the projector light. Stevens shook his hand.

"Joe?" Bob stood in front of him. "Earth to Joe. You still with us?"

Joe shook his head. I can't do everything, he thought. "Lost in the fog," he said.

"Even Super Heroes get tired," Bob smirked. "Can

you spare the time to join us? Lexie and Canfield and some others. My office, fifteen minutes?"

"Can't," he said. "Places to go, people to see."

"Wrongs to right, huh?" Bob looked quickly at Lexan. "We'll give you a pass this time."

"See you at home," Joe said and squeezed her shoulder. "Could be late."

CHAPTER SEVEN

"What would it take to make this all go away?"

Joe looked across the table at the two women. They were opponents on a playing field or opposing sides in a courtroom, but this was no game and certainly not a trial. He smiled to himself, hell, it's not even legal.

"There's not enough money in the world." Joe shook his head. "Besides, I can ruin you without having to deal with you."

He watched his words fly across the table and land in front of Mayor Kimberly Hellauer Horvath. Her hair looked two days late for a dye job, and her face looked like she had recently puked. Next to her, Pamela Holmgren bore her eyes into him and opened her mouth to speak.

Kimberly laid her hand on Pamela's arm and squeezed. Keeping her eyes on the teacher, she felt the muscles in her friend's arm relax a bit.

Joe grinned again. This couldn't be going better. Meeting at an open table in the middle of the public library had been a good plan. Everyone had to watch their manners; even Fr. Jerry would approve.

"How many more times are you going to strong-arm us, Lehrer?" Holmgren hissed.

Joe wanted to make her repeat her question, but he had already done that twice before. An Avenging Angel didn't have to use his sword every time. The threat of it would provoke them enough; the trick was to provoke them positively.

He ignored Holmgren and said to Kimberly, "There's not much more to ask for, Mrs. Mayor. You've been co-operating beautifully." He counted to five. "So far."

"You expect us to deal with you, and then we still have to negotiate with the Teachers Association?" Horvath would have sputtered like an indignant Donald Duck if she could have raised her voice. As it was she sounded slurred and drooly.

Joe suppressed his laugh. "Yes, I'm here to make things easier for both sides. Let's get two things off the table now, salary and the state tests."

"But the Board still has to negotiate," Holmgren repeated.

Joe noticed her normally elegant voice was ragged. It sounded to him that the gray-haired cosmetics heiress was tired. He smiled inside again. "Mrs. Holmgren, I didn't know you were on the negotiating team or the Board of Education."

Horvath had to restrain her friend once again. "She's not, as you know. Her point is that negotiations will be a sham if we supersede the process."

"It's to save face, Kimberly, mostly yours. It would behoove you to accomplish something positive for the people of Stradford." If her eyes had been lasers, he would have burned to death. "If you agree to these conditions, I can guarantee you that negotiations will be a painless proposition," he said. "I'll even promise that I won't be involved at all."

"You're involved now." Horvath's harsh voice increased, and several heads turned. Behind her a child grabbed her mother and pointed.

Joe waited several seconds and said calmly, "I'm involved with you because of your involvement with Governor Stanic."

He turned his attention to Holmgren. "Yes, I still have the pictures, several copies in different locations, and frankly, I'm getting tired of talking about this. I'd just as soon send them to the media and be done with it."

The owner of PamLeeCo cosmetics swallowed a curse, but the Mayor said with a sigh, "What do you want?"

"Keep the salary structure as it is. Do not connect them to the state test results."

"That's coming from the State Board of Education. We have no choice."

"No, it's coming from your friend the governor. It's an absolute non-starter for us."

Pamela looked closely at him. "Not that I care, but what bothers you so much about this? It seems fair to me."

Joe paused a moment. "It's like firing a coach because one of his players fumbled. Or missed a tackle. Or forgot the play."

"They lost the game," Pam said.

"But that doesn't mean the coach didn't do his job. It means they're kids, they make mistakes. My salary should be based on my performance, not held hostage to human nature."

They looked at him as if he were speaking German. He sighed and slid a paper across the table. Horvath turned it over and held it so the other woman could see it. Holmgren shrugged.

"The salary is a little above the county average. I'm not trying to gouge you."

"You're not?" Horvath managed.

"No, I want to humiliate you and embarrass you."

Horvath's eyes flattened into stones. "It's time someone taught you a lesson."

"I see what you did there." Joe smiled and flipped her a salute. "Teacher, lesson, sort of a play on words. *Ein Wortspiel* we would say in German class."

This time Pam had to grab her friend's arm and hold her back. She said, "We gave the job to an amateur last time, Kimberly. Now we know better." The Mayor gritted her teeth and nodded.

"Good to know." Joe slid back his chair. "Ladies, as always, it's a pleasure doing business with you." He knit his brows and lowered his voice. "Or as you ladies used to say, it's a business doing pleasure with you."

Bob looked across his desk at the three people crammed into his tiny office. Outside, the school halls were clear; the kids left long ago and the staff after the faculty meeting. He didn't keep the door closed because of the noise.

It reminded him of their days as detectives, devising schemes to break up the prostitution ring. Those days had been scary but exciting. He and Lex and Joe. Now Roberta and Lexan faced him, and BCI agent Doug Canfield sat to his left. He both missed Joe and was glad he wasn't there.

It wasn't his fault he had been unconscious and couldn't help Joe fight Weigel. Maybe then he would have been up on stage with him, instead of watching from the audience. It's not like he hadn't done anything to help save the girls; he had combed the files to prove the mayor was running the prostitution ring. Now his friend was a hero choosing which battles to fight. It wasn't as if Joe didn't deserve the attention, but maybe it was better he wasn't here.

"So, Dougie, what can we do to help you guys?"

"Eyes and ears." Agent Canfield looked at them closely. "The BCI focuses on the big picture. We rarely if ever get involved in a single town, let alone one school."

Roberta squinted as she did when concentrating. "Then why are you here?"

Canfield looked around as if sharing a secret. "Couple of reasons. One, I'm a Stradford kid. This is my school. Two, I'm playing a hunch. I think what's going on here is part of a state-wide scheme."

The teachers nodded.

"And three, maybe most importantly, I got lucky with a major case last year. Now they trust me. They're giving me a little discretionary power to run with my hunch."

"How do we fit in?" Bob sat up straight.

"We need on-the-ground information." He looked at the teachers around him. "You guys see the kids on a daily basis. You have access to information that we can't easily get."

"What kind of information are you looking for?" Lexan asked.

"Monday morning homerooms," Canfield said.

The teachers looked at him blankly.

"Unless things have really changed since I had Mrs. Turner in homeroom," Canfield said, "kids will say everything you need to know when they talk to their friends about the weekend."

"Parties, who was there, how late." Roberta nodded. "They say so much stuff that I try not to listen."

"Me, too," Lexan agreed. "I know who is going out with whom and way too many details."

"Like you guys were in the locker room," Bob said. "You get together and forget there's anybody else in the room. You tell way more than you need to."

"I wasn't like that, was I, Coach?" Canfield said.

"Son, not one of you could keep your mouths shut."

"Exactly what I want," the Agent said. "Listen to them. Find out where the party was. Who was there.

Were they drinking or smoking or popping pills? Shooting up? Were any parents around? That kind of stuff."

Bob looked at the teachers. "You guys have homerooms, and I'll bet the same stuff happens before classes start." When they nodded, he continued, "I get different information in here, usually one on one. Not as public, I guess."

"Yes, Coach, that's right." Canfield's face lit up. "When I was here, we'd call you narcs for doing this."

"Didn't somebody paint 'McCauley's a narc' on the back wall?" Bert said. "Couple years ago?"

"Misspelled two of the three words," Bob said and laughed. "But hey, this is serious. Kids are dying."

"I get the joke," Bert said. "But some of those kids really trust me."

"We're doing it for their own good," Bob said. "We have to keep them alive to teach them. Right?"

"Yes," Canfield said. "No single piece of information is going to put anyone in jail. We need to piece many together, from many sources, and do our own investigations before anybody acts. You guys are part of the process, that's all. Does that make sense?"

"We're in," Lexan said and Roberta nodded.

Canfield stood up. "The main thing, well one of the main things we want from you, is the source of the drugs. Who is getting the drugs to the sellers in the building? We know kids are selling, and we could round up a couple right now, but we need to find their sources."

"Reeling in the big fish, right Dougie?"

"That's right, and that's my job. Don't think about

that, and don't ask about that, because I won't tell you." Canfield frowned. "We're taking a risk here, so keep in your lanes, all right? I don't want anybody getting hurt."

Bob looked at his colleagues. They returned his nod.

"Thanks for your help, you guys." Canfield reached for the door. "I'll be in touch."

"I'll walk you out," Bob said and the two men left.

"Seems odd without Joe here, I bet," Roberta said. When her friend neither answered nor made any move to leave, she said, "You guys OK? It's none of my business, I know."

"Does he seem different to you, Bert? You've known him forever."

"Maybe a little, I guess. Stronger maybe. But that's a good thing."

"It is. I'm happy things are going so well for him."

"But now he's on top isn't he." Roberta squinted as she thought. "All the years I've known him, he was out there tilting at windmills, fighting the big guys."

"Now he's the big guy. He's got the power." Lexan clasped and un-clasped her purse several times.

"But he's doing good things with it, Lex. He got rehab money for those girls."

"He is. He is definitely doing good." Lexan nodded in agreement. "But you know what? It's hard being in love with a saint."

CHAPTER EIGHT

"I don't want to hurt him, Uschi. You know I'd never do that."

"If you go stomping out of here, Karl, in the mood you're in, he will be hurt," she said. "Alfred will definitely be hurt."

"He shouldn't be, it's not his fault," the big white-haired man said. "He didn't do anything wrong."

"It's his sister, you big fool. He loves her like a daughter."

Karl stepped to the screen of the lanai and looked at the boat bobbing in the canal at the end of the dock. "She's ruining everything we did."

"He gave it to her, Karl. It's hers to--"

"--Stradford is not hers to ruin. No. We, I, put too much work into it."

Alfred came out of the kitchen carrying a tray with drinks. "The sun is past the yardarm, my friends. No more business talk." He skirted the diving board end of the pool and held the tray in front of his wife. "My dear, your Old-Fashioned." She took the drink, and he set the tray down.

He picked up the remaining two drinks, but when he saw the look on Karl's face, he returned them to the tray. "We are not having this conversation again."

Karl took a slow breath and settled his weight on the balls of his feet. He loved the man, but he didn't know where this was going or how it would play out. "Did you hear what she did?"

"She settled the teacher contract. No sweat, no conflict. Pretty good work if you ask me." Alfie retrieved his Tom Collins and took a sip. "A little tart."

Karl looked down at his drink on the tray, Uschi's bare knee next to it. "Aside from giving them way too much money, she signed a three-year deal. We always did two years."

"Things change. Details changed. No biggie, big man." He moved to clink his glass but saw that Karl hadn't picked up his. "Come on, Karl."

"Boss, she made the deal outside of the process. That's not legally binding. That's subverting the law." He grabbed the beer and took a long swallow.

"After all the shit we've pulled, you're having a hissy fit about legality?" Alfie looked at his wife and they both laughed. Neither saw the look in Karl's eyes.

When they stopped laughing, Karl said, "There's a system, Alfie, you and I set up a system. Everybody knew what was expected. We only dealt with somebody when they deserved it. Like she should do with Lehrer. That's what we would have done."

"Karl, dammit, I'm getting fed up with this all the time."

"I'm getting fed up with looking like a fool." Karl jammed a finger in the other man's face. "You should be, too!"

Alfred set his glass down. "We're not looking like fools, because we're not there. We're not involved."

"Be that as it may," Karl struggled to control his breathing. "There is no way in hell that you would leave yourself open to blackmail. Neither of us would."

Alfred looked to Uschi. She shrugged.

"Now she's letting two gangs fight a turf war in Stradford. All she's got to do is pick one and get rid of the other. It's not that hard."

"I trained you, and you're explaining this to me?"

"If you're not going to take care of it, I will," Karl said.

"You work for me, Karl. I give the orders."

Karl grabbed his crotch. "Yeah? I got your orders right here. Fuck. You." He hurled his bottle into the pool and strode out of the lanai.

Governor Thompson Stanic spoke carefully into the cell phone again. "We'll figure it out." He placed his hand over the mic and raised his eyebrows to his aide, Lance. "She's having her period." His aide covered his lips and tittered.

He removed his hand. "Don't worry, Kimberly, we can make it go away." She had called him several minutes ago, and he had had few chances to say anything else. Her life was a wreck, somebody blew up a house, teachers were running amok, she gained two pounds.

"Are you done?" he said into the phone. "Have you gotten it all out?"

Lance could hear her response. "I'd say she hasn't."

Stanic lifted his feet to the desktop and settled back into his chair. "Coffee?" he mouthed, and Lance left the room to fetch it.

"Yes, I'm still here. Uh-huh, no, I didn't want to step on your feelings." The Governor paused and gave the phone a snarky smile. "Well, that's how much I respect you. You don't have to thank me. It's part of the package." He nodded as Lance set the coffee cup next to his feet, then grinned. "No, not that package, but I like the way you think." He waved Lance away and waited until the office door closed.

"OK, I think we have a couple of options." Stanic shook his head. "No, we don't have to decide right now, but let's lay them out." His silver pen twirled around his manicured nails. "I think it boils down, basically, to two."

"Come on, Kimmy, let's be rational." He held the phone away from his ear. "I have my status to consider, and, and, wait a minute, you do too. Certainly. I didn't mean that." She can be a pain in the ass, he thought.

"No, I'm not recommending one over the other. For now, I'm just laying them out." He listened to her. "Right, either we pull out the weed or we fertilize a different garden."

Stanic held the cell away from his head.

"You remember why we're talking about

gardening, don't you?" he said after the noise dropped several decibels.

"Uh-huh, we could do it from your end or from mine," Stanic continued. "As long as we keep it quiet. Right, in fact, I probably do know a landscaping service. You?" He nodded as he listened.

"Either way. Uh-huh. Your preference?"

"No, exactly," he continued. "That's the issue. There are plusses and minuses to both. We have to balance beauty in both the short and long terms, with ease and satisfaction. A whole raft of things to consider, so we should take our time deciding."

He waited and he fiddled some more with the heavy Mt. Blanc pen. "OK, how's this? How about you explore the weed pulling option, and I gather some thoughts on finding another plot for our garden. How'd that be?"

He nodded to her and said, "Listen, I got a call I have to take. Talk to you soon. Right. You too, Babe."

"You look exhausted, Boss." Lance appeared and cleared away the coffee cup.

"She's worth it, my friend." He nodded. "But that is one feisty broad."

CHAPTER NINE

Bob didn't want to be jealous of Joe. They were best friends and he knew the ribbing he got from not being there during the Weigel shooting was good-natured. Jokes like he'd make if the roles were reversed. But the roles weren't reversed. Joe was the hero, and he was the butt of the jokes. In his absence Lexan had been hurt and Chelsea had been forced to pull the trigger.

Now was his chance to redeem himself. While Joe was wielding the sword of justice and accepting awards, Bob could take the lead in fighting the opioid crisis. Lexan and Roberta would help and Canfield would be there of course, but if he could find a way, the jokes about buying beer during the shootout would cease.

He glanced through his office window and keyed open the website for Cardinal Educational Services. He searched names of officers and whistled when he saw how many different products they supplied. Floor wax to roofing tar and everything in between. He found it funny that the only product they supplied for the State Tests were the pre-test workbooks. He could check to see who sold the other test materials.

He sat back in his chair and looked at his poster of Payne Stewart. Poor slob, asphyxiated in an airplane. His eyes caught Cardinal's shipping address. Blacklick, Ohio. He clicked Google maps and there it was, an industrial park off I-70 not far from Columbus. He changed from the map to the satellite view and dragged the cursor over the images. Cardinal owned several small buildings and a larger one he assumed was the warehouse. The cursor ran across another building and the name Murgatroyd lit up. He had seen it someplace before. He thought, frowned and bobbled Tiger Woods' head. Answer sheets. Scanable answer sheets like they use to grade the State Tests. He wondered if it could be a coincidence.

Most villages and small towns have a local spot for their residents to meet and socialize. Many larger towns and cities have neighborhoods with bars or restaurants that serve the same function. In Stradford, like many suburbs, people live in one place and socialize in another.

When the Stradford High School faculty gets together for a session of 'paper-grading,' they generally meet at *Competitors* in a strip mall on Center. It's not classy or charming, but offers extended Happy Hours drink specials on Friday afternoons.

Joe Lehrer clearly didn't have to worry about half-priced drinks or paying for any drinks at all. His role in securing more money for all of them in the new teacher contract made it unnecessary for him to reach for his wallet or even to have a wallet in his pocket.

Roberta nodded at the enormous plate of loaded nachos the waitress set between the Buffalo wings and pot stickers in front of Joe, and said to Lexan, "Girl, you won't have to cook for a month."

Lexan grinned as the waitress handed her another glass of Pinot Grigio. "He does most of the cooking anyway."

The French teacher stared at her. "He cooks, too? I thought he was kidding about that."

Lexan sipped her wine. "No joke."

"Joe can do everything. Almost anything." Bob's mug clattered when he set it down and the others looked at him. "You guys know why Radburn's been in the building lately?"

"What did Joe say?" Roberta asked.

Bob pursed his lips and shook his head.

Roberta thought he was mad at her. "Sorry, I thought he would know." She shrugged. "He or maybe Gene."

"Joe has no idea."

The women looked at each other.

"Radburn's in the building railroading Hoskins, and St. Joe doesn't even know it's happening."

Lexan started to speak. Bob shushed her and drained his beer.

Roberta looked from one to the other. "Wish my husband--"

"We're not married," Lexan said quickly and

banished a curl from her face.

Roberta looked back to Bob. "Anyway, I wish my 'significant other' knew where the heck our kitchen was." Neither Bob nor Lexan laughed

Lexan jabbed her arm across the table to where Joe was taking a selfie with some teacher from Raub Elementary. "Want me to take it for you?" Lexan held out her hand for the girl's cell phone.

"Got it under control, hon," Joe said as he gave the young woman a hug and returned to the table.

Roberta nudged her with an elbow. "He can do it all, can't he?" When Lexan didn't respond and Bob balled up his napkin, she leaned across the table to Joe and said, "You must be exhausted."

Joe whooshed out a long breath and wiped his hand across his forehead. "That was selfie number fourteen, but who's counting?"

"You're the darling of social media." Bob looked at Lexan.

Joe smiled and finished his drink. "Bert, it's tough, but somebody's got to do it. Right, Lexie?"

She tipped her glass to him. "You seem to be coping."

"Actually, for once it's pretty good to be me." Joe leaned closer to Roberta.

A round of applause interrupted them, as Association President Gene Phillips stepped gingerly onto the bar. "Ladies and gentlemen! Oh, wait a sec." He shaded his eyes with his hands and scanned the crowd. "I don't see any administrators or board members, so I guess I can say that!"

The crowd laughed and several whistled. "You all know why we're here--"

"--you're buying drinks!" someone shouted, probably Zimmerman.

"No, no freebies tonight," Gene said as the room quieted. "I don't want to interrupt the celebration, but I wanted to clarify why it is we're here tonight." Someone handed him a beer. "Our Association Representative, Joe Lehrer, has brought labor peace and financial stability to Stradford. Let's raise a glass to Joe!"

The crowd cheered and applauded, and several people pounded Joe's back.

"We all want peace so we can continue to work with the young people of Stradford." Gene's calm voice was hard to pick up in the crowded room. "But the Association thought you might like a little more prosperity in your paycheck twice a month as well!" He toasted Joe again with his mug.

"Joe, Joe, Joe!" the others chanted.

"Maybe we can get him up here."

"Speech, speech!"

Joe shook his head, but hands prodded him and he stood up. He reached his hand to Lexan, but she held back, and the crowd swept him to the make-shift stage.

Lexan watched teachers grab his hand, hug him, and pummel his back. Strangers, teachers she didn't know, hugged Joe, and told her how proud of him she must be. Roberta watched her face, and thought about what Lexan had said last week in Bob's office about living with a saint.

"This was no big deal," Joe was saying from the top

of the bar next to Gene. "I'm just an Association member like you all and was happy to be able to do it."

The crowd cheered him. He paused a moment drinking it in, then said, "Listen, really. Thank you, but I just did what any of you would have done."

They raised their glasses to him and gave him the ultimate Cleveland tribute: they woofed like they were in the Dawg Pound rooting on the Browns.

Lexan leaned her head closer to her friend's. "Meanwhile, kids are dying from opioids."

"Mixing that synthetic Fentanyl into everything." Bob tossed the paper wad toward the bar. "And teachers are getting fired."

Roberta squinted her eyes as she did when she was confused. "He can't do everything, Lex."

"Sure he can. He's Joe Freaking Lehrer." Bob stood up.

"He's drinking shots, and kids are dying." Lexan crossed her arms. "He could help us do something."

On the bar, Joe was holding his hand to his ear as if he couldn't hear the cheering. He didn't see Bob leave, or hear Lexan's comment. Gene clapped enthusiastically beside him.

In the parking lot outside, Oskar turned on the heater of his truck to clear the fog from his windshield. He had been waiting a long time now, and it was cold. He rubbed his hands together, then pulled his leather work gloves back on. He would wait as long as he needed to.

CHAPTER TEN

From 32,000 feet above Ohio the sun looked as warm as it had in Florida and the sky nearly the same blue. Karl knew better. He rubbed his hands together and turned away from the window. Same color but different temperature. The disembodied voice of the stewardess, he knew that's not what they called them now but didn't care, had just announced they would be landing soon. Good, he thought, I've had enough of this seat. He wondered for a second how the people in the back managed.

It was a rhetorical question. He didn't care about the people in the rear cabin or those with him in first class either, for that matter. He cared about a small number of things, and no one on the plane was on the list, except maybe the pilot. He settled his long legs and cinched the seatbelt.

Forty minutes later he tossed his bag into the back of the Mahindra XUV500 they had given him at the rental counter and worked his way out of Hopkins International toward I-71 south. One of the things he did care about was Stradford. Not the town itself, but the way it used to be. Neat, orderly, controlled. He had to pause on the on-ramp as the wash from a semi buffeted the puny import. It wouldn't have bothered the Caddy he'd requested. He flashed a bird to the driver and shot around the truck.

"Fucking learn to drive, would you?" he muttered. Interstate lanes were supposed to be based on speed. The left lanes for the fastest, the right for the slowest. "Get out of the way and let the merging traffic enter."

The driving was not really what was making Karl angry. He was used to disorderly driving having lived here twenty years. It was the disorder in Stradford, and that couldn't be cured with a couple of well-aimed curses and a burst of speed. He exited the expressway at Center and worked his way into the Deer Woods Creek development. He parked in front of one of the McMansions where he could see the house on the corner of Hill Valley.

Not much was left of what Kimberly called the Wish Fulfillment Center; collapsed roof, blackened walls, shattered windows, a door in the front yard. A rotten tooth in a mouth of pearly whites. He appreciated her choice of words but didn't like what it meant. When he was in charge, this house was maintained as if it belonged in this area. It was neat and orderly. It had to be, because the people who supported it were neat and orderly. Drug addicts in this town liked to think their habit was as normal as a mowed lawn and freshly painted shutters. When he was in charge, they distributed product here but didn't make it. He kept the product separate from the money.

Now there will be questions. Karl drummed the steering wheel with his thumbs. Ownership had been buried in a series of shells, so that would hold for the moment. If they had any sense, they'd call the explosion a gas leak. But now the cops will start asking the neighbors about activity at the house: who was coming and going, what they looked like, when the lights were off, if the lights in the house ever were off. He stopped drumming. If Kim had the sense to keep a lid on this. If she had a clue.

He muttered a curse. All the time he had spent making sure the sellers dressed the part. Making sure they made their pick-ups when most of the neighborhood was at work or asleep. Keeping the bulk materials in the mattress store. He bit his lip. The products we moved through here maybe weren't neat and orderly, but dammit, my process was.

The engine raced when he punched the ignition, and he forced himself to pause and take a breath. It was time to talk to Kimmy.

Joe Lehrer hated lesson plans. Knowing last week where he'd be this week, with this group of kids, was at best a guess and at worst a deliberate deception. Reducing what 'the student' would learn, as opposed to what a real student did learn, was a hope or a dream. Submitting a paper copy to Nancy and posting it on-line for the parents was simply a waste of time.

Joe taught best when he took the pulse of the class and directed his lesson from where they actually were to where the curriculum needed them to go. That worked when he was observant, and when they were open with their questions and sincere with their efforts.

In his rational moments, he knew neither method worked every time for every kid. He had turned in his lesson plans for this week, but consulting them now and looking at his German II class, he wasn't sure they were going to work. They had been ready last week when he ran out of time, and it was hard for him to re-establish that feeling. He finished taking attendance and stood up.

"You'll need notebooks today, class," he said in German. Those that understood did so, and those who didn't followed their lead. He reached for the Nerf ball on his desk.

"Ooh, ooh," Jodi nearly squealed. "Direct object! It's a direct object!"

Chuck dropped his pen onto his notebook. "Grammar? Again?"

"Actually, Jodi, the ball is not a direct object at the moment. It's just sitting in my hand."

She screwed up her face and paged through her notes. "No, no I wrote it down, Herr." She jabbed her finger at the page. "See, right here. 'The ball is the Direct Object'." She shoved the notebook onto TJ Teeple's desk.

"Read her notes, TJ," Joe said holding the ball for the class to see. "Is the ball moving?"

"Direct Object is the receiver of the action," TJ read. "Man, your writing is so neat."

"*Danke*," Jodi said and blushed a little.

"Action," Joe repeated and looked at the ball. "Anybody see an action? Is the ball moving?"

"Predicate Noun," Ketul announced.

"What?" Chuck tossed his pen again. "Man."

"Thank you, Ketul," Joe said, "but let's stay on track here." That was the thing about lesson plans. The kid was absolutely right, but now was not the time for it. He was so far ahead of the others it would muddy everything up for them if he pursued that angle. He handed Ketul his favorite grammar book, *The Deluxe Transitive Vampire.* "Take a look at this. We'll catch up with you later."

He turned back to TJ. "Keep reading."

"Yeah, so the Direct Object receives the action."

"And the Subject does the action!" Jodi said.

"*Sehr gut,*" Joe said, "but again I ask, where is the action?"

"Karaoke night at *Competitors,* Herr." Chelsea did her Mona Lisa smile. "So I've heard."

"What is going on?" Chuck said.

Joe turned to the board to hide his grin. "OK, everybody," he said as he picked up a marker. "Check your notes. Do you have a definition for Subject and for Direct Object? The do-er and the receiver of the action. Got it?"

He walked to the front of the room and held up the spongy ball. "No action, no Direct Object. Questions?"

"No? OK, let's move on." He tossed the ball up and down in his hand. "That's an action, now we have a

Subject and a Direct Object." He paused. "Right?"

Several heads nodded and he tossed the ball to Irwin. The kid dropped it, picked it up and tossed it in the neighborhood of the bookcase. Several kids snickered. Joe retrieved the ball and threw it again. "OK, I'm throwing it, so I'm the Subject. Now Irwin is throwing it, so he's the Subject."

"Right? OK, so what?"

"I got it," TJ said reading from Jodi's notes. "That means they, uh, they have different forms."

"Right, like *ich* and *mich*."

"Personal Pronouns!" Chuck said. "Nailed it!"

Joe checked their faces for comprehension. He held most of their eyes, and decided to keep going. He tossed the ball once again to Irwin. "Fine, we got the Subject and the D.O, but what about Irwin?" The kid tossed Joe the ball. "Now what am I?"

Joe looked directly at Chelsea and wagged a finger. "Not one word about the second baseman, young lady." She raised her hands in surrender.

He spoke as the ball flew back and forth across the room. "Is Irwin the D.O? Am I throwing Irwin? No. The ball is the D.O. But who is the receiver of the ball?"

"Right, the thrower is the subject, the ball is being thrown, and the guy catching it, or not," the class looked at Ketul and giggled. "The guy who catches the ball is the Indirect Object."

"Chuck, does that make sense? Do you see three different things going on here?"

Chuck called for the ball. Joe tossed it to him. Chuck said, "Now I'm the Indirect Object."

TJ slapped his palm. Jodi clapped. Joe knew he had them.

"What's the bottom line? Huh?"

"Indirect objects have a different form?"

"Yes, exactly," Joe said and grabbed a stack of papers from his desk. "OK, gang, I'm giving you these papers." He paused. "I, Subject, papers, D.O, you, I.O. Got it?

"Homework." He waited for them to look up. "Identify the Subs, the D.Os and the I.Os."

The bell rang and he smiled. *"Auf Wiedersehen!"*

CHAPTER ELEVEN

Karl looked at the buildings of Cookies' Cookies spread out below him. They ran along the southeast quadrant of the Cleveland Avenue intersection with Center Street, forming a capital ell with a serif. He remembered when the complex was a single building, just the serif itself.

The tall, white-haired man turned from the window in Kimberly's office and looked at his watch again. Her perpetual tardiness had been a source of humor when Alfie was in charge, and Karl had enjoyed poking the old man about it. "She's your sister, for Pete's sake," he'd said. "Why can't you control her?"

It wasn't funny now. It was just another example of her incompetence.

"--thought the meeting was in my other office," Kimberly was saying as the door crashed open. "I brought bagels, sorry I'm late." She shoved a Panera bag into his hands and pecked his cheek. Before he could say anything, Kimberly Hellauer Horvath, Mayor of Stradford and CEO of Cookies' Cookies was seated behind her desk, beaming up at him.

"Nice flight?"

Karl calmly set the bagels on her desk and sat down. "Not particularly."

"It's so nice to see you, Karl. I miss you." Kimberly made a pouty mouth.

"Me, too." She's dancing with who brung her, he thought, still playing the wide-eyed little girl. "That's not why I'm here."

"You're not happy to see me?" Her eyes joined the pout.

"Of course I am," he snapped. "But we have business to discuss."

"You don't have to be rude." Her pout faded and her eyes set.

"You can drop the little girl shit," he said. "You got major problems here."

She relaxed her body and slowed her breathing, the way her therapist had showed her. "The key word here is 'you'," she said. "Any problems in Stradford are mine to deal with." When the man didn't respond she added, "Not yours."

Karl's first thought was to shoot the ungrateful, ignorant bitch. He matched her long, careful breath. "Can you handle a gang war?"

To his surprise she slapped the table top and laughed. A deep, whole-body laugh. "The house burned down because of a gas leak, Karl. You came all the way up here because of a gas leak? You thought it was part of a gang war?" She tried to hold back another laugh.

Karl forced his pulse rate to steady. "I don't know who told you it was a gas leak, or who you're listening to, but--"

"It's sweet that you care about fire safety, but really." She waved a hand and tried to straighten her face. "No, that's all under control."

She looked at Karl and realized nothing had changed. He still thinks he's running Stradford. He looked at Alfie like that, and Alfie had let him. Not me. "Look," she said. "I've talked to the people in charge, as well as my 'off-book consultants' as you used to call them." She noticed his eyes brightened a bit at that. The lower part of his face didn't.

"Indications from all sources are that it was just that. An accident," she said.

"That's too much of a coincidence." He shook his head. "No way six adults died in an accident. They were working, not paying attention, and somebody took them out."

Part of her enjoyed watching Karl, especially when he was irritated. "Go on," she said.

"Thank you." She's playing with me, Karl thought. "First of all, you need to verify who they were."

"Karl, they were our people. You know that. It was our house." She checked the calendar on her phone and waved her hand. "Your wish fulfillment place. Whatever."

When she finally looked up, he said, "I've heard someone's moving in on us. Probably think there's a power vacuum here."

"You leave and it's a power vacuum?" She shook her head and dropped the phone onto her desk. "Self-absorbed much?"

He strangled the arms of the chair. "It's probably the Russians. Your father and I helped get them out of the Cleveland market, now they want it back." he managed to say. "They're not our friends."

"So, we let our friends, as you call them, handle it themselves. They're armed, you know," she said not bothering to look at him. He actually was pretty well-informed. "Save me the history lesson. We'll let the mobs kill each other and keep the survivors under control."

"You can't even keep the teachers under control," he said angrily. "You're still being blackmailed! Just kill the guy!"

"I abhor violence," she said to make his face darken.

"You gave them everything they wanted!"

"Maybe I did, maybe I didn't," she said. "I bought us some labor peace."

"Labor peace maybe." He looked out the window, took a breath, and tried again. "Kim, they blew up a house in a good neighborhood. If you don't do something to stop them, they'll be shooting each other in the mall."

"But nobody's shooting anybody in Florida, right?"

She was leaving him very little choice. "I also hear they have a new product."

She looked up, startled, but kept her face closed. Karl continued, "Now you listen? Way cheaper and way, way stronger."

"Oh, that? The Holy Grail of drugs?" Kimberly dismissed it with another wave. "They're always chattering about some new super drug. Probably blew themselves up making it."

"Worth taking a look," he said.

"I have looked. Besides, you hear all this stuff from 1000 miles away. Your information's not any better than mine. Come on, give me some credit."

"I trust my sources. Been working with them for years."

"One of mine was one of yours. Oskar Blattenfelter, whatever his name."

"Oskar's alive?" Karl spat, all attempts at self-control forgotten. "I, I gave explicit orders to have that piece of shit slob taken out. He, he's a loose thread, a loose cannon."

"Explicit orders?" she said. It delighted her to see the man squirm. "See, that's the thing, Karl. I give the orders in Stradford, explicit, implicit. All of them." She stared until he looked at her. "You're not in charge anymore."

"He can hurt us, Kimberly."

She was expecting his don't-fuck-with-me expression and matched it with her own. "Then you should have taken care of it before you left town."

He started to say something, but she held up her hand. "Time's up, old man. You had your chance. Say hello to my brother in sunny Naples, would you?"

"You can't--"

"Yes, I can." She pointed to the door. He hesitated, thought of Uschi, and left the room.

The door closed and her office quiet again, she released a breath to loosen her shoulders. When her muscles relaxed and her breathing slowed, she scrolled her cell for Governor Stanic's private number. *Does every man I know have to be an asshole?* She giggled and reached for her phone.

On a normal teaching day it wouldn't be so bad. Lexan could immerse herself in the activities, focus on the kids, and before she knew it the day would be over. But today was Chapter Eight test day, decreed by the Spanish Department, Nancy Turner, Chair. That meant every section of Spanish II was taking the test today, and that meant Lexan had time to think about Joe.

She heard a rustling in the room and looked up. Eyes returned to tests, and she continued thinking about him. It wasn't as if they knew each other all that well before she moved in with him. They had agreed this was a trial and getting to know each other was part of the fun. What she had learned about him was great. She loved his openness and honesty and vulnerability. He was not afraid to admit he needed her. She wasn't used to those qualities in a man. The lack of them had burned her more than once.

The sound of a desk sliding across the terrazzo floor interrupted her. She froze Chandler with a stare. He lifted his hands in a 'who me?' gesture before lowering his eyes.

Lexan hated everything about cheating: the deception, the lying, the covering up, the basic wrongness. She hated having to talk about cheating with her students.

She didn't think she was good at it, but did so anyway, hoping it would dissuade a couple of them at least. The thought of entering a zero in the gradebook nauseated her. And on top of it all having to explain the concept to the parents.

She tallied the score, wrote it on top of the test and circled it. Halfway done grading the previous class. Won't have too many to take home and grade, she thought. She dropped the red pen onto the pile. The thing is, it felt to her as if Joe had changed. It wasn't his openness and honesty, it seemed he was actually different. Now he was the top dog, not the underdog. He was more aggressive, more confident. More vengeful.

He really believes he's Michael the Archangel. She shook the thought from her head, but it returned, unbidden. Was he always like that? She didn't think so; that wouldn't have attracted her. He was clearly still in love with her, she knew that, but he was a winner now. He had power and for what she could see, he enjoyed using it. Had he been like that before he started blackmailing the Mayor?

Her eyes jerked up at the sound. Might have been whispering, she wasn't sure, but the looks on the boys' faces convinced her. Lexan kept her face blank and stood up. It was time to take a walk.

She arranged the desks in rows on test days and spaced them far apart to make it hard to see from one to the other. "Twelve more minutes," she announced. "If you haven't started page three, you better get at it."

It was always the last row. The farther they were from the teacher's desk, the more invisible they became.

Thought they were ostriches. Somehow the last desks in two of the rows were closer to each other than the front desks. The same thing had happened in the last hour, and she had made sure to set them right before this group came in. My Lord, she thought, it's a chapter test, not the final exam. Just study!

Lexan stopped at the end of the row and didn't circle the room as the miscreants expected her to. Instead she turned her back on them and looked out the window. "Good," she said and extended a finger to the glass. "The custodians are plowing the faculty lot. I'll be able to drive home tonight." She turned her body slightly to see the reflection of the two boys in the back seats. One was leaning over and examining the other's test paper.

"So, Kenny, do you think Blair's answer to number 14 is right or wrong?" She started speaking with her back to the class, then slowly rotated toward them. "I mean, you're just checking, right?"

Blair reddened. His fingers scrabbled on the slick desk top trying to pull his test away from the edge. "I'm not cheating, Ms. Warner, I mean, we're not, I mean--"

She took the tests from each of them and stood between their desks. "Mr. Mazur, Mr. Chandler, these desks are too close to one another."

"That's where they were when we got here. We just sat down."

"No, Mr. Chandler, they weren't." She looked up to the rest of the class. "Turn around, there's nothing to see here."

"We weren't cheating." Kenny Chandler stressed 'cheating' as if it were the stupidest thing in the world. Or as if Lexan were. He was a big lug of a kid, overweight, sloppily dressed and very sure of himself. Popular too. She wondered what the other kids saw in him.

"I'll look at these tests and compare the answers. If I find a pattern--" Lexan dropped her voice.

"Weren't cheating." Kenny arranged his arms as a pillow and lowered his head.

"We weren't, Signora," Blair Mazur said. "Really." He was thin and looked tired. Pretty bright and usually eager to please. She pushed the two desks apart and walked up the aisle. "Couple minutes left."

The bell rang. Kenny pretended to wake up from a nap, stretching and groaning. She collected the test papers as the children filed from the room. She let Kenny past, but held Blair.

"We need to talk, Mr. Mazur."

"I didn't cheat," he mumbled to the floor. "Those are my answers."

"All of them?" She stood in the doorway and held the handle so the next class wouldn't interrupt them. The boy nodded.

"Why did you let him do it?"

He looked up at her. "I didn't do anything wrong. I didn't cheat. You didn't see anything. I have to get to my next class."

She held his gaze as he fidgeted and looked away. "I hope not, Blair, I really do. You've got a lot going for you. Don't blow it."

"Yes, Ma'am," he blurted and escaped into the corridor. Lexan straightened the rows of desks.

CHAPTER TWELVE

Kim kicked off her shoes and squeezed the little toe on her right foot as Stanic's phone rang. She sighed. Just before it went to voice mail, he picked up. "I'm in for option one," she said.

"No foreplay?"

"Sorry, sir, how's this?" She feigned a giggle. "How are you? I'm fine. Let's kill--"

"Not funny!" Stanic covered the phone and motioned for Lance to leave. The aide did, but slowly and grudgingly. "OK, I can talk now. You can't joke around, Kim, we don't know who's listening."

She sighed and rubbed her foot again. The man was a worry-wart. "Yes. No. I don't know. I just want it to be over."

"That would be faster, I agree."

"The faster we get Stradford under control, you can run for congress and I can move on down the road to the statehouse. That's our plan and I'm ready for it."

Stanic could feel the heat from her smile through his phone. He looked at it in his hand, then said, "Well, I've been thinking."

Her mind flashed white hot. He was trying to dump her. "Oh? Thinking about what, dear?"

"Well, option two for one thing."

"Uh-huh." She drawled the word out.

"Yeah, look, if we get caught, we're toast."

"That's it?"

"No, no, not at all. I've got a plan that will achieve what we want, prove to be more than satisfactory, and," he paused, "it will make us some money, too."

"You're not getting me out of this shithole suburb? Is that what you're saying?"

"No, no, I am, I promise." He rubbed a cloth over his forehead. She could control his body temperature from a hundred miles away.' Just not this election cycle. Evanko won't leave his seat."

"You're not running for congress?" She let the hysteria rise in her voice. "I can't be governor?"

"No, you will, you will. I'll run for Blankenship's Senate seat in two years. He's 106 now, and hey, come on, the Senate is way better than the House."

She let him stew for a minute before saying, "That pushes back my election."

"But only for two years, two years, and in the meantime, I got a way for you to hurt Mr. Teacher and Little Miss Barbie, and make us a whole shit-ton of money."

"This had better be good."

When I'm *avtoritet*, Iosif thought, things will be different. He gunned the car up the rutted excuse for a driveway. Gravel spat into the undercarriage, and Dima grabbed the armrest. I won't have to do the grunt work and I won't have to babysit the 'newbie.'

He fishtailed into the street and gunned it again on the smooth surface of the state road. The young man beside him was scared to death. He wouldn't be any help, but at least he'd gotten away from the farmhouse.

Filya, the man keeping him from his rightful position as the head of the team, had found a farm in Wayne County for the Bratva. It had plenty of room for all of them and their vehicles, but was too far from Stradford. Nothing to do but look at cows and their weird-looking Amish neighbors.

Iosif's headlights flashed on an orange triangle. He cursed, swerved into the other lane and shot around the black horse-drawn buggy. He couldn't believe this was America. Dima's face was ashen even in the weak dashboard light. He smacked the kid on his knee and grinned.

"Filya won't be happy if you wreck the car. He told me to drive," the kid mumbled.

"Filya doesn't trust you, that's why I'm driving."

In the buggy behind them Karl raised the device Jacobs had given him. It looked like a garage door opener.

"I'm wounded, that's why I can't drive.'"

Jacobs snapped the reins. "Push the button." Karl did.

Two small explosive charges blew out the left side tires as Iosif sped into the right-hand curve. He slammed the brakes, and yanked the steering wheel, but the rear end didn't hold. He managed to keep from rolling over, but slid across the other lane and crashed into a huge maple tree.

Jacobs tugged the horse to a stop. "See, modern technology works."

Steam rose from the hood of the wrecked car. Karl looked at the small plastic object. I could have shot the tires out, you know."

"There was a time you could have." Jacobs gestured at the wreck. The driver lay on top of the steering wheel. The passenger sprawled half outside the car. "They dead?"

"Doesn't matter. Old Sasha will get the message either way."

Jacobs didn't understand, but nodded. He clicked to the horse, and they continued down the darkened road in silence.

It was a two-for-one message, Karl thought. Sasha had been the head man in the Youngstown mafia, the Bratva, whatever the Russians called it. They had come to an agreement years ago, the result being Sasha's gang stayed out of the Cleveland market. Karl had known Iosif, Sasha's son, for years, and whether the kid lived or died, the former 'authority' would know what it meant. The new *avtoritet* would, too.

Karl noticed the patches of snow where the

moonlight illuminated the softly rolling hills. The other person he could leverage with the message was Mayor Horvath. Kimberly was just a girl in Karl's view, but her words had stung him. The reality that he was not in charge and that she was, stung even more. More importantly, it had distracted him from the main point: the Stradford he and Alfie had spilled blood to create.

So he had taken her shit and meekly left her office. He swallowed the bile that rose as he thought about it. He had made a plan to keep Stradford safe like the ones he and her brother used to make. Whether she would be impressed was not the concern. He had come to realize that Kim really didn't matter. If she climbed on board, great, it'd be like the old days. If not, she could be dealt with. She was his best friend's sister, but she wasn't more important than Stradford.

CHAPTER THIRTEEN

"Why can't you get a good night's sleep and drive down in the morning?" Lexan stood in the bedroom doorway.

Joe finished folding a shirt and laid it in his overnight bag. "First of all," he grinned, "I'm not so certain that I'd get all that much sleep."

He turned to her when she didn't smile or unfold her arms. "Look, Lex, I gotta meet with these guys. I'll drive down after school today, have dinner tonight, then meet early on Saturday. I'll be home late afternoon. We can do something tomorrow night."

"You don't have to spend your weekend with the Ohio Education Association in Columbus. It has nothing to do with Stradford."

"The OEA and the National Education Association," he said. "It does have a lot to do with

Stradford, in the long run."

Her right hand swiped a curl from her face then sped back to its place around her waist. "In the long run."

He balled his socks and tossed them into the bag. "OK, maybe that's a stretch. It is an honor. These are the guys that negotiate teacher contracts all over the country. They're in Columbus, and they want me to share what we've done in Stradford."

"What you've done."

He sat down on the bed and patted the space beside him. She hesitated, then sat down, her arms still tight around her. "What I've done, you're right."

"What is your topic, 'How to use blackmail for the greater good'? Is that about right?"

He put his arm around her and she shrugged it off. "Come on Lex, should I not go?"

"No, go, go ahead. You need to get credit for what you did."

"But then why the attitude?"

Her hand darted out again, this time across her eyes. "It's the Winter Formal tonight. You promised to chaperone."

"It's another dance, Lexan. That's why you're mad?"

"I'm not mad."

"Oh, oh, it's worse than mad," he nudged her with his elbow. He tried to keep his voice light and make it sound like he was joking. "You're disappointed."

She got to her feet and faced him. "Actually, I am. I am very disappointed in you."

He ignored the blush rising up her face.

"Disappointed that I got us a great contract or disappointed that I can't dance the night away with you?"

"It's not about dancing."

He stood and put the rest of his clothes in the bag. "Then why's it so important?"

"You forgot, like you always do when you're caught up in your saving the world shit. Stuff."

"What did I forget?"

"No, don't worry about it, go on to Columbus and get a good night's rest." She took a step toward the door. "Share your expertise with the big shots."

"Damnit, Lexan, what is this about?"

She turned and he saw the tears in her red-rimmed eyes. "There will be kids doing drugs tonight, Joe. We're not going to be dancing." She paused at the word. "We're going to be looking for opioids. Bob and Bert and Canfield and others."

"Oh, man," Joe began.

She held up her hand. "This isn't the first time you've let us down. We keep thinking you're going to show up."

"I can't do everything, Lex, I can't."

"You don't have to do everything; that's what I'm trying to tell you."

He furrowed his brow and looked at her.

"But you do have to appreciate what others are doing," she said.

"That's not fair. Bob and Bert are my friends, and I love you."

"No." She waved her hand and took a breath. "Ever since--"

"--ever since I saved your life?" he shot back.

She squared her shoulders to him. "Can we be done with that? I've thanked you a million times. That's not what I mean."

"Then what do you mean?"

She blew out a breath. "Ever since you decided you were the winner, the only winner, the rest of us are, I don't know, redundant."

He turned away and grabbed his bag. The zipper jammed as he tried to close it, and he cursed. "I'm just trying to do the right thing. I only have so much leverage to use. If you can't understand that--" His voice faded.

"No," she said. She stood by the door, her feet apart, her arms still clutched around her. "I understand that. We all do."

Joe turned to her. "So the problem is what?"

"You're not the only one trying to do the right thing." She shook her head but the look remained on her face. "Get over yourself, Joe."

"No, I agree with you," Pamela said for what seemed to her the seventh time. "I do agree we have to do something."

"This is intolerable," Kimberly repeated. Each time was louder and more staccato than the previous, so by now the six syllables were sharp as the spikes on her heels. "We can't let that man think he can run my city!"

Pamela was tired, but this conversation could be her last chance to get Kim under control and in control of Stradford. She fixed a pleasant smile on her face and said, "Karl does have his uses, but let's not put all our faith in him."

Kimberly paused her rant and offered a slight smile. More of a smirk, but to Pamela, who fancied herself the expert on Kim's moods, it was enough. "Of course," the Mayor said. "Anything we do with him is on a contingency basis."

Pamela nodded. "When the contingency is no longer in effect--"

"--neither will he," the Mayor finished. "Show him in."

Maybe I don't have her quite under control, Pamela thought as she pushed her chair under the table in the basement bar of Shelby's Country Inn.

Kimberly watched her weave through the dark room and return moments later with Oskar. She waved 'no' to her friend's expectant look and motioned for the man to sit.

"Fancy place," he said. "I don't get in here much."

"Quiet place," she said. "Keep it that way."

He leaned his beefy forearms on the table and picked at one of several dirty fingernails. "Not a problem. Ma'am."

"Good." She expected him to smell bad. He looked like he smelled bad, but she couldn't tell. "I have a proposition for you."

The eyes in the man's porcine face expanded in delight. "I'm not that kind of man, but if you're--"

She realized her mistake and raised her palm. "A deal, Oskar, I have a deal for you."

"Oh." The fat around his eyes oozed back and the pupils recovered their normal size.

"Something for you and something for me," she said and waved to the waitress.

After she'd ordered him a beer, he said, "What do you want me to do?"

"Don't you want to know what you'll get out of it?"

He put his hands in his lap. "Not the way it works around here. People always want something from me. Usually they never pay me back."

"Well, Oskar, I will. That's what makes it a deal."

His lips tightened at her pedantic tone. "What do you want?"

She had to look away. "Information."

"What else?"

"Just information. It's not the kind of stuff I can get from my staff." She looked back at him. "Or from the police."

Oskar's mind scrabbled at what that could mean. "Why me?"

"It's street level information," she said. "411."

He looked at her blankly.

She coughed and cursed Pamela. "It's stuff that the Mayor can't be seen finding out."

"Illegal stuff?"

"Getting the information is not illegal." She looked at him sincerely. "Even if it were, we could probably find a way to help you out."

"Probably's not good enough." He took a swig of his beer.

"No, we'll cover you. Absolutely," she said and told him what she wanted.

Oskar finished the beer and placed the bottle

deliberately on the coaster. "I don't work for free, Mayor."

Kimberly looked past him at the darkened bar. ESPN played on one screen, Fox on another, but no one was watching. The waitress was cleaning glasses at the far end of the bar, and Pamela, she knew, was watching the door. "Karl or the teacher." she said. "Either one."

The fat man smiled and his eyes widened. She knew she had him.

"Make yourself at home." Bob hoped he could update Joe on his Carnation research as his friend closed the office.

"Whew."

"Bad day at work, dear?" Bob saw the look on Joe's face as he collapsed into the chair and knew it was not the time.

"Bad day at home is more like it."

"Even super heroes have bad days, you know." Bob gave him a grin.

"OK, bad day at the Fortress of Solitude, then."

Bob waited, then said, "You want me to interrogate, or do you want to share?"

"Asshole."

"True, but when you get down to it, that's about it: you talk or I pry."

"I came in here for some advice," Joe said.

"You'll get it, but come on. Is it the Board, the Mayor, Shirley Temple? Who's raining on your parade?"

"Who's on first," Joe said, but Bob shook his head instead of laughing. "OK, it's Lexan. You've been working with her. What's her problem?"

"That's what I was afraid of," Bob said, stalling. "How 'bout them Cavaliers?"

"Spill it," Joe said. "I'm serious."

"You said it yourself, Joe. I've been working with her. You haven't."

"I've been busy."

"Of course you have. No one is doubting that. You're probably doing too much."

Before Joe could speak again, Bob said, "No one else could do the things you have, for the girls, the teachers. That's not the problem."

"What then? I don't understand her. She's moody and won't talk."

"She's moody?"

"What's that word for it? Snappish. She's very snappish."

"Here's the thing, the major point, Joseph. Listen to me." Bob sat up straight and rearranged his face. He was totally serious. "In a relationship, the most common fault you find in your partner, is the fault you find in yourself."

"I think I saw that in a fortune cookie once."

"Asshole." Bob waited for Joe to lose the grin. "I'm serious. You're the snappish one. You're the one who's stopped communicating."

"You didn't hear her; she ripped me a new one." Joe's face darkened. "You weren't there."

"That's where it started, Joe. You haven't been there. All that good stuff you've been doing--"

"She called it shit."

"She was in the middle of a rant. Give her a break."
Bob opened his palms. "Look, you've been busy, and
you've been doing it all on your own."

"I have to do it alone! It's illegal! I can't let her get
caught in it!"

"That's true, and noble and loving. Angelic even.
But that's not the kind of gal she is."

Joe looked at his hands. "Maybe."

"No maybe about it. Who dragged our sorry asses
into the prostitution business? Who was going to do it
with or without us?" Joe looked up and Bob nodded.
"You know I'm right."

"So I'm trying to protect her, and she wants to
help."

"Bingo. You're saving her, and all she wants is to
be needed."

"You know, Bobby, you may not be an asshole."

"Oh, I'm an asshole all right." He pointed to his
heart, then his head. "But I'm also your friend and pretty
damn smart."

After Joe left, Bob leaned back in his chair and
snorted a breath. Great, he was one for two. He helped
Joe with his Lexan problem. His own problem with Joe
would have to wait.

David Allen Edmonds

CHAPTER FOURTEEN

Not every teacher volunteers to chaperone school events. Some don't like the unorganized feel; it's different when you don't know the kids and they're not neatly sitting in rows. Plus you don't have a grade to hold over their heads, and they know that. Others have little kids of their own at home and just don't have the time or the energy.

In some schools teachers are assigned outside activities to chaperone; in others they are allowed to select their own. Some are part of the contract and therefore mandated. At Stradford High School, it seemed that some teachers worked all the events, and some teachers worked none. Agent Canfield had suggested that Lexan, Bob and Roberta use the dance as an opportunity to observe the students. Maybe they would be lucky.

"Oh," Lexan said and stopped in the doorway

leading to the gym. "I don't know what I was expecting, but it wasn't this."

"You were thinking maybe snowflakes, or snowmen, stuff like that?" Roberta said. "Wintery things for a Winter Formal?"

Lexan scrunched up her face. "Was that stupid?"

They looked at how the gym had been decorated. A giant rainbow covered the wall above the home bleachers. That was reasonable enough, but the other three walls were infected with what looked like a multi-colored case of chicken pox. That, or a monster had puked up his breakfast of Froot Loops. A giant mirror ball rotated above, sending more colored dots scurrying across the walls. Helium balloons on sparkly ribbons floated above the tables surrounding the dance floor.

"White, twinkling lights, dark sky, maybe some stars sparkling on snow?" Lexan said.

"A sleigh definitely, a sleigh with bells," Bert said.

"Instead we got colored dots, lots and lots of colored dots. I don't get it," Lexan said and stepped aside as Bob entered.

"Wow, great decorating job, huh? I mean, none of that white crap. This is colorful. I like it!"

The women looked at each other and shook their heads.

"No, really," he said. "This is what they wanted, a Skittles party. Terri was in charge and she let them do it the way they wanted. Voila!"

"Wait, those aren't polka dots? They're Skittles?"

"The candy Skittles? How old are they?" Lexan said.

"Come on," Bob said and they followed him into the room. "Look at the tables. Instead of some dopey favor, a coffee mug or a vase, they have candy, look." Skittles candy in the familiar red bags had been piled on each table. "Everybody likes candy."

He grabbed one and ripped it open. "See, the colors of the candy are the colors of the dots on the walls and on the curtain behind the DJ."

"It does all tie together, Lex," Bert said. "Maybe it's not so bad."

"It's awful."

"But tasty," Bob said and popped several in his mouth. "Here ladies, grab some."

"Save one for me," Terri Dieken said and stuck out her hand. "Thanks for helping us out tonight, you guys."

"Our pleasure," Bert said, and exchanged compliments about their dresses, ending with, "Even Bob is wearing a suit."

Lexan was going to ask Terri about the decorations, but she didn't as the short-haired English teacher launched into what could only be termed a happy rant about the glory of the Skittles theme. When it subsided Lexan said, "OK, so what exactly do you want us to do tonight?"

"Like we always do, we sniff them," Bob said. "Right?"

Terri nodded. "It's easy to catch smokers. Drinking isn't really much harder."

"More sniffing," Roberta said. "A great time for the Tic Tac industry."

They laughed and watched the kids dance. Then

Lexan said, "How do we catch the pill poppers?"

"The high highs and the low lows," Bob said. "But they're teenagers. A lot of them act that way normally."

"Unless we actually see them swallow something and catch what it was, we're pretty much out of luck," Terri said. "Just keep your eyes open. Oh, and remember, if anyone leaves, they can't come back inside." The others nodded. She said, "I'll catch you later, I gotta get back to my rounds." She waved and began circling the dance floor.

"We have no chance," Lexan said.

Roberta nodded glumly. "We can watch their behavior and we can listen. That's all."

"I got an idea," Bob said. "Not real well thought out."

"How unusual." Lexan grinned.

"Look, if they're intent on getting high, they need to get out of their own houses, right?"

Roberta nodded and Lexan pointed to the dance floor. "Got that part covered."

"Sure, but if we're diligent, they can't pop anything here," Bob said. "And they can't go out to their car and come back in."

"So, they leave the dance and go somewhere safe," Bert said. Lexan kept her gaze on a table full of kids.

"A house where no one is home," Bob said. "Or dare I say, they get a room at the Marriott."

Roberta shook her head. "The Marriott has to have tightened up their security, but there are lots of other motels in town."

"Yeah, so they take pix with mom and dad, get to

the dance, post more pix on the interwebs, and leave."

Bert screwed up her eyes. "How can we stop that?"

"My big idea was to keep track of the kids who leave early." Bob opened empty hands. "That's all I got."

Lexan turned back to them. "Better than nothing," she said. "But they don't even have to leave. Look, the table to the right of the DJ."

A girl, it was hard to tell who in the flashing lights, was trying to open a pack of Skittles. Finally, she handed it to her date, who tore it open. He looked around, put his hand into the pack, and handed it back to the girl. Lexan started walking toward them, and the other two followed.

The boy saw Lexan and said something to his date. She looked at the teacher then tossed the contents of the candy bag into the air. Candies flew up, then splattered down to the floor. The other kids at her table chanted, "Bailout, bailout," and several other handfuls of Skittles joined the first.

Lexan stopped several tables away, pretending not to have noticed. The kids at the first table applauded, as Bob and Bert joined her. "They're throwing the candy around, Lex. What's the problem? They're slobs, right?"

"They are, Bert, sure. But what if they're hiding pills in with the candy? Nobody could find the Oxy's in the mess on the floor."

"Even if we could," Bob said, "there's no way we could tell whose they were."

"I still don't get it," Roberta said.

"Just a spoonful of sugar helps the medicine go down," Bob sang, and stopped as Lexan slapped his arm.

"Bert, they could be taking pills with a handful of candy in plain sight."

The French teacher looked from Lex to the kids to Bob. "Oh, my God."

Bob stepped into the hall outside the gym and checked the time on the cafeteria clock. It was an excuse to get away from the din inside. Another hour to go, then clean-up. He might be able to make it home by midnight.

Many of the kids had left and the cafeteria was nearly empty. He stuck his head through the gym door and told Bert he was checking the men's rooms for smokers. He glanced down the hall to his office.

Bob checked the first bathroom. Cloudy, but no one there, and nothing was burning. He crossed the hall to the Guidance Department and unlocked the door, shut it behind him, and opened his office. He didn't turn on the light. Instead, he removed his suit coat and set the wastebasket on his desk. He moved his chair out of the way and pushed the desk against the wall. He stepped from the chair to the desktop. A sound startled him, he froze. No one there.

He lifted a tile from the suspended ceiling and carefully slid it up and out of the way. He climbed onto the overturned metal wastebasket and stuck himself into the open space. He reached over the top of the cinderblock wall and removed a ceiling tile from the room next door.

It was dark, but he could see the file cabinets of the records room. He hoisted himself onto the cinderblock, twisted, and lowered his feet onto the nearest metal cabinet. He stood stock still. No sounds. He dropped to the floor. The records room had no window; he flipped the switch. The fluorescents hummed and the room lit up.

Bob had been in the tiny room many times, mostly finding or returning student files. He knew business files were catalogued here as well. The last time he had tried his own key, and found it also worked in the other cabinets. He stepped to the cabinet with the business contracts, unlocked it and pulled the third drawer toward him. It was heavier than he expected.

The files for Murgatroyd Educational Supplies were halfway back. He pulled out the one headed "Answer sheets,' and laid it on the small table. He shuffled through it until he found several receipts for the scan-able State Test answer sheets. It seemed to him an amazingly high amount. He froze again as the gym door opened and music blared out.

He pulled out the paperwork he had received with his free roll of paper towels. Cardinal Educational Supplies, Blacklick, OH. What a name. He laid it next to the receipt from Murgatroyd. Blacklick, OH. He stood up and furrowed his brows. Zip Code the same for both, 43003. Same street, Eastgate Parkway, the addresses a few digits off.

"Find what you're looking for, Mr. McCauley?"

He dropped the folder and spun around.

Mel Radburn stood in the doorway.

Joe punched off his cell and carefully laid it on the night stand in his room at the DoubleTree in suburban

Columbus. He'd considered tossing it onto the floor.

What did he expect? He'd asked relationship advice from a celibate guy. Fr. Hastings had even joked about it. Joe kicked off his shoes and dropped onto the bed. We don't have enough faith? Come on.

At least that's what he thought the priest had told him. Joe wasn't sure. What he remembered most was the priest prodding him to keep talking. And he had. He'd spoken about the closeness he and Lex shared. How they'd worked together to help the girls. How he'd known he loved her when he saw her being attacked by Weigel. How his anger had given him strength. How they were so comfortable living together. How she helped him heal after his wife's death. How she hadn't pressured him about anything.

Until now. For the life of him he couldn't understand what she was worked up about. He hadn't changed. He was like he always was, tilting at windmills, maybe, sure, but that's why he'd saved her, wasn't it? His job was to protect her, and he certainly wasn't going to let anyone hurt her now. He should get over himself and let her get hurt? No way.

He picked up the TV remote and jabbed it on. I have to keep her out of harm's way. The danger's not over; Kim or Karl or hell, Oskar maybe. Any one of them could come after me. After us. For Christ's sake, he thought, they blew up a house right down the street.

She wants me to get involved in the opioid thing and make some more enemies. Like I need more? He almost smiled, then frowned instead. Great, now a drug cartel would be after me. Maybe two.

He scrolled past the Cavs game. They'd traded most of their team and still wouldn't play any defense. He found an episode of 'Hunting Hitler,' but he'd seen it. Then he remembered how Jerry had ended the conversation by telling him to marry her.

Not enough faith, according to the priest, meant they were afraid to commit. They weren't being open enough with each other. They weren't sharing everything. "I'm a fucking open book," Joe muttered and jabbed the remote.

Four reality shows and three heads talking to screwed-up couples about their screwed-up lives. No, he thought, that's not us. We don't weigh 350 pounds and we don't throw chairs.

He should have met Fr. Jerry in the rectory, face to face. The priest's tone had been off, something that Joe couldn't decipher. Was he baiting him? Was he dissing him? Joe couldn't believe that; they'd known each other for years. He'd always been there for him. But there was something different about him tonight. It seemed like the priest was giving Joe enough rope to hang himself.

That's what I get for always asking for somebody's opinion. I ask for help and they tell me. Then I bitch about it. First I ask Bob, now Fr. Jerry. Why can't I decide for myself? Besides, Joe continued telling himself, I'm not ready to marry her, or anybody else. He gave up and turned out the light. Not yet, anyway.

CHAPTER FIFTEEN

S eeing Mel Radburn in the records room, Bob's first thought was to berate himself. Not just for getting caught; the man was a known lurker and could find anyone. No, his first thought was that this happened because he was jealous of his best friend. He wanted to be like Joe, and he screwed the pooch. His cheeks reddened fiercely.

"I asked if you needed help, Mr. McCauley. You didn't answer."

Bob followed Radburn's eyes and they flitted to the open drawer, the files on the table, the file in his hand, the missing ceiling tile. He was completely trapped. He would lose his job, maybe his pension. His family would suffer.

"Actually, I do need help, sir."

"What are you doing in here?" Radburn's eyes

narrowed to black pin-pricks. "You are clearly breaking and entering. Stealing public documents."

Bob took a breath and played his last card, his only card. "Someone is stealing, sir, but it's not me."

Radburn reached for his cell phone.

"Five minutes, Mel. You got me. All I ask is five minutes."

Radburn looked like a kid using a magnifying glass to fry a bug. He set the timer on the cell. "Five, no four minutes, fifty-two seconds."

Bob swallowed. "Look at these files. Receipts, orders, check numbers. Years of them."

"I'm the business manager. I know what they are."

Bob picked up several folders.

"This company, Murgatroyd, provides answer sheets for the State Tests. They sell us maintenance supplies, paper towels, soap, cleaning products."

"I am familiar with the system." Radburn reached into another cabinet and pulled out a file. "This firm, Western Ed-Tek, provides software for the Tests."

Bob raised his eyebrows. "Right. Different companies provide other products for the State Tests, scoresheets, make-ups, statistics, the test booklets themselves."

Radburn pushed his Buddy Holly glasses up his nose. "Go on."

"Seven or eight companies supply all the testing materials for the state tests."

The big man peered through his glasses at his phone. "What is your point, Mr. McCauley?"

"That's an awful lot of money flowing through this

school for the normal supplies and the state tests."

"The school system is the largest employer in the city."

"And there are over two million school kids in the state; they test nearly every grade."

Radburn sighed. "Again, what is your point?"

Bob tried to control his hands as he explained. "Add that money flow to the wave of drugs across the state."

Radburn looked at the time. "And?"

"Drug gangs could be using the schools to launder their cash."

"Since the money is routed through my office, you are accusing me of conspiring with drug dealers." Radburn turned to the door.

"No, God no, I didn't mean that."

"Time's up. What do you mean?"

"I, uh, I mean, I need help, your help. Because you know how this works."

Radburn hesitated as if thinking. "If I don't help you with this idiotic idea?"

"I'll take it to Agent Caulfield, see what he thinks."

Radburn took a step toward Bob, filling the space in the small room. "We'll not bother the agent, Mr. McCauley. Let's you and I have a little chat."

When Kramer was a young patrolman, he had wondered why the police didn't simply set up sobriety check points near the popular bars in town. Everyone knew people were drinking and everyone knew where, so it would be easy, he had reasoned. Certainly easier than driving around looking for DUIs. He shook his head. Or pulling bodies out of wrecks.

He sat in the Burger King parking lot across the street from *Competitors Sport Bar* and watched another couple weave out the door and flop into their seats. As a Detective it wasn't his job anymore, and tonight he had another assignment. After eight years on the job he knew the answer, the always answer, the only answer. The-it-didn't-matter-what-the-question-was answer: money.

He slipped the car into drive, prowled across the street, and into bar's parking lot. Most of the plates he could read by the security lights, but twice he had to roll down his window and use the searchlight. He punched the Franklin County plates into his computer, furrowed his brow, and headed back into the street.

Roberta looked at the crowd inside *Competitors.* "I thought Bob said he'd meet us."

"That's what he said." Lexan's voice was flat and difficult to hear.

"Another undependable male, huh? Bob's not here, Joe's not here." Roberta hoped Lexan would smile. She didn't. "Probably afraid we'd make them pay."

Lexan stared at her drink and shook her head.

The French teacher squinted at her friend. "You OK?"

"I'm fine."

"I don't know. The look on your face when I mentioned Joe."

"I need more wine," Lexan said.

Roberta rubbed her hands together and grinned.

"OK, girlfriend, give me the good stuff, dish the dirt, lay it all out there!"

Lexan stared down at the table. Roberta turned away and signaled the waiter. When he returned with the wine and filled their glasses, she handed Lex the Pinot Grigio and said softly, "If you want to talk."

Lexan shook her head but accepted the glass and tasted it.

"As much as we hang out," Roberta said, "there's a lot I don't know about you. I don't even know where you're from. I mean, I know this year has been kind of a blur, the stuff last fall, the girls, the contract, all that--"

Lexan looked at her. "I think I'm leaving Joe."

Roberta nearly spit out the wine. "You're what? Why?" she managed.

"It's like you said, Bert. You don't know me at all."

"No, I do, I know the important stuff about you."

"No, you don't. I'm living in a shadow."

Roberta narrowed her eyes to slits as she did when concentrating. "Joe's shadow. It's funny to hear. Ironic."

"I don't see it." Lexan offered to refill Bert's glass.

"Thanks. For years Joe didn't have a shadow. He worked, did a great job with the kids, but he had no power at all. He'd try like a madman but never managed to win."

"Except in the classroom."

"Right, like I said, but politically, no."

"Then Cathy dies." Lexan's voice was flat. "Pregnant."

"I thought we were going to lose him," Bert said. "I really did." She looked at Lex through her squinty eyes. "Wait, I get how you mean it."

Lexan held the glass in front of her and shrugged.

"Shadow, what you mean about Joe's shadow. We started talking about you, and now we're talking about Joe."

Lexan finished her sip. "Now you're going to say I saved him."

Roberta straightened as if shocked. "I was. You did, Lex, you did save him."

Lexan looked around the bar, mostly groups of white men watching NCAA hoops. "Now you're going to explain why I'm unhappy?"

Bert's eyes squinted more. "He's changed, that's for sure."

"Yeah, now he's a big shot and--"

"--he's got no time for you." Bert nodded. "Makes sense."

"He's in Columbus tonight and doesn't have to be. He's not helping us with the opioid thing. He's never home." She set the glass down too hard and had to keep it from falling.

"You're pretty busy yourself," Bert said.

"Yeah, I am, and I don't want to be Suzy Homemaker. That's not me."

Bert unlidded her eyes and arched her brows. "Does he pay attention to you when he is home?"

"Pay attention? That's a laugh. What he wants to do is protect me. Thinks I can't take care of myself."

"Well, you are in danger. You both are."

Lexan put her purse on the table. "There it is. Joe's friend coming to his defense. I should have known."

"Wait, Lex." She put her hand over the other's.

"I can take care of myself." Lexan pulled her hand free. "I don't need an Archangel."

"He saved you once, though, didn't he?"

Lex stared directly at her. "And I saved him. I gave him hope." She air-quoted the word. "Doesn't that make us even?" She reached for her coat, but Roberta snatched it from her.

"What are you doing?"

Roberta put Lexan's coat on the opposite chair and stared at her. "Sit down."

Lexan hesitated, then did so. "Look, it's late and--"

The other woman raised her hand. "We still haven't talked about you."

"I don't know what to say; this is so weird." Her hands flitted around the table until they found her purse.

Roberta kept her eyes on her as she sipped her wine. "Joe's my friend. I don't want to see him hurt."

"He's hurting me, Bert."

She nodded. "I want to be your friend, too. I hope I am."

"But?"

Roberta sighed. "But I know him so much better than I know you." She held the bottle over Lexan's empty glass.

"Thank you." Lexan took a sip.

"Thing of it is." She pursed her lips beneath her pursed eyebrows. "I just can't imagine him hurting you."

Lexan appeared to relax a little. "No, not physically, I agree. But I'm in his shadow, remember?"

"That doesn't fit." She looked at her. "Joe and I have worked together for ages, and I'm not an expert."

She stopped. "That's kind of creepy, sorry." When Lexan smiled slightly, she continued. "But I can't believe he would hurt you intentionally."

"Either way, it still hurts. I have to get away so I can grow."

Roberta looked around the bar. All of the servers and bartenders were female. "You've been hurt before."

"What? Where did you get that?" Lexan's words came out in a rush, her eyes wide.

"The only thing that makes sense to me."

"That's so ridiculous, I don't even know what to say."

"No, him hurting you is ridiculous. What are you hiding?"

"I'm not the one hiding things."

"Yes, you are. You're hiding behind Joe. To use your word, hiding in his shadow."

"That is such bullshit!" Lexan looked around and lowered her voice to a hiss. "I don't want to be in his shadow, remember?"

"I think you do. It's good cover. You talk about Joe so you don't have to talk about yourself."

Lexan stood up. "I've listened to this because I thought you wanted to be my friend. I'm not talking anymore."

"Fine. You don't have to talk to me. But you do have to tell Joe what the problem really is."

Lexan's eyes darted left and right. "You're back to Joe again."

"You're hiding behind Joe again. Tell him."

"There's nothing to tell!" She slapped some bills

on the table and grabbed her coat.

Roberta looked up from the stemmed glass in her hand. "I'm not going to let you hurt him."

"That makes no sense at all." She jammed her arms into her coat. "He's hurting me."

"Just tell him the truth," she said, but Lexan was several steps away.

CHAPTER SIXTEEN

A cross Cleveland Avenue in a parking space in front of Subway, Karl looked up from his tablet. He had parked there so he could keep his eye on both *We Are Mattresses* and *Competitors*. It was early for the delivery, so he'd been watching the sports bar more closely. Several minutes ago he had noticed Kramer stopping at the dark Impala just as he had earlier, and now he watched Barbie storm out the door and stomp to her car.

Stomp was the word for it, but stalk and march were close. "Little missy is peeved, is she," he muttered and turned on the engine. As he pulled up to the street, a second set of headlights flashed on in the parking lot. He cursed.

Lexan's car passed him heading north, and Oskar's dented blue truck revealed itself as the second car. Karl pulled out behind them. He didn't see the two large men leave the bar and get into the Impala from Franklin County.

Several hours later a non-descript white van parked in the space Karl had vacated. Two Italian men with short-barreled AR-15s under their long coats stood guard, as two others unloaded several plastic-wrapped packages and carried them up the loading ramp into the store. If Karl had been there, he would have appreciated their efficiency and congratulated them on their attention to security. Karl would also have congratulated himself for noticing that mattress stores were so common as to be invisible, and using them as wholesale delivery hubs was in fact brilliant. It was one part of his plan that Kimberly had not changed.

On the other hand, Kramer thought, why should they bother with DUI checkpoints at all? The statistics were clear, and everybody in law enforcement knew them. If you see a car between 2:00 and 6:00 am, the driver has been drinking, especially on the weekends. He glanced at the clock in the corner of the GPS display. Kids probably get started earlier.

He followed the twists and turns through the development, and parked the cruiser at the entrance to the *cul de sac.* Most of the houses were dark, but the lights were on in the one at the end, the one keyed into his system.

The detective made sure his lights were off and the computer screen faced away from the house. Mangione had given him the address. He shook his head. It did nothing but irritate him. "Why the hell am I even here?" he muttered.

Kramer had been inside the house several times. Complaints about this address came into the department on a regular basis: too loud, cars squealing tires, parked on tree lawns and across driveways. He once wrote up a kid who'd parked so close to a fire hydrant that he'd scratched the car door. Knucklehead wanted him to help with the insurance claim.

Those complaints came from neighbors, and he could probably list their names and addresses from memory. Most of it was minor-league kids' stuff; he was more interested in the anonymous tips.

Those tips concerned traffic in the *cul de sac* late at night. Weeknights. Men coming and going in cars with headlights off. The tips were from men and from women, and the voices on the recordings always dropped to a whisper at the end when they mentioned 'drugs'.

He should be here to catch the guys moving the drugs, but that wasn't his assignment. He was here to watch the Chandler house where a party was obviously going on with underage drinking and probable opioid abuse. The house where the kids had a sleepover nearly every weekend. The house where the parents monitored the doors and were probably watching his car now. The house where the evidence would vanish as soon as he hit the doorbell. Chandler, whatever the hell the owner's name was, Kent or Kenneth, had more clout in town than he did.

Kramer had hoped that the new chief would at least make a pretense of establishing control, but it appeared that wasn't going to happen. As soon as Michalik was fired, Mangione slid in, and whatever agreement there was with the dealers remained in place. He had laid it all out for the new chief in black and white, but here Kramer was, wasting his time.

The computer bleeped with the results of his license plate search; no name appeared, because the car was registered to the State of Ohio. He thought a moment then jabbed the ignition. Maybe his assignment had nothing to do with this house.

Karl let another car pull in front of him so he wouldn't follow too closely behind Oskar. The oaf wouldn't notice me if I jumped up and down in the truck bed, he thought, but decided as he usually did that discretion was the wisest course. Besides, Oskar's days upon this mortal coil were limited.

Oskar bounced along Cleveland Avenue intently following Lexan. He didn't care if she noticed him or not because the way she was driving had convinced him she was drunk or close to it. The first couple times she changed lanes he followed her, but now he was content to keep her in sight.

Got you in my gunsights, he thought, and fired his finger pistol. As if avoiding the phantom shot, Lexan's car swerved into the left lane and back to the right. "Get a grip, girl," he said aloud. "Got to make sure you get home."

Lexan braked for the light at Center a little too hard and the car slid on the snow-dampened street, but she kept it out of the crosswalk. Behind her, Oskar adjusted his mirror to keep the headlights from blinding him. Behind him, Karl brought his car to an easy stop, a safe two lengths behind.

The three-car parade, four if you counted the Impala, proceeded north on Cleveland until Lexan turned off into her development. Oskar realized if he was being blinded from behind, maybe she was too, and backed off a little. By the time they reached Joe's house, the street behind Oskar was dark. He waited as she lurched into the driveway and the garage door chugged up. Lehrer's car wasn't there and she parked her car in both spaces. "You made it girl, barely, but you made it," he muttered. "Tell your boyfriend I'll catch him later." He fired his finger again and drove away.

By the time Karl had circled the block, Oskar was gone and an upstairs light burned in Joe's house. Karl settled the car into a space across the street where the weak glow from the street lights didn't reach. He opened his tablet and waited.

"Dammit, dammit, dammit!" Lexan yelled and collapsed on the bed in the spare bedroom. She pulled her foot over her knee and rubbed her toes where the closet door had crunched them. "I told him to sand the door so it would open, but did he do it? No, he didn't. He didn't and my toes hurt! Damn it to hell!"

Lexan had been talking to herself, yelling to herself actually, since she had left the bar and Roberta. It was impossible to lose a fight with herself, but now it occurred to her it was impossible to win either.

She limped back to the closet and yanked her

suitcase off the shelf. It came out faster than she expected, but she managed not to hit herself with it as she had done with the door. "I just emptied these; now I'm filling them," she muttered as she dragged it, a smaller case, and her hanging bag into the room she shared with Joe.

Her cover was blown and she had to leave. Roberta, of all people, Roberta had found out. Not Nancy, that bitch. Not Bob, too stupid, too male, not any of the others. Joe neither. He was the one closest to her, the one hardest to deceive.

"What are you hiding, Lexan?" she said in a voice she thought sounded like Roberta's. "I don't want you to hurt, Joe, Lexan." She hurled a handful of clothing into her suitcase. "What about me? What if you're hurting me? You don't even know it, but you're hurting me!"

She dragged the small case into the bathroom to collect her toiletries. "Why can't you leave me alone? All of you. Why can't we just be together, do stuff, but no, we have to get to know one another and share our inner thoughts. What about my privacy?"

One of the bottles she slid off the shelf broke, and she cut herself as she grabbed it too quickly. Red drops of blood splashed onto her blouse before she could get her hand into the sink.

"Shit shit shit!" she yelled at herself in the mirror. She squeezed her finger under the water and was surprised, then relieved, as it slowed to a stop. She took a deep breath and looked at her face.

Her hair was fine as it always was. It was hard to convince her hair to do anything other than curl up, and the heat from her reddened, sweaty face had probably helped. Her eyes were another matter, red-rimmed and teary, and her skin way out of control. The full range of colors from pale pink to dark red blotched her face from forehead to chin. She forced herself to take another breath and relax.

"Plenty of time," she told herself. "Joe won't be home tonight." Again the dichotomy. She had time to pack and leave him, because he wasn't coming home tonight. His not coming home tonight had been what provoked her. It was the opening that had allowed Roberta to get inside. If there was one thing she knew, one thing both sides of her could agree on, it was this: if she let someone inside, she would be hurt.

She put a bandage around her finger and took off her blouse. The flowing water sluiced the blood from the pale ivory fabric and she relaxed a little. Until she looked at the reflection of her arms in the glass.

That's what happens when you let somebody inside. The marks where he had bound her wrists were gone, but not the burn marks on her arms. Surgery had reduced them. The sight of the brownish circles brought back the smell of her burning skin and the raggedness of her screaming throat. And above all, obliterating everything else, the pain. The searing, awful pain.

That's how she knew. That's why she'd promised herself to never let anyone inside. It was why she had quit her job and moved up north. It was how she kept herself safe. She zipped her cosmetics bag closed and laid it on the bed.

She couldn't explain why she had let Joe in, even to the extent that she had. He was trusting and kind, and she was a sucker for that. But what had gotten her was his pain. She knew that pain, she felt it and understood it. She opened herself to share his pain with hers.

Now he's inside and I have to leave. She had had to lie to him. Chicken pox scars she'd said, and he believed her. He'd kissed her scars, and she'd let him.

But it will only get worse, she thought. He's on a mission to protect me. He'll want to marry me and I'll have to say no and that will kill him. I have to leave. It'll be better for both of us. She wiped a tear from her eye and carried the hanging bag and the small case down the stairs.

She dragged the luggage down the hall and turned to the door leading to the garage, but light from somewhere caught the wall of pictures in the family room and she stopped. The bags fell from her hands. She walked toward the pictures as if drawn.

Shortly after she'd moved in, Joe had mounted her family pictures on the left side of the fireplace and his on the right. Some of his, of course, were of Cathy. Others were of his parents and cousins, and even two of his grandparents, old oval black and whites.

Her pictures had been defaced when her apartment had been ransacked, and he had painstakingly restored them and had them reframed. She looked at her life portrayed on the wall, from infancy to tenth grade. She dropped onto the sofa and cried.

CHAPTER SEVENTEEN

Politically it had been worth it, Joe reminded himself. The National Association people had been impressed by the gains he had made for the teachers of Stradford. They'd even hinted about a job for him on the national level. It was a chance to be in the room where it happens, a chance to be Hamilton, not Burr.

He punched the garage door opener and checked the clock. Little over an hour and a half from Columbus. He'd cut the meeting short and left right after dinner, hoping that hadn't hurt their opinion of him. But he had to get home.

He carried his overnight bag from the trunk and reached for the door into his house. It was locked. His first thought was she was locking him out, but he replaced that with a smile. She was keeping herself safe. Good girl, he thought.

It was quiet in the house, and he stumbled over something as he stepped into the kitchen. Her hanging bag, and two suitcases lay on the tile. He toed the bigger bag. It was heavy, packed. He set his own beside it.

He found Lexan on the sofa in the family room. Asleep on her side, curled into a snail. He sat down next to her and touched her arm.

She woke with a start, her eyes open in fear before she recognized him. "Joe." Her hands ran across her mouth and her hair as she unfolded herself.

"Home again," he said. "Got here as fast as I could."

"I fell asleep. Stopped to look at the pictures and just passed out." She sat up and her hands continued their inspection. "Slept like I was in a coma."

Joe put his hands on his knees and gave her another minute to collect herself. "Going somewhere?"

"What? I, oh."

"Nearly threw a hip tripping over your bags."

"Listen, Joe, I can't talk about this now." She started to stand and he took her hand.

"You're leaving?"

"Yes, I mean, no, I mean I am. But." She pulled her hand away.

"You thought you'd be gone by the time I got home." He moved from the sofa to a chair.

"Look, if I start talking about it, I'll cry and you'll be upset, and we'll fight and say things we don't mean." Her voice started forcefully before fading off.

"Sure. We wouldn't want that."

Lexan stood up. "Besides, we've said everything before. Nothing's changed."

"Nothing will change if you leave. We'll lock our doors and pretend."

She took several steps away from him. "I can't stay here. With you."

"I'm hurting you?" He shook his head. "No, I am not hurting you Lexan. I love you."

"I don't mean like that." She swiped away a tear.

"Then?"

She fought her face into control. "We've been over this. I told you."

He held up a hand. "And I didn't listen, right?"

"No, you just don't get it." She stepped across the kitchen floor and picked up her bags.

He followed her. "I'd do anything to protect you."

She took a breath and opened the door. "I know you would. You would do everything to protect me."

"How is that hurting you?" He opened both palms. "What the hell, Lex? What am I supposed to do?"

"What you always do," she said. "The right thing."

"What's the matter with that?" Joe's voice was louder than he intended.

"I want a man, not an angel."

He was still holding his hands apart as the garage door rose and fell. He was alone.

Parked on the street outside, Oskar nodded with satisfaction. She was leaving and the teacher would be alone. He stretched his back and shook his hands to loosen his fingers. It had been a long wait. She piled several bags into the trunk and he wondered if she was moving out. He didn't care. It was more interesting that she was on her cell phone as she drove past. He pulled the slide back on the gun and waited till she was out of sight.

Roberta had to yell into the phone to be heard over the wail of the siren. Another ambulance screamed into the ER bay. She looked at Bob and turned her back to the sound. "Lexan, sorry to bother you after our last conversation."

Lexan jerked to a stop at the end of Joe's block. "What do you need, Bert? Kinda busy right now."

"I, we, Bob and I thought you would want to know."

"Where are you? It's so loud."

"At the hospital, South West."

Lexan focused quickly. "What happened?"

"The Chandler boy, Ken I think his name is. He's in your class."

"I know, yes, he is. What's the matter?"

"They brought him in, to the ER last night. Friday night. After the dance."

Lexan shook her head. Could she just get to the point?

"Overdose."

"What? Is he OK?" Lexan jammed her foot on the accelerator.

"No. He's still in ICU."

"On my way." Lexan screeched around the corner onto Cleveland Ave. "Thank you, Bert."

CHAPTER EIGHTEEN

J oe looked around his empty house and said, "Fuck."
It wasn't the stillness or his coat on the floor or his duffel bag in the kitchen. It was the future, yawning before him in a dizzying gyre of gloom. It felt like Cathy's death.

"What the hell do you want from me, Lexan?" He tried to yell the words to clear away the dark thoughts, but they dribbled from his lips, defeated and without energy. As he picked up his coat, he felt the gun in the back of his neck.

"You're pathetic." Oskar's words were a guttural growl.

Joe let the coat drop. "You got that right."

"Walk slowly to the sofa."

The gun prodded him and he stumbled forward

"Gonna make it look like a suicide. Sit down."

Joe did so. "Oskar? You?"

"You were expecting someone else to kill you?" The fat man smiled and pulled the coffee table out of reach with one meaty hand. The gun in his other didn't leave Joe's face.

"Never gave it much thought." Joe kept his weight on the edge of the couch. "Who's paying you?"

"Prick. Always the smart guy. Think I can't do anything on my own?" Oskar swung his leg and crashed it into Joe's kneecap. Fire spurted up his leg.

"Yeah, you're a big man all right. You kicked me." Joe massaged his knee and wondered why he had to have the same argument again.

"Can't leave many marks, smart guy. Gotta look like you did it yourself."

"I get that, but I don't get why you want to kill me. What did I do to you?"

The fat man's eyes diminished into pin pricks. "Laurel Ann. My Laurel Ann."

"I didn't kill her, Oskar. You know I had nothing to do with that."

"She's dead. Weigel killed her. Don't you think I know that?"

A random death, Joe thought. He looked down the hall to where he had fought Weigel. That killing made sense. This didn't. "Who was Weigel working for? Kill him, not me."

"Karl? I can't--"

Joe dove off the sofa into the man's body, wrapping his arms around him. Oskar scrambled back, but stumbled and they fell to the floor. Joe put both hands on his gun arm and forced it aside. Oskar slammed his other hand into the healthy side of Joe's head. He saw stars and rolled to his side. Oskar freed his legs and stood over him.

"Get up, asshole, I'm tired of talking."

"Just shoot me here." Joe thought of his own weapon safely stored upstairs.

"Get up on the sofa!" Oskar screamed. The gun shook in his beefy hand.

"Screw you." I'll never get the chance to apologize to Lexan. He rose to all fours.

Oskar fired the automatic, and Joe stopped thinking.

Oskar nodded at the blood leaking from Joe's head. He tried to pick him up with the gun in his hand, but Joe's limp body was heavier than it looked. He put the pistol on the coffee table and leveraged Joe's body into a seated position on the sofa against the arm. He stood back, then toppled Joe's body forward onto the floor.

"That'll do her," Oskar muttered. "Looks like he shot himself and fell down." He pulled a rag from his pocket and reached to wipe off the gun.

"Nicely done," a voice said from the hallway behind him.

"Karl," Oskar gasped and took a step.

"Don't even think about it." The tall, white-haired man gestured with his gun. "Step away from the table, please."

"I can explain, I can." Oskar's eyes darted from the window to the door to the hall.

Karl looked at the stain growing around the crotch

of Oskar's pants and shook his head. "No need, my friend. Come with me, we're going upstairs." Karl directed the man into Joe's bedroom and found the gun safe in the closet. He handed him a slip of paper and told him to open it.

Oskar turned the tumbler and hesitated with his hand on the door. Karl poked him with his gun and told him to step away. Karl reached in and pulled out Joe's pistol. "Downstairs."

"Come on, Karl, we been friends a long time." Oskar's voice was tiny and high-pitched. "I always done what you told me." They went down the hall to where Joe lay face first in a pool of blood.

When Karl didn't respond, Oskar said, "We had some tough times, I know, but in the end I always did what you--"

"Shut up, Oskar, and turn toward me." The fat man looked surprised as he saw Karl on one knee and the gun aimed up at him. The look remained on his face as the bullet from Joe's gun entered his forehead. He never heard the sound.

Karl stood quickly and caught the body before it fell. He walked it to where the coffee table had stood and let it crumple in front of Joe. He inserted the gun in Joe's hand, and laid Oskar's gun near his body. The white-haired man stood and looked carefully at the room, paying attention to the trajectories of the bullets. Joe's hand lacked gunshot residue, but Mangione would cover it. Or the suburban knuckleheads would just miss that detail. Either way, He nodded, satisfied, and returned upstairs.

In the bedroom Karl carefully shut the gun safe, wiped it down, and began his search. Methodically he combed each room and found two sets of the pictures Joe was using to blackmail Kimberly, one in the bedroom and one near the computer. He ripped out the hard drive and left the cables dangling. Oskar was messy, he reasoned, so he left a mess in the rooms behind him, emptied drawers, clothing, even food from the freezer. Joe surprised the junk man ransacking the house, they shot each other, and everything fits.

Karl put the pictures and hard drive into his backpack, removed his gloves and thumbed a text message. It was a good day's work; he had solved several problems. When the 9-1-1 operator answered, he laid Joe's landline on the table and left the house.

Lexan sped down the access road into the hospital parking lot. On a normal day she, or Joe, would have wondered why the road was called 'Old Oak Blvd,' when there wasn't a tree in sight. That didn't' occur to her today.

The car rocked as she slid into two spaces and took her foot off the brake. She was here, Bert and Bob were waiting in ICU, but she couldn't get out of the car. Joe. She had left Joe. It was the right thing to do, the thing she needed to do. She knew that. But she couldn't open the car door until she had willed her breaths to lengthen and her heart to slow down. She laid her head on the steering wheel and took one more deep breath. Kenny Chandler.

Lexan found Roberta, Bob and Doug Canfield huddled around a table in the ER waiting room. "Sorry I snapped at you," she said. Bert gave her a stiff hug.

She turned to Bob. "Thought you'd be at the bar. What happened?"

"Had a strange conversation with Mel. Tell you later." He looked away.

"Canfield called him," Roberta said. "Bob called me."

The BCI agent held out his hand. "Glad you're here."

Lexan returned his handshake. "Kenny's in Intensive Care?"

"Yeah," the agent said. "They're only allowing family to see him."

"Not a good sign," Bob said.

They sat in a cluster of dark-blue sofas. "Is there anything we can do?" Lexan couldn't find a place to rest her hands.

The others shook their heads. "Joe home yet from Columbus?" Bob asked. Roberta shot him a look.

Lexan shook her head and looked past them. "I see some of my students." She got up quickly and crossed to where a dozen kids stood huddled in small groups. Several of them were crying. Bert nodded to Bob and they followed. Canfield left to find the nurse.

"Blair," Lexan said sharply. "What do you know about this?" The gangly sophomore shuffled to her. "Nothing, Ms. Warner." The other teenagers shrunk from her, their eyes wide. Bob noticed Chelsea among the others and gave her arm a squeeze.

"Were you at the party with Kenny?"

"Yes, Ms. Warner." Blair's face was bleak, more gray than pink, his eyes furtive.

"What happened to him?"

"I don't know. One minute he was joking around, then someone called the ambulance." He shook his head.

"They must have had a reason to call the squad, Blair."

"I called the emergency squad, Ms. Warner." Chelsea stepped forward. "He passed out and we couldn't wake him."

"Chelsea, good for you. Where were his parents? Weren't they at home?"

"Upstairs. Like always," Blair muttered, and the girl nodded.

Lexan stood in front of her student. "Look at me," she said. The boy did so.

"What did Kenny take, Blair?"

"I dunno."

"Yes, you do. Look me in the eye and tell me."

Roberta put her hand on Lexan's arm. She snatched it away. "Pills from the medicine chest, Blair? Skittles? Isn't that what you call them?"

"We can do this later," Bob began.

The boy mumbled something. Lexan grabbed him by the shirt front and yelled into his face. "Damnit, Blair! Kenny is your friend! We can't help him if you don't tell us what he took!"

Roberta and Bob hugged Lexan away from the boy. She burst into tears as their arms surrounded her.

CHAPTER NINETEEN

"**H**ome invasion thwarted?" Patrolman Kennedy said again, hoping to keep the irritation from his voice. It was the second time he'd tried impressing Lt. Kramer.

Kramer was squatting near the blood splatters in Joe Lehrer's family room where the two men had been shot, and had heard the young patrolman the first time. "Hmm," he said.

"That's what it looks like to me," Kennedy offered. "We have clear signs of a struggle, and the rooms have been ransacked, like someone was looking for something. Home invasion, for sure, but he picked on a homeowner with a gun."

"Which one is which?"

Kennedy's eyes dashed from the floor to the sofa to the coffee table. "This is uh, Mr. Lehrer's house, so, um, I'd say he was the homeowner, and um--"

"I knew that," Kramer said. "Does that mean he shot first? Does that mean the other man ransacked the rooms?"

"Um, uh, yes, I'd guess so."

"You'd guess?" He stared until the younger man lowered his eyes. Then he said, "What about the foot marks where the blood was tracked? Are you sure there's only two sets?"

"Wow, Detective Kramer, I just assumed. I mean two bodies was all there was."

"Uh-huh. That's why I had them take so many pictures." Kramer handed him the samples from both blood sources. Take these to the techies, Kennedy, and take a look outside for signs of forced entry."

"Windows and doors. Tracks in the snow. Got it, sir."

Kramer's phone beeped. He noted the name and quickly headed to his cruiser. He turned on the siren and lights and sped down the street. Minutes later he squealed to a stop in front of the *We Are Mattresses* store across from *Competitors.*

He saw Chief Mangione huddled with two officers and hurried to them. "Quite a night, fellas," he said.

Mangione looked at him for a moment. "Three dead here. Two at yours, isn't it?"

"Yes sir. Five. I can't remember--"

"Stop with the history lesson, Lieutenant, I know I'm the new guy in town."

Kramer looked away. Bodies strewn all over town and the guy has to be a prick. "Sorry, Chief."

Mangione stared several seconds longer, then said, "What do you have at your scene?"

"Early to tell, sir. Could be a home invasion gone wrong, but I don't see anything missing."

"I heard the house was trashed."

Kramer wondered how he had found out so quickly. "Doors emptied, mattresses slid off, closets emptied. Gun safe locked."

"So?" Mangione's tone was impatient and pedantic; he wanted the student to prove his point for him.

Kramer looked to the EMT's loading a body into their van. "It looks like a B and E gone wrong, and maybe it is. But I can't get my mind around what the teacher could have that was worth killing him for. It sure wasn't bags of cash."

"Murder/suicide?"

"Maybe." Kramer had never considered that. "Looks like the guns we found match the wounds. Like they killed each other. But we haven't done the ballistics." Kramer thought for a moment. "Could also be a third shooter. That would mean no home invasion, OK, but it would also mean a guy with a motive for killing the teacher and Brummelberger. I don't see how that fits."

Mangione nodded. "Blood matches, footprints, all that?"

Freaking Kennedy must have been on the phone as soon as I left, Kramer thought. "Looks like there could be a third footprint in the blood. Working on it. Nothing yet on fingerprints."

Mangione looked like he expected him to say

something more about the shootings. Instead Kramer stepped toward *We Are Mattresses* and said, "So what do we have here?"

Mangione sighed. "Thought this was a quiet suburb, not the Old West. Shoot out at the mattress store."

"Lot of brass," Kramer said and toed several gun casings. Numbered triangular signs marked where the spent bullets lay. Three dozen at least. He looked at the Chief. "A firefight? They keep a lot of cash here?"

"Don't know about motive," Mangione said. "We got shot up cars and three bodies."

Kramer scanned the area. "I gotta believe there were more than three."

Mangione shrugged. "Might have carried off their wounded."

"Gang on gang?"

"Can't tell. Don't look Hispanic."

Kramer's brow furrowed. "Why would the cartel be shooting its own people?"

Mangione turned to him. "That's an interesting question."

"If we can ID them, we can--"

"A question that we will keep to ourselves."

Kramer wondered what the chief was hiding. "I'll get back to the Lehrer house. Sir."

"That's good, Lieutenant."

Mangione watched the taillights of Kramer's car head south on Cleveland. *He asks too many questions for his own good.* He nodded as if agreeing with himself and started across the parking lot toward the mattress store.

"Chief Mangione," a voice called out.

The policeman turned and recognized Stephanie Sanders. "How's my favorite lady of the press?"

Sanders held back her grin and extended her hand. "The *Stradford Star* at your service, Chief Mangione."

He gave her hand an extra squeeze. "Out late for a young lady, aren't you?"

"The news never rests, sir." She turned on the recorder strapped around her neck and opened her notepad.

"Going all official now, are we?" He ramped up the sincerity in his smile.

"What can you tell me about the shooting?" She put herself directly in front of him,

"There's no cause for alarm, Steffi." He kept his voice calm as his mind raced. "Why do you think it was a shooting?"

She swiped hair off of her face. "The ambulance I passed on the way here, and the second one I heard on the scanner. Are you saying there was no one shot?"

"No, there were casualties, but I see no need for concern."

"People died and you're not concerned?" The pen in her hand jabbed at the notebook.

Mangione reached a hand to her shoulder. She jerked away. "How many dead?"

He stared at her until the color rose in her cheeks. "Three."

"And that doesn't concern you? What about the other shooting tonight? Are they related? What is happening to our city?"

Mangione shook his head as if he were sad. "Let's focus on this event; we're still investigating the other shooting." God, he thought, do I miss the days before the internet. "Yes, three men died here tonight, and it does concern me. That's not the Stradford anyone wants."

Sanders watched the man's eyes as he spoke. When they flicked down and to the left, he was probably lying. "Go on," she said.

"I am more concerned that I'll open the paper tomorrow, your paper, and see some wild, crazy headline that we're all doomed. That's not in anybody's best interest."

"We don't go to press tomorrow, Chief Mangione. We'll have a story on-line tonight."

"Yes, so what I'm proposing is that you and I sit down tomorrow and discuss this. We'll have more facts by then and your story will be more accurate."

Sanders gave him a look. "What can you tell me about the three people killed?"

She needs a lesson, he thought. "Three males, 20-30's, appear to be Latinos, probably illegals."

"Any names or nationalities?"

"Hispanics, like I said." He looked away. "I have more work to do here tonight."

"Last question, Chief. Does their being 'Latino' or "Hispanic" make you more concerned or less concerned about the safety of the citizens of Stradford?"

"There is no cause for concern. The Stradford Police have the situation under control. Good night, Ms. Sanders." He walked across the parking lot and entered the store through the loading dock.

She flicked off her recorder and held the notebook in the light. He hadn't said very much, and she would have to try again tomorrow. She was tired of being stonewalled.

It would have been more apropos to have met her in her office tomorrow morning, Karl thought. That was the scene of his humiliation, where she said he was too old. Obsolete would have been better, but he wasn't sure she knew the word.

As it was he was hunched down in his car, parked across the street from Kimberly's house, waiting for her guests to leave and her husband to go to bed. The Holmgrens and the Horvaths were notorious partyers, in their own minds at least, because he knew they were equally famous for their short nights. They drank a lot in those nights, but they were almost always tucked in bed by midnight.

He checked his watch. He was safe here in the inappropriately-named neighborhood of Stradford Heights. The name didn't fit as the houses lined a valley, more of a gorge actually, and were well below the level of most of Stradford. Being the first of the exclusive developments also meant the trees lining the windy streets were fully grown. That made him feel safe enough to reload his weapon and relax.

The two couples were in the driveway now, waving and hugging. It must be nice to have friends you can be seen in public with. He had made his choices and would live with them. The Holmgrens maneuvered away. Karl watched the lights go on, then off in Tom's wing of the low house, what he would call California style. The living room light stayed on, as Kimberly, he presumed, was having a last glass of wine. Probably an oaky Chardonnay. He sent her a text.

Several minutes later she opened the door a crack. "Karl, it's late."

"Can't wait," he said. "May I?"

She stepped away and led him down three steps into the sunken living room. In the daytime, he knew, they would enjoy a great view of the valley. Now the large expanse of glass reflected the light from the few lamps and their faces. He sat down and said, "I have news."

"Good, I hope." She bundled her arms around herself as if cold. Only the wine glass protruded.

"So good I had to let you in on it ASAP."

Really? Who says that anymore? "Get at it, Karl."

"I will, but I don't want to rush it," he said, clearly enjoying being on stage.

"While we're still young." She looked at him pointedly. "At least while I still am."

That hit home, but Karl brushed it away. "First of all, I realize that you lied to me."

"What?"

Karl held up a pacific palm. "No, you did, and it was the right thing to do. I would have done the same in your position."

"God, Karl, this had better be good, because you're irritating me." She slurped some wine and set the glass on the coffee table. "What'd I lie about?"

"The house fire and the gas leak. It was clearly a hit. My sources are sure, and that would make sense, because there is in fact a new gang moving in on you."

"Do tell."

"But it's OK, more or less, because I am here to help you and--"

"As I told you before, I don't need your help."

"But you have it, my dear. It's all good. I retaliated for us, for you."

"Wait, you're responsible for that accident in Wayne County? That was you?"

"It wasn't an accident." Karl beamed. "It was a message for Sasha."

"You did it alone." She drank some more wine. "How'd you manage that?"

"I got ways," he said. "I want to help you, Kimmy."

She nodded. Probably got help from the Dagos in Cleveland. "That explains what happened tonight. They tried to rip off the mattress store because you attacked them. That only worsened the problem, Karl."

"Not to worry; we killed another three of them. Probably more. We knew they'd come at us, so we trapped them. Didn't lose an ounce of product."

"Wayne County was one thing, but you shot up the main street in Stradford. That will make it harder to keep hidden."

"We put the Russkie bastards back in the grave, Kim. Back to Youngstown."

She lowered her voice. "You did this without my permission."

"You got plenty on your plate, Mayor." Karl grinned. "Well, you did have."

"Quit talking in riddles."

He pulled a brown envelope from his bag and spilled the contents onto the low, smoked glass tabletop.

She moved her wine out of the way and poked at the pictures, the disc and the green thumb drive. "Are these what I think they are?"

"Absolutely! Found two sets of them, Kimmy. Lehrer can't blackmail you anymore!" Karl leaned back into the long couch and spread his arms wide. "You're clear!"

"He said he had seven sets of them." She flipped through several pictures before tossing them back down.

"Bullshit. Found one set in his closet, the other by the computer. He just said that to scare you."

Kim sat up straighter. "He gave them to you? Just like that?"

"Not exactly, but he won't be bothering you anymore, with pictures or anything else." Karl smiled broadly.

"He's dead?"

"Kim, the first thing you're going to need to do is stay better in touch. That police scanner I gave you?"

"You killed Lehrer?" She looked up sharply. "Can they trace it back to me?"

Karl appreciated her reaction. She must have actually listened to him.

"Got it covered, Mayor. A masterstroke, I must say."

The man could draw out a story like no one she knew. Especially a story featuring him as the hero. "Well?" she prodded.

"Oscar shot him, not me. I'm clean."

"Whose gun?"

"Oscar's gun. Come on, what did you think?"

"But then Oscar can--"

"Not from the grave he can't. Our fat friend is no longer speaking. Or breathing."

"You killed him?"

"Joe's gun killed him. See, we're in the clear." He slapped his hands together as if shedding dust.

"No mess, no fuss, no bother," she said. "Like Alfie used to say." She gave him a warm smile.

"Exactly right." He laughed heartily and slapped his thigh. "Just like the old days."

Just like I'd planned it, she thought, or nearly so. She fixed the smile on her face and moved beside Karl on the sofa. "Thank you, Karl, thank you."

Predictably, she thought, he wasn't finished talking about himself.

"The way I see it, I got rid of your problem, Joe Lehrer, and I got rid of my problem, Oskar. A twofer, you could say."

She toasted him. "My hero."

"The bonus is the pictures. Gone for good, you're in the clear."

"No, Karl really. That was a heroic thing you did." She bowed her head and laid a hand on his leg. "After I treated you so abysmally."

"Not to worry, my dear, not to worry. I was happy to do it for you."

"How can I repay you?" She looked at him closely.

"You can't, Kim, and you don't have to." He smiled at her. "It was the right thing to do."

"Thank you, Karl," she said and pecked his cheek.

"Aw, shucks."

He said aw shucks? This guy is un-real. "No reward?" she said. "Then you'll have to do me a favor."

Yes, he thought. "Anything you want, Kim. Name it."

"Come back and work for me." She set her glass down. "With me. Be my guy, my right hand."

"Your *consigliere*."

"I don't know what that means, but it sounds right!"

Karl smiled broadly. It's Italian for 'I'm in charge'.

"I want us to work together, like you and my brother used to. I can use some help and after what you managed to do tonight." She shook her head in amazement. "Say yes, Karl, please."

"Yes, of course, Kim. Yes. I'd consider it an honor," he said. Now things will run as they're supposed to.

CHAPTER TWENTY

The uncomfortable silence of the hospital waiting room was shattered by the shriek of an ambulance. Nurses sprinted past, lab coats billowing behind. One turned and shouted, "Bring another gurney!" The high school kids stepped out of their way, both fascinated and repulsed. Bob glanced up. Bert and Lexan spoke quietly and barely noticed. The doors from the ER bay burst open and a body was wheeled inside, one nurse pulling, another pushing. A third was hanging an IV bag on a stand. The sheet covering Oskar was splotched with blood.

Lexan looked up, not knowing why, or realizing she had. Bert held her hand, and Bob sat close by, but she didn't realize that either. As the kids separated in front of her, she rose and saw the second gurney. The sheet covering the victim slipped away as a tech in purple scrubs pounded the chest. The kids turned and looked at her. Bert squeezed her hand. It was Joe.

Lexan ripped herself away from Roberta and lunged for him. She tried to call his name but the others heard a tortured scream. She lunged for his hand. It flopped away as Bob tried to catch her.

"Let me go, let me go." Lexan elbowed herself free and ran after the gurney until it disappeared behind the heavy double doors leading to the ER. She pounded the wall button, but the doors wouldn't open. Bob and Bert gathered her in their arms and walked her slowly back to the waiting area.

"He's dead, I know he's dead," she said as Bert hugged her.

"We don't know that, Lex, we don't know that."

"He's dead because I left him." Lexan's words were garbled by her tears and her raspy breathing. "It's my fault."

"You didn't hurt him, Lex."

"I did, I did hurt him. I love him and now he's dead."

"We don't know what happened. Let the nurses help him." It was hard for Roberta to speak as well, but Lexan needed her, and she tried to hold her own emotions in check.

"He never leaves me alone." Lexan's words came out in choking sobs. "I made fun of him for protecting me."

Bob looked questioningly at Roberta. She shook her head. "You didn't do this to him."

"No, I didn't do this." Lexan sat up straight. "No. I

just left him alone so someone else could hurt him."

"Lexan, sit back down, you're--"

Canfield returned with a nurse. "Please tell his friends, if you can, what you told me," he said to her.

The nurse glanced at her clipboard. "I don't have much to tell you, really."

"He's dead." The words broke through Lexan's mouth as if expelled.

"He's in a coma, Ma'am," the nurse said. "I don't know how long--"

"--what do you know?" Lexan stepped toward the nurse, her face red and her eyes wide. Bert grabbed her elbow, and Bob stepped in front of the nurse. Canfield herded Chelsea and the other students across the waiting room and spoke to them quietly.

"Let's sit down, why don't we?" The nurse took a breath. "Apparently it was a gunshot wound."

"Shot? With a gun?"

The nurse knew better than to respond to Bob. She leaned over and spoke closely to Lexan. "At the moment he's non-responsive, but that is typical with head trauma. Don't be overly alarmed."

Lexan shuddered. The nurse patted her arm and stood up. To Bert she said, "Keep doing what you're doing. I'll keep you informed." She pulled Bob aside. "Are you family?"

"Close as he's got." Bob swallowed and kept himself from yelling 'Fuck!' "What else can you tell me?"

She spoke calmly. "It is good that the bullet appears to have glanced off. We don't think it penetrated the skull, but bone fragments may have. Mr. Lehrer is unconscious. You and your friends should prepare yourselves." She gave Bob a kindly nod and looked around to find Kenny Chandler's parents.

"I don't know why you need to run everything by him," Pamela Holmgren said to the Mayor. "We're perfectly capable of making our own decisions."

Kimberly's hand still held her cell phone. "It's more of a courtesy than anything else."

Holmgren looked at her closely, wondering if she should go along or push it a little farther. It was worth her while to consider her words, because the plan was for her to be Mayor when Kimberly ascended to the Governor's mansion. It was why she had gotten out of bed at this ungodly hour and was sitting here without even a cup of coffee. Ultimately it was up to the governor of course, and she would have to tread softly. "What did the man say?" she asked.

"We read him right," Kim said. "The Governor merely fine-tuned the plan." She wondered again how much she could trust Pam. Her cosmetics firm, PamLeeCo, made a lot of money so that wasn't her motivation. "Rest assured that we are continuing not to kowtow to the man, my dear."

Pam looked out the windows of the Mayor's office at the black night outside. "He gets the first move, of course."

"It's state money and he's the governor. He gets the first move."

"And?" Pamela pressed.

"In a week. If that's soon enough for you."

"Yes, thank you Ms. Mayor, that will do nicely." She folded her hands in her lap and smiled theatrically. "The hired help won't be calling the shots anymore."

"Lance and Thommy's staff are working on the press release tonight; it'll be ready Friday for the weekend news cycle." Kim nodded. "You do realize however, Mrs. Holmgren, that it was a man who gave us this opportunity."

"Karl is functional, I can admit that," Pam said. "In this case he has helped us out."

"He will be staying on," Kim said. Holmgren's eyes darted to hers. You don't know everything, dearie, she thought.

Pam re-arranged her features, hoping to hide her shock. "In an advisory capacity, I assume."

Kimberly nodded, holding the other's gaze.

"Hopefully on a short leash." Pam noticed a crease in her skirt and smoothed it.

Kim held her thumb and forefinger several inches apart. "This short enough for you?" She laughed as she said it.

"Said no man ever," Pam said and they both laughed some more.

Kim gave her a minute. Pam was her friend and deserved that much. "Back to business. The Governor will announce that the expected tax revenues did not reach the forecasts, and that he has no choice other than to cut funding to the schools."

"He was actually expecting lower revenue, correct?"

"He was ready to go either way, so the cuts have

already been laid out. That means--"

"--let me, let me," Pam interrupted.

Kim smiled and nodded.

"That means Stradford won't receive enough state money to fund the teacher contract."

"So sad," the Mayor said.

"So sad," Pamela agreed. "No more blackmail, no new contract."

"One more thing, my friend."

Pamela raised her eyebrows.

"The funding cuts are so severe, we are forced, unfortunately, to lay off teachers."

"Reduce the staff?" Pam dabbed her eyes. "My eyes are welling up."

"You'll get over it," the Mayor said with a contented smile. The phone buzzed and she picked it up.

Holmgren tried to catch the voice as a smile broadened on Kim's face. "Who?" she mouthed.

"Mangione." Kimberly clicked off the phone. "This keeps getting better and better."

Holmgren looked at her expectantly. Kimberly loved seeing the need to know on her face. "Guess who they just wheeled into the hospital with a gunshot wound?"

"I surely don't know."

"Your little friend Joe Lehrer." The Mayor heard her friend's gasp as she strolled to the sideboard. "This calls for a drink," she said over her shoulder.

Lexan gave herself ten minutes to grieve for Joe. They had finally let her see him in a curtained bay in the

ER after what had seemed to her hours. Most of the kids had left the waiting room, leaving Roberta and Bob alone. Canfield had taken a phone call and disappeared.

Lexan looked at the intubation tube attached to Joe's face and listened as the machine breathed for him. His head was bandaged, blood spotting the right side and leaving his left eye uncovered. It was closed, but his eye jerked beneath the lid as if finding its way. The skin she could see on his face was grayer than pink. She wanted to touch him, but was afraid of hurting him more.

She was giving herself ten minutes because that was when the nurse told her they would be taking him for the CT scan and there would be nothing for her to do except wait. She listened to the machine beep and watched the graphs of his respiration and heart rate. Beeps and lines. She was sure he was going to die, but pushed that thought away, consciously and often.

Waiting and listening and watching, Lexan checked off boxes in her mind. Denial. Check. Isolation. Check. Pain. No check, she was determined not to feel pain.

Guilt. Check. Two checks. If she would have been with him, Joe would not be lying here more dead than alive. But no. She made her point. Stood up in front of him and won the argument. She was right in what she had said, she still believed it, but she had walked out, and now he was here. Motionless. No smile on his face, no twinkle in his eyes. It was her fault.

The nurse pulled aside the curtain, followed by an orderly. "Time to get your friend a CT scan," he said as he unlocked the wheels of the gurney. "You can wait outside."

When she looked past him as if she hadn't heard, he said, "I'll find you in the waiting room and let you know what's happening."

Her head turned to him, but her eyes remained on Joe. "We'll take good care of him, I promise."

Lexan nodded as they wheeled Joe from the alcove. He was as safe as he could be and she wouldn't know anything more until the tests were done. She walked past her friends in the waiting room. They would hold her back. Sitting in the darkened parking lot she checked the next box.

Anger.

CHAPTER TWENTY-ONE

K imberly tilted her glass and drank the last of the wine. She toasted Pamela and said, "I think we should call it a night."

"Yes, and a most rewarding night it has been." Pamela stood and reached for the crystal. Kimberly said, "Leave them. That's what my staff is for."

The Office of the Mayor of Stradford is in the same building as the Police Department and most of the municipal offices. It faces Center Rd., while the PD looks toward the gazebo and Cleveland Ave. to the west. Kimberly led her friend through the warren of offices to the back door and the parking lot. There were few cars parked there at this time of night, only the policemen working the night shift, and Karl guarding his boss.

In the ER waiting room, Bert elbowed Bob awake. "She's leaving."

"What? Who?" Bob shook his head.

"Lexan, she's leaving the hospital."

Bob grabbed his coat. "She's leaving Joe here? She wouldn't do that."

"She left him once tonight," Bert said.

He stopped buttoning. "She what?"

"Long story, I'll tell you later."

He took a step towards the door and turned around. "I got something to tell you, too. Remind me."

"I will." Bert frowned. "She's a grown woman. Give her some space."

Bob paused, then said, "Almost lost one friend tonight. Not losing another." He hurried through the maze of furniture in the waiting room and jogged out the exit.

Roberta wrapped her arms around herself and sighed. She would stay here with Joe.

The two women turned the last corner in the hallway and approached the exit of the Municipal Building. Pamela stepped in front of Kimberly and held the door for her. "Allow me," she said and waved her friend through.

"Thank you, Mrs. Holmgren," Kimberly smiled as she exited.

Lexan's fist struck her flush in the left eye. The Mayor tumbled backwards through the door and onto the hallway floor.

"Oh, my!" Pamela said. She let go of the door and it swung closed, striking Kimberly's head with a thud.

Lexan followed her prey into the building, banged

the door into Pamela and pushed her away. "Get up, bitch," she cried and pulled the mayor upright. She reached her right arm back to punch the woman again, but her arm caught and she dropped the Mayor.

"Hold on, wildcat, that's enough," Karl said. He held Lexan's arm with both hands. She flailed her legs trying to turn around. "Lemme go!"

Karl wrapped an arm around her waist and twisted her down the three steps. "Stop! Now!"

Lexan stepped back, nodded, dropped her arms and launched herself back up the stairs.   The Mayor had propped herself up on one arm, covering her eye with the other. She screamed, "Karl!"

The white-haired man grabbed Lexan's coat with both hands and lifted her off the ground. He carried her down to the sidewalk and dropped her on her feet. He held her with one hand and pointed his gun into her face. "Do that again, Ms. Warner and I will kill you."

"Kill me? She tried to kill Joe."

"No, she didn't," Karl said calmly. He poked her chin with the gun. "Think about it. If you're dead, you'll never see your boyfriend when he comes out of his coma."

"Take your hands off her." Bob stood behind her, panting, cell phone in hand. "I just called the police."

"The other Boy Scout is here, I see." Karl nodded. "You probably did." He said to Pamela, "Stop crying and inform Sergeant Jacoby at the front desk, that the Mayor has everything under control." Pamela scuttled into the building.

"You can't do that," Bob said.

Karl sighed. "Yet, in fact I did." He pushed Lexan into Bob and climbed the steps. "Your turn. Don't let her get away." He bent down to look at Kimberly's face.

Lexan pulled her arms away from Bob. "I'm fine."

"Silly me. You were clearly winning, three against one."

"She killed Joe," she whispered fiercely.

Bob slipped his arm around her shoulder. This time she didn't flinch. "He's not dead, Lex."

Her eyes filled.

Kimberly was now seated, her back against the heavy glass door. "Why did you send the police away?"

"Throw a pretty mean punch, Ms. Warner." Karl dabbed his handkerchief against the cut above the Mayor's eye.

"Damn it, Karl! I'm going to throw her in jail. She hit me. In the face."

"A shiner for sure." Karl rose and offered her his hand.

Kim jabbed her hand at Lexan. "Don't let her get away! Arrest her!"

Karl reached out both hands and pulled the Mayor up. He stood ready to catch her, but she regained her balance. "Thank you, I'm fine."

The white-haired *consigliere* walked down the steps toward the teachers. "Take her home, Mr. McCauley."

Bob tugged her sleeve.

"No. If she didn't try to kill Joe, then it was you." Lexan's eyes bore into Karl.

"Keep her quiet," Karl said. "If you can."

"No." Lexan's curls jounced as she shook her head.

"Come on, he's letting us go." Bob kept hold of her hand.

"I'm not going! Joe, they hurt Joe." She stomped her foot down.

"Let's get back to the hospital and see how he's doing, OK?" She mumbled something, and leaned her head into Bob's chest. Bob nodded to Karl over her head.

Karl returned to the Mayor. "I told you to arrest her," she said. Pamela had returned and was holding a mirror for her friend to assess the damage.

"No, that's not how we're going to handle this. Ouch, that hurts!" Kimberly snatched the mirror from Pamela.

Karl waited. "You hired me to do a job. Let me do it."

"Look at my face, Karl. Look what she did."

"A flesh wound, Ma'am. Considering what we're going to do to her and her friends, I think we're good. Right?" The women looked at each other, then back to him.

"Fine," he said. "Now, let's get you two ladies home without further ado."

CHAPTER TWENTY-TWO

"**Y**ou look tired," Roberta said. "You should go home and take a nap."

Bob wondered why Lexan had even come to school. She looked worse than merely tired. Her face was pale, the skin under her eyes splotched dark blue, and she slumped in his office, as if she could barely hold herself upright. How she had managed to teach six classes today was beyond him.

"Home? Right, you mean Joe's house. I walked out of his house, remember?"

"I didn't mean that," Bert said. Bob looked away, hoping they wouldn't go back to that again.

"No." Lexan waved a tired hand. "I know you didn't. Let's just get this meeting going, OK? Then I can get to the hospital."

The door opened and Agent Canfield entered Bob's small Guidance Department office. He found the open chair and said, "Well, this is a fine-looking group. Considering the weekend you had, I'm surprised any of you are here."

"We're not all here, but we're here." Bob hoped that was a joke; he wasn't sure.

"OK, I'll make this fast." Canfield opened his *portmanteaux* and withdrew a notebook spiraled across the top like reporters carry.

"First of all, the dance theme, Skittles Party." He looked at Roberta. "You were right, the kids were playing us." He narrowed his eyes. "They were having a pretend pill party. They drop whatever pills they can get a hold of into a bowl, mix them up and grab a handful. Eating bags of the candy was their way of mocking us."

"They acted like kids with candy. Skittles." Bob said it as a curse.

"The joke's on them," Lexan muttered. "Ha, ha. Kenny's dead." She again waved a limp, dispirited hand.

Bob tasted vomit in the back of his throat. "They don't even know what pills they're taking."

"They don't care. At least at the dance they were just pretending." The Agent shook his head. "At the Chandler house it was worse."

"How could it be worse?" Lexan nearly screamed. "Joe's fighting to live, and these kids, oh my God, these kids are killing themselves. Deliberately! I can't, I can't stand it." She slumped back in her chair.

Bob waited a moment. "What happened at the party?"

"Apparently the skittles thing has become too

tame." Canfield furrowed his blond eyebrows and turned to Bob. "Now they're into heroin."

Canfield looked from Bob to Lexan. "It killed the young man."

Lexan reached for her coat.

Canfield stood up in front of her.

"Get out of the way! I'm going to the hospital! All we're doing is spinning our wheels."

"Sure," he nodded, keeping contact with her eyes. "But at least hear some not so bad news."

"Joe's alive? Kenny's alive?"

"No." Canfield fought to keep himself calm. "We have found some information that may help. Thanks to you guys and the kids you spoke to at the hospital."

Lexan let Roberta hug her. The Agent kept his voice steady. "What we've been able to confirm is, the heroin the kids had at the house party came from two different sources."

"So what?" Lexan demanded. "And how could you possibly know that?"

"The gangs buy the heroin in powdered form, then press it into pills."

"Why bother?" Bob looked confused. "Why not sell it in baggies?"

"They can cut it for one thing. Get more volume by adding to it."

"Fentanyl?"

"Luckily not in this case. Doesn't have to be narcotic, just white powder."

"Why do we care?" Lexan's voice sounded to Bob like a cry.

"Because each gang marks the pills as their own. They mark the pills when they're stamped."

"Logos. On pills. That's all I can bear." Lexan struggled into her coat. "Let me out." The Agent stepped aside and closed the door behind her.

Canfield looked to Roberta then Bob. "She has got to get some rest," the counselor said.

"She'll be fine," Bert said.

"I hope so." Canfield took a breath. "Two different batches of pills means two gangs are operating in Stradford. Now we have two trails to follow."

Bob nodded. "I hope that means the odds of catching them have doubled."

Buddy Kramer was cooling his heels in the Police Chief's reception area, wondering why he wasn't being received, or even acknowledged. He tried to catch the secretary's eye as he had before, but she was intently concentrating on her computer screen, or shopping on-line, he didn't know. He also didn't know why he needed to make an appointment to see his boss.

He checked his cell. He'd been here almost twenty minutes. "You may go in now," the secretary said and pointed to her right. Her eyes remained on the computer.

"Thank you," he mumbled and opened Mangione's office door. The Chief was behind his desk, his eyes on a screen as well. Maybe they were texting each other.

Without looking up Mangione gestured to a chair. "What do you have?"

"Which death?"

"Not the kid, the other one, with the multiple victims in the house." Mangione's tone suggested that Kramer was an idiot and the question was, too.

"It looks like our initial thought; intruder shot by homeowner shot by intruder."

"I agree. Let's move the paperwork along. We have lots to do." When Kramer didn't respond, the Chief raised his eyebrows. "Well?"

"I said it looked that way, but I'm not sure."

"Ballistics?"

"The weapons and brass and wounds match up. The entry angles are within bounds."

"What's your problem?"

"My problem, sir, is the GSR."

Mangione scrolled through the file on his screen. "There is gunshot residue on the fat guy's hand, Oskar."

"Correct. He definitely fired the weapon." Kramer waited as Mangione searched the file. After several minutes he said, "But none on the teacher's hand."

"Gloves?"

"No gloves found at the scene."

Mangione looked up. "What are you thinking?"

"Another shooter. A third person in the room."

"You think someone staged this? Figured out the trajectories? Positioned the bodies? Wiped off his own print? Put the guns in the proper hands? All that?"

Kramer nodded.

Mangione shook his head. "Any physical evidence a third person was there?"

"No."

"Thought I heard something about footprints in

the blood."

"Didn't pan out."

"You got nothing."

"Got a gut feeling, sir."

Mangione smiled a grim smile. "Take a couple Tums."

Kramer tried to smile back as he stood up.

At the door Mangione said, "Just so we're clear, drop your third shooter idea and get the paperwork completed. *Capisce*?"

CHAPTER TWENTY-THREE

The woman walked like a zombie.

Janice had seen her in the room yesterday and the day before. She had spent Saturday night curled in a chair next to her friend's bed, and assumed she'd never left the ICU. The RN hurried to the desk so Ms. Zombie wouldn't have to explain herself to Margie. Margie was a rules stickler.

Lexan didn't pause at the desk and didn't answer Margie's questions. She knew Joe was in the third room on the right. Janice reached the desk as Margie was coming around it, saying "You can't--"

"I'll handle this, Margie," Janice said and took Lexan's arm. "I know her." She guided the woman down the corridor and stopped at the door to Joe's room.

"Have you slept at all?"

"I don't need to sleep," Lexan said and freed her arm.

Janice put herself in front of her and noticed the blotchy complexion, the obvious fatigue. "You have to help yourself before you can help him."

"I'm fine," Lexan said and pushed past the nurse into the room.

Janice watched her drop into the chair like a heavy load. "I'll bring you some soup, hon."

Lexan leaned her forearms onto Joe's bed and rested her head. Joe looked like he had the past two days. Arms at his side, pillow beneath his pale face, fluids dripping down plastic tubing into the ports in his forearms. The ventilator breathed for him, adding its whooshing to the beeping of the monitors. The eye she could see was closed; he could have been sleeping, but he wasn't. He had been shot. By Kimberly or someone who worked for her.

What did I do? I punched her. I ran after her like a kid on the playground. I made it worse. I wasn't there for him when he got hurt and now I made it worse.

She raised her head and looked at the bandages covering the right side of his face. She imagined what lay beneath, but hadn't seen it. She thought about how close the bullet must have come to entering his brain. The jokes they had shared about his hard head did not occur to her.

I can't let that bitch get away with this, but I have to have a plan. He needs me to have a plan. She laid her head back down on her arms and closed her eyes.

She was still asleep when Janice returned with the soup. The nurse paused at the door, then placed the tray on the table. *The girl needs sleep more than food,* she thought. She checked the monitors and was turning to leave when Dr. Burton entered.

"Ms. Warner," the neurologist boomed, looking at his handheld screen.

Lexan jerked awake. "Ssshhh!" Janice held a finger across her lips.

"We met the other night." The doctor raised his eyes as he heard the nurse whisper.

Lexan stretched her shoulders. "It's OK." Her voice was garbled. She wiped drool from the corner of her mouth. "I'm fine."

"It's good you're here," Burton said, "but I can come back." Janice glared at him.

"I'm awake now." Lex pushed off the bed to stand up. "What do you have to tell me?"

"No, really, I can come back later. You look like you--"

"Dr. Burton, if you have something to tell me, please do." She gestured with her arm. "He looks the same as he did Saturday night."

The doctor was surprised by the edge to her voice. "OK, I'll tell you what I have, and then I'll let you go." His voice was hard to pick up as he scanned Joe's file on the tablet. Janice caught Lexan's eye and shook her head.

"The CT scan results," Lexan said.

"Yes, the tomography scan indicates a GCS score of 12-13. Between a moderate and mild concussion, resulting in, as you know, a coma."

"Is his brain swelling?"

"It was. We drained off some fluids and he's stable. That's good news." Janice nodded.

"How long will he?" Lexan's voice caught. She

tried again. "Will he be like this?"

Burton glanced at the nurse, then Lexan. "He has several things working in his favor. His age for one, and he is in pretty good condition otherwise. That and the level of severity."

"How long?"

"One more thing to test. We want to run an MRI to be sure there are no bone fragments."

"Bone fragments?"

"The surgical team knows there was no major fracture, but they want to see if any small particles of bone are floating around in there." He looked up from the screen. "I concur. Probably nothing, but we need to make sure."

"How long will he be in a coma, Dr. Burton?"

"Tough to say." When that didn't satisfy her, he added, "Too soon to worry, but tough to pin down."

She put her face in her hands and seemed to shiver. She unclenched her face and said, "Ballpark it for me."

"We'll know more after we run the MRI." He patted her arm. "The ventilator will stay on another week and a half, then we'll see if we need to do a tracheotomy."

"Give me an answer."

"Could be a week, could be a month." He closed the tablet and left the room.

Janice led her to the table and removed the lid covering the soup. "First, you eat, then we'll talk."

Lexan sat down dumbly, and put her spoon into the soup.

"You know, Kim, I can get one of my girls to come

177

in and she could make your face look like it never happened."

The Mayor looked at her friend across the desk in her office at Cookies' Cookies. Then I'd be indebted to you, Pammy, she thought. That's not going to happen. Aloud she said, "No, thank you though. That's very kind of you to offer.

"I've seen the work they can do, I mean, they're good." Pamela beamed. "Why one time, the funeral home, um--"

"DiBello-Blaha?"

"Yes, that one. Anywho, there was this big accident, over on the Interstate, and they called in my team of cosmetics specialists, and they put these faces back together. I mean, there were broken bones and everything, and when my gals were done--"

"You're saying I look like I've been in a car wreck?"

"Oh, no, no, no, not at all. I just mean they could help you with the stitches and the black eye."

"Pamela, please stop. While we are still friends." Kimberly was almost happy that the office door opened and interrupted Pamela's response. Except it was that other loudmouth, know-it-all Karl.

She stood and gestured to him to sit in the chair next to Holmgren. He kissed them each on the cheek and said, "Ladies, it is always a pleasure."

Before Kimberly could start, the white-haired old fart leaned to Pamela and said, "I suppose our Mayor told you about the pictures I recovered? The blackmail pictures?"

"Oh, my yes," she said patting his knee. "So happy that awful blackmailing is over."

"You're quite welcome," he said and turned his head to Kimberly.

Drama queens. Everywhere I look, there's a damn drama queen. "I am quite thankful, Karl, for what you did for me. For us. But that is not why I called you today."

She arranged some papers on her desk and glanced at the screen to give him a chance to think. "How does my face look to you, Karl?"

Pamela's hand flew to her mouth. To his credit, Karl didn't flinch. "Not that bad," he said.

"It's bad enough that Pamela here is getting a mortuary cosmetician--"

"--aesthetician, they're called aestheticians."

"Shut up, Pam." Kimberly kept her eyes on Karl. "The point is, I can't show my face around town, the town you may recall I am the mayor of, because apparently I look like I died in a car wreck."

Karl knew he needed a joke to break the female tension here, but couldn't come up with one. "I am so sorry. She came out of nowhere."

"You were supposed to be guarding me."

"Truth be told, Ma'am." Karl knew how much she loved the Ma'am shit. "I was there in time to stop her from hitting you again."

Kimberly gave Pamela a 'can you believe this guy?' look. "That's the standard now, is it? Stop the second punch? What if she had used a gun?"

Would have saved me some time, he thought. "Fortunately, she didn't. Ma'am."

"I'd be dead, Karl. Not looking dead." She gestured to her face. "Dead dead."

He squared up his face to hers. "Won't happen again, Mayor."

She held his gaze several seconds like Alfie had instructed her. "It had better not." She paused again. "No one would vote for a mayor who looks like Rocky Raccoon."

That's the joke, he thought, and laughed along with the women.

"Now then, the real reason for meeting today, Karl, is to make sure we are clear on your assignment."

"Absolutely." I've taken my ration of shit for the day, bring it on.

"The gang situation. We, you, need to find a solution."

"One state or two?" Karl smiled warmly.

The man was such an ass. "This is Stradford, Karl, not Palestine."

"What?" Pamela said.

"Do you want to back one and eliminate the other?"

"I don't want the streets to look like Aleppo."

"Our old friends could take out the rest of the interlopers," he said. "I've reduced their strength the last couple weeks."

"You have, but that's cost us politically. Too obvious. Too much blood."

"I have carte blanche?"

"For god's sake Karl." She waved a hand to dismiss him. "Take care of it. Discretely."

"As you wish, Ma'am." He stood, bowed, and left.

Pamela watched the office door close. "Think he can handle it?"

"Now that he's properly motivated, sure."

"Why does he want to work for you, Kim? I'd think he'd be tired of doing the hard work."

"I don't really know. I thought he'd stay in Florida with Alfie and Mrs. Alfie."

"Maybe he thinks he's the boss. Men are like that. My husband surely is."

Kimberly knitted her brows. "You know, men are like that, aren't they."

CHAPTER TWENTY-FOUR

Lexan lay somewhere between awake and asleep.

Monday night in Joe's hospital room it had been hard for her to keep her eyes open, even with the flood of friends coming and going, hugging and crying. When they finally left, after convincing her to take a personal day Tuesday, she'd thought she'd fall into bed and pass out.

But it was Joe's bed. The bed they had shared in Joe's house, and it smelled like him. She clutched his pillow, her eyes wide, her mind racing. She had left him; she was here safe and warm, he was alone in a coma in the hospital. He didn't respond to her voice, to her touch, to her plea for him to just open his eyes.

Around and around her mind spun, repeating the same words, the same pain, the same guilt. Sometime after midnight Lexan had stumbled to the bathroom and swallowed an Ambien. She didn't know what time it was, but the pill worked.

She didn't know what time she awoke either. She did know she was clearly to blame, she knew that in her heart, even though someone else had pulled the trigger. She also knew she needed a way to get back at the people who hurt Joe.

Forty-five minutes later she found her hand frozen to the door of the Stradford Police Department, her body poised and ready, but unable to pull it open. She couldn't bring herself to talk to Det. Kramer.

Her first thought was for her friends. She couldn't allow them to be put in danger, like she had done to Joe. She'd considered Agent Canfield, but didn't know him well enough to trust him. That left Kramer, the man who had pursued Joe for months, trying to get him to admit that Chelsea had killed Weigel, not him. The short cop with the crew cut was abrasive, but on some level, she felt him to be an honest man.

There was no other choice. The door swung open from inside and a man held it for her. She didn't hesitate, and now found herself on the other side of Kramer's gray metal desk, sitting on the same gray metal chair she had several months before.

"How did you manage to avoid being charged with assault, Ms. Warner?" he said.

"People are being assaulted and killed all over town. How do you manage to keep your job, Detective?"

He gave her the police stink eye for several long seconds. Lexan considered admitting a bad decision and leaving. Then he leaned back in his chair and laughed.

"That's funny? People dying and you're laughing?"

"Hey, come on, I'm backing off." He held his hands up in mock surrender. "You could too, you know."

She found herself leaning across his desk, and sat back into the hard chair. "OK, I'll admit to being a little stressed out. Sorry."

The detective took a cleansing breath. "Good, let's start over. How is Joe doing?"

Her words tumbled out too quickly. "Stable. It doesn't sound like much, but it would be a whole lot worse if the bullet had entered his head."

He saw she was floundering and said, "It surely could have. Joe's lucky to be alive, and he's getting good care. Burton is top notch."

"I don't know, I hope so." She dabbed a tissue across her eyes.

Kramer smiled warmly. "What can I do for you, Ms. Warner?"

"Joe didn't kill anybody, Detective."

He tapped a file folder on his desk as her mood switched. "Evidence says he did."

She held his eyes. "Evidence showed he killed Weigel. You didn't believe that."

Kramer pursed his lips. "He killed one guy, why wouldn't he kill another?"

"He shot Weigel to protect Chelsea Larkin."

"He shot Oskar Brummelberger to protect himself."

She kept her face on his several seconds. "Do you believe Joe shot Oskar?"

He looked down and to his left. He wasn't sure. "I

believe the evidence."

"That's not what I asked." She waited a beat. "Do you have any doubts about the evidence? Does any of it not fit?"

He noticed the pallor of her skin, the sunken eyes, the aura of desperation. Clearly she was not herself. He thought about Mangione and said, "It fits."

She didn't believe him. "Why would Oskar want to kill Joe? What was his motive?"

"If Joe didn't kill Oskar, who did?"

"Exactly. The same person who wanted Joe dead." She stared at him. "Come on, Detective, you know what's been going on around here."

Kramer shrugged.

"You have to know why Joe has so much power in town."

Kramer folded his hands on the file folder.

"Or else you're not much of a detective." She waited. "You know who wanted Joe dead. Oskar killed him for someone--" She bracketed the word with her fingers, "--unknown."

"I could lose my job." His eyes darted to the door.

"Just do your job."

"I don't have any evidence." He let out a breath. "But I do have a theory."

Karl hated the idea of meeting in the bar of the Stradford Marriott. The hotel at the intersection of I-71 and Center Rd. reeked of prostitutes and shady dealings. And it simply reeked. He inhaled and nearly gagged.

"You all right there, Karl?" Mangione grinned and

extended his hand.

Karl nodded and sat down at the tiny table in the WWI aerodrome-themed bar. "Out of all the gin joints in all the world," he began, then noted the blank look. "Why'd you choose this shithole?"

"I did it for you, *consigliere.* I thought it would bring back memories."

"It does," Karl said and rolled his chair away from the table so he wouldn't have to touch it. "Unfortunately so."

"Doesn't the site of her coronation hold a special place in your heart?"

Karl directed his eyes at the Chief of Police. "You have to know what is transpiring here, my friend, so I ask why you are hosing me around."

"Hey, *pisano,* no harm intended, you know?" He opened his palms to show he had no weapon other than his tongue. "What can I do for you?"

For me or to me? Karl asked himself. He considered leaving, but he needed to deal with this man one way or the other. "I need your advice."

The scantily-clad waitress approached and took their drink order. Karl recognized her as one of his former employees but didn't mention it. Mangione practically drooled over her long, shapely legs.

"Not bad, hey?" he said and smacked his lips.

Karl despised how badly he needed to work with this idiot. "I want to run something by you."

"Glad to help," Mangione said.

Karl explained that Kimberly had given him the task of dealing with the drug gangs in Stradford. Mangione nodded as he spoke, and Karl got the surprising impression the man was comprehending the importance of the assignment.

When Karl was finished, Mangione arranged his face as if thinking. "I believe your instincts are correct."

Karl nodded, satisfied.

Mangione sipped his drink. "In fact, you may be the one guy that could pull it off."

"I appreciate that."

Mangione set his drink down. "Listen, Karl. I've heard some very impressive things about you." He shook his head. "But you never really know a guy."

"No, you don't."

Mangione's brows tightened. "But your plan is well thought out. Audacious--"

Karl grinned.

"--yet doable," Mangione continued. "You are the only one around here who could bring both gangs together and broker a peace deal. Truly impressive." He tipped his glass across the table.

Karl beamed. "It's simple, really. There is plenty of money to be made."

"You got that right," Mangione agreed. "They do throw their money around."

"They do. The only real issue is who gets what."

"Or where," Mangione said. "We can divide it up by product or by territory. What do you think?"

"I think I'm not the only genius around here. Very prescient comment, sir." Karl smiled at the Chief. His plan was working and he didn't notice Mangione's use of the word 'we'.

"Which way do you want to go with it?"

"It doesn't really matter; I'll propose one and use the other as a trade-off."

"A tool if you need it," Mangione nodded. "You are quite the negotiator."

"That I am." Karl finished his drink and winked at Mangione. Now you, he thought, will go running to the Mayor and convince her to go along with it.

CHAPTER TWENTY-FIVE

"We don't need a plan to retaliate, Lexan, we need to get Joe healthy." They had moved to the ICU waiting area across the hall, but still Roberta had to fight to keep her voice lowered. Bob looked from one woman to the other and kept quiet; both had already yelled at him. Lexan bounced on the balls of her feet like she was going to slug someone.

"I'm not a doctor, Bert, I can't help him. You can't either. Or Bob."

"Joe knows we're here," Roberta said. "He can sense us, and we don't want him to pick up negative vibes."

Before Lex could shout something in reply, Bob pointed across the hall. "Yeah, he's listening raptly to the advice Nancy is giving him right now. You know, like he always does."

The women looked into Joe's room, then spun back to him. "You're an asshole, Bob," they said together, then looked at each other and laughed. Bob hugged them both and said, "Works every time."

Lexan wriggled out of the hug. "But I need to do something other than watch him and listen to those damn machines."

Bob gave her shoulder a squeeze. "I know you do. You've been with him 24/7."

"Very brave," Roberta said.

Lexan shook her head. "I have to do more. I'm the reason he's here."

"You didn't shoot him, come on."

"I didn't protect him either, did I?" Lexan spoke so fiercely Bob stepped back from her. "You were going to do, what, take a bullet for him?" he managed. Bert looked worriedly from one to the other.

"I don't know, Bob. What I do know is that I wasn't even in the same house. I left him alone, and now he can't even breathe by himself." Roberta reached for her hand, but she pulled away.

"I have to do something to make up for it. I don't know if he'd ever take me back. I don't deserve it, but I can't just let him lie there and do nothing."

"So what, we form a posse?" Bob began. "Good that Nancy's here, she can saddle up, too."

Roberta shushed him as Nancy came out of Joe's room. "Let's give Lexan some space, shall we?" She took his arm and the other teacher's, and guided them down the hallway.

Lexan took Joe's hand and watched them leave. She pressed his fingers to her lips.

"Sorry to interrupt." Dr. Burton stopped inside the doorway. "I can come back later."

"No, please, tell me how he's doing." Lexan stepped away from the bed as the neurologist drew closer.

"Yes, the MRI results." He looked at his tablet. "We were concerned about the bone fragments."

Lexan nodded.

"Good news then. Didn't find any. The wound is clean." He smiled warmly.

"No need for surgery?"

"None at all. Mr. Lehrer is a lucky man." Burton snapped the tablet shut.

"But he's still in a coma."

"A little over a third of patients with this condition survive. He is clearly in that group, Ms. Warner. He's making progress, but you can't see it."

"When will he wake up or come out of it, whatever?" Her voice raced and she stepped toward the man.

"We just don't know. He is as I said fortunate to still be alive. He was shot at point blank range."

"I know, I know, but--"

He laid a reassuring hand on her arm. "We'll give him a couple more days. If there's nothing more we can do for him here, we'll transfer him to a re-hab facility."

Salt crystals crunched as Bob crossed the wide, open space under the arched Quonset hut of the Stradford Schools Service Department. He shivered both from the cold and the feeling that someone was watching him. The crunching echoed and his breath puffed out in clouds.

He grabbed the dark blue railing and hauled himself up the handful of steps to the loading dock level. Most of the offices where dark; he headed for the one with meager yellow light straining to escape the lowered blinds.

He was meeting Mel Radburn in his lair. That was enough to scare him normally, but this meeting was nowhere near normal. First, he was alone. The man had made it clear that he would only speak to Bob. Second, this was not the Office of the Business Manager in the Board of Education building. Third, after all the years of head-butting, Mel was volunteering to help. He couldn't get his mind around that. He hoped working with his enemy would be worth the reward.

He opened the door marked 'Supervisor'. "Nice place you got here."

"It's a dump, McCauley. Sit down." Behind a shabby desk covered in file folders, Radburn pointed to a wooden straight-back chair.

"Why are we meeting here?" Bob pulled out a yellow pad.

Radburn looked over his glasses. "I know you're not that dumb." He waved at the pile of papers. "Maybe you're lucky. That would explain it, but you're not dumb."

Bob wrote the date and time on the pad. Dealing with Mel had taught him that habit. "That's a compliment, right?"

The large rumpled man snorted. "I've been researching these test suppliers for years. You noticed the similarity of their billing addresses."

"It is a compliment." Bob beamed a smile.

Radburn glared at him. "What crime is it you think they are committing?"

"Like I told you before. With their access to the community, the volume of money they move around and the drug crisis, it's simple. They're laundering drug money."

"Shell companies?"

"Exactly." Bob smiled. Maybe this was going to work.

"You're wrong. They aren't shell companies."

Maybe not. "It's a perfect way to launder money. They got to put it somewhere, right?"

"Do you even know what a shell company is?"

The man could be an ass. "Yeah, they put cash in different accounts so it looks like they earned it."

Radburn took his glasses off and massaged the bridge of his nose. "Shells are companies that don't really exist. Or only exist on paper."

Bob gestured to the files on the table. "You're saying these companies are legitimate."

"Yes. I've been working with the regular suppliers for years. When the state tests were mandated, we vetted them thoroughly." He folded his hands. "It's time for you to drop this and walk away."

Bob unclenched his jaw. "We know the government is corrupt. Maybe they're adding the drug money to legitimate monies."

"That's not happening. Drop it, McCauley." Radburn snapped his briefcase shut.

"No way." His plans were going down in flames. "You could even be in on it."

"Be careful," Radburn hissed.

"You got access to all the numbers and you write the checks."

"Do I look like I'm in on it? Do I look like one of them?"

"You seem pretty chummy with the rich and famous."

"Maybe you are that dumb. It's my job to bow and scrape. Schmooze or lose."

"If you're so good at schmoozing, Mel, why did you lose your job at the high school?"

Bob knew the answer for he had exposed the scheme. He watched Radburn's fingers clench. "What you did was juggle the attendance figures to jack up the test scores. Was that bowing or scraping?"

"You are astoundingly out of control, Mr. McCauley. And I am out of patience."

"If you want me to trust you."

"I should earn your trust?" Mel huffed a breath. "I needed to get closer to them, the elites, and to the numbers. I couldn't do that from the high school."

"Wait. You're saying you planned to lose your job?"

"I did it to make the school look better. The higher test scores moved our Report Card to 'Excellent'."

"I don't believe you. We're done here." Bob yanked the zipper on his pack. "I'll expose what I've got so far."

"You got nothing."

"What I got is a whole lot of drug money and the mechanism to launder it."

Radburn's face opened. "We'll look bad if we don't have all the facts. More importantly, we'll hurt the people we're trying to help."

Bob nodded. "That I agree with. We have to stop hurting the kids."

"There's hope for you yet." He spoke slowly and softly. "Your hunch about money laundering is what I've been working on for years. We were both wrong."

Bob returned self-deprecating half-smile. "What do you think is going on?"

"Plain old theft, Bob. Taking money away from the kids and stuffing it in their pockets."

He used my first name, Bob thought. "Let's nail them for that."

"We have to find out where the money is going. It's complicated."

"We can work on it together."

Radburn's stare was stern but not menacing. "If you can keep your mouth shut about it."

Bob watched the man thumb through the folders and shoved several across the desk. The others Radburn slid into his case. This wasn't what Bob had planned, and it would take time to make a splash even if they were successful. But it was something. Radburn rose.

"What do we do next?"

"You do your job, I'll do mine."

"But?"

"We're different. I work from inside, you and, your friends--" He managed make the word sound distasteful. "--work from the outside."

"I don't get it."

"You may never." Bob started to speak; Radburn waved him silent. "Before you ask, this conversation never happened. I was not involved. If there is any credit to be had, it's yours."

"I have to ask one more question." Bob stood up and looked at Radburn squarely. "Why would you help me and Joe and Lexan? You hate us."

"No, I hate your methods." Radburn glanced at the time on his cell.

"Nope. I'm not buying that."

Radburn took a step toward the door keeping his eyes aimed at the teacher.

Bob blocked his path. "No way. You enjoy antagonizing us and belittling us."

Radburn's eyes held Bob's for several seconds then dropped to the floor. His voice softened again. "What they're doing is not right," he said. "You and your friends are obnoxious, and I don't agree with your methods, but those people are hurting children."

Before Bob realized what Radburn had said, the man had hurried out the door.

CHAPTER TWENTY-SIX

F r. Gerald Hastings, Pastor of Holy Angels parish, found Lexan huddled into a ball in the corner of Joe's room. "Looks like you could use a cup of coffee." He extended her one foam cup and sipped from the other.

Lexan looked blankly at the coffee, then at him. "Oh, Fr. Jerry. Sorry, I'm in kind of a fog. It's nice to see you again."

"You, too." He looked at her from beneath his wrinkled forehead. "Is he doing any better?"

Lexan kept her eyes on Joe. "Not really. Stable. I guess that's good."

"Comas are strange. He could wake up five minutes from now."

"Or lie there like a vegetable for a year."

"Could be worse."

"How, exactly, could it be worse?" She turned sharply to him. "I can't do anything to help him, and nobody knows how long he'll be unconscious."

He waited several seconds before saying, "Where there's life, there's hope."

She grimaced.

"Lexan, he's not dead." The priest tried to catch her eye. "And it's not your fault."

She glared at him. "What?"

He sipped some coffee. "You think it's your fault because you weren't there when it happened."

The coffee sloshed in her hand. "How, why did you say that?"

He gestured toward Joe. "You're like him, you're blaming yourself."

"I'm not like him."

"Maybe." Hastings knew she was more like Joe than she imagined. "You didn't shoot him either."

"What do you know about it?" Her hands shook as she set cup on the table. "Or about who I am?"

"You're playing the-I'm-a-priest-so-I-don't-know-anything-about-real-life card?" He took another sip of the coffee.

"You come in here and tell me what to do, what to think." Lexan's voice rose and she rocked forward on her feet.

"I haven't done either of those things, Lexan." He faced her. "Look, I don't want to stress you out. I'll just give him a blessing and get out of your hair."

He took the purple stole from his pocket and unrolled it. "You know, I just now figured out why you remind me so much of Cathy."

Lexan looked up, but didn't speak.

"Joe had all these girlfriends in high school, but he never got serious with any of them." Hastings pursed his lips. "Don't know why I'm talking about this. Sorry."

"Tell me about him." Lexan kneaded her knuckles. "You've been friends a long time."

Hastings smiled. "Since third grade."

"I assumed he was popular, but he never had a real girlfriend?"

"Not until Cathy." He arched his eyebrows. "Do you really want to know?"

She looked at Joe as she spoke. "He may never be able to tell me himself."

Hastings lowered his voice. "He always kept part of himself hidden."

She shook her head. "He's not like that now."

"Cathy changed him." She looked defeated, and he wondered how far he should take this. "Before he met her, there was a wall he wouldn't let people through, girls especially."

"She was different?"

Hastings nodded. "I don't know all the details. I was at a parish downtown. But she got him to open up."

Lexan's eyes left his face and returned to Joe. The priest put on the purple stole and made the sign of the cross over his friend. She still hadn't moved when he finished praying. He turned as he left and blessed her silently. He hoped she understood what he was saying.

Lexan fumbled and dropped her keys trying to

unlock her car door. When she finally managed to get inside and back out of the narrow space, the line to pay at the hospital exit was long and she had forgotten to have her ticket validated. The seat belt clanged against the window as she reached to the passenger seat floor to retrieve her wallet from the pile that had slid out of her purse when she had hit the brakes too hard. She cursed again when the machine spit out first her ticket, then her credit card. Finally, she managed to insert enough bills, the gate lifted, and she sped out of the parking garage.

Lexan would never get used to people judging her. She was beyond crying about it, she just needed to get away from everyone else's opinions. They didn't come out and criticize her face to face, like she would if the situations were reversed; no, they couched their barbs in platitudes and false kindness. Platitudes, fricking platitudes. Almost 34% of coma victims survive. That's not comforting. Two out of three don't.

She drove south out of Stradford, across the county line to a bar in a strip mall at the top of Liverpool hill. She didn't know anybody here and could think uninterrupted.

"Back so soon, honey?" Brian or Benny, whatever, stopped wiping the bar and smiled. "The usual?"

"A double," Lexan said and dropped onto the bench of her usual booth.

"Ladies, we are gathered here to celebrate a birth." Karl pulled the bottle of champagne from the metal bucket on the stand next to his chair.

"We could have met at one of my offices," Kimberly said.

"Or mine, or in the library for goodness sake," Pamela said.

"Mundane," Karl said. "Prosaic, run of the mill, drab. This is big."

Pamela smirked. "If we agree that this is a momentous occasion, would you at least explain why you called it a birth?"

"Pam, the gentleman has our best interests at heart. I believe we should let him speak." Kimberly gave her friend a look that told her to hold her tongue.

He finished filling their flutes and settled his hands in his lap. "It is a new beginning, akin to a birth. The drug war will be over, all impediments to Kimberly's smooth sailing will be removed, her path will be clear." He raised his glass. "That deserves a toast."

They clinked and smiled at each other. Kimberly looked around Shelby's Country Inn and said, "Now would be a good time to hear some details, sir."

Karl downed his champagne and rubbed his hands together. "Basically, it is your plan Kimberly; I work for you." He bowed his head to her, Pamela noticed, and covered her grin with her fluted glass.

"As you suggested, we'll get the two sides together, divide the turf--" He nodded to the ladies as he said the word. "--split the proceeds. Plenty for everybody, no one has to die."

The women nodded and he continued. "Peace doesn't mean we're stepping away, peace means everything will be back under cover like it was before. No more blood in the streets. Problems hidden, profits ensured."

"Mangione?"

"On board."

"You talked to him? Well done, Karl."

"Thank you, Ma'am. I like to cover all my bases."

Pamela narrowed her eyes. "What about manpower?"

"I have given you the strategic overview." Karl carefully re-filled their glasses. "I will however keep the tactical details to myself, to protect you. You can plead ignorance, if the need arises."

"The need had better not arise, Karl."

He tipped his glass in the Mayor's direction. "Not to worry."

The three smiled at each other and sipped their champagne.

CHAPTER TWENTY-SEVEN

Because Bob had known his tiny office wouldn't accommodate this meeting he'd scheduled it in the guidance department conference room. The empty chair he had left for Lexan meant they could have stayed in his office. "Bert, should we wait for her?"

"I doubt she's coming," the French teacher replied. "I couldn't get a word out of her today. Hope she went home to bed."

"I'll bet she went to the hospital." Bob turned to Agent Canfield. "Do you want to introduce our guest?"

They all laughed. The usually dour Detective Kramer grinned humorlessly. "I think we've all met one time or another."

The door opened. "I thought we were meeting in your office." Lexan's voice was brittle. "Like always."

Bob watched as she drooped into the chair and let her things slide to the floor. "No prob, Lex, we're just getting started. I believe you know the detective."

She nodded vaguely. "Let's get on with this, I have to see Joe."

"OK, we will." Bob turned to Canfield. "Explain your connection with the police department."

"Buddy and I meet on a fairly regular basis," the BCI agent said. "It's good because we are each familiar with a piece of the puzzle, but were having trouble making sense out of the whole thing." He nodded to the detective who gestured for him to continue.

"We are now fairly certain that there are two drug gangs working Stradford."

Bob looked up expecting more. Neither officer spoke. "That's it?"

Canfield cleared his throat. "It's a big deal." Kramer agreed. Roberta squinted. Lexan exploded. "You drag us here for a meeting when I could be with Joe? For this? I already knew this."

Bob put a pleasant expression on his face. "Come on, gentlemen, you can tell us more."

Kramer sighed. "Actually we can't. You're not deputized."

Lexan stood up. "We get you evidence about the party, we do your stupid legwork and that's it?" She snatched her book bag from the floor.

"Why even meet with us?" Bob fought to keep his voice calm.

Canfield gestured to Lexan at the door. "If it weren't for you guys, we wouldn't know about the second gang."

"And that's important why?" Lexan yanked the door open.

Canfield looked at Kramer. The Detective said, "Please shut the door. Sit down. We can give you some more information."

Lexan glared at them. "I'll stand."

Kramer looked from her to Bob. "To answer your question, the recent violence in town seems to be the result of the interaction between the two gangs."

"I don't care! Joe's in the hospital!"

"It may be why he is in the hospital, Ms. Warner."

"Go on," Bob said.

Canfield shuffled his notes. "We believe the friction between the two gangs is causing the violence."

"Did Joe get between the gangs?" She looked from Canfield to Kramer. "Did they kill him? Did they?" Her voice was high pitched. Desperate.

"We don't know, Ms. Warner," Kramer said. "But it may be part of it. He could have been involved--"

"Whatever." Lexan grabbed her coat and books and stormed from the office.

Bob shut the door. "Sorry. She's been under a lot of stress."

Roberta paused before asking, "Was the house fire part of this?"

"Maybe the shootings at the mattress store as well." Kramer made a decision. "The recent activity indicates two groups. I'm familiar with the old Cleveland Mafia, the Hill gang, and Agent Canfield's sources link to the new gang. They're Russian. Call themselves the Bratva. They lost their turf to the Hill gang years ago. Now they're trying to re-claim it." He bunched his lips. "That's all we can tell you."

Karl was stress free and happy. Happiness to him was not a feeling exactly, like some would get from a good bottle of wine, a nice car, or a good lay. For Karl, happiness was the state of things being in their proper place. Stradford was on the brink of true happiness. When the sun came up tomorrow everything would be returned to order the way he and Alfie had intended.

Kimberly would be Mayor, as she was now, but in her proper role; she would be the face of Stradford. She would be the one to rally the troops, chair the meetings, and speak to the press. After he brokered the deal, their main revenue stream would be simplified, expanded, and safely hidden beneath the surface. The façade of peace would descend again.

He would remain in the shadows, unseen, but efficient. The way it had been when Alfie was in the big chair. Like *Game of Thrones*, he would be the Hand of the Mayor. Karl chuckled at that thought. He needed one of those gold pins to wear on his lapel.

He had chosen the site of the meeting for one good reason and one that was admittedly sentimental. The old Pemberton factory was secure, out of the way, and for him accessible from many directions. It had been abandoned years ago when Alfie had sold part of its acreage for the Interstate right of way. The company had been one of their first shells, and they'd made money selling the equipment and writing off the loss. The one road leading to it was bumpy and weed-choked. The highway cut off the other routes that had led to the factory, but he knew where the tunnels still led underneath I-71. He would be using one to enter the property tonight, and had made sure another was usable if he needed it when he left.

In all likelihood he wouldn't be needing to make a covert getaway, because he had planned the meeting carefully, vetted it, and most importantly it made sense; there would be no need to flee because there would be no losers. It would be lucrative for all sides.

Lucrative always brought a smile to his lips. Lucre, filthy lucre. The smile reminded him of the sentimental, and he had to admit, the real reason the meeting would be held here. Years ago when he and Alfie were stealing money from the state for the highway, some asshole had tried to stop the sale for environmental reasons. Karl shook his head at the idiocy. A creek leading from the property across the future path of the highway was polluted. Carcinogens from the factory, they claimed. That led do-gooders, he had plenty of other terms for them but he was in a good mood, to an inspection of the factory itself, where they found the storeroom filled with 40-gallon oil drums. He nodded as he remembered. There wasn't much oil in the drums, but they did hold a variety of toxic waste, including the carcinogens.

It had cost them a lot of money to divert the investigation. It was a cost of doing business, so that wasn't why he remembered the incident so fondly. Two things: first, they had inserted the head rabble-rouser into one of the steel barrels and welded it shut. That took the sting out of the group. Second, the look on the faces of the workers years later when they unearthed the barrel during the construction of the elementary school on the other side of the woods. He laughed aloud and had to focus on the path through the darkened tunnel. The forklift driver had hoisted the drum up, but lost control, and it cracked open when it fell. The skeleton had floated out, pieces of it anyway, some tatters of clothing, a little flesh. Made a great front page for the *Stradford Star.*

The lesson to be learned? Because Stradford was being properly administered at that time, he and Alfie had walled themselves off from the investigation, and the incident faded away. As incidents should.

Karl was now at the tree line, where he could see the factory and not be seen. He opened his lawn chair and sat down. The sun was setting behind the ruins as he began a methodical sweep with his military-grade binoculars. He had some time before his men would show up, hopefully before either of the gangs did. They were men from his old team like Jacobs, and he could rely on them. He probably wouldn't need them, but part of planning was to cover all the bases. He hung the optics on the back of the chair and opened his notebook to the agenda. When satisfied it was complete, he began another visual sweep.

A branch snapped behind him and Karl looked at his watch. By the time he stood, the five men had exited the tunnel and lined up for his inspection. He nodded at their dark clothing and blackened faces. He looked through the scope on the second man's weapon, and checked the night vision goggles of the fourth man. He looked into the eyes of each one, nodded at Jacobs, but did not speak their names. At his gesture, they followed him across the field.

The Pemberton Tool and Die Factory hadn't aged gracefully, but still reminded Karl of the old days. The main floor was low and dirt covered, surrounded on three sides by a walkway. The second floor held offices, the lower floor held work spaces and storage. He chuckled that several oil drums had survived. The roof was open in several places, but for the most part the spider web of metal supports held firm. The middle portion of the large rectangular roof was raised; yesterday it had admitted light through the mostly broken panes. The remaining glass was dirty, nearly opaque.

The triangular table in the center of the floor had been Karl's master stroke. Inspired by the round table of King Arthur, he would use symbolism to his advantage. One side for him, the head of course, but it wouldn't appear so, one for the gang from the Hill and the other for the Russians. Room for two men per side; he would be alone.

It was time. He directed the two-man firing teams to their positions on the second-floor. In the pre-op meeting yesterday, they had determined the high corners afforded them the best fields of fire. They had pulled file cabinets and desks from the offices to use as cover. Jacobs, the man he trusted most, took his place at the loading dock where he would ensure weapons stayed outside. Karl sat down at the table facing the door and checked the time on his cell.

"The Cleveland boys are here, boss," Jacobs called.

"Two in, no guns." Karl stood up. He extended his

hand. "Tony, no you prefer Anthony, right, and, wait, you're Guido. Did I remember that correctly?"

The men looked at each other.

"Good, it's been a long time." Karl extended his hand. "Please, have a seat."

"We'll stand," Guido said.

"As you wish." Karl looked toward the door, where Jacobs was patting down one of the *Bratva.* He believed the word meant brotherhood. They had been forced out of Cleveland by the Italians, but that was before his time and he had never had to deal with them. He assumed they would respond to reason. "Send them in and we can get started."

When the Russians arrived at the table, the four gang members glared at each other, neither side wanting to move first. After a long minute of glaring and posturing, Karl said, "Thank you for attending, gentlemen. I believe we can come to an agreement here." He sat down and the others grudgingly followed suit.

"There is no reason for a meeting." Guido squared his shoulders and said to Karl, "This is our turf, you should protect us. That was our deal."

"True enough," Karl said and looked to the *Bratva.*

Filya spoke. He was not a large man, but his voice was heavy and deep. "You have killed many of my people. I will kill you next."

"That's a good start," Karl said. "A summary of our positions."

Jacobs racked a round. The four men reached instinctively for the weapons they had given up at the door. They are all so predictable Karl thought. Their four heads rotated to him.

"If I may continue," Karl said. "We are in this together. We don't need to kill anybody else. We have the same goals." He spread open his hands. "Money, am I right?"

Anthony, the younger Cleveland mobster said, "That is always how it has been. Why should we let these *putas* into Stradford?"

"Excellent point." Karl looked at Filya. "Your response?"

"You are old, worn out." He turned to the big man beside him. Vadil said something in Russian. "Da, that's it. You are past your use-by date." The two Russians laughed.

Anthony and Guido glowered. Karl wondered how much they would take. "But it is kind of true, gentlemen. You've had this market to yourselves for quite a while."

Guido started to rise. Anthony held his arm across his chest. "There is no need to change. Get rid of these animals."

The four men stood up. Chairs clattered to the floor as they paired off. Karl and his men had rehearsed this scenario yesterday, and he knew that each of the gangbangers was in the crosshairs of one of his shooters, and Jacobs covered his back. The primary targets were the Bratva, of course, but all four were sighted. "Have a seat, let me explain," he said. They listened but kept their eyes on the other gang.

"Five minutes." Karl stood up and smiled at them. "If we don't have an agreement then, you can all go back outside and kill each other. And lose all that money."

"Five minutes." Guido pointed at Filya. "Then I kill him."

"But not here," Karl said and sat back down. "Join me, please. Five minutes.

"Thank you, gentlemen." He paused as he had rehearsed. "Anthony, Guido, listen. Filya and, Vadil, am I right?" The man nodded but kept his eyes on the Italians.

"Anyway," Karl continued, "our friends from Youngstown have a new product." He rotated to the Hill gang. "You have an old product. Both are good, both make money. Let's do both.

"My proposal is not to divide Stradford into separate turfs. No, there's plenty for all. Cleveland, you do the coke, and Youngstown, you do the heroine. Like car dealers, huh? Separate stores, but they all make money and nobody dies."

"Is that all you have, Mr. Karl?" Guido said. "We are to share with these? No."

Karl sat up straight and pulled the lobe of his right ear. He had wanted to get along with both groups, but the new gang didn't want to play ball, so they would be taken out. At least he had a good relationship with the Hill gang. He pulled his earlobe again.

Anthony stopped talking to Guido when a red hole appeared above his left ear. The Russians dove to the floor. Karl didn't hear the sound. Guido's face exploded across the table.

No, you idiots, you shot the wrong guys. Karl struck the lantern from the table and scuttled away as Guido's body spasmed on the floor. Anthony sat slumped as if sleeping.

Karl had cleared the clutter away from the table yesterday and had no place to hide. He looked to the door. His guard was sighting up into the catwalk. Karl waved up at his shooters. "Hey, what are you doing?" A shot hit the ground near his feet. He ran to the right. Jacobs turned and fired into the door as something exploded outside

Another shot from above ricocheted off the table and Karl ran back. "You shot the wrong--" He ran toward the door as it burst open. His guard fell under a stream of gunfire. "It's me, wait, don't--"

Karl stopped running. A shot to the shoulder spun him around. Another tore two fingers off his left hand. He didn't fall down. Another shattered his shoulder blade, another gashed his cheek. He raised his whole fist to the shooters in the darkness above him. "I gave you jobs and you turn on me? You get in bed with those immigrants! Fuck you! Your ancestors and your children--" He never finished as shot after shot ripped into his stomach, back, groin and finally, his face. He wobbled a step, screamed "Ursula," and fell to the floor, dead.

The gunfire at the door ceased. Filya and Vadil sprang to their feet and embraced. The shooters clattered down the metal steps and joined them. The rest of the Bratva poured in and the celebration began. On the dirt floor Karl's blood was staining his white hair red.

CHAPTER TWENTY-EIGHT

Lexan arranged her legs beneath herself and rolled the table closer. Joe's water cup and the remote were on the end table where he could reach them. If he would only reach for them. She turned her eyes to the laptop in front of her and pulled a stack of Spanish II quizzes from her school bag. She uncapped her red pen.

"Joe," she whispered. "Wake up."

He didn't answer, like he hadn't when she'd greeted him an hour ago. He hadn't responded to her kiss either. She hoped he knew she was here.

There's nothing I can do for him, she thought. Might as well try to keep up. She sighed and managed to keep herself from crying.

Looking into Joe's room from the ICU hallway, Janice gestured to the other nurse on duty, Margie. "She's a machine that one."

"Like she never sleeps. I offered her a sleeping pill and she turned it down."

"I tried that, too. Told her to get herself home, but she snapped right back at me."

"If it wasn't a gunshot wound, I'd think she was blaming herself." Margie's eyes grew wider. "She didn't, did she?"

"Well, she's not in jail," Janice said. Margie watched her go into the room down the hall with the burn victim, and returned to her seat at the desk.

Lexan entered the last quiz grade and stretched. Joe? She hoped, then looked at his bed. No movement, no voice, only the beeping and whooshing of the machines.

"Joe, I don't know what to do. I know you'd tell me not to worry about retaliation or revenge. You would take care of that for me. For us. But you can't now and I can. I can, and I want to, but I, I'm lost.

She glanced away from him. "I'm lost without you. I know I made fun of you for always protecting me. You were my guardian. My angel.

She looked at him. "You are my angel. I want to protect you. I didn't, and you're here, and I'm sorry. Joe, I should never have left you alone. You wouldn't have left me.

She wiped a tear from her eye. "I'm not very good at this, Joe, but I'll try."

"I talked to Detective Kramer today."

She nodded. "I know, he's not your favorite person."

She shook her head. "No, he was fine, helpful really."

"Uh-huh. But he thinks you didn't shoot Oskar."

"No, really, but he can't prove it."

"Joe, I didn't know who else to ask. I'm desperate. She sighed. "Anyway, Kramer has this theory, only a theory, but he thinks somebody shot Oskar and you. A third guy. Right, not you."

"Uh-huh, and set it up to look like you shot Oskar after Oskar shot you."

Margie had ordered a dinner for Lexan from the cafeteria but stopped in the doorway because it felt like she was interrupting a conversation.

"Ms. Warner, it's late and I know you haven't eaten."

Lexan said goodbye to the man in the coma and kissed him before turning to her. "Thank you, nurse, that's very kind."

Margie took a step inside the room.

"Oh, sorry," Lexan said. "Let me make some space for the tray. Now that you mention it, I'm starving."

Margie set the tray down, then turned to check Joe's tubes and monitors. The numbers were within range. When she turned back the woman was eating the Swiss steak and checking her emails. "Anything else you need?"

"Thank you, no, this is great," Lexan said without looking up,

When Janice stopped at the desk later, Margie said, "Sister, you've got to hear this."

216

* * *

The two men in the dark sedan with Franklin County plates leaned forward as lights flashed through the windows of the old tool and die factory. "Starting to happen," one said. He cinched the Velcro strap on his Kevlar and flipped off the safety on his weapon. The other nodded while peering through the windshield. They were parked on a mound with a good look down at the loading dock door.

Several vehicles appeared from the left, headlights waving wildly as they bounced down the rutted road. Automatic fire flew from the open windows. One car burst into flame. Tracer fire ripped through the dark night air. The Cleveland Hill Gang fell back to the advancing Russian Bratva. Several figures appeared out of the gloom and ran into the light of the doorway.

"Time for us?" one of the men from Columbus said.

"We're backup," the other said. "They'll call us."

The first one slipped the safety back on.

They watched the factory windows flare several more times. The firing in the yard sputtered out. Men, they hoped they were Russians, streamed into the factory. After a minute or so of darkness, one man said, "What do you think?"

"Looks like the good guys won. No one called for help."

"Let's go take a look."

"Then I'll update GOTSOO."

"Why does the Governor like that?"

"It's presidential. POTUS, you know?"

"Whatever. I hate it."

They exited the vehicle and worked their way down the slope to the factory.

Mangione pulled off the balaclava and stepped out of the smoky air inside the factory. He wiped the sweat off his face and coughed. Like Karl, he'd hoped there wouldn't have to be shooting. He didn't like the clean-up. Unlike Karl, he had prepared for shooting by paying the shooters more than Karl had. Also unlike Karl, he was still alive.

Several bodies lay in the grass and one car burned sullenly. Other vehicles had been used as shields, their windows broken out and doors unhinged. Mangione had held his men back and allowed the Russians to kill the Italians outside the factory. Now the Russians were celebrating inside. The Hill gang was finished, and the one man that could connect the dots had bled out inside.

"Gentlemen," he said and extended his hand.

One of the men from Columbus shook it, the other mumbled something and walked past him into the factory. "Gotta take a look around," the hand shaker said.

"Be my guest," Mangione said. "But be back out here in five minutes.'

The man looked at him dumbly.

"Five minutes," he repeated.

Mangione wasn't finished. He had ridden himself of one gang but knew he couldn't control the other one. Sooner or later he would have to weed them out as well. He watched the Governor's guy leave the factory, then motioned to Kennedy and lit a cigarette. He'd decided on sooner.

The patrolman and his team jogged to the door and barricaded it closed. The laughter and shouting diminished along with the light. Other Stradford policeman spaced themselves around the factory. Mangione fired a shot into the air. Kennedy and two other patrolmen activated small devices that resembled garage door openers. Three explosions followed. Orange light flashed. A larger explosion thundered. The roof shuddered and collapsed.

Kennedy jogged back to his commander. "Just like you planned, sir. All that C-4 we put in there last night, Man, you had it--"

"--shut up, Officer Kennedy." Mangione looked past him to the orange billows of flame.

The shock slipped off the young man's face. He stood up straighter and saluted. "Sir. Yessir."

CHAPTER TWENTY-NINE

Lexan was exhausted.

After visiting Joe at the hospital, she had fallen into bed with her clothes on and slept as if drugged. Or dead, she thought as she tried again to work the kink out of her back. The kids in her Spanish II class who were paying attention looked at her funny. "That brings us to question 17 on the quiz."

"How can there be so many questions on a quiz?" Carlos asked.

"When all the level II's have the same quiz, it gets to be long." She held a hand over her mouth and yawned.

"Are you OK, Senorita Warner?"

"I'm fine, Marita," she said. "*Numero 17?* Anybody?"

They finished class, she assigned the homework, and found herself on the sofa in the Faculty Lounge several minutes later.

"You look like crap," Nancy Turner said. "How'd your group do on the quiz?"

"You, too, fine thanks," Lexan said.

Nancy made a sniffy face and left. Bob McCauley held the door for her. He rushed in and sat down on the sofa.

"You all right?"

"I would be if everybody would stop commenting on how bad I look."

"Sorry, you're fine, you look great. When exactly did you sleep last?"

She sighed. "I was hoping to get in a few winks now. This is my prep period."

"Oh, OK, I'll let you go." He tried to stand up; she put her hand on his leg. "Spill it."

Bob looked around the room. "We should go to my office."

"I can't move."

He lowered his voice. "Just got off the phone with Canfield. He's hot."

Lexan opened her eyes. "What's going on?"

"His job as drug liaison with the school is over. He's being transferred."

"How can that be? No more drugs in the 'Ford?"

Bob grimaced. "It can't be that. I don't know, but he is angry about it."

"They can't just stop the program, can they?"

"His funding goes from the state to Stradford. The city filters it down to him." He looked at her. "The school funds us."

"Kimberly is trying to save money? That sucks."

"I don't know." He stood up. "I'm going to tell Bert."

"You could give Kramer a call, he might know something."

He nodded. "Get some sleep."

Lexan slumped back into the sofa. Bob stopped at the door and said, "Wait, I forgot. Canfield said something about a news conference this afternoon. The mayor and the police chief are speaking."

"Maybe that's it." She closed her eyes until the bell ended the period.

The three teachers met in the parking lot behind the police department and threaded their way through the crowd toward the Gazebo. Situated in the open area in front of the municipal complex at the corner of Cleveland and Center, the Gazebo was Stradford's living room. Alfie had championed that homey idea and convinced Council to build it. It was decorated according to the current holiday. Today's theme was springtime; it looked to Lexan as if a gigantic Easter Bunny had puked pastel flowers all over the octagonal structure.

"Don't think I've ever seen this place used for a news conference," Bob said.

"Just festivals," Bert said holding her coat together in the wind. "Fun stuff and celebrations."

"What could we be possibly celebrating?" Lexan muttered. The other two exchanged looks.

"We could check it out, Lex," Bert said. "And you could go home and crash."

"I'm fine, really. I'll get to bed early."

"Take another sick day, kid, that's why we have them."

Lexan stopped. "Bob, I'm fine. Besides, I used most of them up first semester, remember?"

A small stage had been erected in front of the Gazebo, as its floor space was overrun with rabbits and daisies. A city worker thunked on microphones behind the podium and on a stand beside it. The big speakers screeched, then hummed. He made a thumbs-up.

The area closest to the stage was cordoned off. Nearest the yellow rope, reporters and cameramen jockeyed for the best spots. Bob recognized Steffi Sanders from the Stradford *Star* among them.

"Pretty big crowd for a Thursday afternoon."

Bert narrowed her normally squinty eyes further. "Never seen it like this."

"Won't have to wait long." Bob pointed to the police department as the doors opened. Mayor Horvath and Chief Mangione followed two patrolmen through the crowd to the stage.

"Thank you all for coming," the Mayor said. "I have important news to share with you all, and we--" she gestured to the policeman next to her "--decided not to wait to share it. We'll start with our Chief of Police, Garrett Mangione."

"Thank you, Mayor. It is indeed great to be with all of you because we do indeed have good news. Usually I'm only in front of the cameras when I'm talking about a disaster." He looked straight forward and said, "This is definitely not a disaster."

He arranged his folder on the podium and opened it. "Last night, officers of the Stradford Police Department and the regional SWAT team participated in a raid on the Hill drug cartel. In the exchange of gunfire, seven known gang members were killed; no law enforcement officers were killed or wounded. Large quantities of drugs and weapons were captured or destroyed. Following on the heels of the recent activities related to this gang, we can confidently say--"

Kimberly elbowed the man quiet and said into her mic. "What the Chief means is, they killed each other over the past several weeks, and our police department took care of the rest of them last night."

Mangione looked at her. "The bottom line is, the Hill gang, working out of the east side of Cleveland is out of business. They are dead and gone."

"They will no longer bring death and destruction to our city ever again!" Kimberly raised her arms and urged the crowd to respond.

Respond they did. Clapping, cheering, high-fiving, the citizens of Stradford congratulated their Mayor, their police department and themselves. The drug crisis might remain a problem for other communities, but for us, for Stradford, we are free! Kimberly and Mangione descended from the stage and waded into the adoring crowd.

One citizen did not agree or celebrate. Lexan didn't shake her head as Bert did, or curse like Bob. She ran.

Bob reached for her and missed. She pushed people away, slipped between others, and kicked one.

After passing through the cordon of reporters she scrambled up the steps and grabbed the mic.

"No, they're lying to you! The drugs are still in town. There are two gangs--" Before she could say any more, patrolmen grabbed her from both sides. She pushed one off and kicked the other. They pinned her arms to her sides and led her off the gazebo. The pack of reporters and cameramen left Mangione and Kimberly and followed at a trot. Mangione ushered the Mayor through the crowd and into the safety of the building. The focus gone, the onlookers didn't know what to do. Some ran toward the police door, others followed the mayor. Most stood around in confusion and talked loudly.

Bob had lost Lexan in the thick crowd of bodies. Now he worked his way back through them to Roberta. "I knew she was upset. But, man."

"She's asleep on her feet, Bob We shouldn't have let her come." She crossed her arms and glared at him.

"Hey, you ever try to tell her what to do?"

"What should we do? We can't leave her in there."

"I hope they don't arrest her. This isn't the first time she's gone after Kimberly."

"At least she didn't punch her."

"Again." Bob put his arms on her shoulders. "I'll let it simmer down, then call Lt. Kramer. Maybe he can help."

CHAPTER THIRTY

Ursula Hellauer carried the silver tray through the sliding glass doors and down the short step onto the lanai. She carefully avoided stepping on the overflow hose that controlled the water level in the pool, and stopped in front of her husband.

Alfie sat slumped in his chair, his chin on his chest. His white hair standing defiantly in tufts across his weathered, mostly bald head. His breathing was ragged. She set the drinks on the table between their chairs watching his chest rise and fall. He wasn't dead, merely sleeping.

Uschi, his pet name for her, put the empty glasses on the serving tray and scanned the tiled floor. She found yesterday's *USA Today* and a half full water bottle. She stopped with one foot inside the house and turned back.

Still sleeping, still alive. Keeping the place tidy was all she could do.

She had thought the news of Karl's death would kill him. It hadn't quite. She re-cycled the bottle and the paper, and put the glasses in the dishwasher. He had taken it far better than she'd expected because part of him was still mad at his life-long friend. The insulation of resentment and anger had protected him. She shook her head and admitted to herself that their argument about Karl's death had come closer to ending his   life   than the actual news.

He wanted to fly right back to Stradford, guns blazing, and take out everyone who'd killed Karl. Like he'd have done thirty years ago. "Like Karl would've done for me!" he yelled, his face bright red, his mouth gasping for breath.

She had her phone in her hand ready to call 9-1-1 when she said, "You told him not to go."

"I did, didn't I?" he yelled. The air drained from his lungs. His face sagged.

"He walked out on you, Alfie."

Her husband shook his fingers loose as he remembered.

She should have stopped there, but she said, "He was very disrespectful."

"Grabbing his crotch? No, that was just his way."

"He disobeyed your direct order, Alfie."

"I should have gone with him."

"Then you'd both be dead."

His eyes narrowed. "He was a good man."

"Yes. And he was pig-headed, you know he was."

He looked her straight in the eye as his face reddened and the anger returned. "Don't you speak that way about my friend."

"He'd still be alive if he'd listened to you!"

He stepped toward her and raised his fist.

"He was my friend, too!" she screamed. "I loved him!"

"We both loved him." He'd spoken quickly. He dropped his fist when he realized what she had said.

She had covered her face with her hands and sobbed. He had slumped down onto the chair. Now she stood in the kitchen of their condo in Naples, wiping her hands with a towel and counting the many ways her life could have turned out.

"She was drunk." Nancy Turner frowned. "That would explain it."

Roberta shook her head. "She wasn't drunk, Nancy."

"Well, you were with her, you'd know better than I." She burped her Tupperware container. "Either that or on drugs."

"Damn it, Nancy, Lexan wasn't drunk or high or anything else."

Nancy's eyebrows raised. "To make a scene like that? I just don't know."

"She's stressed out about Joe. She's barely slept," Roberta said.

Nancy carefully inserted her tableware, cloth napkin and the food container into her lunch bag. It was dark blue with her name and a heart embroidered on the sides. "I'm sure she is. But she interrupted the Mayor's very positive message; that I can't understand."

Bob looked at Bert. "She thinks the Mayor didn't tell the whole story."

"The Mayor and the Chief of Police?" Nancy gathered her things and stood up. "She knows more than they do? I think not," she said and left the Faculty Lounge.

"I don't know what else I could have said." Bob shrugged.

Roberta patted his arm. "Did you get a hold of Kramer?"

Bob tossed the wadded paper napkin onto his lunch tray. "He's not answering. But I did talk to Canfield for a couple minutes."

Bert too was glad the room was nearly empty. Wosniak was doing the Sudoku on the sofa in the corner. "Good news or bad?"

"Both. It looks to him like the City will let her off with a hand slap."

"It's good the Mayor didn't file anything when she punched her. Bob, I really am worried about her."

"I hope it's only the stress and the lack of sleep."

"But?"

"I'm not sure Nancy was off base." Bob let out a breath. "That would explain it."

"That's not what you told her."

"That's right. I'm not laying her out there in front of Nancy or anybody else. Especially if we don't know."

"I had my arms around her before she took off," Roberta said. "I didn't smell anything."

"I didn't either, and she'd just come from school."

Bert looked at the giant round clock on the wall. "Gotta get moving. Wait, was that your good news? What about the bad?"

"The Board suspended Lexan this morning. Pay is on hold; she can't enter school grounds. Has to turn in her laptop."

"Damn." Bert kept the volume down but not the venom. "How long?"

"Gene told me 'pending investigation'. He checked the contract, and that's the way to handle it."

"She didn't actually do anything wrong."

"You mean she didn't hit anybody. It's bad enough." Bob managed a small smile.

Bert squinted across the table. "I want to know who's going to help the kids if everybody thinks the drug war is over."

CHAPTER THIRTY-ONE

"That skinny little bitch came at me, Pam. I can't let that happen."

Kimberly and Pamela Holmgren were ensconced in her office at Cookies' Cookies, having fled city hall after yesterday's fracas. It wasn't that Kim felt unsafe in that big leather chair, but she felt safer in this one. She glared at her friend over the rim of her wine glass.

"All I'm saying is, it did happen. And what?" Pamela looked theatrically around the room. "Were you wounded? Are you dead?"

"If she'd had a gun, I would be."

Pamela pursed her lips. "She didn't really go after you, Kimmy, she ran to the microphone."

"Little-Miss-Think-She's-Hot had something to say, did she?" Kim glared harder. "What was it she said, hmmm? Did you hear it? Did anyone?"

Across the large table Pamela sighed and took another sip. "No. In all the chaos, no one heard a word she said."

"She didn't say anything, Pam, she screamed and whined. Out of control."

"Exactly. That's my point exactly. She failed in attacking you, so you don't need to attack her."

"She's come at me twice. I took your advice and didn't crush her the first time. She hit me, remember?"

"You did the correct thing then, and you should do the correct thing this time."

Kimberly shook her head. Pamela continued. "Lehrer is in the hospital. She's upset. She didn't attack you physically. Her message was not heard. Therefore, nothing bad happened to you."

"She's a bitchy little know it all."

Pamela nodded. "That's true, but she looks like a victim."

"She attacked me!"

Pamela waited for several seconds, then twisted the top off the next bottle of grocery store Merlot. "Is that the end of the rant? Finally?"

"Remind me why you're my friend?" Kimberly held her glass out and nearly grinned.

"OK, so we're past the drama. For a least a couple minutes, right?"

"I'm cool." Kimberly held her hands level, fingers spread.

"Good, very good. My bottom line is this. You can afford to be the adult here. Warner, your little bitchy friend, lost control. You can look like the bigger person."

Kimberly cocked her head to the side and raised her eyebrows.

"OK, the better person, not bigger." God, she's a piece of work, Pamela thought. "You look like the adult, she looks like the kid. We win."

Kimberly appeared to be in thought. "I hear you. For that little piece I agree."

Pam nodded satisfied.

"The only thing I regret is not being there to see the look on Karl's face when he realized what we'd done." Kimberly gave a sideways glance at the dark red wine. "Pompous ass. So worried about the gangbangers, he never gave us a thought."

"Who us? We're just women." Pamela returned her toast and drank some wine. She wondered again if Kimberly really didn't understand what had happened at the factory. If she actually thought that only Karl and the Hill gang had been wiped out. Did she even know about the Russians? Could she be that dense?

Kimberly tipped her glass. "But I am also remembering the advice Alfie gave me."

Pamela looked up, confused.

"When you get someone down, finish them off," Kimberly said.

Pamela's glass wobbled as she set it down. The things she had to do to keep her somewhat under control. "Mayor Horvath, things are going according to our plan. Karl is out of the way. We've made it appear the drug war is over. Oskar is gone. We're not suspected of anything. There are no more enemies left to finish off."

"There's one more." Kimberly's mouth became a thin slash across her face. "I don't care if he's in a coma. I don't care if he's dying. He pushed my face into the mud, and he will pay for that."

"No, Kimberly, it's time to relax and consolidate our victories."

"Relax? Consolidate? No." Her calm was more unnerving to her friend than her rantings. "OK, hands off bitchie-poo. Great for public relations. I get it."

"Lehrer hasn't moved in a week; he can't hurt you."

"Think big! That's the other thing my brother told me. Kill all of them and think big."

Holmgren spun the skinny glass in her fingers. Think big, like how we get Stradford back to the quiet little suburb it was. Like where we're getting our drug revenue with both gangs gone. Like not worrying about petty feuds. She looked the mayor in the eye. "What are you going to do?"

"I really can't kill them all." She shook her head. "But I can make them all pay."

Pamela pursed her lips and made her decision.

Margie gestured to Janice to look through the window of Joe's room. "She's doing it again." The other nurse grimaced.

Margie checked the clock in the hall of the ICU. "For twenty minutes."

They watched as Lexan spoke to Joe and reacted as if he were awake and having a conversation with her. He was doing neither; the only sounds from his side of the room were the machines beeping and the ventilator whooshing. The two nurses sidled closer to the doorway so they could hear:

"Looks like I got myself in trouble again."

"Uh-huh, suspended. Guess I won't have to pay my share of the mortgage this month."

"No, I know I don't, but I want to. That's the part that makes me mad."

She snorted a laugh. "Now that's a tradition we should retire, Joe."

"You think we could actually go a month? One of us would do something stupid."

"OK, maybe a week. Two tops." She laughed again and dabbed her eyes with a tissue.

"Probably me. I know, I know."

Outside the room, Margie said, "We have to get her help."

Janice shook her head. "Were you on shift when I suggested that? She almost ripped my face off. No, thank you. Just let her be."

"But she's speaking aloud, gesturing, and changing her expressions."

"I know, Margie. In cases like this I need to remind myself that Mr. Lehrer is not the only one injured. It's her way of coping."

"I know, but--"

"Excuse me, Nurse. I'm looking for Herr Lehrer, sorry Mr. Lehrer's room."

They turned at looked at the gangly blonde girl, wearing a winter coat, scarf, heavy black boots and a mini skirt.

"Are you a relative, Miss?" Margie said.

Chelsea shook her head, no. "I'm one of his students. In German class."

Janice said to her colleague, "Let her go in. This might be what she needs."

"The girl?"

"I meant Ms. Warner, but sure, both of them."

Margie patted Chelsea's arm. "Be sure to sign the register when you leave."

"Thank you," Chelsea said. She took one step into the room and stopped. She listened as Ms. Warner continued speaking to the Herr and acting like he was answering. Without thinking, she stepped farther into the room until she was between the two.

Ms. Warner said, "Excuse me, we're talking."

Chelsea swiped away a tear. "No, Ma'am, you're not."

"That is so rude, young lady."

"He, Herr Lehrer, can't speak, Ma'am. He's too sick to speak to you."

Lexan was rattled. "That's not true, that's--" Her eyes focused. "You're Sea, Chelsea Larkin."

"Yes, I am," Chelsea said and extended her arms toward the woman.

Lexan stood up. The girl wrapped her arms around her. They stood that way for nearly a minute. Lexan's shoulders began to heave. Chelsea patted her back. "It's OK, he's going to be fine. It's OK."

Lexan was still sobbing on Chelsea's shoulder when the nurses passed by. "Maybe you were right," Margie said. Janice nodded.

CHAPTER THIRTY-TWO

"**A** faculty meeting on a Friday?" Bob shook his head. Seated next to him on the oddly-tilted chairs in the choir room, Roberta let out an exasperated sigh. "I assumed it was a joke," he continued.

"If he had a sense of humor," she replied, referring to Principal Gale Stevens.

"There's that," Bob said, then raised a hand to beckon Gene Phillips. The Association President sat down next to Roberta.

"I put up with a lot," Gene said, "but having to sit on these chairs is beyond the Pale."

Between the men, Roberta shook her head. Bob chuckled at the history teacher's phrase. "Couldn't they just use a tanning bed?"

Roberta elbowed him. "That's not what it means."

Nancy Turner poked him from the row behind. "Sshh. I want to get out of here as soon as I can."

"Why's everybody hitting me?" Bob said. "I didn't call the meeting."

Roberta turned to Gene. "Why did they call it? Is it about the state tests?"

Nancy's head appeared between their shoulders. "That's what I heard. The state test results." Having answered the question to her satisfaction, she rocked back into her seat and nodded.

Gene twisted his head toward Roberta, then Nancy, then back to the French teacher. He rubbed his neck. "I don't think it's the tests. The results aren't due yet, but, truthfully, I have no idea."

Bob leaned across Roberta. "Ever had a Friday meeting before?"

Gene's round face twisted like a cinnamon roll as he thought. "No, I've only been here twenty-eight years, but I don't think so."

Terri Dieken's head leaned forward. "Could be about discipline. Faculty discipline."

Bob's head snapped around. "Shut up, Terri, it's not about Lexan."

The English teacher held her hands like ping pong paddles. "Just saying, Bob, relax." She raised her eyebrows. "Why else would Radburn be here?"

Bob started to speak, but stopped as he felt Roberta grab his arm.

Principal Stevens and the Business Manager approached the podium, and the room fell silent. It wasn't quite full; several coaches were at practice or preparing for games.

"I don't want to keep you any longer than I have to," Stevens said in his reedy indoor voice. "I know it's Friday."

Bob whispered to Roberta, "Quit poking me, would you?" She pointed to the doorway.

"If we can settle down?" Stevens said.

Mayor Horvath walked through the door into the choir room.

"And maybe get started?" the Principal continued.

"Didn't even bring a board member with her," Bob muttered. "This is gonna be bad."

"We, uh, don't really have an agenda today," Stevens said. The room quieted again. "Thank you. But we do have a special guest, the Mayor of Stradford."

Three or four people clapped. The rest waited. She walked briskly to the podium, her spiked heels clacking against the terrazzo.

"Thank you, Mr. Stevens." She waved an arm at him and nodded to the hulking business manager. "And Mr. Radburn."

"I have just received news from Columbus that I feel I need to share with you." She looked at Gene Phillips. "Although I am no longer a member of the Board of Education, I do have a strong connection to Governor Stanic."

Roberta turned to Bob. "Low hanging fruit," he said and kept his eyes on Radburn.

"I admit further, that while I was not at the bargaining table for the last negotiations between the Board and your Association, I am cognizant of many of the details." Kimberly looked from Gene to Bob.

"It saddens me, truly, to have to be the bearer of bad tidings." She looked to the administrators behind her. "Although it will spare these gentlemen from this odious burden."

Bob looked to Gene. The older teacher's face was ashen.

"My hope is that the community will work with the administration to make the upcoming changes as palatable as is possible."

She paused to let the bubble of nervous energy grow. "I will come to the point." She waited another beat. "The Governor has told me that the state tax revenue did not reach expectations. As a result, the amount of money the state can allocate to school districts is less than anticipated."

Nearly every teacher reacted at the same time. Some shouted, some raised questions, some turned to their neighbors, some sat silent as stones. Bob tried to catch his eye, but Radburn leaned his massive head toward Stevens. The Principal raised his arms above his head. "People, please."

Kimberly opened a folder, but kept her eyes on the teachers until they fell silent. "The bottom line is, the Stradford City School District does not have enough money to fund the latest contract with the teachers."

She looked again at Gene. "I know you have questions, Mr. Phillips. We can leave the details to the lawyers, but--" Her voice faded and she looked away as if she were actually troubled. "--but the old saying is true. You really can't get blood from a turnip." The Mayor gestured vaguely to the men beside her, said, "Gentlemen," and marched from the room.

Lexan took a deep breath, more of sigh than a breath, looked at Chelsea Larkin's red-rimmed eyes, disheveled hair and the snot oozing from her nose. She grinned weakly. "I sure hope I don't look as bad as you do."

Chelsea was sitting on the chair in Joe's ICU room and the teacher was perched on the edge of his bed. They had spent most of her visit crying. The girl laughed as she dabbed her nose with a Kleenex and ran the back of her hand across her eyes. "It's not how we look, Ms. Warner, it's how we feel."

Lexan was amazed once more at the girl's empathy. She knew from the events the past year that she was strong, nearly fearless, and had a firm moral compass. Lexan swallowed the lump forming in her throat. The aura of comfort and understanding the young woman radiated was extraordinary.

So extraordinary that Lexan finally felt safe enough to cry. Finally let the hurt escape after holding it inside for a week. She'd appreciated the kind hugs of her friends and Joe's as they paraded through the hospital room. But this was the first time she had fully cried, and it was because of the way she felt in Chelsea's presence.

She looked to Joe's face behind the whooshing ventilator mask. She wondered if she would ever get the chance to cry with him again.

When she returned her eyes to Chelsea's, the girl took her in as if reading her emotions. "How are you feeling, Ms. Warner?"

"I feel pretty good," Lexan said. "As long as you keep me away from a mirror." She realized as the words came out that she had tried to make a joke. That was also a first. "I think so anyway."

"Sometimes all it takes is a good cry," Chelsea said, rummaging through her backpack for her compact.

"Thank you." Lexan handed her a small comb.

"You don't have to thank me." Chelsea paused the comb in her nearly chin-length hair. The bottom inch was its original black, the rest blond. "You helped me when nobody else would. I still owe you for that."

"You don't owe me anything, Chelsea."

The young woman tossed the compact into her pack and stood up. "I do, I still do."

Lexan stood and hugged her. "Thank you, thank you, thank you!" They both laughed. "You can't stop me, but you can do one thing for me."

Chelsea cocked her head.

"Please call me Lexan. Maybe not in school, but 'Ms. Warner' is a little stiff after sharing all those gallons of tears."

"Lexy?" Chelsea's eyes twinkled.

"Not even once." Lexan hugged her again and the girl left the room. She sat back down on Joe's bed and laid her hand on his leg. "I love you, Joe," she whispered.

Bob and Roberta entered the ICU minutes after Chelsea left, but didn't see the girl. They paused at the door of Joe's room. Lexan lay with her back against the footboard and her feet alongside Joe. Her eyes were closed.

"Should we bother her?"

"At least she's not talking to him." Bob shook his head.

Lexan jumped off the bed as they approached. Roberta engulfed her in a hug. Bob looked at his friend's face, then at the flashing and beeping monitors. His lips gathered in frustration.

Lexan freed herself from Bert's hug. "Thanks for coming, you guys. What's new at school?"

Bert pulled the chair closer and sat down. "You missed a faculty meeting."

Bob paced. "On a Friday."

"Makes me glad I wasn't allowed in the building."

"Wait till you hear." Bob explained what had happened, ending with the possibility of layoffs.

"Good thing I'm suspended then, isn't it?"

Bert heard the venom in her voice. "Bob didn't mean that."

"No, Lexan, there's nothing specific. But I am worried about you. You went after her. Twice. You're lucky you're not in jail."

"Bob, leave her alone!" Roberta wrapped her arm around Lexan's shoulder.

"No, I can't." Bob looked from Roberta to Lexan. "You have to get a grip. Joe needs you. We need you. You can't flip out now."

Lexan levelled her glance at him. "What's this really about?"

"What? I don't know, it's just, shit." Bob looked away.

Lexan stepped out of Bert's hug. "Spit it out."

"I've heard that you're drinking." He turned to her. "It's a small town. Drinking alone at *Competitors.* Some other place in Beebetown."

"I'm a grown-up."

"Yeah, a suspended grown-up who punched the mayor. For God's sake, Lexy."

She let out a deep breath. "That's it then? I'm a terrible person with no self-control and a drinking problem? I shouldn't be allowed to interact with children and should really be in jail? That about cover it? Huh?"

"Shit, Lexy, I don't mean--"

"It's all true." She looked from him to Bert. "But let me give you some news."

"Damn it, Bob," Bert said.

"No. I'm fine. Really. I know I don't look it." Lexan tried a stiff smile. "Maybe I shouldn't have been the one to punch Kimmy, but someone sure as hell should. I'll bet she enjoyed delivering the bad news from her love-buddy, Stanic, didn't she? Uh-huh." She nodded. "They have to cut staff, right? Guess who is on the short list." She hooked a thumb and jammed it into her chest. "This guy, right here."

"I didn't mean--"

"True or false? She's a bitch, she loves using power, and I'll lose my job. All true." She turned to Joe. "At least he's not doing any worse. Did I tell you they're sending him to rehab?"

The other two shook their heads.

"Tomorrow or the next day. The Pflegeheim. Where his dad was in hospice."

Bert's hand flew to her mouth. Bob looked at the

ground.

"Until he died. Yeah, they're taking Joe to where his dad died."

Bert reached out to hug her again. Lexan flinched. "No, that's how it is. It's OK. I'm fine, and Joe will be, too.

Her face brightened wildly. "And it's all true, all those things Bob said. Don't be mad at him, Bert. He's telling the truth."

Bob thought of Radburn's warning to keep his mouth shut.

"I know you guys love me." Lex darted from one to the other. "I know you do, but this is my problem."

Screw it, Bob thought, she needed to know.

Lex's voice raced. "I know you've known Joe a lot longer than I have, but he's my guy, and I'm going to deal with it."

"Not alone--" Bob managed.

"-- appreciate that, I really do." Her eyes flew around the room as she tried to focus. "I am strong enough to handle this. Joe, the job, the whole thing. You guys don't really know me. Joe barely does, so don't give me advice."

"But you're hurting yourself," Roberta said.

"Right, myself. I am hurting myself. Or not."

Bob touched Roberta's arm. "Come on. She's tough, she knows what she's doing." Bert started to speak, but Bob led her out of the room.

CHAPTER THIRTY-THREE

Detective Kramer watched as Agent Canfield maneuvered the non-descript g-ride nose first into the parking place next to his own non-descript government-provided vehicle. Kramer nodded approvingly; the young man had backed into his place so they could speak through their respective windows.

He keyed his window down. "Good to see you, Agent." He kept his eyes on the door of the bar as he spoke. "Don't get much of a chance to see you anymore."

"You don't see me now," Canfield said. His eyes continued to scan the traffic on Liverpool Hill Parkway, the southern extension of Cleveland Ave.

"New case?"

Canfield shook his head. "Still transitioning. They haven't given me anything to do."

"You're not supposed to be in Beebetown, are you." Kramer intoned it like a statement, his eyes on the bar. "Welcome."

"Thought this was Liverpool Township."

"No one knows where the borders are. Beebetown is like an archipelago in a sea of Liverpool Township."

"That is acutely boring," Canfield said.

Kramer didn't look at the BCI agent, but grinned. "Probably want to know why I reached out."

"Thought it was about time you bought me a drink."

"When I buy you a drink, it won't be in a hole like this." Kramer nodded at *The Dew Drop Inn*, lodged in a strip mall at the top of Liverpool Hill, a quarter mile south of the county line separating Stradford from Beebetown. He adjusted the mirror to keep watch on the street behind them. "Need to touch base with you."

"Why here?"

"That's where Warner drinks." He jabbed his finger. "In there now. Just came from the hospital."

"Shame about Mr. Lehrer. He OK?"

"No," Kramer said. "She's not taking it well."

Canfield gave him a minute then said, "Where does that put us?"

"Up shit creek." Kramer turned toward him. "Everybody we need to talk to is dead. The Hill gang and the Russians."

"I'm not shedding a tear about that." The younger man turned to Kramer. "Did you know that was going to happen?"

"What, that the thing was a double trap?" Kramer's

head snapped to the younger man's. "Hell no, I was way out of the loop."

Canfield nodded. "You got good contacts here."

"I do," the policeman said sharply. "Mangione plays it close. The SWAT guys showed up at the last minute."

"Told you they were for back up, right?"

"He did, so when shit started blowing up--" Kramer's voice trailed off.

Canfield noticed a dark SUV slowing in the street. "Should be good news. Like the Mayor announced."

"Would be, but someone else will show up. The community wants to buy, somebody will sell it to them."

"Good news, bad news."

"We lose the familiarity, the contacts, the business models. Back to square one." Kramer faced the BCI man. "What you got?"

Canfield returned the look. "The new players are not as violent as the old gangs. Don't follow the same pattern. Not as much top-down. Sellers more independent."

Kramer nodded. "Unpredictable."

"That, and the drugs they're pushing are way more potent. Just breathing the dust from this synthetic fentanyl they're mixing with the heroin will kill you."

"You got any time for this?" Kramer checked the door of the bar.

"They'll assign me something soon. Couple days max."

"You could rest, take a break, see your wife."

"Girlfriend. Thanks, good idea, but hey, I'm from

Stradford, you know?"

"I do," Kramer said. "Something else bothers me. Coupla things really."

"Uh-huh."

"The next day I found out that the Governor had some people there."

Canfield's eyes narrowed. "State police?"

Kramer shook his head. "His Ready Team. Apparently they were there to observe, but I don't like it. Smells funny."

"Stanic should know what's going on, right?"

"Observing and being involved are two different things."

"Another loose end."

"At least that." Kramer's eyes flicked from the bar to Lexan's car. "Probably starting Mojito number two by now. Then there's the other thing."

Canfield checked the traffic. "Go on."

"Why is Karl dead?"

"Caught in the firefight."

"He was practically the head of the Hill gang. Cleveland loved him."

"That's why he's dead. Along with the rest of his gang."

"You don't get it. Look, Karl was Alfie's man in Stradford. The prostitution, the drugs, the gangs, all of it. His sister is now the mayor. She called him back to town. And he's dead? Her brother's main guy? He was family."

"I see." Canfield worked the cuticles around his thumbs. "Could have been an accident."

"Theoretically. Took eight or nine rounds. Never

drew his weapon."

"Then they blew the place up. Somebody wanted him dead."

"You're brilliant, Canfield, a freaking genius."

"You're not all that fun to work with, Detective. What I'm asking is, who benefitted from him out of the way?"

"That's what I don't get. First, he's family, second, I think he's the one who killed Oscar and shot Joe Lehrer."

"You got any proof?"

"Trajectories are close. Not enough to convince Mangione."

Canfield glanced at the traffic in front of him. "If Karl got those two out of the way as a favor for the mayor, or did it on her orders, why would she want to kill him?"

"That's the question." Kramer peered through the windshield at the wooden Indian standing beside the door of the bar. "I don't suppose you have the answer, do you?"

The *Dew Drop Inn* was decorated to fit its tacky name. A modern bar with an old-looking plastic surface ran the length of the shoebox-shaped storefront. Behind it a garish painting of an overly endowed nude was surrounded by old-looking mirrors and more pressed fiber 'wooden' trim. Several raised booths lined the other side, and four or five tables were scattered in the rear. Old-fashioned neon beer signs hung cheek by jowl along the walls under the pock-marked ceiling tiles.

Lexan Warner found it perfect for her late

afternoon drinking. She pulled her second Mojito closer and adjusted it on the tiny napkin. She deserved to drink watery drinks in a crappy bar because, as she reminded herself, her life sucked.

Her life sucked mostly because of Joe. It was one thing to fall for a guy, to let him under your radar, to open yourself to him. But he got himself shot. To just lie there in a coma? To get deposited into the old folks' home?

To leave her alone?

She stabbed at a piece of mint floating in her glass, missed again, and finally grabbed it between her thumb and finger. She sucked the sweetness off the leaf and followed with a sip. She scraped the leaf off her tongue and wiped it onto the napkin.

Being alone wasn't exactly the problem. She liked the freedom. No, she shook her head as her internal dialogue continued. She had opened herself up, and he'd left her. That was way worse.

She gazed around the skinny room from her seat in the last booth. Not crowded, she was starting to recognize the regulars. The two red-faced old guys at the end of the bar were making love to their Lite beers. She had checked the digital juke box and knew there were no Billy Joel songs. A couple of after work ladies had their heads together at one of the tables in the back, probably discussing their husbands. She took another drink. Like I am. Sort of.

The guy that didn't fit was younger than the others, probably younger than she. Light weight, smartly cut leather jacket, black jeans, white shirt, not a dress shirt, open a couple of buttons. She had seen him before. She noticed the gold chain at his throat as he swaggered past her to the men's room.

Joe was only the first on her list. She finished her drink and held up her hand. Bernie caught her eye and nodded. Three was her limit. She could handle three.

Bob and Roberta were also on her list. They meant well but were always getting up in her shit. Telling her what to do, how to act, how to feel. She hated that. They didn't know her. They didn't know what she'd been through. They thought they had all the answers. They didn't.

She thanked Bernie and pulled the new drink closer. They had no idea how strong she was. She could handle this. She'd handled much worse, she told herself again. She took a drink. No, she didn't hate the two teachers, she just didn't need them. The ladies in back were arguing with Bernie about their bill. Probably wanted separate checks.

She couldn't hate Bob and Bert, they were truly nice people. Maybe that was their problem; they were too nice. She took a sip. Kind of like Joe. Too nice to shoot Weigel and too nice to take on Kimberly.

I'm not too nice. I can kill the bitch myself. She chugged the rest of the third mojito and was reaching for her purse, when the young man in the leather jacket sat down across from her.

"Been talking to yourself," he grinned. His warm brown eyes were partially hidden by strands of longish black hair. He brushed them aside. "I do that myself."

"Who gave you the right to sit down?"

He stood up quickly. "Sorry, I forgot to introduce

myself. I am Hector. May I please sit down, Madam?"

She heard his over-the-top politeness in a Ricardo Montalban accent and returned the grin. She extended a hand, and he sat down.

"I've seen you here before and don't want to know your name." His head swiveled. "It will be better for both of us."

"Your name's not really Hector." She fished her sunglasses from her purse. "Better?"

"I'm not a secret agent." He smiled and pointed to her empty glass. "I thought you might like something a little mellower. Drier."

"I'm listening."

"And more portable." He gestured to the bar. "You wouldn't have to drink in this place. Or alone for that matter."

So it goes, she thought. I'm sitting here thinking about how screwed up my life is, how empty and hurt I am, and how much I want to kill somebody. She pulled some bills from her purse.

"No money, Miss." Hector pushed the bills back to her. "Introductory special." He checked that no one was looking, and slid a white envelope across the table beneath his hand.

Lexan slipped the pills into her purse. "Next time?"

"When the Indian man is holding something in his hands, I'll be around. When he has nothing, so do I." He got up and spun toward the door.

Lexan felt a shaft of the setting sun and a gust of wind as Hector left the bar. The light glared on the white envelope, and she quickly snapped her purse shut. Adjusting her sunglasses, she paid her bill and stepped outside.

CHAPTER THIRTY-FOUR

"Ghe went ahead with the news release against your wishes?" Lance tsked three times as he set the silver coffee service on the Governor's desk. He frowned at a spot on the shiny mahogany surface and wiped it away.

"She's headstrong," Stanic said.

Lance put a teaspoon of sugar into the coffee and added the right amount of almond milk. "It's part of her charm."

The Governor's brows bunched together. "Normally it would be kind of cute. Another example of her quest to shatter the glass ceiling."

Lance shivered. "The lady has no concept of timing."

Stanic nodded. "We could call it that, that's what we've done before. But she orchestrated a bloodbath up there, for Pete's sake."

"After you told her to keep things quiet." Lance shook his head sadly.

"Yeah, remember? I told her not to off the teacher, so she offs the teacher and seven or eight other guys."

"She said Karl killed Lehrer as a favor to her."

"A favor. Right. I thought she was supposed to be in charge. That's all she talks about. 'Don't tell me what to do'." Stanic slumped back into his enormous black chair. "If she wasn't such a great piece of ass."

Lance didn't want the conversation to take this turn again. "Even if she's right about Karl, how does she think a gang shoot-out is keeping things on the down low?"

Stanic waved his hand in defeat. "I know, I know."

Lance pressed on. "I hate to think what the fallout would have been if the Ready Team hadn't been there to handle it."

Stanic nodded. "And put the right spin on it. Made her the tough-on-crime-crusader."

The aide didn't like this tack either. "That's just lipstick on a pig, sir."

His boss looked up sharply.

Lance cleared his throat. He had to be careful here. "What I mean, Governor, is although we'd planned it all out for her, she made three mistakes." As Stanic's face darkened, he spoke quickly. "First, she didn't do what you told her. Second, she put herself in danger. Third, most importantly, she exposed you to risk."

He's a faggot, Stanic thought, but he has great instincts. He let his face relax. "Thank you, Lance, you've given me food for thought." He waved at the coffee tray, and the aide picked it up. The Governor watched him leave, then punched a number into his cell.

"Know this guy?" Kramer nodded toward the door of the *Dew Drop Inn.*

Agent Canfield squinted. "Hector. That's his street name."

"Messican?" The BCI man kept looking through the windshield, but the policeman noticed a grin at the edge of his mouth.

"Mexican wannabe. If you can imagine that," Canfield said. "Name's Ernie, Greenfield, Gruenfeld, something like that. From somewhere down state. Portsmouth, maybe."

Kramer turned his head. "New gang moving in?"

"Reasonable assumption."

Kramer pointed to Lexan exiting the bar. "Speaking of which."

"Could be a coincidence," the agent said. "We know she drinks here."

"I don't believe in coincidences," Det. Kramer said.

"No, just clichés," Canfield said.

Kimberly H. Horvath, Mayor of Stradford, looked at the little man trying to make himself appear taller on the other side of her desk. She gagged at the cheap cologne and glanced at the time on her phone. She'd had to endure a laundry list of statistics from the Police Chief's monthly report: traffic tickets issued, B & E's, domestic disputes, hopefully culminating in the J-walking report.

She'd had enough. "Anything I need to know about?"

"I saved the best for last." Chief Mangione's expressions ran the gamut from A to B. This time he used his impish little boy look.

"There's more?" She waved a hand to get him started and to disperse the cloud of scent.

He snapped his leather case shut and grinned again, more impishly than before. "You are going to love it."

I am going to suffocate if he doesn't get out of here soon. "Garrett, I have a full schedule."

Mangione gazed around the Mayor's office. "I have a way you can get rid of Ms. Warner."

Kimberly's eyes lurched from her cell to his face. "You, what?"

"Just doing my job, Ma'am." He sat up a little more and adjusted his gray silk tie. She had to admit the man could tie a neat Double Windsor. "Your little friend has a drinking problem--"

"No shit, Sherlock. She's losing her job, her boyfriend is in a coma, and she's drinking. I hate the little bitch, but come on, I need more than that."

"If you'd let me finish." Mangione now wore his second expression, the heavy-lidded, intimidating Don Corleone. He waited a second, then said slowly. "She is also using drugs." He stared at her some more, enjoying the control. "I think that is more than enough. Don't you?"

She returned his stare and forgot the scent. *This could be her chance.* "Where?"

"The *Dew Drop* in Beebetown. Top of the hill--"

"I know where it is." She thought a moment. "Why did you think to look for her there?"

"I'm a cop."

Don Corleone on max, the little imp discarded. "Paperwork?"

"Of course not. Too early to leave a trail." He lifted his eyes as if thinking. "I needed to know if you would be on board."

She considered whether the man knew how simple and un-subtle he was. Just another run-of-the-mill, control-freak male. "Thank you for your consideration."

Mangione nodded graciously. He was overplaying his hand, but he had given her a worthwhile piece of information. "I may be interested," she said. "Bring me some evidence and we'll see."

They looked at each other until they were interrupted by a soft knock at the door. Mangione stood up. "That will be Pam," Kimberly said. "Let's wrap this up."

Pamela Holmgren held the door knob. "Oh, I'm sorry, I didn't know your meeting was still going on."

"Come in, please, we're just finishing." If you knock, she thought, why can't you wait for an answer? She shook Garrett's hand and thanked him for the meeting.

The Chief nodded curtly to Pamela and left. The women dropped down into chairs on opposite sides of the desk. "My, but that man does smell sweet."

Kimberly pulled a can of aerosol spray from her desk. "He does, but he has his uses." She spritzed several times and returned the can to the drawer.

Pamela leaned forward. "Does he?"

Kimberly dropped her voice and summarized Mangione's report, finishing with, "My dear, I think we got her."

Across the desk Pamela nodded but didn't smile. Now what's wrong, Kimberly thought.

Pamela sighed and clasped her hands in her lap. "Overkill, Kimmy."

"Yes, exactly. Finally we can be rid of little Barbie."

"We already are rid of her. She is about to lose her job."

Kimberly waved away the last remnants of Mangione. "She can get another job. I'm talking jail time."

Pamela shook her head. "Too risky. Too emotional, and really, unnecessary."

"Damn it, Pammy, why have power if you don't use it? She hurt me, I'll hurt her back!"

The older woman stared back before turning away. "It's too much. You're kicking a dog when she's down."

Kim brushed the statuette as she jabbed her finger into the desktop calendar. "That's what I'm talking about. Kick the bitch!"

Startled by the Mayor's vehemence, Pam managed to catch the crystal neutered Stradford Stallion before it hit the floor. "I agree with your sentiment, but violence will bring more exposure."

Kimberly slowed her breathing. "This is good exposure. I'm acting on evidence brought to me by our police department. It is my job to act on it."

"We have plenty more pressing concerns," Pamela said. "We put the teachers back in their place. The Hill gang is gone. Let's move on." She looked up. "That's all

I'm saying."

"Thank you for your input." She glared at the overly made-up cosmetics czarina. Knows everything. Rains on my parade. "That's all for now," she said and waved toward the door.

"But, really, I--"

"Thank you, Pamela." Kimberly keyed her cell. It was time to share the good news.

CHAPTER THIRTY-FIVE

I don't need a man to help me, Pamela Holmgren told herself the next day. She glanced across the table at Chief Mangione. Especially this one. Thinks he's a rock star. She watched him adjust the tails of his jacket as he sat, then worry the enormous knot on his silk tie. She giggled.

He ran a hand down and up the length of the blue paisley fabric. "Something amusing?"

"I'm just taking in the ambiance of this place," she said. Quit playing with yourself, she thought.

"In the old days, before my time, they tell me anyway." He paused to make sure she noticed how young he looked. "O'Rourke's would have been called a cop bar. You know, off-duty uniforms and officers letting off steam after a shift."

She wondered again if putting up with his shit was worth it. She smiled encouragingly. "But it's not in Stradford."

Mangione had expected the question. "Best not to drink where you work." His wave took in the wood-paneled room. "Usually owned by retired cops. There'd be police memorabilia on the walls, probably patches from different departments."

"Are you telling me this is a cop bar or it isn't? All this technical stuff gets me so confused." She put on her I'm-a-helpless-female face.

"No, you got me." He held up his hands in surrender. "I confess. I was just waxing nostalgic."

"Civilians are allowed, I presume?"

"Encouraged," he smiled. "Although I really do think some retired cops own the place."

A waitress arrived and took their order. Mangione said, "Nostalgia aside, Mrs. Holmgren, why did you want to see me?"

She nodded, satisfied that the competent version of the man had returned. "I'm worried about our Mayor."

"You cut right to the chase." He nodded as well. "It's good we're not meeting in the 'Ford."

She looked at him over the rim of her glass.

He increased the sincerity in his eyes and the concern in the lines around his mouth.

"It's a fragile time."

"I agree." He moved his head fractionally toward her.

"She's bringing too much attention to herself."

"She's in a public position. It's part of the deal."

She shook her head but kept her eyes on his. They were a deep brown, flecked with gold. "Too much. I don't mind that she preens, it is, as you put it, a public position."

Mangione arranged his face to convey the impression he was deep in thought. "Overkill."

"She wants revenge."

"She's taking it personally." He shook his head slowly. "Can't do that in this line of work."

"She should relax and let Stradford go back to sleep." Pamela rolled the olive from her martini into her mouth. "It's bad for business."

"You're afraid she'll expose us."

She smiled inside at his use of the first-person pronoun. "I'm not afraid," she said. "I just want to be prepared."

He folded his hands and placed them on the table. "You came to me."

She looked at his thin manicured fingers, the hint of polish on the nails. "I came in our mutual best interest." She smiled at him.

"You did the right thing."

Detective Kramer wiped a speck of yig off the windshield of his g-ride and peered at the *Dew Drop Inn* through the smear. It was hard enough to see with the sun setting behind the strip mall. Tailing a person of interest to a bar on a Sunday afternoon was something he would normally assign to an underling, but there was nobody in the department he could trust. Kennedy maybe, but he was safer doing it himself. It would have been easier if Canfield hadn't been re-assigned.

A large black SUV pulled slowly across his sightline and blocked out the sun and the bar. "What the--" he began, but stopped as a man got out and slid into the seat beside him.

"You should know better than leave the doors unlocked during a surveillance, detective." The man kept his eyes forward.

Kramer snapped his holster closed and let his hand relax. "Stanic's Stalwarts still in town."

"The official term is Ready Team."

"Whatever." Kramer tried to look into the man's face, but could only see his profile.

"We can't leave until Stradford settles down." The man slid his sunglasses from his face to the top of his nearly bald head. "What's the matter with you clowns up here?"

Kramer let out a breath. "It's a suburb. Everybody's a star."

"Car's too small." The man rearranged his bulk in the seat, keeping his eyes on the bar. "No one takes orders, huh?"

"Just want to give them."

"Too many moving parts," the man said.

"Need a program to tell who is working with who," Kramer said.

"Whom," the man said. "Working with whom."

"Cut the crap, and get to it, would you? Why are you here?"

The man turned to Kramer. "We'll handle the surveillance. You may leave now."

The detective looked from the large man next to

him to the vehicle blocking his path. He needed to keep track of Warner, but saw no way to do so. "Get out of my car," he said.

"I like that. Dirty Harry defending his lawn," the man said. "We'll be in touch. Clint."

Inside the bar Lexan also adjusted the sunglasses on her head. She waved her hand to Bernie behind the bar, and he pulled a fresh glass from the rack. Does quite a business on a Sunday afternoon, she thought, as she scanned the tastelessly decorated room. The regulars at the corner of the bar, housewives at the tables in back, and nearly all the booths full. She couldn't see into them, as the seat backs were too high, but had noticed them when she passed by.

She traded glasses with Bernie and glanced down at the purse on her lap to be sure it was closed. Hector had sold her a larger number of pills than the first time. He'd been here when she arrived and left out the back. There had been no talking this time, other than the purchase price and her not leaving the bar for twenty minutes. She lifted the mojito to her lips as a shadow fell across the end of the booth.

"Mind if I sit down?" Kimberly Horvath said and did so. "Oh. Let me get that." She grabbed a napkin and wiped the drink that had sloshed from Lexan's startled fingers. "We don't want to get anything on that cute handbag."

Lexan clutched the bag and pushed herself away from the mayor.

"Or anything inside the bag either." Kimberly

wiped the screen of the younger woman's cell and slid it to her "Certainly not that."

"What do you want?"

"A drink." Bernie had appeared and snatched the wet napkin away. The Mayor ordered a Manhattan and looked expectantly at Lex. The younger woman shook her head.

They sat silently until the drink arrived. Kimberly took a sip and slid her cell closer to Lexan's. "Take a look."

"What? Why?" Lexan struggled to keep her voice under control. Her hands flitted as if looking for a safe place to land.

Kimberly let out an exasperated breath and keyed the photo app. "Take a look."

Lexan's mind raced. Her hands darted to the bag, the cell, the sunglasses.

"Go on, Ms. Warner." Kimberly smiled at the woman's distress. "You're brave enough to hit me, you can certainly look at some pictures I took."

The phone shook in Lexan's hands as she scrolled. There, in eight consecutive frames was Hector selling her the pills. Clear shots of both their faces. She was ruined.

"You're done, Ms. Warner. Your career, such as it was, your political power, your relationship with that poor comatose angel. All of it."

Lexan pulled herself into the corner of the booth and jabbed at the cell. If she could delete the pictures--

"Go ahead, honey, I've got plenty of copies." She picked up her iPhone. "Why don't I just air drop them to you?"

Lexan looked at her, her eyes wide with horror.

Kimberly calmly set down her phone and reached for her glass. "You're a teacher, excuse me were a teacher. You must appreciate the irony."

Lexan forced her hands to obey. They wanted to tear the woman's face off.

"My, I feel like a teacher myself." Kimberly fanned herself. "That or a hot flash." She took another sip. "You know, like Joe had so many copies of the pictures of me, now I have copies of you. With your little friend, Hector."

Lexan wiped away a tear as Kimberly licked the rim of the glass. She wouldn't let the bitch see her cry. She thought of Joe in the hospital. "What do you want from me?"

"From you? Nothing. You mean nothing to me."

"Why don't you go to the police? You've got your evidence."

"Oh, I will, honey." She ran her tongue across her lips. "Right now, I just want to gloat."

CHAPTER THIRTY-SIX

J oe turned his head and rubbed the back of his neck. Must have slept funny, he thought as he kneaded the stiff muscles. The rest of him ached as well. He tried to flex his legs and his lower back, but they seemed not to respond. He sighed and settled into the pillow.

His room in the Pflegeheim faced a spacious lawn with gardens, and beyond, the MetroPark. He had seen none of it since being wheeled in several days ago. He was in the skilled nursing section of the facility which sprawled several blocks down Cleveland Ave. south of Cookie's Cookies. The facility had been established by German immigrants in the 1890's when Stradford was not much more than a country crossroads; *pflegen* their word for 'care' and *Heim* a cognate of 'home.' Joe appreciated the care his father had received in the memory unit, and donated regularly to the non-profit organization. If he had known where he was, he would have appreciated that, too.

A green light flashed and an alarm sounded in the nurses' station. "He's awake!" Nurse Jenke sprang from her seat and sprinted down the hall to his room.

"I don't need to hear this," Lexan said. She lowered her sunglasses into place, dropped her phone into her purse, and bent to stand up.

Kimberly clamped her hand down on Lexan's wrist. "Sit down. Sip your drink. You're not going anywhere."

The younger woman snatched her hand free. "I am, too."

The mayor lowered her voice. "Hector just left, missy. He told you to wait. A half hour, wasn't it?"

How had she known? Lexan sat down on the bench and tapped the table with the tinted glasses.

"You're probably asking yourself how I knew about Hector and what he said to you." Her eyes probed Lexan's face. "That just shows how far out of your element you are."

"You know nothing about me." She returned the stare.

Kimberly swallowed some of her drink, then sadly shook her head. "I know you're an abused woman."

Lexan fiddled with the sunglasses to keep her hands from shaking.

"Touched a nerve?" Kimberly smiled, a cat torturing a mouse. "Here's another one you thought was a secret."

"You bitch."

The mayor waved for another drink, keeping her eyes on the teacher. "You poor thing. Those aren't chicken pox scars on your arms, are they?"

"How did you--?" The only person she'd told was Roberta.

"You think you're so smart." Kimberly's voice hardened. "You're not. You're so obvious I can read your mind." She dropped her voice to a whisper again. "It wasn't Roberta who told me."

Lexan squeezed her hands together instead of reaching across the table and strangling her. "I give up. Not even Joe knows that." She forced a sigh. "At least you can buy me a drink."

"Bernie, all around," she called with a smile. "Now then, we can get down to the business of gloating."

"That's not what you've been doing?"

"Just messing with you. Got to be sure you're paying attention."

"I'm listening." Lexan hated the woman.

"Good. You need to leave Stradford quickly and quietly." She glanced around the bar. "You can't really hurt me, you know that's true, but you and your little friends are a distraction to me and the good people of Stradford."

"Might be best for everyone." Lexan slumped her shoulders. "There's nothing left for me here."

"Exactly my point. You have no job and your friend is a vegetable."

Lexan balanced her weight and slid forward on the

bench. Every single thing Kimberly said galled her.

"So then, we're making progress." Kimberly saluted her with the Manhattan.

"You got me." Lexan returned the salute and took a long drink. "I actually have to admit a certain amount of respect."

"Excuse me, Lexan, but I find that extremely hard to believe."

"No, you're despicable." Lexan managed a small grin. "Through and through."

"I am who I am," Kimberly said and slurped from her glass.

"But you have managed to achieve quite a bit in spite of all the males in your way."

The mayor paused mid-sip. "My greatest accomplishment. Thank you for noticing."

"I realize you took over your brother's--"

"--expanded it, improved it." Kimberly waved one hand and pointed her Manhattan with the other.

"No, I agree. That was what I was going to say. You took something good and made it better." Lexan crunched an ice cube from her drink.

Kimberly nodded. "Exactly. The cookie business was all mine, Alfie thought it was a joke."

"But that turned into your power base. Brilliant." Lexan returned the alcoholic salute.

"They never even consider women." She furrowed her brow and stared across the narrow booth. "I appreciate your words, but what is this change of heart?"

"What do you mean?"

"I thought my actions violated your sense of

morality."

"Me?" Lexan laughed. "I'm the abuse victim, remember? No, that's all Joe."

Kimberly cocked her head.

"Joe's the one with the Christian guilt, not me."

"I don't think I buy that, Ms. Warner." Kimberly peered from her hooded eyes. "You two are thick as thieves."

Lexan set down her glass nearly where she'd aimed it. "Sure, like you and your brother, you and that white-haired creep, you and the gov. We're women, we do what we have to."

"To survive in a man's world." The mayor nodded. "We do what we have to."

Lexan smiled conspiratorially and waved to Bernie. "Let me buy the next round."

"I may have misjudged you."

Lexan returned her small smile. "Thank you."

"No, you are a total pain in the ass."

"Takes one to know one, Mayor." Lexan clinked her glass.

"An immature pain in the ass who definitely needs to get out of town." Kimberly grinned. "But that's pretty much what they said about me."

"I knew it," Lex said. "Especially the men, right?"

She looked at Lex closely. "You know, under different circumstances." She shook her head.

"I thought the same thing," the teacher said.

"Did you?" Kimberly's face relaxed into a genuine smile. "Too late now, but you never know." She tried to clear her head. "You're getting me drunk."

"Not me," Lexan said. "It's Bernie's fault, all Bernie."

They laughed together, hard, eyes watering, breaths gasping, until Kimberly said, "I haven't laughed like that in years. Honestly."

"It's a fact," Lexan said solemnly. "Men are always trying to get us drunk."

That started another wave of laughter. When it ebbed, the mayor said, "This is not how I imagined this conversation going."

"Us girls have to talk to each other."

"We do, and since you've been so much fun, I think I can tell you a little story."

"I am fun, and soon will be out of your hair."

"True, true." Kimberly plucked the cherry from her drink and stuck it in her mouth. "What you said before about the prostitution and morality. I still don't believe you." She yanked out the stem.

Lexan shrugged and fidgeted with the sunglasses.

"Anyway, I thought I should explain myself about that." She took a drink. "That was mostly another male thing. Alfie set it up. Karl ran it."

"The white-haired guy?"

Kimberly nodded. "I inherited it. I was never interested in it, or those girls." Her voice faded off. "I'm not that upset that it's over."

"It made you an awful lot of money, Ms. Mayor." Lexan grinned.

"Some." She dropped her voice. "It's one of the reasons I took care of Karl."

"Karl's dead?"

The mayor's eyes scanned the bar and returned. "He thought he was in charge. He wasn't."

"You were." Lexan's fingers toyed with the glasses. "Thank you for that."

"You're welcome."

"It was a blow for women everywhere."

"It was, wasn't it." Kimberly nodded and finished her drink. "While we are on the subject, I had nothing to do with Joe being shot."

"I hope not." Lexan screwed up her face. "I know we're BFFs, but that would be hard to take."

"I should hope so." Kimberly started to giggle. "Even if he is a man."

Lexan giggled along with her. "So if Karl didn't shoot Joe, who did?"

"That was Oskar. You know him, don't you?"

She nodded. "The dump guy. Probably killed Chelsea's sister."

"I don't know about that," Kimberly said. "I do know he had it out for your Joe. That's why I had Karl kill him. To even the score a little bit." She reached across the table and laid her hand on Lexan's. "I'm sorry, I really am."

Lexan returned the squeeze, then slid her hand away. If you're not sorry now, you will be, she thought and replaced the glasses on her head. "I better get going."

"I know what you mean," Kimberly said. "Two women spending the afternoon together drinking."

"They'd never allow that in Stradford."

"They have laws against it," the Mayor agreed.

From their stakeout position in the parking lot, the Ready Team watched the Mayor, then Warner leave the *Dew Drop Inn*. The bald agent cursed himself for sending Kramer away, realizing now that he could use the second vehicle to follow Horvath. His orders were to keep tabs on the teacher; he put his car into gear and followed her north down the hill into Stradford. He and his team, like Lexan, had made another mistake twenty minutes ago. None of them had noticed Agent Canfield slip out the rear of the bar behind the drug runner, Hector.

CHAPTER THIRTY-SEVEN

Agent Canfield parked just north of Stradford in an apartment complex nestled beside the I-71 interchange. He had verified Hector's gang affiliation and now had an address that fit the pattern; the Mexicans don't work where they live.

Canfield pulled down the visor and opened the mirror. He smiled at the strange man in the reflection, then removed the glasses and peeled off the goatee that had hidden his youthful face. The disguise had helped him answer one question, but raised another. He mussed his hair back into shape and raised the visor. What the hell was Lexan Warner doing in a bar with Hector?

The obvious answer was buying drugs. Probably the fentanyl mixture the Mexicans were selling now. The recipe that had nearly used up Stradford PD's supply of Narcan. No, he told himself, that didn't add up. The girl was a wild card, sure, but he hadn't picked up the user-vibe from her. He looked at kids on a jungle gym in a green space near the door Hector had entered. Still, that answer connected the most dots.

Warner's boyfriend was in a coma. She had punched the mayor. She went off at a news conference and the school had suspended her. She wouldn't be the first person to try and ease the stress that way. He checked himself in the mirror again and punched the start button. She was certainly drinking. He crawled through the parking lot and re-traced his path from the bar. Maybe she was still there.

Gov. Stanic's Ready Team followed Lexan up Cleveland Ave. through the center of Stradford and into the Police Department parking lot. "The fuck she doing here?" the man in the passenger seat said.

"Not turning herself in for speeding," the bald man said.

"No, it's Kramer. She's talking to Kramer."

"About--?"

"She just spent twenty-eight minutes talking to the Mayor. Think she knows anything?"

The furrows on the bald man's face reached past where his hair line would have concealed them. "Why else would she drive straight here? She must know something."

"That means the Mayor told her something." He turned to the bald man.

"Which means she's ratting out GOTSOO."

"We don't know that for sure."

The bald man ran his hand from the top of his skull down across his eyes. The furrows disappeared as if erased. "Maybe she did, maybe she didn't." He keyed the Telegram app on his cell. "It's his call."

Lexan looked across the gun-metal gray desk into the bland eyes beneath Detective Kramer's buzz cut. Pale blue and distant, she reminded herself they saw much more than they revealed. "Funny," she said, "we've been talking this whole time and haven't mentioned Joe once."

The policeman removed his eyes from her for a second, then brought them back. "Not the normal pattern for us." He gauged her reaction, then said in a softer tone, "How is he doing? I should have asked about him sooner."

She fiddled with her sunglasses before laying them on his desk. "The same, nothing's changed. They moved him to the Pflegeheim."

"I heard that."

"I think he can hear me so I keep talking to him, but, I don't know." She looked away.

"I didn't want to dredge it all up, Ms. Warner. But I did want to express my condolences."

Lexan snapped her eyes onto his, not believing his sympathetic tone. When she saw his expression, she thanked him. "It's not really about Joe today, but it does concern him."

Kramer nodded.

"Now that we have observed the pleasantries, what are you going to do with the information I just gave you about Mayor Horvath?"

The concern in his eyes for Joe disappeared. "What do you expect me to do?"

"Your job." She focused on a spot in the center of his forehead. "She admitted to two murders and the prostitution."

"She admitted that to you."

Her hand slapped the desk top before she could control it. "What does that mean?"

"Do I have to spell it out for you?" The cold returned to his eyes. "You're *persona non grata* around here."

"Great, you use Latin. But are you going to let her get away with it?"

"I need proof." The detective's calm voice irritated her.

"I'll testify."

"You and your axe to grind? Who'll believe that?"

She strained to check her tone. "Perhaps if you investigated, you could find corroboration." She paused. "Now that you know what she did."

"I don't need you to tell me how to do my job."

She rejected a smart come-back. "OK, I'm sorry, Detective. Just tell me one thing. Whether or not you can prove it, do you believe what I told you?"

His eyes may have thawed a bit.

"You had doubts about Oskar and Joe shooting each other, didn't you?"

"Go on."

"Kimberly told me she had Karl kill Oskar. Doesn't that support your theory?"

"It might." He hesitated. "If that's true, you're in danger." He watched doubt cloud her face.

"What do you mean?"

"Two things. One, your story needs verification. Two, your story gives her a reason to keep it quiet. The easiest way for her to do that is to eliminate you."

She hadn't considered that. "You want to put me in a safe house?"

"Or give you a ticket out of town."

Lexan forced herself to think. She didn't fully trust Kramer, and either option would take her away from Joe. She couldn't leave him, and she wouldn't leave Stradford without Kimberly being punished for what she did to him.

"Look, Detective," I can't be pushed to the side, I need to keep--"

"--safe. Ms. Warner, if you're not safe you can't help anybody."

Another man telling her what she could and couldn't do. She slowly unclenched her teeth. "I'm not hiding and I'm not leaving."

Kramer gave her the full cop deadeye. "Let me put it as clearly as I can, OK? If you're dead you can't help Joe."

She pulled her face back as if slapped. "Let me put it as clearly as I can. OK?" She wiped a tear away before it could trickle out. "I have nothing left to lose. They've taken Joe and my job. You want me out of the way." She bit her lip. "They can't hurt me any more than they already have."

"You'd risk your life?"

Lexan's phone tweedled. She glared at him until the third sound, then at the sender. "It's the Pflegeheim." She leapt to her feet and raced from the office.

Kramer leaned back in his chair and exhaled. That girl was a piece of work, he had to admit. Crazy, but brave, too. Ran out so fast, she left her sunglasses on his desk blotter.

CHAPTER THIRTY-EIGHT

In the shade of a maple tree beneath the mint green water tower, the bald man spoke on the encrypted app. "Wait, sir, she's coming out now, running, and hold on, Agent Canfield--" He followed his partner's outstretched arm to where the BCI agent held open the door for Lexan, and obviously said something to her. The girl ran past without answering and jumped into her car. Canfield watched her drive away, shook his head, and entered the police station.

The thin voice on the phone startled the bald man, and he adjusted it over his ear. "Yes, sorry about that, Governor. Yeah, I think more bad news. Uh-huh. First the girl spoke to Kramer, now it looks like Canfield is doing the same."

He started the car as he continued to listen. "Yes, sir. Will do." He nodded across the phone at his partner. Seconds later they were following Lexan south on Cleveland Ave.

"You'll never guess who I ran into on the way to your office."

Detective Kramer gestured to the chair and Canfield sat down. "Literally," the BCI agent said.

"Probably the same woman who ran out of here like a shot."

"If I hadn't held the door open, she would have run through it." Canfield grinned. "Where you suppose she's going?"

"Only thing could make her fly would be Joe. Got a phone call from the Pflegeheim."

The agent nodded. "Alive or dead?"

"Dead? Don't think so. Dying maybe." He checked the younger man's expression and wondered if he cared about the answer or was just covering the bases. "I'm guessing he's conscious."

"Makes sense."

"What brings you here, Agent Canfield? I thought you'd be at your brand-new post in West Bumfuck."

Canfield saw the twinkle in Kramer's eyes and relaxed. "I'm here to report what I've been doing, and I am expanding department protocol."

Kramer almost smiled. "Proceed, Agent."

"I'll do the easy stuff first." The young officer crossed his legs. "The drug runner, Hector, is definitely with the Mexicans."

"Thought so."

"Followed him from the *Dew Drop* to a known residence outside Stradford."

Kramer leaned closer. "Without notifying the local LEO's."

"Hey, I wasn't in Stradford and his gang does have a connection to my new post. Which is actually East Bumfuck."

The police officer suppressed a grin. "Off book?"

"Not quite, but here's the thing." He looked directly at Kramer. "Apparently Ms. Warner was buying drugs from Hector."

Kramer's eyes widened. "She told me she was in a bar talking to the mayor. Pills?"

"He slid an envelope across the table and she pulled cash from her purse." Canfield paused to think. "I didn't see Horvath. Must have shown up after I left. Looked to me Warner was just getting lit. She was into her third mojito."

"You didn't stay."

"No, I followed Hector." He re-crossed his legs. "Did she seem drunk or high when you spoke to her?"

Kramer turned to the 'Loose Lips Sink Ships' poster on his wall. "No. She talked fast but she always does. Didn't smell anything."

Canfield waited. "Are you going to tell me what she said?"

Kramer looked from the closed office door to the BCI man. "She told me our Kimberly admitted to two murders."

"Oskar was one, right? Like you thought." Canfield dropped his leg to the floor. "The other has to be Karl, but I thought that was a gang hit."

"We all did," Kramer said. "But nobody knows. The Columbus guys covered it up."

"Kimberly took credit for it, didn't she?"

Kramer agreed. They sat quietly for several moments. "A lot of moving parts."

"Too many," Canfield said. "She's in the middle of it all."

Kramer looked across the table. "Right smack dab."

CHAPTER THIRTY-NINE

Lexan skidded to a stop in a handicapped space in front of the nursing home. She raced between the white columns and flung open the outside door. She yanked the second door and let out a yell of frustration when it didn't budge. Inside she could see the dark hall extending away from her and sitting areas to the right and left, but no people. She pounded on the glass. A sign with white letters on a red background informed her that visiting hours on Sundays expired at 8:00 pm.

She stomped her foot and looked for a call button to get the damn door open. Nothing but a white board with meals in different colors. A signup-sheet for pickle ball. A calendar with daily events. "For God's sake," she spat. "Joe's awake, let me see him!"

She spotted a button and jammed her finger into it. A voice slipped from the small speaker. "Visiting hours are--"

"I know, I know. You guys called me to come." She stepped from foot to foot as if waiting in line to use the bathroom.

"Oh, wait a sec. Are you Lexan Warner?"

"Yes, yes."

"To see Mr. Lehrer?"

"Yes, room 118."

"The last four digits of your social?"

She recited the numbers, listened as the voice repeated them, and finally heard a rasping buzz. She ripped the door open and raced down the hall.

"Get out of the way," she said to a nurse at Joe's door and pushed past her.

Joe was sitting up against a pile of pillows. His expression brightened and he opened his arms. She fell into them. "Joe, I'm sorry, so sorry."

The nurse, Carol Jenke, smiled. "Be careful."

Joe patted her back and spoke haltingly. "God, it feels good to hold you."

His voice was scratchy and she had to listen closely. She burrowed into his neck and cried. He patted her some more. "Hey, I'm the one in the hospital bed."

She pulled back to look at him. "It's my fault you're here." Her face was already puffy and flushed. She wanted to wipe her eyes but didn't want to let him go.

"Carol told me I got shot. You didn't pull the

trigger, did you?" He looked at her closely. Her head had bumped the left side of his face. He winced. "Why would you say it's your fault?"

"I wasn't there for you when you needed me." She lost her voice and swallowed. "And, and when you were in the hospital, I thought I'd never--" She grabbed onto him and sobbed.

Joe reached around her head to wipe a tear from his own eye. "I'm not real sure where I am, or how I got here. The only thing I remember is I was looking for you, in the family room, and then nothing. Now I'm here."

Lexan jumped from the bed and spoke to the nurse. "Does he know who I am, can he remember anything, is he OK?" Her eyes darted from Carol to Joe, frantic.

"The short-term memory is the last to come back." Nurse Jenke spoke calmly as she handed Lex a box of Kleenex. "We ran some tests before you arrived and he's doing really well."

"But he doesn't know who shot him."

"Give him some time." She patted Lex on the shoulder. "I'll get you two some coffee and leave you alone for a bit."

"Hello, I'm the patient, over here in the bed." Joe gave them a sloppy a grin.

"See, he's coming around," the nurse said. "Keep talking to him, he'll be fine."

The bald Ready Team operative looked up from the phone and shook his head at his partner. The whiney voice of the governor's aide, Lance, filled the space in the front seat. If they would only make up their minds.

Stanic came back on the line. "Gentlemen, we have come to a decision. A temporary decision, pending further developments." The men in the car focused.

"Get yourselves in position, targets in sight, and wait for the go order."

"Tactical dress?"

"As previously discussed." Stanic muffled his phone and said something to Lance they couldn't understand. "No action, of any kind, without my order. My order alone."

"Understood." The connection clicked off and the bald man turned to his partner. "We're going in. Sort of."

CHAPTER FORTY

urse Jenke entered Joe's room with a coffee cup in each hand. Ms. Warner had pulled a chair as close to Mr. Lehrer's bed as possible, and he had slid to the very edge. She cleared her voice. "I'll just check our patient, then continue my rounds." She set the cups on the rolling tray table and listened to his heart. She nodded and reached for the blood pressure cuff.

"How long can I stay?" Lexan asked as the nurse ripped the Velcro.

"I'm probably in trouble for letting you in." She inflated the bulb and listened. "BP's good." She hung the hose on its stand. "You can stay until I finish my rounds. Maybe an hour."

Lexan followed her to the door and lowered her voice. "Any idea how long he'll have to stay here? I'd like to get him home."

"If the doctors clear him, only a couple days. We can talk about it later." She squeezed Lexan's hand and disappeared into the dimly lit hallway.

Home, Lexan thought as she sat down next to Joe. He smiled and another wave of shame washed over her. I left his home. I left him to face death alone. He reached himself up and kissed her. I don't deserve him.

"You look so serious," he said. "Not even a smile?"

"I thought you were going to die."

"Just because a bullet creased my skull?" He hooked a thumb at the bandage on the left side of his head, then rubbed his neck. "Must have slept funny."

She put a smile on her face. "You've been asleep more than a week."

His right eye widened. "Was it that long? Didn't seem like it."

"Seemed longer to me." She interlocked her fingers with his.

"Do you remember being shot?"

"That's the stupid thing. I remember a bang. Just a noise and a flash. Didn't even feel it. Someone told me it happened, but who, where? No idea."

Lexan watched him strain. She didn't want to re-open the wound she had caused by leaving him. They could talk about it and she could beg forgiveness when he was strong enough to take it. If he could remember it. If he didn't think he was an angel. "It doesn't matter." She squeezed his hand. "You're here now."

He caught her eye and grinned. "Yeah, and I'm not dead."

* * *

Her brother would call it 'feeling no pain,' Kimberly Hellauer Horvath thought as she maneuvered her Lexus down Liverpool Hill into Stradford. He'd also say something about 'ducks in a row' and she wouldn't. But she had to admit Alfie would have summed up the situation with those two expressions.

She lurched to a stop in time to see a woman spin the front wheels of the baby stroller out of the crosswalk and shoot her an evil look. Kimberly lifted her hands toward her and bowed her head. Not gonna spoil my day, bitch.

Her jaw clenched shut, the woman pushed the stroller past the car with one hand and led a 4 or 5 year-old with the other. Kimberly flashed a smarmy smile, but the woman didn't look at her. Shouldn't be walking her kids in the dark anyway.

I have a right to be happy. I do have my ducks organized: I nailed little Miss Barbie dead to rights and Lehrer is good as dead. A horn blared from somewhere behind her.

She waved and continued her happy thoughts. Those two dead-ish, and the others actually, truly and forever dead. She laughed and stopped at another red light. She held up fingers and counted: Barbie, Joey, Oskar, Karl, all those drug dealers. Nobody left but me.

She lowered her fingers except for the middle one when the jerk behind her pounded his horn. She waited until the light changed from green to amber, then turned right. Three blocks later, she crossed the four lanes of Center Road into the PamLeeCo parking lot.

The four-story brick building stood on a large wooded property across from the Mall, bordered on the east by the interstate and the north by the Park. Gold reflective glass on the windows and doors lent an additional level of privacy to the secluded setting. Kimberly usually felt relaxed when she visited the offices of the cosmetics company, but not so today. She jerked to a stop in the space reserved for Pam's husband and burst through the revolving door into the Atrium. Today she was on a roll.

She yanked open the door of Pam's office and raised her arms over her head. "Remember my Evita pose? At the party? My silver dress?"

Pam and Chief Mangione stopped talking and looked up in surprise.

"Don't cry for me, Ashtabula. Oops." The Mayor stumbled as she spun around, her hands still raised. "I love Evita."

Pamela and Mangione exchanged looks. Kimberly pranced around the desk and enveloped her friend in a hug, "I love this gal, too."

Pamela wiggled herself free. "I love that guy, too," Kimberly said, "but since I'm his boss, I shouldn't be hugging him." A thought worked its way across her forehead. "Oh, what the hell." She ran around the desk and hugged the chief of police.

Mangione protested, succumbed, and managed to extricate himself. When Kimberly was finally settled in a chair, Pam said, "Well, you are certainly one happy cowgirl."

"I am." Kim looked around the spacious office.

"You guys got anything?"

The other two exchanged glances again. "Haven't you had enough?"

"I'm your boss, Garrett, and I'm thirsty." At Pam's nod he mixed her a weak drink at the sideboard.

"What brings you two here on a Sunday night?" Kim looked from the policeman to her friend.

"I was about to ask you the same thing." Pam forced a smile. "Why the good mood?"

"The. Best. Mood. Ever!" She tasted the drink. "All water." She set the glass on Pam's desk. "But I don't mind, because I got the little bitch. Barbie, Lexan whatever the hell her name is. I nailed her ass!"

Mangione furrowed his eyes. "What do you mean?"

"Can't hurt me, us, anymore." She snatched the drink from the desk and drained it.

Pam looked from him to her. "What happened?"

Kimberly explained the story to them, ending with, "and that just leaves us with the, what do you call it, collateral damage."

Mangione raised his palms. "Slow down a second here. Ma'am." He looked to Pam. "It sounds like you have Warner cold. That's good."

Kimberly held out her glass to him. "A double, please."

The police chief took the glass. "But collateral damage? What do you mean?"

Pamela watched his butt tense and relax as he walked to the sideboard. "Things should settle down now, Kim. What else is there for you to do?"

"I say let it die down." Mangione tossed some cubes into her glass. "Too much violence around here already. That will mean more questions."

The Mayor sighed. "When it's all done we can relax."

Pam watched him deliver the drink. "But who's left? You've removed them all."

"Much better." She set down the heavy crystal. "Bob McWhatever for one. And the French teacher."

"The guy who slept through the Weigel shooting?"

Pam looked at him. "At least he was involved. Why the French teacher? I never heard of her."

"You got the ones who attacked you," Mangione said. "Everything's calming down. Let it go, Mayor."

Kimberly looked at him as she took another swallow. "You two don't get it. When you have your opponents down, you keep them down." She moved her attention to Pamela. "So they can never hurt you again."

Pamela nodded her head to Mangione as Kimberly finished her drink. "Well, you're the Mayor, I guess you can do whatever you like."

"Damn straight!" Kimberly's face lit up. "And what I'd like to do right now is take my two besties out for a celabbatrory dink."

"However you say it." Pam laughed. "I'm in, but I think poor Garrett has some work to do tonight."

Kimberly wobbled to her feet. "He's a model public employee, that one." Pamela took the Mayor's arm and steered her to the door. She winked to Garrett before it closed. He nodded, then picked up his phone.

CHAPTER FORTY-ONE

The bald man screwed the suppressor onto his Glock Model 19 9mm pistol and looked up. Beyond the open space where the middle row of seats would be, his partner was tugging a black balaclava into place. "When you think about it, it's just like any other infiltration."

The other man adjusted the straps on his body armor. "Suppose it is."

"Very little security." They had timed the guard's rounds and had a comfortable window of time. "Very quiet," he added when the other didn't respond.

"You'd expect that in an Alzheimer and re-hab unit." His partner turned to him. "Hospice patients don't usually put up much of a fuss."

"That's enough," the bald man said. "Let's just do our jobs."

"Always do." They stepped out of the SUV into the night.

The two dark figures moved across the open area of the gardens when a bank of clouds drifted in front of the moon. As they approached the cluster of buildings, the ground sloped down. They kept close to the fruit trees placed decoratively along the curving pathway. The leader paused by a hedge at the corner of the main building. His partner followed him into the shadow.

The main building housed meeting rooms, the cafeteria, and the physical therapy area. A three-story square tower stood next to the wide, peaked roof structure. Light from the tower windows described trapezoids across the natural wood siding.

The two men skirted the short side of the building and avoided the lights at the entrance by creeping down another short slope of grass into another garden. Keeping away from the lighted path, they slipped between some benches and crouched behind a stone plinth in the raised center of a circular patio.

Heads on swivels and eyes constantly moving, they crossed the patio and ascended another slope towards a gazebo. They hopped the fence surrounding it and stopped in the shadow of a tree. The bald man gestured across the path to the right-hand first floor room in front of them. His partner nodded. The rooms above had balconies; Joe Lehrer's room and the one next to it opened onto a small patio, seven meters away. His partner adjusted his low-light goggles. The curtains were open and provided a clear line of sight to both targets.

The bald man poked his shoulder and continued

toward a service door in the elbow of the three-winged building. He slid a pass card through the reader and grunted when the light flipped from red to green and the bolt slid free. He turned the handle and glanced over his shoulder to his partner's position. He grunted again when he couldn't see him. He entered the building.

He made sure the door behind him shut tightly before tapping his cell. He scrolled the layout of the building and cautiously opened the door into the corridor. No one was there.

Like in the movies, it was too quiet in the Pflegeheim. He crept to the left, running his hand along the protruding rail like an old person. Like all the old persons behind all the doors. Most were cracked open, and when he passed them, he could hear whooshing machines, snoring, and weeping. He turned left at the corner and counted five rooms. Someone was gagging and coughing in the third. He had to hurry past before someone showed up.

He stopped at 116 and listened. Nothing. He replaced the 'Plesac' placard next to the door with 'Unit Available' and swiped the card. The door opened and he slid noiselessly inside.

The bald man felt the length of the wall separating this room from Joe's, and found the proper spot. He attached the listening device to the wall, inserted his earphones, and pulled up a chair. Before sitting down, he made sure the glass doors leading to the patio were unlocked. He clicked his com twice; his partner returned the phrase. He attached the listening device to his free ear, and adjusted the gain. "So sorry," Lexan was saying. "I'm so sorry."

In his office in Columbus, Governor Stanic softly set the old-fashioned receiver into its cradle. Lance leaned forward. "Well?"

"Our new friend in Stradford." Stanic narrowed his eyes.

Lance let his back relax into the deep leather chair. "Agreed with me, I bet."

The aide's smug tone irked him. "Not exactly."

Lance pouted. "He certainly didn't advocate a shootout, did he?"

"No, he didn't think a shootout was in the city's best interest at this time." Stanic wondered again why it was his underlings had to hassle him all the time.

"See, that's my point exactly, I--" Lance recognized the governor's expression and stopped.

Stanic kept staring until the younger man looked away. "Chief Mangione actually had a better idea than you did."

Lance grudgingly replaced his smug expression with his doting servant mask. "What's his plan?"

Stanic tapped the picture of his wife with the pen the Koch brothers had given him. "It's a twofer. Maybe a threefer."

Lance looked at him blankly.

"The violence doesn't bother him."

"Then what is it?"

This time Stanic only had to raise his eyebrows to stop the little prick from speaking. "His plan is to get someone else to commit the violence."

"Mangione can make the bust and make Stradford safe again."

Stanic nodded. "That's the frosting on the cake."

Lance grinned deferentially. "What's the cake?"

He's feeling better about himself, Stanic thought. "The cake is getting the right person to pull the trigger." He could see Lance's mind working.

"That eliminates a problem at both ends." The aide clapped his hands. "We bag the shooter and the shootee!"

A smug sycophant, but the kid was pretty sharp. "Hand me the phone on your way out, please."

CHAPTER FORTY-TWO

The other man adjusted the barrel slightly on the limb of the tree to keep his arm from cramping. He noticed Lexan Warner approaching the patio door and re-adjusted the scope. "Clear shot at the female target."

On the other end of the com, the bald man clicked, 'Understood.'

The sniper felt Lexan's gaze as she looked through the plate glass. He knew she couldn't see him, but it felt like she could. She reached a hand to the curtain and turned her back to him.

"Leave the curtains open," Joe said. "The moonlight is kind of pretty."

In the room next door, the bald man held his Glock to the feeble light and chambered a round.

Lexan released the curtain. "Joe, there's something

I have to tell you."

"If it's not 'I can't wait to get you naked,' I don't want to hear it."

"Never get a better look." The man outside centered on the soft spot to the right of her spine.

The shot itself wouldn't be a problem. The trick was to place the tranquilizer round in the upper back at the base of the neck. He adjusted the crosshairs. He released his breath.

Joe's voice was scratchy from the tube, but the gleam in his eye made her blush. "No, really it's important. Joe, I--"

"Go, when you're ready."

Light exploded in the shooter's goggles.

"Fuck!" The shooter squeezed his eyes closed.

Carol Jenke stood in the doorway, her hand on the light switch. "Sorry to interrupt."

The phone beeped in the bald man's ear.

"Final rounds." The nurse picked up Joe's wrist and counted.

"Stand down!" the bald man shouted into his com. "I repeat, stand down!"

"We can talk later--"

"Sshh." The nurse shook her head at Lexan.

The shooter drew the barrel away the target.

Lexan stood by Joe's bed both relieved and disappointed. She smiled at him.

The nurse let his wrist drop to his side. "Folks, we are way beyond visiting hours."

The shooter removed his goggles and rubbed his eyes. "Fuck" he muttered again.

Lexan took Joe's hand. He winked at her.

The nurse closed the curtains to the patio and frowned. She locked the sliding door.

The bald man spoke softly into the phone.

"Good news," the nurse said. "Looks like they're releasing you in the morning."

The bald man's partner broke down his weapon and stowed the goggles.

"We can go back home." Joe squeezed her hand.

The bald man stuffed the listening device into his pack and crept to the patio door. He clicked his com. His partner acknowledged.

"Home." Lexan covered her fear with a kiss.

"Boys, you know better than this." Mangione glared first at the BCI agent then Kramer. "You especially."

Canfield nodded at Kramer. "Don't blame him, Chief. It's my idea.'

Mangione ignored the younger man. "First thing on a Monday morning you want me to arrest the Mayor?"

Kramer hardened his face. He knew they needed more than Warner's testimony, but Canfield had been adamant. "We, I, didn't say arrest her, Chief."

Mangione froze Canfield with a look then returned to Kramer. "Think maybe I should buy her a nice breakfast before we throw her in a cage?"

"She likes griddle cakes. Sir." Kramer kept his face under control.

Mangione smashed his hand onto the desk. Canfield jumped, Kramer didn't. "You will not play the fool with me, Detective."

Kramer waited until the man's face was nearly purple. "It's a lead, Chief."

"A fucking poor lead is what it is. The Warner broad got herself suspended and she's a pill-popper. Who in the world would believe her?"

"That's why we want to pursue it."

Mangione waved his words away. "You want me to take the mayor into custody. Your boss. My boss." He stood and turned his back on them.

Kramer gave Canfield a shit-eating grin.

"We'll get corroboration, Chief Mangione," the BCI man said.

Mangione shook his head before turning back from the window. "You'll not do anything until I give you the go-ahead." He glared at each of them. "*Capisce?*"

"I could go to my--"

"No, Canfield, you can't go to the BCI. You're not even assigned here."

Canfield opened his mouth, but Kramer poked him with his elbow. "No way, boss, we don't want a pissing contest."

"If Stradford has a problem, Stradford will handle it." Mangione leaned his hands onto the desk and glared. "If is a very large word."

"Yes, sir." Kramer and Canfield nodded.

"Now get your worthless asses out of my office."

Lexan woke with a start and flailed for the alarm clock. It eluded her and crashed to the floor. Red digits blinked 10:42 am at her from the floor. She bounded from the bed. Halfway to the bathroom she realized, yes, she was late for work, but no, she didn't have a job. She flopped back down on Joe's side of the bed, a starfish atop his pillow.

It had been late when she left the Pflegeheim, and she had finally gotten a good night's sleep. She needed more. The pull-out sofa in Roberta's guest room had been lumpy. And lonely. She breathed in Joe's scent and stretched.

She would bring him home this afternoon and she wouldn't be alone. She'd have to talk to him, but they'd be in the same house in the same bed. The conversation could go either way, she thought. If he forgave her, she could stay. If he still thought he was an angel, she could leave. Minutes later she was singing in the shower.

CHAPTER FORTY-THREE

If one were to ask Fr. Gerald Hastings his opinion of the Pflegeheim in Stradford, he probably would offer none. If he were asked his feelings about the facility he would prevaricate unless pressed. Then he would praise the selflessness and skill of the care providers. He would cite awards they had won from the state of Ohio and professional rehabilitation organizations, and he would list the many positive experiences he had been part of.

Most of the questioners would shake their heads and marvel at his ability to spend so much time with people who were certainly going to die. They would say how much they admired him for doing what they could not. They would thank him profusely, break eye-contact and shuffle off to their cars and speed away. They would leave him to care for those whose bodies or minds had deserted them.

Fr. Jerry prayed for those who left as well as those

who lived behind the security doors. He did get down sometimes as anybody would, but he always returned to the Pflegeheim with a smile on his face and his heart full of love. If truly pressured for an explanation, he would shyly explain his faith. "Two things can happen here," he would say, "and both are good." To their skeptical or scornful expressions he would continue, "Either they recover and live longer, or they die and meet their God."

He believed it was a win-win, but as he pulled into a reserved-for-clergy parking space in front of the rehab unit, he hoped Joe was going to pull through. They had been friends since grade school, and losing him would hurt. He said a quick prayer.

Hastings found Nurse Jenke peering at her laptop. She led him to Joe's room and stopped in the hallway. "See for yourself, Father. He's awake."

The nurse retreated and the priest stepped into the room. Joe was seated in the armchair looking into the courtyard. Hastings approached quietly from behind. "Luuuuke, I'm your Faaaather."

"They may call you father, Father, but you're not my daddy."

They laughed and Hastings came around the chair to face him. Joe extended his hand. "Good to see you, Jerry."

The priest reached down, gave him a hug, and quickly ran a hand across his eyes. He turned away and pulled up the other chair. When his face returned to Joe's, there was a smile on it.

"Took you a while to get here," Joe said with a grin.

"Hey Joey boy, I was here, but you weren't. You

were somewhere far far away."

"Yeah, there was this light." Joe let his eyes glaze over. "I was like hovering above it and I followed the light and got this warm, glowy feeling, like love was oozing all around."

Jerry punched his arm sharply and held up his fist. "I got your glowy, oozy love right here!"

They both laughed. Joe said, "Man, it is good to see you. I mean it's good to see anybody, but hey."

"I know, Joe, I know. You gave us a run for it this time."

"It's like I was dead," Joe said. "I don't remember anything."

Jerry noticed the bandages on his head, the dark circles beneath his eyes. "How are you feeling? Really."

"Actually, I feel OK. Weak, can't sit up very long, sleepy all the time. Not much pain."

"That's more than I expected you to say. Usually you slough everything off."

"Not this time." Joe looked at his friend seriously. "This scared me. Part of my life is gone."

"It'll come back, you'll remember more every day."

"Thank you, Father Jerry. I'll bet you tell that to all your patients."

The priest laughed. "No, I talked to your nurse." He stopped smiling.

"Here comes the real reason for your visit." Joe grinned, then noticed Hasting's expression. "What's up?"

The priest kneaded the backs of his wrists. "You've got to drop this Avenging Angel bit, Joe. They tried to kill you."

"Couldn't pull it off though. We angels got us some thick skulls."

Hastings waited. "This is serious. You can't keep poking the bear and not expect to get clawed."

"Really, a metaphor?"

"Damn it Joe! You can't keep putting your life in danger. Too many people love you, too many people depend on you."

"I was at home minding my own business, Jerry. That's the last thing I remember. I wasn't poking anybody!"

"Sorry about my language." The priest massaged the base of his thumb. His face was flushed across his deep forehead. "I know you're not looking for trouble, I know you don't really think you're an angel. But." He looked closely at his friend. "You're a human being, not a super-hero. It's not your job to right all the wrongs in Stradford."

Joe took a deep breath. "I know you mean the best Jerry. I know you love me. You're my friend."

"And I don't want you taking risks and dying! Lex doesn't either, or Bob."

"I'm not trying to hurt myself."

"That's what it looks like."

"Do you see wings or a sword?" Joe looked side to side.

Hastings gave him a thin smile.

"What I'm doing is walking the walk. I can't believe in justice if I'm not ready to work for justice."

The priest opened his mouth, then closed it.

"Sort of like the way you live your life, Father."

"When you explain it like that."

Joe reached up and hugged his friend. Jerry settled him back in the chair. "Just be careful, would you?"

"I will, my friend, I will."

To Garrett Mangione's way of thinking, things were progressing nicely. He accepted the coffee cup from his secretary, ceramic not Styrofoam, and watched her butt until she closed his office door behind her. She'd been a nice addition, one of several he'd made while replacing staff members he couldn't trust; the police department had been rife with people who knew his business and couldn't keep their mouths shut. He took a sip of coffee. He had busted her when he was working narcotics in Cleveland. She knew better than to cross him.

The Chief of Police leaned back in his chair, and wished he was as sure about Pamela Holmgren as he was about his secretary. His plan had been to take things slowly and consolidate his base before making his strike. He took another sip and placed the mug onto his desk in front of the picture of his wife and children. But things had moved so quickly that he feared he had gotten ahead of himself. The damn teachers had forced things. Now Pam was showing signs of wanting him. He was looking forward to the sex; usually pampered, older women were desperate and couldn't resist his uber-masculinity.

The problem with bedding her was, he'd only been in Stradford a handful of months and didn't know how deep her roots ran in this tribal town. That meant he didn't know who was really on her side, or who was in her pocket. He literally didn't know if she was playing him or he was playing her. Was she really that interested in screwing him?

Mangione clanked the coffee mug with his pen. However he put the pieces together, it came out the same: he couldn't trust her. Use her, sure. Let his guard down, never. He grabbed his phone when he heard her speaking with his secretary. He picked up her scent as he scrolled through his text messages.

"Good morning, Chief."

He feigned interest in his cell. Slowly he raised his eyes to hers. "Good morning." He ran his eyes down her body. "*Mon cher.*"

He watched her breath catch and her eyes widen. He ignored his doubt.

She sat down and waved her hand across her face. "Is it hot in here?"

"No, it's you." He gave her the full smile. She melted a little more.

She probably would have thrown herself across his desk right then, but the anonymous cell phone tweedled. Mangione winked at her. "Governor Stanic."

"Are you alone?" The politician's voice was pitched higher than normal.

"No, sir." Pamela noticed his deferential tone and felt his gaze linger on her legs. "I'm here with Mrs. Holmgren."

Stanic waited a beat. "Can you trust her?"

"Absolutely." More than I can trust you. "I'll put the phone on speaker."

"Good of you to join us, Mrs. Holmgren. I value

your input, so I'll get right to it." Even through the tinny speaker Stanic's voice had recovered its usual bombast. "How's the weather in Stradford these days, Chief?"

Mangione looked at her and they both raised their eyebrows. "It's gray and overcast up here, Governor, like it always is."

She made a 'what kind of question is that' gesture with her hands. He shrugged.

"Not that, the temperature."

"Mid-forties, snow's mostly gone." He looked at cars speeding past on Cleveland Ave. "Maybe warmer."

It sounded like Stanic was covering the phone and speaking to someone in the background. His words spilled out anxiously. "I didn't mean the actual degrees." Another pause. "I'm trying to get a handle on the, uh, prevailing conditions in Stradford."

"Conditions, sir?" Mangione looked at Pamela again and screwed up his face. She held up a finger and looked from him to the phone.

"Do things seem to be settling down up there. Is it calmer, more moderate?"

"The temperature? I already--"

"It was much calmer a couple weeks ago, Governor Stanic," Pamela said quickly. "But there may be storms in the forecast."

Mangione frowned and looked out the window.

"That's not good," Stanic said.

"No, it isn't. They're saying spring may be late, and violent."

"But I heard--"

Pam shushed Mangione with her hand. "We'll

need to take precautions."

"I'd like you two to get out in front of this," Stanic said. "We don't want to get caught unprepared."

Mangione tossed his pen onto the desk and slumped back. She reached for his hand. "An ounce of prevention, Governor, we'll get right on it."

"I'm sure you will." Stanic's voice drifted away. "Like you did with that press conference. Nicely done."

She undid the top button of her blouse to catch Mangione's attention. "A little bit of sunshine for Stradford."

"That's what I'm talking about," the Governor boomed. "That's why we keep her around, huh Garrett?"

His eyes remained on her breasts. "Sir, yes, Governor."

"If the weather turns very bad, can Stradford count on help from Columbus?"

"What would that look like?"

"If there were another series of heavy storms like there were last month."

"Mrs. Holmgren, my office would jump at the chance of assisting the good people of Stradford in their time of need. As we always have."

"Hopefully we can handle everything by ourselves." She ran her tongue across her upper lip.

"That would be the best course of action. It always is." Stanic's voice faded and returned. "Garrett, you be sure to keep it all on the down low. We don't want the folks up there worrying when they don't have to."

Mangione jumped as if shocked. "No, yes, on it, Governor."

"We'll keep it mild, like good old-fashioned spring weather," Pamela said quickly. "Maybe one shower."

"One quick shower. No more." The line clicked off.

Pamela sighed and fiddled with her necklace. Mangione's eyes lingered on the pendant, then slowly lifted to her eyes. "Why was he talking about the weather?"

She sighed and jotted a room number on his desk blotter. "4:00. We'll talk about it then."

CHAPTER FORTY-FOUR

It hadn't been as difficult getting Joe out of the Pflegeheim and into his house as Lexan had imagined. She'd brought him some clothes, helped him with the paperwork and prescriptions, set the follow-up appointments, and here they were: she standing, arms crossed by his bed, he under the covers, claiming he wasn't tired enough to take a nap.

"You're not the boss of me."

"That's exactly what I am. Till you're better."

"Oh, I'm better, I'm so much better." Joe lifted the covers from the other side of the bed. "Come here, let me show you."

She backed away. "You're not healthy enough for that."

Joe's forehead crinkled. "How can I prove that I'm better?"

"Seriously?"

"Yes, mostly." He adjusted the pillow against the headboard. "Did they tell you anything to look for? Something I should be able to do? A timetable?"

It had been easy thus far because the physical move wasn't the hard part. She gave him a stern look. "Well, how do you feel?"

"Great, I'm weak, but no problem. Got both eyes open. The head wound's itching so it's healing, right?"

The hard part would be knowing when to tell him that his real wound was her fault. "That's good." She sat down on the edge of the bed. "How's your memory?"

Joe's face darkened. "Nothing there." He looked away from her as if ashamed.

She averted her eyes as well, tensing when she noticed her hanging bag and duffel near the bedroom door.

"Wait, I do remember something." Her face spun toward him.

"But I can't reach it. I know it, it's right there." His voice faded.

Lexan released a breath. "Frustrating. You need to close your eyes and let it come back." She stood and took a step toward the door.

"Hey, Lex, why are your bags sitting over there? You going on vacation without me?"

Packed and ready to leave, she had forgotten to hide them in the guest room. The doorbell rang and she gratefully raced down to answer it. Minutes later she returned with Bob and Roberta. She had never been so glad to see them.

"The man who literally dodged the bullet!" Bob

nearly leaped onto the bed to hug his friend.

"Get off me." Joe's eyes closed as he touched the wound.

Bob jumped up, horrified. "Man, I always screw it up. Always."

The women pushed him aside, Lexan taking Joe's hand, Roberta checking the bandage. Joe struggled more upright. "I'm fine, you guys, really. There's no blood or anything, is there?"

Roberta pulled her hand back and dabbed away a tear. "It's so good to hear you talking."

Lexan put her arm around her friend's shoulders. Bob stepped out of their way.

"The mere sound of my voice?" Joe grinned. "I am still a chick magnet." The women laughed and sat down, bracketing him on the bed. He opened his arms and they both hugged him.

"It's good to be alive, Bobby, it's good to be alive!"

Bob turned to the three on the bed. I'll never be him, he thought. "Yes, my friend, it surely is."

Roberta's grin faded as she looked at Bob's face. She tried to catch his eye, but he was fixed on the scene on the bed. When Lexan broke away and stood up, she said, "Guys, I think Bob has something to tell you."

Bob shot her an embarrassed look. Joe adjusted himself on the pillow, "Before you start, I have to say something."

He's so hard to talk to, Lexan thought, because he always has to run things. It's always him first. "You don't have to say anything, Joe, after all you've--"

"It's my near-death-experience we're celebrating

here today. I get to go first." Joe smiled hoping his friend would, too.

"I've been an ass, Bob. I really have. It's been all Joe, all the time. I must have been hard to live with."

Bob's eyes flickered to him, then away. Roberta said, "No, Joe, really." He didn't notice the flush moving up Lexan's face.

He waved off Bert's comment. "Thank you, Bob. That's all I wanted to say. I know you've been working on stuff, and I haven't paid attention to it. I don't even know what you were up to."

Lexan looked from one to the other.

Bob smiled weakly. He toed a brown leather satchel at his feet. "It didn't turn out the way I thought it would."

"I want to know, Bob."

In between the two men, Lexan let out a breath. She was glad they were talking, for both of them, but she would have to postpone her confession.

"It was a waste of time."

"It was such a big deal that you wouldn't even tell us what it was." Roberta looked at Lexan, who nodded. "You wanted to tell Joe first."

"No, I got ahead of myself. I thought I could be the hero this time."

"That's my job." Joe hoped his light tone would change the look on his friend's face. It didn't.

"I feel like I always disappoint you guys. I don't want to talk about it."

"You spent an awful lot of time on it," Lexan said. "I'm sure you gave it a good shot."

Bob nodded. "But in the end, I'm just a big loser."

"Time out! You can't feel sorry for yourself." Joe sat bolt upright. "You're the guy who always picks us up."

Roberta hugged Bob. "Wait, you told me something good that happened."

"You promised not to tell, Bert."

"You do or I will."

"Well, yeah, one thing. I worked on my theory with Mel."

Joe threw himself back on the bed. "Now I am gonna die."

Lexan whooped. "Mel? Radburn?"

Roberta elbowed Bob.

He grinned shyly. "Hey, he knows stuff. He worked through it and showed me I was wrong."

"He wasn't a complete horse's ass about it?"

"Oh, he was his normal assy self."

"But you actually worked with him?" Roberta squinted.

"Yeah, I know, hard to believe. In fact we're working together on something else." Bob raised his hands. "Don't even ask. No details, no expectations of glory. It'll take a while."

Joe shook his head. "I can't grasp the concept. You're working with Mel. You must trust him."

"I do." Bob grinned. "It just goes to show."

"Oh, oh," Lexan said. "That's his feeling better face."

"Yup, you guys picked me up, so it's time for a joke."

"Now we're going to be depressed," Joe said.

"I don't think so. This joke is based in truth." He gathered his audience. "I was saying that Mel is not all bad, OK? I believe no one is all bad, not Kimmy or any of the other crooks around here."

Roberta nudged Lexan. "Is this supposed to be funny?"

"No, I mean no one is 100% bad." Bob chuckled. "Even a pedophile slows down in a school zone, right?"

The three friends stared at him, trying not to laugh. Grins became smiles, smiles became chuckles and laughter broke free.

Bob raised his arms in triumph. "My work here is done."

Roberta pulled his arm and said to the others, "Time for us to leave."

"Thanks for coming." Joe waved and Lexan followed them out. He settled back into the bed. Bob can't disappoint me, he thought. He's my friend. I can't stand to see him down, but that was one terrible joke.

When Lexan returned, Joe was snoring softly. She adjusted the pillow so he could lie flat. Well, she thought, at least Bob got to confess today. That gives me more time to worry about it.

Pamela Holmgren examined the ceiling of room 472 in the Stradford Marriott and decided the stain looked a little like the face of a clown. She had to focus with the bed thumping up and down and Mangione's greasy head in the way. She didn't have those problems when she lay in the grass and looked up at the clouds.

"Oh, baby, oh baby," the Chief of Police moaned.

She dragged her nails across his back and he pumped faster. No, it wasn't a clown, more like a duck. With an enormous beak. He thrust himself deeper inside and she nearly lost herself.

"Oh, baby, oh baby, oh." Mangione's beak was enormous, too, just not his vocabulary.

She slowed him down so he'd remember this longer. Dear Kimmy had told her that. Control lay in the timing, not the grunting, sweating and pounding. "That's it Garrett, yes. Like that," she cooed into his ear.

He was speeding up again. It had been hard to get him to understand that Stanic wasn't talking about the weather, but the need to remove Kimberly. She explained that this would earn them favor with Stanic, and clear the path for them to take control of Stradford. When the light finally came to his eyes, he took ownership of the plan.

She increased the pressure on his back.

As if the whole thing were his idea, not hers.

She dug her nails deeper into him.

As if she hadn't foreseen how this would play out months ago.

He arched his back.

As if he were in control.

He wasn't. He came, and she released a shuddering gasp.

"Oh, baby."

She held him as if she loved him.

He collapsed on her, spent.

As if he were neither the clown nor the duck.

CHAPTER FORTY-FIVE

"We're fucked."

Detective Kramer flinched at Agent Canfield's choice of words. Not that he was a prude, he'd heard and used worse, much worse. It irritated him coming from the younger man in the confines of his own office, and it irritated him because it was true.

"Sorry, but it's like your office. We're close to the black and white, but all I see is gray."

Kramer rubbed the heels of his hands into his eyes. They'd been at it for days and couldn't see how they could corroborate Lexan Warner's claim that Mayor Hellauer was running the drug operation in Stradford. "I have no idea what gray and those colors mean."

"It means we're close enough--"

Kramer raised his hand. "I don't care what it means

either." He released an exasperated breath. "How much more time can you get away with?"

The BCI had transferred Canfield to an operation in the Mahoning Valley. He'd been helping Kramer by using sick time and calling in favors. "Gotta get back soon. Tonight at the latest."

Kramer tapped his desk blotter with the sunglasses Warner had left, and noticed the gray walls, the gray desk, the gray cabinets and chair in his office. "You got a problem with gray?"

"All fifty shades." Canfield grinned, but saw the confusion in Kramer's eyes. "No, what I meant was, hey, those glasses. Let me see."

The Detective tossed them onto the blotter with a shrug. The kid had energy, but needed direction. Their case was indeed fucked.

"Wait, look at this!" Canfield was jabbing the sunglasses at him. "Here, right here. The temple piece. I thought it was too thick!"

Kramer had thought the glasses gaudy and heavy. Black plastic with rhinestones and pointy corners. Girly glasses. "What?"

"Here, where there should be a sparkly stone, like on the other side, see?" Canfield jammed the glasses into his hand. "Here, on the right side, there's a hole, the left side has a stone."

"There's a bunch of sparkly shit on both sides."

"Look at the pattern. There's one missing on the right side."

"Probably fell out. So what?" First colors, now symmetry. Kramer needed to get some sleep.

Canfield shone the light from his cell phone into the hole. "Look at this!"

"Get on with it," Kramer said, then flinched again at the cracking sound. "Why did--?"

"Just as I thought!" Canfield cracked open the temple like a crab leg. "A camera!"

"Warner recorded her conversation with the Mayor?"

"Bet she did."

"Then we got her." Kramer felt a surge of energy and raised his eyes to the BCI agent. "How do we get the video off that? We have nothing here."

"My guys can do that." Canfield reached for the glasses. "We don't need a warrant if it's abandoned property."

"We know whose it is. It's Lexan Warner's."

"Then?"

Kramer dropped his voice. "It's proof of what she was telling me. She raced out of here before she could show me."

He slid the pieces and the camera into a brown paper envelope, and handed it to Canfield. "Get to your tech guys with this. I'll keep tabs on the Mayor."

Canfield paused at the door. "Maybe we're not fucked."

Kimberly Horvath's blood ran cold as her cell phone continued to beep. Busy, like the other four times she had called the Governor's private number. She jammed her tongue into the back of her teeth to keep from crying.

"We're not lying to you, Kim." Pamela Holmgren congratulated herself on the compassion she lathered onto her words to keep the glee out of her voice.

"I didn't say you were." Someone must have talked. Hector?

On the sofa beside her Garrett Mangione feigned sympathy. "We think it for the best. Your best."

Kimberly couldn't decide which one of them she hated most. "My best."

"This way everybody wins, honey."

"You want me to kill people." She was so distraught she didn't notice 'honey'.

Mangione's patient façade cracked. "Listen, we've been over this and over this." Pamela laid a hand on his arm. "You're toxic. Stanic is done with you. He will have you killed." He jerked his arm free.

Kimberly's eyes darted to the phone. "I want to hear it from his own voice."

"He won't pick up because he doesn't want to talk to you." Mangione fell back into the sofa. "That's it, I'm done."

"Better they die, than you, is all we're saying." Pamela's patience was wearing thin as well. This plan was their entre into Stanic's good graces. She took Mangione's hand in hers.

"What's the guarantee?"

"Garrett will make it look like an accident." Pamela squeezed his hand as he huffed. "Won't you." The man nodded.

"Like you covered up Oskar's death?"

Mangione's eyes flashed at her, but he held his

tongue. "With time to plan, we can do a better job," Pamela said.

Kimberly looked from her cell to the Chief of Police. "You're telling me to kill the teachers."

Pamela put her hand on his chest. "We're telling you to facilitate their accidental deaths."

"I've never killed anyone."

"You've had people killed!" Mangione broke free from Pamela and strode to the window.

"One is nearly dead anyway," Pamela said, "and you hate the other one. You can do it."

Kimberly took a breath. Hector is too smart to get his gang involved. Who else had she talked to? It hit her with a flash. Lexan Warner. She drank too much and ran her mouth. The bitch had ratted her out. Kimberly released the breath.

"You have to do it, or you'll be dead." Mangione spoke with his back to them. "Accidentally, but dead just the same."

The secure phone buzzed again. Governor Stanic glanced at it but didn't pick up. Lance sniffed. He'd never liked the Horvath woman. Never trusted her. Too bold, too opinionated. Cheap. His mother would have called her brassy.

Lance nodded and dropped two spherical ice cubes into the tumbler. The Governor was almost finished going over the sales figures from one of the testing companies and would be ready for a drink. He poured three inches of the amber liquid over the cubes and swirled the glass.

Stanic reached for the scotch without looking up, finished the last page, closed the folder and said. "Thanks, I needed that." He drained off some of the drink and waved Lance to sit down.

"Get yourself something, Lance."

"No, sir, I have to keep my head tonight."

"How so?"

Lance put on his concerned expression. The Gov liked his underlings to be thoughtful. "I'm not 100% sold on Chief Mangione's plan."

"It's a good plan, son, don't worry." He grinned. "Besides, isn't it Mrs. Holmgren's plan?"

Lance shook his head. "Are we really getting into bed with another power-hungry woman in Stradford?"

"Haven't got to that part yet. Might be fun though." Stanic took another sip.

"I'm not kidding, sir, I am not."

Stanic heard the change in voice. "What's bothering you?"

Lance worked the joints of the fingers on his right hand. "I'm not re-hashing your prowess with women, or the difference in controlling men over women. We've been all over that. Bottom line, you're the governor."

"It's my call."

"Exactly." Lance screwed his face into his near-tears expression and gulped a breath. "The plan itself, whoever's name is on it, is a little thin."

"Go on." Stanic set down the heavy tumbler.

"As big a bitch as Ms. Mayor is, sir, has she ever actually taken a life?"

"Now that you mention it." He sipped some Glen

Fiddich. "I don't believe so."

"Think she can do it? Think she will do it when the time comes?"

"I don't know. She hates the two of them. I know that."

"Not enough, Governor. If she botches it, there's no way to save her." Lance let his voice fade off. "More importantly, it will surely lead back to us."

Stanic finished his drink. "What's your idea?"

Lance handed him the secure phone. "We need back-up, that's all. If she kills them, great. If she doesn't or can't, we're covered."

"I'll tell the Ready Team to keep her in sight."

"They provided her with the drugs, right?"

Stanic nodded. "They can help with the cover-up, if Mangione screws the pooch."

"Exactly, I hadn't thought of that, boss. A second back-up." Lance had thought of it; he didn't trust Mangione all that much either.

"See, I'm learning, Lance." He handed the kid his glass. "Get yourself one, too. You've earned it."

Lance fixed the drinks at the credenza, then turned to Stanic. "One other benefit of having your Ready Team on hand."

The Governor looked up. "What's that?"

"If things go completely off the rails, the Mayor could have an accident, too."

Governor Stanic nodded. "She could."

Detective Kramer chewed what was left of his thumbnail and tried not to think about how gray his office really was. It was gray before it was his office and gray the six years his name was on the door. Not until Canfield's comment had he noticed it.

Was his life gray as well? Was his life endless wheel-spinning, energy expending, no forward motion? He switched thumbs. Where the hell was Canfield with the video download?

He'd called an hour ago on his way to the police station. They planned on arresting the Mayor in her office and save her the embarrassment, although neither officer cared about that. But in the meantime, Kramer had checked, and Kimberly wasn't there. Her secretary was vague about where she actually was. He assumed her office at Cookies' Cookies.

Kramer spit the nail fragment at the wastebasket. The BCI had the technical ability to get the evidence in, he checked the time, a little under 24 hours. SPD surely didn't, but still, if Canfield never showed up with it, what good would it do? Another good idea stuck in a quagmire of gray.

What the fuck is the matter with you, he yelled at himself. Quagmire of gray? He ran a file across his jagged nail and strode from his office. Maybe walking would clear his mind. A car squealed to a stop in the parking lot. Canfield jumped out and waved an envelope above the roof for him to see.

Kramer jerked the door open and got in. "The right stuff?"

"Just like we thought." Canfield jammed the video transcript into the console between them.

"Good work." Kramer gestured toward the exit.

"No bells and whistles." Two minutes later they were standing in the anteroom of the Office of the President of Cookies' Cookies.

Kimberly's secretary gestured to the ornate spinning clock on her desk. "It's after hours, Gentlemen. Mrs. Horvath is gone for the day."

"We have important paperwork for her to sign. Do you mind if we take a look?"

The secretary's hand flew to her mouth. "Is something wrong, Detective Kramer?"

Both men gave her the dead-eye. She looked from one to the other and leapt to her feet. "Right this way, her office is--"

They brushed past her and opened the door. Empty. Kramer turned to Canfield. "I should have had her tailed."

"Yeah, maybe. Who could you trust?"

Kramer grimaced. "The place is a sieve."

"Where do we look for her? That crappy bar up the hill?"

"Not there." Kramer started for the door. "Where's the worst place she could be?"

CHAPTER FORTY-SIX

L exan Warner swirled the Pinot Grigio around her glass and checked the time on her cell. Joe was due for the next round of meds and she would have to wake him soon. Her hand shook as she returned the glass to the bedside table. She told herself he was well enough to leave.

As usual, everything around her was turning to shit, and everybody she cared for was being hurt. In junior high it had been a joke. In senior high it gave her a measure of control. In college it had been her escape mechanism. The closer she got to other people, the more she screwed up their lives. Her hands unconsciously rubbed the scars on her arms. The more hurt she caused.

Joe was sleeping peacefully, his breath strong and regular. No machines, no beeping. He's through the hard part, she thought. He'll be better off without me.

"Penny for your thoughts."

She quickly dabbed wine from her lips. "You're awake."

"Maybe half-awake." Joe adjusted the pillows and sat up. "I like to keep my eyes on you when you think you're alone."

She arranged the pill bottles on the tray so the labels all faced the same way. "Reading my thoughts, are you?"

"No, mostly wallowing."

She looked up abruptly. "Wallowing?"

"OK, floating. Floating down the stream of your beauty."

She jammed a handful of blond curls behind her ear, hiding her blush with her hand. "Stop it."

"And thinking," Joe said.

She looked up from the pill containers. "That could be dangerous."

"I don't try it very often." He grinned. "I'm stuck in bed with nothing to do, so I thought I'd give it a try."

She twisted the cap off a fresh bottle of water. "What have you been thinking about?"

"Us."

The water bottle froze halfway to him. He knew she was going to leave.

"Lex, you OK?"

"What? Sure, I'm fine." She should have left when he was asleep. Now he was going to grill her. She gave him the water bottle, then the pills.

He took a second swallow to clear his throat. His head swam. "I'm sorry, Lexan. I've hurt you and I'm sorry."

That's not what she expected him to say. She reached for the wine glass. It was empty.

When she met his eyes, he said, "I've been totally self-centered. I don't know how you put up with me."

"Joe, no --"

"Please, this has been rolling around inside my head for a long time." He gestured toward the wine bottle. "I don't suppose I could--"

"No way, not with those pills."

His arm dropped to the bed. "I'm gonna use my second chance and just blurt this out, Lex. I was never home with you. I was obsessed with power. Never had any before, but that doesn't matter. I actually believed I was the avenging angel. Looking out for everybody else, but shit. You, the one person I really care for, you I ignored."

The pain in his head made it hard to focus. "We agreed to give this a try, and I didn't even give you my full attention."

"Joe, it's not you."

He waved his hand. "Yes, it is me. I don't deserve you." He stopped at the distress on her face.

She waved her hand and looked down. "It's OK."

"Maybe, but I came on too strong about marriage. You weren't ready, hell, I don't know that I am. But I asked you anyway. I didn't take the time to talk to you about it." He sighed. "I pressured you."

Lexan fought not to cry.

"That's why you packed your bags."

Her eyes flashed to his. "I didn't think you knew that."

"You didn't hide them very well."

She spoke softly. "I was on my way out, when the call came from the hospital."

"One way to get a girl's attention." Joe's weak smile dissolved into a grimace.

She twirled the empty wine glass in her hand. "It's not all you, Joe."

He stared at the ceiling for a second. "Seems like we both have something to say."

She swiped at her eyes and tried to smile.

"I know it's hard for you to talk about yourself."

She nodded.

"It is for me, too."

She looked up, her eyes brimming.

"I talk a lot, so people think it's easy for me." He shook his head. "What I'm really doing is hiding behind the words. So I don't have to talk about what I really feel."

"Joe, I--"

"You have the same problem, I think, but instead of talking, you stuff it all in a bag and close it tight."

Her eyes darted to her luggage in the corner.

"I feel guilty."

Her eyes returned to his.

"I should have shot Weigel. I didn't save you."

Lexan slid onto the bed and put her arms around his neck. "Joe, it's my fault you've been hurt."

"You didn't shoot me."

She buried her face in his neck "You think I'm perfect, but I'm not."

"I hurt you." He stroked her back. "You'd never hurt me."

Lexan started to speak, but Joe kissed her.

She pulled back. "No, it's my turn."

"You don't need to say a word."

"I do. I need to tell you the truth."

Please, he thought.

"Joe, I--"

"How sweet. How disgustingly sweet." Kimberly Hellauer Horvath levelled a pistol at them from the doorway. "It's my fault, no it's my fault. No, it's my fault. I may vomit." She stepped toward the bed and pointed the barrel at Joe's face.

"No!" Lexan tried to stand up, but Joe pulled himself in front of her.

Kimberly's eyes burned dark and bright as she swept the gun from him to her. "Stay where you are, Barbie Doll."

Joe wrapped himself around Lexan and whispered into her ear. "She's high."

"Yes, I am. I'm high as the sky." She lifted both hands over her head and danced on her toes. She stopped suddenly and extended the pistol. "But I can't possibly miss from here. Yee-ha!"

Joe inched his legs to the edge of the bed. His head ached alarmingly, his vision blurry. "I hate to ask a stupid question, Mayor Horvath, but why are you here?"

A smile began to fill her face but disappeared like a garage door descending. "An incredibly stupid question. For a teacher." She started to use her fingers to enumerate her reasons, but remembered the pistol in her hand. "Well, let's see. You've been blackmailing me, your little honey ratted me out." She pursed her lips. "And I hate you both."

Joe stretched higher against the headboard and dropped his right leg over the edge of the bed. "Get ready," he whispered.

"Shut up, I'm talking here!"

"Now you're going to give one of those evil madman speeches to justify what you've done?" He squeezed Lexan's shoulder. She elbowed him back.

Kimberly's face narrowed. "You two had no reason to get up into my business. All I was doing was trying to live the American--"

"You're a greedy bitch, Kimmy." Joe threw a pillow at her and dropped both feet onto the floor. Lexan rolled across the bed the other way.

Kimberly hopped backward and aimed at Lexan. Joe took a lunging step to get his balance. Kimberly stumbled but fired the pistol. She shoved Joe in the chest and he crumpled back onto the bed.

When Joe could focus his eyes, Lexan lay face down on the carpet and Kimberly was taking a second gun from her vest. Why didn't the shot explode like Weigel's? Why did she have two guns? He tried to rub the pain out of his head.

"Awake?" Kimberly jammed the bolt closed and gestured to the floor with the second pistol. "She's not. I filled her full of Valium."

"If she's hurt--"

She stared at him over the barrel. "You'll what, hurt me? You can't even stand up."

Joe forced himself to laugh. "Tell me something to cheer me up. Like you being the victim."

"I got a good one for you." Nothing on her face smiled. "She ran out on you again. Look, her luggage is at the door. How does that make you feel?"

Joe twitched involuntarily. How had she known? "No, she's just catching a quick nap."

Kimberly thought for a second. She held the gun on him and kicked Lexan's arm. It didn't move. "Nice try."

Joe tried to keep the panic off his expression. "How much time do I have?"

"None." She squared herself in front of him.

The fog in his head cleared a little. It wasn't a gun with a bullet. The point of a dart peered at him from the barrel. "Come on, tell me the rest of the story. You know you want to."

"You're stalling."

"Of course I am." Joe spread open his hands and leaned back on the pillows. "I give up, you have the gun. Just answer one thing for me. One last request."

Kimberly loved the defeated look on his face. She kicked Lexan's body again and stepped closer to the bed. Lexan murmured something.

"What the hell. Why not?"

"Why aren't you using a real gun?"

Kimberly's eyes wavered to the gun, then back to his face. "I don't want to kill you, I want to humiliate you."

"With a CO2 pistol and a tranquilizer dart? Come on."

"You are so arrogant. Think you know everything. If I kill you, you're dead.'

"Duh."

"I'm counting the seconds, Lehrer." She wiped the sweat from her forehead. "If I kill you, you're dead once. But if I ruin your life, I'll kill you every day you spend in jail."

He shivered as if someone stepped on his grave. "What did you put in the dart?"

"Besides the Diazepam? Nothing. But these." She pulled a handful of red-fletched darts from her vest pocket. "These have a little heroin for you. The sleepy stuff will fade out, the opioid won't, and *voila*, you'll be another victim of the drug crisis, Mr. Lehrer. You and your girlfriend." Kimberly's face brightened. "Wait, more than a victim. We'll spin it that you were selling drugs to those precious children we entrusted to your care. You are totally screwed."

"You must have learned that from your drug buddies." He shook his head. "No way you figured that out all by yourself."

"That's it, ladies and gentlemen," Kimberly announced. "Mr. Joe Lehrer's last smart-ass remark." She trained the pistol on his nose.

Lexan jabbed her foot into the back of Kimberly's knee.

The dart slammed into the headboard.

Joe scrambled off the bed.

Lexan yanked at Kimberly's arm.

Kimberly swung her elbow at Lexan's head.

Joe dove into Kimberly.

Lexan fought for the mayor's gun hand.

Joe planted his fist squarely in Kimberly's face.

Her head smacked the floor. Her eyes fluttered,

she lay still.

Lexan drew back to hit her.

Joe grabbed her arm. "She's not worth it."

Lexan's eyes flashed at him, then widened as she drooped to the floor.

Joe pulled the dart from her leg.

Lexan rubbed the spot and slowly raised herself to all-fours. "We. Got. Her." She spoke as if asleep.

Joe held her face. "I thought you were out of it."

"I didn't want to miss the fight." She let out a breath and smiled.

On the second-floor landing, the bald man screwed a suppressor onto his pistol and muttered, "She can't do anything right."

"She can talk." He looked to the RT leader.

"It's like we're making this up as we go along. I hate it."

His partner re-fastened the Velcro on his vest. "We're not using dart guns?"

"We can't because she didn't want the pistol we had for her. Now we have to kill all three of them and stage it like a shoot-out."

The other man nodded. "What about the drugs in the girl's system?"

"Just a barbiturate. That's what the local LEOs are for."

At his hand signal, the two men silently crept up the rest of the stairs to the bedroom door.

"I'll call the police." Joe panted the words. "Get

that crap pumped out of you." He levered himself to his feet using the corner of the bed. He wobbled, balanced himself, and tried to rub the pain from his head.

Joe's cell phone lay on the night stand. He carefully stepped over Kimberly's outstretched legs. He barely managed to shield his face as he struck the floor.

Kimberly kicked him again. Pain raced from Joe's head to his kidney. He curled up. "Thought I was dead?" She stomped on his hand. "I'm not."

Outside the bedroom, the bald man halted his partner. "What the fuck's she doing now?" They backed down the hallway into another bedroom. The bald man keyed the encrypted app.

Joe didn't know what part of his body hurt the most. Kimberly stood above him in a haze.

"Miss Barbie appears to be out of it. But she pretended to be asleep before. I better check." She lashed her foot into Lexan's stomach and nodded. "That'll do, donkey." She laughed shrilly.

Both sides of Joe's head hurt. Lexan lay in a crumpled ball; he didn't know if she was alive. The Archangel had regulated Joe's rage since Weigel had hurt her. Now he stepped aside. Joe took a breath and owned it.

Kimberly's dart gun hung open and she was trying to organize her fingers to reload it. "Damn it!" Kimberly ran off a string of unintelligible words. She yanked a dart out of the breech and threw it at Joe. "Shitshitshit!" She pulled another red-tipped dart from her vest.

"I'm sure your drug supplier has a help-line. Maybe you could--" She kicked her foot at his crotch. He rolled aside and took the blow on his hip. Another dart fell to the floor.

"Why didn't they just give me a gun?" She yelled the words in a high-pitched screech. "You just point and shoot! You don't have to load!"

"Got darts? I'm sure they deliver."

Joe fended off the spinning dart gun but fell back as Kimberly launched herself onto him.

"Get off him!" Somehow Lexan had thrown Kimberly aside. As he crabbed toward her, his hand found one of the heroin laced darts.

"She's, trying, to, kill, us." Lexan's words were still blurry, her eyes too bright.

"You OK?"

She nodded, rubbing her side where Kimberly had kicked her.

They struggled to their knees. Kimberly bounced from foot to foot, waving the marble bookend she had snatched from the dresser. "Who goes first? Who's the hero, huh, which one of you?"

"Shut up Kimberly." He didn't know how he managed to speak clearly. "Drop that and we'll all be--"

"Aagghh!" She stepped toward him but whirled and swung the bookend at Lexan. Blood spattered as she took it flush in the face and dropped.

Joe reached as high as he could from his knees and aimed the dart at her neck, but she twisted and it landed in her shoulder. Maybe the narcotic would slow her down.

It didn't. Jerked as if by an electric shot, Kimberly shoved him back down and raised the marble piece over her head again.

Lexan lay awkwardly on her side. Blood pooled around her face.

"Fuckyoufuckyoufuckyou!"

"The amphetamine was a bad idea?" His voice rasping and his head splitting, Joe reached to ward off the bookend.

The barb dangled from Kimberly's back. Spittle dripped from her mouth. Hatred gleamed in her eyes. Kimberly drove the bookend down into his head where Oscar's bullet had struck. Joe dropped to the floor, motionless.

Watching from the bedroom doorway, the bald man said, "That's it, we're out." The black-clad RT holstered their weapons and disappeared down the stairs into the darkness behind the house.

Joe woke to pain unlike anything he had ever experienced. His first thought was Lexan. He couldn't turn his head, but managed to open an eye in the direction she lay.

An undulating police siren split the air. He tried to focus. She wasn't there. His vision tilted and swam as he rolled his head the other way. Kimberly's head was a mere two feet away. It hurt when he drew a breath.

The Mayor's mouth was open in a scream, her gums exposing her teeth, her tongue lolling uselessly. A red-fletched dart protruded from her eye. The only sound was a police car sliding to a stop in the driveway.

Joe wrenched his head farther. Lexan's luggage was gone, too.

CHAPTER FORTY-SEVEN

gent Canfield spun the SUV around the corner and slid it into the driveway of Joe's house. He flipped off the siren, left the reds and blues on, and yanked the door open. Detective Kramer grabbed his arm. "Go around back."

The BCI agent drew his weapon and crept past the garage toward the backyard. Kramer waited several seconds. It was 1:30 and lights were on downstairs. He hoped the siren and lights hadn't awakened gawkers, but could feel eyes on his back as he stepped onto the front porch. He didn't like how it looked inside.

Canfield felt something, too, as he rounded the corner of the garage. He kept in the shadows and scanned the backyard. The wind or something else rustled the bushes on the lot line in back. He waited; nothing else. He crossed the patio and up the wooden steps. The lights in the room beyond were on, the sliding glass door open. He thumbed off the safety.

Kramer looked through the narrow window next to the front door. The hall was dark, the room beyond it lit. He held the knob and shouldered the door. Surprisingly it opened and he stumbled in. The hairs on his arms pricked awake. He levelled his weapon.

Blinking green dots from the computer and Wi-Fi were the only lights in Lehrer's office. Canfield crept past them into the family room. A floorboard creaked, and he saw Kramer approaching in the hallway. They nodded, cleared the rest of the ground floor, and crept up the stairs.

In the master bedroom Joe Lehrer crouched on his knees peering underneath the bed. In front of the low dresser lay a body, a woman, the face covered in blood. Kramer pulled out his cell and the two men holstered their weapons.

"Mr. Lehrer, Joe, can you hear me?"

Joe looked dumbly at the young officer. "I can't find her."

Canfield noticed the blood streaming from the man's forehead. His clothes were ripped, his arms and chest scraped. "Who is missing, sir?"

"Her luggage is gone. It was there, right there."

Canfield extended his hand and helped Joe to stand. When he tried to take a step, the younger man kept him from pitching forward. "Hold on, there. Who are you looking for?"

Joe's face spun to his and he snapped, "Lex, Lexan Warner. She's gone."

From his knees Kramer probed for the pulse in Kimberly's arm. He shook his head at the BCI agent.

Canfield led Joe to the edge of the bed. "Are you wounded?"

Joe shook his head. "It's her blood."

"Whose? The Mayor's?"

Kramer pulled Kimberly's arm away from her face. Canfield swallowed a scream. "There's something jammed in her eye!"

Sirens whooped. The front door banged open. Footsteps pounded up the stairs. "One dead." Kramer stood up and worried the knuckles of his right hand. "One needs transport."

"No one's going anywhere." Garrett Mangione's voice roared in the hall. He burst past an EMT into the bedroom. "Leave everything where it is until I tell you otherwise."

The Chief of Police scanned the room as he walked directly to the policeman. "Detective Kramer, you know better than to disturb evidence in a crime scene."

Canfield slid to Kramer's side. An EMT knelt peering at the mayor's face. "I know the rules, Chief." Kramer tried to keep his tone respectful. "Not moving any evidence."

"Nothing without my direct approval. *Capisce?*"

Kramer ignored Canfield's elbow nudge. "Yes. Sir."

Mangione jutted his face closer. "That includes questioning the suspects, Lieutenant."

▪▪▪

Governor Thompson Stanic grumbled as he rolled over to answer the cellphone. It was the middle of the goddam night. A chill passed through him as he noticed the sound was coming from the secure app. "What is it?"

The words were clear, amazingly so. "Bad news, but good news, Governor."

"What on earth does that mean?" He remembered too late to keep his voice down. His wife rolled toward him.

"Mayor Horvath is dead, sir. That's the bad news."

Stanic did the math in his head. Obedient sex, minus. No one to testify against him, plus. "That saddens me."

"Yes sir." The bald man shook his head at his partner. "You have my condolences."

"Did you follow the rest of the plan?"

The bald man paused. "Of course. The other two are alive."

"They'll pay for killing her."

"When we find them."

"What does that mean?"

"Lehrer's still here, banged up pretty good. The broad flew."

Stanic grimaced. "Not really our problem."

"Yes sir. We made sure Mangione will be at the scene. His detective didn't call him, only an ambulance."

"Thank you for your good work." Stanic clicked off.

"Anything the matter?" Stanic's wife asked.

The governor rolled toward her. "Nothing I can't handle."

Several hours later Joe's house was empty and dark. Blood stains, forensic markers and an outline of the mayor's body littered the bedroom carpet. Crime scene techs had set up light stands and taken videos and stills of the room and its contents from every conceivable angle. Trace evidence had been collected and secured in plastic bags. The darts Kimberly had dropped had been found. The dart guns and the bookend had been dusted and tagged. A patrolman sat in his cruiser outside.

Joe sat in a holding cell in the Stradford jail. Lexan was gone. Kimberly's body lay on a table in the basement of the police station. Mangione, Kramer and Canfield sat in the conference room upstairs.

"They killed the Mayor, that's obvious. We have to charge them." Mangione looked across the table expecting a fight.

"Until we match the blood, we don't even know how many people were there."

"Warner was there. That's what Lehrer said." Mangione frowned. "Anything else?"

"Maybe they had cause."

Mangione ignored Canfield and kept glaring at Kramer. "Two against one. They overpowered her. Her blood is all over Lehrer."

"A near invalid and that little teacher overpowered a woman with a dart gun? Two dart guns?" Kramer stared back at the chief.

"The book end only had one set of prints," Canfield added. "The Mayor's."

"They killed her. She didn't kill them." Mangione

shook his head. "I thought you were better than this, Detective."

Kramer kept his eyes locked on Mangione's. Canfield reached the envelope from his pocket and slid it across the table. "You should read this."

Mangione stared at Kramer several seconds before looking down. His eyebrows furrowed as he noticed the writing on the outside. "What's this?"

"Open it, sir."

Kramer and Canfield watched the color drain from Mangione's face as he read the transcript from the video of Kimberly Hellauer Horvath, then return above a forced and broad smile. "Come on, fellas, a camera in her sunglasses? What is she, Inspector Gadget?"

Neither man on the other side of the table smiled. "The video corroborates Ms. Warner's oral testimony."

"The testimony you told us to sit on. Sir."

"The Warner broad is a known crazy. She attacked the Mayor. The school suspended her." He stopped as if he were hearing his own words.

"Ms. Warner has video of Mayor Horvath admitting to making money from the prostitution ring." Kramer kept focus on his boss. "She admitted cooperating with a drug gang."

Canfield leaned forward. "After telling the world there were no drug gangs in Stradford."

Mangione looked away to hide his grin. This couldn't have come out better. Radburn's discovery that Kimberly and Stanic were skimming would have stunk the whole place up. Now he could shift the blame to Columbus and let the governor deal with it. Kim's death left a nice convenient hole which he was glad to fill. He set his face and turned back to the police lieutenant.

"She admitted orchestrating Oskar's death and Karl's." Canfield stared, but again Mangione wouldn't look at him.

"What do you want me to do?"

"You can start by not charging the teachers with murder."

"We don't know where Warner is."

"Lehrer at least. We'll know more when we find Warner."

"But they killed the Mayor!"

"Could be she was trying to kill them. She brought the weapons."

Mangione smiled to himself. "I expected more from you, Buddy."

"It's not about me, Chief." The Lieutenant looked at his hands. "Do you want all this other stuff to come out in court?"

When he didn't answer, Canfield tried another tack. "She hired you to clean this place up, didn't she?"

Mangione turned to the BCI man, his mind calmly re-assembling the pieces. It was too late to save Kim's life, and Warner's video took care of the Mayor's reputation. Time to cut bait. "Opportunity." The words escaped his lips before he could stop them.

"Pardon me?"

The Chief shook his head and forced a grim smile to his lips. A fresh start with him and Pamela on top. "It's an opportunity to finally rid Stradford of the drug trade," he said.

Kramer looked at him blankly.

"You're going to admit the Russians were selling in Stradford?"

"Exactly that, Agent Canfield. It's the perfect time. We took care of the Hill gang, then quickly removed the Russians. Yes, indeed, the Mayor hired me to clean this place up."

"But we took both the gangs out at the same time."

Canfield looked at Kramer. "He never announced it. All he mentioned was the Hill gang."

"You two go ahead with the evidence against the mayor." Mangione drummed his desk with a ball point. "Drop the charges against Warner and Lehrer."

Canfield opened his mouth, but stopped when Kramer grabbed his arm.

"Yeah, that'll work. Small potatoes."

"Sir?"

Mangione dropped his gaze to them. "I'll give the citizens of Stradford what they want. Two things: a bad guy, Mayor Horvath, and another drug cartel out of business." Mangione grabbed some papers from his desk and stood up. "It's what they hired me for."

Kramer turned to Canfield. "That's what he's doing? Really?"

The BCI agent nodded. "It is why they hired him."

Mangione's satisfied smile followed them out the door.

CHAPTER FORTY-EIGHT

Joe sat in his car in the driveway looking at his house. A strand of crime scene tape lay on the bushes next to the door. No lights were on, but he knew what lay in the darkness inside.

Memories. Life and death memories. Hope and loss memories. Cathy. Weigel. Lexan. Kimberly. For each positive, a negative. For each good, a corresponding evil. A good he had turned evil. A hope he had turned into a loss.

He turned the key and stepped into the dark hallway. He stood in the spot where Weigel had died and turned on the light. He glanced up the stairs toward the bedroom where Lexan had killed Kimberly. The last place he had seen Lexan.

He continued down the hallway to the family

room. What would have been the family room if Cathy and the baby in her womb had lived. He dropped down onto the easy chair and turned on the lamp. Across from him was the sofa where he had been shot and Oskar had been killed. The police had returned the pistol to him. It lay on the coffee table in an evidence box.

Wind brushed a tree branch against the window over the deck. He glanced across the darkened room. Nobody out there. He was alone.

He was toxic. He was involved with all these deaths, all this loss. He touched the new wound on his forehead; he deserved the pain. He laughed darkly at the useless weapon. He hadn't pulled the trigger either to kill or to protect.

Told himself he was the Avenging Angel, the hero, the good guy, but no. He didn't kill Weigel to protect Lexan, and he didn't protect her from Kimberly. Chelsea killed for him, Lexan killed for him. Instead of him. They did the killing, he did the talking. He didn't even protect himself.

The doorbell rang. His head jerked up, his eyes danced furiously. A longer, more persistent ring. Again as his hand reached the door. Mel Radburn filled the opening. "Let me in."

This day just cannot get any better, Joe thought.

Radburn pushed past him into the house.

"Sure, what's one more home invasion?" Joe followed him down the hall.

As the fat man lowered himself to the sofa, his eyes swept the room. "You fucking coward. Now you're quitting?"

"What?"

"We finally make some headway in this burg and instead of celebrating, you're having a one-man pity party."

"I don't let my friends talk to me that way, Carmelo, sure as hell not you. Get the fuck out of my house."

Radburn gestured at the gun. "Should I be scared?"

"You think I'd kill you?"

The fat around his stomach rippled. "It crossed my mind."

"Go away." Joe waved his hand dismissively.

"Listen."

"To what?"

Radburn's eyebrows arched over the dark rims of his glasses. "To yourself. Listen to yourself."

Joe dropped his hands to his knees. "Just leave me the hell alone."

"I will if you promise not to kill yourself."

"What difference would it make to you?" His voice faded and his shoulders slumped. "You're not my friend. We can't stand each other."

"It's not my job to be your friend." He looked around the dim room. "I don't see any of them around."

"God damn you."

"You got that right."

Joe stood up.

"Sorry to offend. Just listen."

"You've got nothing I want to hear!"

Radburn sighed. "Listen, Joe, the world is better off

without Kimberly. Without Weigel. It doesn't matter who pulled the trigger. They were evil, now they're gone."

Joe sat back down. "I have no idea what you're talking about."

"I'd say let's have a drink and chat, but the way you've been hitting the bottle the last couple days, that's probably not a good plan."

"I have a very short list of people I truly hate, but you're on it."

"That's more like it."

Joe looked at him coldly. "Five minutes."

"Fair enough." Radburn narrowed his piggy eyes. "Don't quit."

"What?" Joe grimaced.

"Don't quit teaching and don't kill yourself."

"Why the hell would you care?"

"We need you."

"You need someone to bully, that's what you need. Find somebody else."

"I'm not getting through to you."

How the hell does Bob trust this jerk? Joe thought.

"I understand how you feel, but you're wrong."

"No, you don't." Joe checked the time.

Radburn let out a breath. "Look, teaching is a hard business. Too many human interactions every day. Too many problems we can't solve, and we try to solve them all anyway. It takes a toll."

"You don't give a flying fuck about human interactions."

"You think I came out of the womb a bully?"

"Yes."

"I really could use a drink." Radburn shrugged his beefy shoulders. "No, this is a learned behavior."

"Right, and you love babies and puppies." Joe waved his hand for him to get on with it.

"First year I taught." The big man's voice came from far away. "Kid in my class. A girl. Freshman, I think. Never smiled. Too many days absent. When she did show up, bruises every place I could see."

Joe wrapped his arms around his chest.

"Knew she was being abused at home. Knew it for sure. Knew it in my heart."

"What did you do?"

"Followed procedure, that's what I did." Radburn's voice sharpened, his eyes flared. "I followed god-damn procedure. To the letter!"

"Like you were supposed to."

Radburn nodded. "Up the ladder, every administrator in the district."

"Took too long."

Radburn stared at him. "She died before we could get her out of that house. She died because the procedure took too long."

Joe looked at the Colt on the table. "Helpless."

Radburn followed his eyes. "I vowed I would never be again. Put in my classroom years, kept my eyes open." He moved his eyes to Joe's face. "And my mouth shut. Eventually got my own building. Made sure that kind of crap doesn't happen anymore."

"How's that working for you?"

"Don't go snarky on me, boy, I came here to help you."

"Hard to believe," Joe said. "But for Bob's sake, let's say I accept your story. How does that jive with the bully shit? Why do you have to be like that?"

"Why do you have to be a quitter?"

"Answer my question."

"I am. You know why you're even in this situation?" Half the former principal's face lay in shadow. "Because you laid it on the line for your kids, your girlfriend, everybody, but you did it all by yourself."

Joe's hand touched the wound on his forehead, then the wound on his temple. "You're a bully because you like it."

"No, I'm not making myself clear." He let out a breath and seemed to shrink. "I do it to distract people, so I can see who they really are. That makes them better."

"You intimidate people so you can help them? That is such bullshit."

He slapped his knee in glee. "See? Nobody would suspect it."

Joe knitted his brow. "You're saying you ran Hoskins out of the building to make him a better teacher? You made him so miserable, he quit. He's not the first you've run off."

"Yeah, I ran him out because I had a good reason; he was hurting kids." He jabbed a meaty finger at Joe. "I'm trying to keep you. Why do you suppose?"

"We can rule out friendship."

Radburn nearly grinned. "Like I said before, Joe, I need you. Stradford needs you."

"You don't need people who fail," he said.

"You know, for as smart a guy as you are, you are

really a dumbass." Radburn shook his mammoth head and glanced at his watch. "You can't end evil. You can't kill Weigel and the Mayor and think everything is all better. That's not how it works."

"But--"

"Shut up. What you can do is keep fighting. Fight for what you know is right. The one thing you can't do is quit."

"So we're fighting and we know we're not going to win. Can't win." Joe shook his head. "That's supposed to make me feel better?"

"Damn it, it's supposed to make you stop feeling sorry for yourself."

"Nice human interaction there, Mel. Well done."

The large man leaned his forearms onto his knees. "OK, I'll give it one last shot, then I'll leave."

"Alle-fucking-luia."

"You, Mr. Lehrer, are either a jerk or a narcissist. You think you can obliterate evil all by yourself. Then you get all boo-hoo-hoo when life doesn't work out the way you imagined it. Get over yourself, you pansy quitter."

Radburn walked down the hall and left Joe in the dark.

Pamela Holmgren stood at the podium in the Stradford City Schools television studio, the same podium used by the Student Council President for reading the morning announcements, bus route changes and the cafeteria menu. She had chosen television to limit the number of reporters, and this venue because it was easier to control. Controlling the oil spill, was the way

Mangione had put it, and she believed him. Get it said, get it over, get on to the next news cycle.

She looked at the one reporter they had allowed, Steffi Sanders of the *Stradford Star.* "You have a question?"

"Yes, ma'am. You are saying that the drug problem in Stradford is now over. Is that correct?"

"Yes, under the excellent leadership of Chief Garrett--"

"Yes, yes, that's in the hand-out. What I'm asking is, isn't this the same message Mayor Horvath delivered last month? What exactly has changed? Was the late Mayor misinformed?"

Chief Mangione pushed past Pamela to the podium. "The drug crisis, especially when referencing opioids, is constant and on-going. New gangs spring up overnight. We have to be vigilant."

"But Mayor Horvath reported that the gang had been eradicated." Sanders looked up from her notebook. "Last month. Now another gang was eradicated this week? How could that happen?"

Mangione leaned onto the podium and unleashed his seductive smile. "As I said, the drug war is constant. Gangs are like mushrooms, popping up all over the place."

The reporter didn't smile. "In a period of one month, the Hill gang is wiped out, the Russian mob moves into Stradford and takes over the drug traffic, and that gang is wiped out? Is that what you're saying?"

"What I'm saying is this." He warmed up his smile and centered his face in the camera. "Good police work from the SPD, help from the BCI and, most importantly, leadership from Mayor Horvath led to the end of the Russian drug cartel known as the Bratva. Now we're safe."

"That's what Mayor Horvath reported last time. Why should we believe you now?"

Mangione wondered if the young woman got her style from watching the fake news on CNN. "The Mayor may not have been entirely clear. There were in fact two gangs. One was terminated in the firefight at Pemberton Tool and Die, the Hill gang, and the other, the Russian Bratva, was captured in yesterday's raid."

Sanders tapped her notepad with her pencil. "Why was the Mayor involved in a police operation?"

Easy question, Mangione thought. "She loved this community and wanted to protect us."

"What exactly did the Mayor do?"

"Mayor Horvath provided the critical evidence that crushed the gang."

Sanders looked up from her notes. "The sunglasses?"

"With the tiny embedded camera." Mangione allowed himself a smile. "Sounds like James Bond stuff, doesn't it?"

"Did the Mayor use the glasses herself?"

"We had verbal testimony against the drug pushers from another source. The video from the sunglasses provided corroboration." Mangione rubbed a hand across his eyes. Keeping the lies, the half lies and the truths in order was tiring.

Sanders scanned the press release. "But she died in a drug raid."

Mangione changed his expression to sad. "The Mayor died as a direct result of her engagement in bringing this ruthless gang of immigrant thugs to a quick and speedy end."

"I can understand her sharing evidence, but why was she--"

Pamela stepped in front of the Chief and handed him a handkerchief. "Mayor Horvath gave her life finding the truth and protecting the good people of Stradford. No more questions for now."

CHAPTER FORTY-NINE

Lexan always ran. She ran when people made her angry. She ran when people got close. She ran when they hurt her. She ran when they loved her. She ran when she couldn't tell the difference.

She ran to protect herself.

Lexan pressed the accelerator and her car sped past the 18-wheeler and leapt down Interstate 71.

She had awakened during the fight in the bedroom with one thought in her mind: helping Joe kill the woman who had hurt so many people. The woman who had profited from child prostitution.

The sound of the bookend striking Joe's head and Kimberly's manic shriek had shocked her awake. She wiped the blood from her eyes and struggled to her feet.

The Mayor was laughing or shouting. Cheering maybe. Lexan yanked Kimberly's neck into the crook of her arm from behind, and jerked her to the ground.

Kimberly flailed her legs.

Lexan increased the pressure on her throat.

Kimberly racked her nails at Lexan's arms and face.

Lexan gasped at the pain and increased the pressure on her throat.

Kimberly jabbed a thumb at her eye.

Lexan twisted away and saw a red-fletched dart on Joe's chest.

He lay motionless; Lexan swallowed a sob.

Kimberly jammed an elbow into her stomach.

Lexan drew the dart toward the Mayor's face.

Kimberly grasped her wrist with both hands.

Lexan shook her neck like a dog with a bone.

Kimberly heaved her hips off the ground.

Lexan inched the drug-laced dart closer to Kimberly's face.

"Please!"

Lexan thought of Joe, and Amber, and Chelsea.

"I. Beg. You," Kimberly croaked.

"No!" Lexan tugged the dart into the killer's eye.

Kimberly's body jolted as if electrocuted.

Lexan plunged the dart as deep as she could.

Kimberly spasmed and fell limp.

Lexan rolled out from under the dead woman and fought her breath under control. She checked Joe's pulse, struggled down the stairs with her bags and drove through the development to the highway. Sirens followed her, red and blue lights flashed off her mirrors, but no one stopped her. She ran south.

* * *

Bob dropped the tailgate and pulled out the 4' x 8' sheet of plywood. He caught it as the weight shifted and wobbled toward the front door. He couldn't believe this was what Joe wanted him to do.

Joe held the front door open. Bob avoided hitting the frame and marring the paint as he managed the unwieldy plywood up the stairs. He set it down against the wall long ways, the end jutting into the master bedroom. He avoided looking at the blood-stained carpet.

"Hey, you're up and moving."

"Barely." Joe extended his knuckles. "Thanks for coming over."

Bob avoided looking at the purple blotches under his friend's eyes. "You sure you want to do this?"

Joe seemed to shrink.

"No, I'm glad to help out, you know that, it's just. Hell, I don't know."

"Creepy."

Bob waited until his friend's eyes returned. "I was going for 'eccentric'. You do a great eccentric professor thing."

Joe didn't smile. "I can't stand to look at it, Bob."

"You, da boss, Boss." Bob turned the board upright and fit it over the bedroom door. "Like this?"

Joe reached past him and held the board. "That's fine."

Bob pounded nails in the top corners then stepped back. "Anything you need inside?"

"Got everything this morning."

"Someplace to sleep? A bed?"

"Lexan was already packed." Joe grunted something else and disappeared down the stairs.

Bob didn't know what to say. He reached into his pocket for more nails.

Bert was running a sponge across the counter around the sink. She turned and hugged Joe. "You must be ready for this to be over."

He nodded. "More than ready."

She squeezed her eyes together like she did when she was concentrating. "You won't have to see it. Won't have to think about it."

The hammering upstairs ceased, and Bob walked past them to the fridge. "You got beer." He pulled out several bottles and followed the others to the dining room.

"Thanks, you guys."

"Glad to do it." Bob tapped the neck of Joe's bottle with his own.

Roberta took a drink. "You're selling the house?"

"Already listed." Joe squeezed her hand. "Hired somebody to clean and paint it. I'm never going in that room again."

Bert looked at Bob. He shook his head. She turned to Joe. "But you already had a death, in the hallway. When Weigel died."

"This is different."

Bob looked away.

"I'm not arguing, Joe," she said. "But really, you got through that."

"Not this time."

"You're the strongest man I know, Joe. You got over Cathy--"

Bob set the bottle down hard on the table. "He'll be fine, Bert."

Joe saw the expression on her face. "Maybe if I get out of this house and leave Stradford. Clear my head."

"But the school? How are you?"

Bob squared himself to her. "I thought I told you. The Board gave him sick leave through the end of the school year. Hadn't accrued enough, but they mysteriously found him the days."

Joe nodded.

"See, it's all good. What he needs is to get away." He drank some beer.

"I don't want to be insensitive, I usually leave that to Bob." Bert looked from one to the other. "What about the police?"

Yeah, I'm the insensitive one, Bob thought. "That's even better," he said. "They dropped the charges."

Joe spoke to his hands. "One minute I'm in jail, the next in the Marriott."

"That's great, Joe." Bert smiled encouragingly.

"They didn't want to talk about it." Joe finished the beer.

"They want it covered up, don't they?"

"It's the Stradford way, darling, obla-di-obla-da." Bob rubbed his hands together. "So, can we help you pack?"

"I'll call you when I'm ready."

"Great." Bob stood up and looked to Bert. She

turned to Joe. "I know I'm prying, really, but what about Lexan?"

Bob glared at her. "Come on, Bert."

"It's OK, Bob," Joe said, and his friend sat back down. "They're not charging her either, but they want to talk to her."

"Since you didn't kill the Mayor, she must have, right?"

Bob slapped his hand on the table.

Bert jumped. "They're going to ask me about it at school. I want to say the right thing."

"Bert, ask me anything you want." Joe met her eyes. "As to not charging her, yeah, they want it covered up. Only thing that makes sense."

"Happy now?"

"Men." She furrowed her brows. "How can I be happy? I don't know where she is. I mean, Joe's here and that's great. But."

"But where is she?" Joe pursed his lips. "Safe, I hope."

"Any word?"

"No." Joe looked at the crabapple tree he and Lexan had planted in the front yard. "Here's what happened, and to a certain extent, it's why I'm fine." He picked at the label. "You know our relationship has been in trouble. She had her bags packed, literally. The first thing I noticed after I woke was her bags gone."

"I'm sorry, I don't mean--"

"No, it's OK. We had a great talk. I apologized. She apologized. On the same page. Then Kimberly shows up and all hell breaks loose."

"Bert, come on, let's leave him alone."

"No, Bob, that's the thing. I felt really good about our talk. Really close to her." He looked at his friends. "At least she's away and safe. Hopefully." He shook his head. "I'm fine. I just can't stay here anymore."

Lexan always ran, but this time it was different. This time she wasn't running away from pain. This time she was running to inflict it. To hurt as she had been hurt. To kill as she had learned to kill.

Lex knew where he would be. Where he held court, where he gloated, where he bragged about hurting people. Where she would kill him. She pulled her car into a space across from the bar and turned off the engine.

The bar stood on a corner clinging to the streets that framed it. Old, like the rest of the neighborhood, a bar below, and the apartment she hated above. The door was set in a rounded turret that rose to a conical point. The three windows of her mother's room looked onto the intersection from above the door. Lexan's tiny room was down the hall.

He wasn't her father, but he shared her mother's room. Lexan lowered the seat back and her eyes fell shut.

First she noticed her mother crying. Drying the dishes, doing the wash, drinking a cup of coffee. The crying didn't bother Lexan, for when she hugged her, she would stop and say she was fine. It became normal.

Then he noticed Lexan. Sly comments and lewd words. Touches that could be taken two ways. Personal space infringed. Doors opened accidently. Personal space invaded. Touches that could be taken only one way.

Visits in the night. Threats. Cigarette burns. A drink to calm his nerves. A drink to ignore her nerves. Threats. A hand over her mouth. Alcohol fumes. Her legs wrenched apart. Crushing weight. Tearing pain.

"Go ahead and tell her, she won't believe it."

He was right. Her mother didn't believe her.

"You're just like your mother." His grin a toothy leer.

Her mother lowered her eyes and said, "I love him."

Lex was older when she noticed the bruises on her mother's arms. The crying was normal as far as Lexan could tell, but still, she wanted to see her mom happy. Lexan believed her stories that she had tripped, had drunk a second glass of wine, was getting clumsy.

The girl believed her mother until she inadvertently opened the bathroom door and saw her stepping from the shower. Her back and legs were covered in blue, green and purple blotches. Red scabs dotted her shoulders and upper arms. Her mother covered herself with a towel and said nothing. They didn't speak about it.

When Lexan came home early from school and found him raising his fist over her mother's face, she couldn't move. She stood paralyzed as he brought his fist down, again, again, again. Lexan ran.

When Lexan returned, her mother lied about it. Said she'd tripped. Lexan told her mother she had seen it. Her mother denied it. "Besides, what happens in our family is nobody's business but our own."

They didn't tell friends, neighbors or family. Lexan

continued smiling in her softball pictures, her band pictures, her mathlete pictures. The same smile; no one knew. They never spoke about it.

Lexan stirred in the uncomfortable car seat. The second time she found him hurting her mother, she ran at the man. She flailed wildly, uselessly. He calmly backhanded her across the face. Lexan ran to her room. She shut her door and covered her ears. She could still hear the blows and her mother's cries.

Several months passed. Lexan was late getting home and found her mother crumpled at the foot of the stairs, a suitcase and clothes strewn around the circular foyer. Her neck bent crookedly. She was too late to save her mother.

It was ruled an accident. Her mother was a known drinker. He lied that he had been at work in the bar. Customers covered for him. He feigned sorrow. He smirked at her across the desk in the police station. She ran.

She ran through social services. She ran though foster care. She ran till she was eighteen.

She ran through college. She worked three part-time jobs. She got her teaching certificate. She committed to nothing except her vow to protect children. She had failed to protect her mother.

Joe hadn't been in the rectory office of Holy Angels for months, but it felt familiar. He sat on the leather sofa, Fr. Hastings on the matching chair. The soft glow from the lamp on the end table fell on both of them. Coffee gurgled through the pot. The statue of St. Michael the

Archangel stood outside the office window. Helmeted, armored, a sword in one hand, the scales of justice in the other. Joe looked away.

Hastings set down two mugs. "Glad you stopped in, Joe. I was getting tired of following you around."

"I wasn't avoiding you."

The priest sipped the coffee. "Kinda looked like it."

Joe drew his glance away from the statue again. "I couldn't talk to myself. Didn't see the point in blubbering to you."

"That's how you get to what makes sense, Joe, you know that. We did it before."

"I know. It worked. I got through Cathy's death, and what good did it do me? More death, more killing. Lexan's gone." Coffee slopped onto the table as he picked up the cup.

"As long as you're strolling down memory lane, why not throw in the part about you being the avenging angel?"

"Take your best shot, Jerry." Joe's eyes snapped to the priest. "Damn it, I tried to do the right thing! You know I did!"

The priest waited for his friend's anger to simmer. "You're a noble man, Joe. You tried to do good."

"And all your God gave me was a ration of shit."

"He's my God now?"

"He doesn't seem to be on my side. Took Cathy, took Lexy, I don't know where she is or if she's even alive. Got me shot, beat up, thrown in jail."

Hastings counted to five. "Yet here you are."

Joe returned his eyes to the priest. "Here I am."

"Why?"

"I don't know. It worked before." His words faded.

Fr. Hastings let out a breath. "It did. You came here with a problem and left with a solution. Pretty straightforward."

"Now look at me."

"I am." He sipped some coffee. "What I see is a guy whose solution didn't work, and now he's blaming God for it."

"My solution? You led me to it. Maybe it was God, but I came out of this room thinking it was all set."

Hastings nodded his head toward the statue outside. "St. Mikie?"

"Yeah, I sought justice. That's one of the Virtues, right?"

The priest nodded.

"It was God's work I was aiming at. I had the power to do something good."

"Turned to shit, didn't it."

Joe shook his head. "Sounds like you knew it would."

Hastings opened his hands palms up.

"You let me go out there and you knew it wouldn't work!" he yelled.

Hastings finished his coffee and carefully set down the cup. "First off, you're talking in absolutes. Nothing perfectly good followed your decision, and nothing perfectly evil happened." He saw Joe's expression. "I know, there was more bad than good. Surely.

"Second, it was not my decision and it was not

God's decision. It was yours."

"He led me to it. You did, too."

"I never told you to pick up the sword, symbolically or otherwise."

The statue caught the corner of Joe's eye. "But to defeat evil we have to fight it."

"Literally?"

Joe didn't respond. Hastings said, "Literal defeat, like Michael standing on the dragon outside, is only accomplished in heaven. The fight is the daily struggle to be kind to others."

Joe sat quietly several seconds. "I thought I had God's power in my hand."

Hastings held up his hand. "It's all about how to use it. We'll get to that later."

Joe let out a frustrated breath. "So what's the bottom line?"

"Wrong question. The bottom line is only important at the end. You're still alive." The priest's face tightened. "Look, Joe, you were trying to do the right thing. That's fine. Don't stop."

"Then what am I supposed to do?"

"Stop keeping score. Four good deeds doesn't get you four gold stars. This isn't a game."

"If it is, I'm losing."

Hastings kneaded his fingers. "Losing them does not mean God is angry at you."

"Sure as hell feels like it."

"Bad choice of image, but I'm sure it does."

Joe smiled weakly. "Thanks, Jerry, but this doesn't make a whole lot of sense to me."

Hastings nodded. "Get away from here if you can, and think about it."

"Leaving tonight. Someplace warm." Joe pursed his lips. "Sorry for the angry words."

The priest waved them away. "Stop in for a chat when you get back. I don't think we're done here."

"If I come back." Joe stood. "It's a lot. I don't know."

"I'll be here, my friend." Hastings clasped him in a half hug. "Keep your ears open, would you? I don't think He's finished talking to you."

She awoke in her car when the sun hit her face. She stretched, then raised the seatback. She had solved a problem in Stradford by killing the Mayor, now she would kill him.

The neighborhood was showing signs of gentrification; the bar was stubbornly resisting. She kept her eyes away from her old room upstairs and climbed the three stone steps. The door protested as she drew it open.

"Couldn't stay away," his voice phlegmier but definitely his.

Her shoulders tightened. A couple of drunks sprawled on the bar. Two women slumped at a table in the corner.

"I knew you'd come back."

"No, you didn't." Her right hand squeezed the baggie in her pocket.

"Sure I did." He coughed wetly. "You're just like your mother."

She spun around. "No, I'm not! I--"

He was a lumpy pile of flesh in a wheelchair. A few strands of white hair wandered across his pock-marked scalp. One hand lay in his lap, the gnarled fingers of the other clung to the joy stick. Half of his face drooped uselessly. The eye in the other side glared at her. He spat something onto the floor.

"You don't look well," she said.

He nodded her to follow and aimed the motorized chair at an empty table. She sat down.

"I know why you're here," he said.

He had been a big man, athletic, long limbed. He never could have fit into the chair. "You can't know," she said.

"Ruth, clean up this mess." He waved his good hand at the waitress, then glared at his step-daughter. "You're here to do me a favor."

A moldy scent wafted from him. "You think I'd do you a favor?"

"Ruth! A beer and a white wine." He smirked.

"You killed my mother!"

His laugh rasped into a wet cough. "Never charged me, did they?"

Lexan's mind raced as she stuffed some bills into the waitress's hand.

"Hey, my place, my treat." He lowered his bulbous lips to the straw and slurped. Ruth scuttled away.

"I don't want anything from you." Lexan looked at the beer and fingered the powder in the baggie.

"Don't get all pissy, girl," he said. "You're here to help me, that's what I'm saying. Like your mother would."

Lexan tamped down her anger and slowed her speech. "She hated you. You killed her. I hate you."

"She always did what I wanted her to."

Lexan had ground up some of the pills Hector had sold her. She could easily slip the powder into his beer.

"You burned me. You, you abused me."

"Your mother liked it."

"You're insane." She managed to keep her chin from quivering. "You cannot believe I would do anything to help you."

"You will," he leered. "You'll help me die."

His laugh turned into a coughing choke. Ruth rushed to him and turned the wheelchair away. Lexan's fingers ran across the burn marks on her arms. She looked at his beer glass.

"Call 911! He's having one of his fits!" Ruth was sopping drool and phlegm with a bar rag. His face had turned ashen. Behind her someone wheeled up an oxygen tank.

Lexan stepped back. She felt the drugs in her pocket and saw the waiting beer glass. She could do it now when no one was looking. The fool would drink the beer as soon as he could breathe. He'd be dead in a couple hours. If his heart was as wrecked as the rest of him, probably quicker than that.

Or Lexan could let him die slowly. It wouldn't be as satisfying. It would be like Joe ramping up to kill Weigel then not doing it. She understood now what that felt like. The man would linger longer in pain. She set the empty wine glass next to his beer and spoke directly into his ear. "I will not help you die."

CHAPTER FIFTY

Lance McCracken chatted with the clerk about the books he had just purchased for longer than he normally would. He had feigned forgetting his cell to help her remember the time; they would surely ask her about the time. He finally finished discussing the leitmotiv in *Gone Girl*, as if there were one, and took his purchases through Gramercy Books into Kittie's, the coffee shop next door. He ordered a red berry scone and decaf-skim latte, schmoozing this clerk like the other. He plopped into a stuffed chair by the window and opened one of the books. The book wasn't to read, it was a prop. Governor Stanic was dying and he wanted to be able to verify his whereabouts.

He had killed the Governor of Ohio for several reasons. Some of them he would admit to; others lay deep inside where he wasn't sure about them himself. He had learned to be "a bottom-line kind of guy" by working for Stanic, and now it would serve him well.

He had to kill the governor, because the governor was weak. Stanic's paper trail was so obvious even that idiot teacher could follow it to Columbus. He'd returned the school funding to Stradford, and now wasn't running for re-election. Lance would do his job and write the teary eulogy or fight the pitchfork-wielding mob. But either way it went, Stanic was out, and Lance wasn't taking the fall for him or with him.

The scone was dry and stale. He'd been told that's how they were supposed to taste. Why couldn't they put a sweet glaze on them? Lance sipped the latte and turned the page of the book he wasn't reading. Besides, he told himself again, by doing it this way, his mentor would be spared either ignominy. He took another sip and wondered if the barista had used the pink sweetener instead of the yellow.

It was all true, but in his heart he knew the real reason was jealousy. The old man had thrown himself at every available skirt he could find. He'd explained it to Lance as a course in power politics, as if he'd actually believed it. He'd put up with it because at the end of the day or the end of the romance, Stanic always returned attention to him. Lance didn't mind the Governor's wife, she was merely a piece of stage craft. Kimberly, however, was the last straw.

That stupid bitch from the suburbs. Dumb as a rock. Brassy, cheap, low-class. He whisked crumbs from his trousers. The Sturm and Drang had been a powerful aphrodisiac, and Stanic had fallen hard for her. He pacified her with money from the state test materials. For what? Kimberly was only holding them back.

Lance slammed the book closed. Then she'd had the gall to die and leave us on the hook. We couldn't even pin it on her. His hands shook as he dipped the scone in the latte and into his mouth. When you get right down to it, he used me like he used her. More so. I was the sounding board and the whipping boy. I stuck my neck out for him, he got the praise. I did the work and he got the status, the money, the Mansion. He forced a six-second cleansing breath.

Lance checked the time again as the barista appeared at his table. He shook his head no as she removed his plate and the paper cup. She nodded, and he continued scrolling through e-mails. Enough time had passed. He left a tip big enough to be noticed.

He punched the ignition and carefully checked his mirrors. A traffic accident would be another way to verify his whereabouts, but he didn't need the hassle. Thommy's body would be starting to cool on the bathroom floor. They'd find the note he'd written and believe it to be the governor's own. He'd signed Stanic's official correspondence for years.

He drove down the tree-lined main street of Bexley past Capital University. They would find the clues he'd left for them, but they wouldn't find the poison he'd used. He began working on the expressions he would need when speaking with the police, his sad, caring, and vulnerable expressions.

* * *

This place really is a dump, Garrett Mangione thought. Long, open shoebox with the warmth of a warehouse. He couldn't imagine Pamela had suggested the place until her hand on his thigh reminded him. She gets off on this stuff.

The stuff at hand was taking a meeting with the new drug guys. Since the proclamation of the end of the Bratva, Stradford needed to make other arrangements in a timely manner to continue the traffic for everyone's sake. He and Pamela took their new responsibilities seriously.

Shutting down the drug trade was out of the question. There was too much demand, there was too much money. The question was how to return to the days when drugs were available but out of sight. The problem wasn't the deaths or the violence or the despair that surrounded the drugs. It was the disturbance of the peace, the publicity that followed the drug trade and reduced Stradford to any other place. To lose the specialness that the people of Stradford prided themselves on would be intolerable.

Mangione stifled a gasp as the pressure from her hand increased. He turned his face to her, but she wouldn't meet his gaze. Bitch thinks she's in control. But hey, it certainly doesn't hurt.

A thin Hispanic with a thin moustache slid into the booth across from them. Pamela's hand clenched. "I believe I have business to discuss with you."

Mangione waved to Bernie behind the bar. Pamela reached her free hand across the table. "I'm Pamela Holmgren. I like to do business face to face. Your name is?"

"Eugenio, ma'am." He kept his eyes on hers as he pressed her hand to his lips. Mangione edged away from her and made eye contact with Kennedy nursing a drink at the bar.

Pamela retrieved her hand and brought it to her mouth to cover the blush. She took a breath. "I believe it to be in our best interests to continue the terms of our relationship as they have been."

Eugenio shook his head.

"The rate stands." Mangione dropped his hand to his pistol and leaned toward the smaller man.

Eugenio raised his eyes to Mangione's face. He waited several seconds, then said, "I think you misunderstand me, Jefe."

"You understand my gun, don't you?"

The young Mexican spread open his hands. "My friends and I do not need to carry guns. We don't threaten. We don't fight over turf because we own it."

Mangione grinned at Pamela. "They mow it, they just don't fight over it. Isn't that right?"

"Garrett, be nice."

Eugenio kept his face calm. "Violence isn't good for business, Jefe. My employers don't allow anything to get in the way of business." He smiled. "I am here because Hector has gone back home."

Pamela started to speak, but Mangione glared across the table. "Why did he leave? Didn't he like making money?"

"He did and now he's spending it in Mexico." The young man glanced around the bar. "It was time for him to go. Now it's my time."

Pamela put her hand on the policeman's arm. "Better to leave before getting caught."

The young man nodded. "That's part of our business model."

"What else can you tell us, Eugenio?"

"He better be telling us the money stays the same."

"We are here to make money. At the present rate, we both will." Eugenio looked from one to the other. "Our way is to stay out of sight, carry only small amounts of product, no guns, no violence."

"Less work for me." Mangione turned to Pamela. "After all the shootings, this is a good plan."

She kept her eyes on the man across the table. "Tell us more about your employers."

Eugenio's face tightened and he looked older. "You won't see them, just like you won't see us. We don't look like drug dealers. We don't drive beaters. We look like we live here."

"I like that," she said. "And the small amounts keep you out of jail."

"Often that is so, Mrs. Holmgren."

"Wait, a second." Mangione leaned toward the drug dealer. "If you only carry so much product, how can you sell enough to make any money?"

Eugenio lifted his cell phone. "With this. Customers call, we deliver the product. Safe places like the Mall"

"Customer service," Mangione grinned. "How about discounts? You got those, too?"

"We do. We offer discounts to good customers."

"It's just like selling pizza." He beamed at Pamela. "This guy is OK. I'm in."

"If you're sure." She kept her eyes on the young Mexican for several seconds before extending her hand.

CHAPTER FIFTY-ONE

A pair of EMT's forced Lexan to step back as they ministered to her dying stepfather. She twisted between them to keep her eyes on his. He tried to speak; she thought he said her name, but an oxygen mask was jammed across his mouth and she wasn't sure. What could he possibly have to say to her? Sorry I raped you? Sorry I beat you? Sorry I killed your mother?

"Please, Miss, let us do our job," a paramedic said and gently pulled her to the side.

She slumped into a booth and watched them pound his chest to re-start his heart. She had taken the course and recognized the pattern of compressions the EMT was using, but couldn't remember the song the trainer had used. Ruth handed her a glass of water and sat down with her. "Maybe this time," she said.

Lexan looked at her dumbly.

"Maybe this time he dies."

Lexan took the glass from her lips. "Has he been ill a long time?"

"Long as I been working here," the waitress said. "Son of a bitch had the EMTs on speed dial."

Two of the paramedics wrestled the man onto a gurney, like returning a beached whale to the ocean.

"Thought he was dead three, maybe four times." Ruth's eyes followed him. "Keeps coming back."

"Heart?"

She looked closely at Lexan. "Doesn't have one of those. Bad lungs, kidneys, busted liver. You name it."

"Was he on medication?"

"Too bull-headed to take it."

"Too mean to die."

Ruth put her hand on Lexan's. "Maybe not." Her eyes narrowed. "Why are you here? You his kin?"

The EMTs maneuvered the gurney through the door and down the stairs. Lexan stood up, then turned her gaze to the old waitress. "No, ma'am. I am not related to that man at all."

She watched them load her stepfather's body into the ambulance and drive off. No siren, no lights. She fingered the baggy in her coat pocket and climbed into her car. There was no reason for her to stay.

This time Lexan ran east. She didn't have a destination in mind; she followed the urge to move. She had to get away from here, from Stradford, from drugs and death. And from Joe. A vague notion of warmth became a picture of a sunny beach. A place she could insulate herself.

Joe did have a plan. Not one he had thought of himself; he followed the suggestion of Fr. Jerry. A seminary buddy of his had a summer place on the east coast that he could use, and since his sick leave covered the last months of the school year, he agreed. He turned off the ignition and looked through the windshield at the Christian Conference Center in the center of Bethany Beach, Delaware.

He picked up the house key at the desk inside, and walked down First St. toward the ocean. The April sun was not summer-strong, but much warmer than the sun behind the leaden skies of Northeast Ohio. He sat down on a bench and watched the small waves curling onto shore. He felt the muscles in his neck loosen.

His head jerked and his eyes snapped open. He heard a crowd of kids tugging their parents toward the water, and he laughed. Not a hearty laugh, not much more than a giggle, but a sound he hadn't made for a long time. He drove his car a few blocks to the summer house and schlepped his luggage up the porch steps. He dropped onto a rocking chair and discovered an even better view of the ocean.

Lexan refused to stop and rest until she had powered herself through the freezing rain and twisting turns of the Pennsylvania Turnpike. South of Breezewood the weather broke; she found a small motel and slept a few hours. It was late morning when she skirted Washington, and crossed the Chesapeake Bridge in the early afternoon. The Delmarva Peninsula stretched before her, beckoning her to the ocean.

Her un-plan was to get to the beach and work her way south until she found a job in a quiet place. She knew she needed to keep herself busy and was sure easy summertime work would be available. It had been before.

She hoped she'd find a quiet place before reaching Ocean City. There would certainly be work on its lengthy boardwalk, but it would be packed with tourists. A good crowd to hide in, but she preferred to hide in the quiet.

Her un-plan didn't work in Rehoboth, where the man at Dogfish Head Brewing told her he was looking for someone younger, nor in Dewey Beach where the man never raised his eyes to her face. She guessed he wanted a server with bigger boobs. Or one without a cast on her forearm and fading bruises on her face. She sighed and continued south on US1 through the Delaware Seashore State Park.

The sign leading into Bethany Beach described the little town as "A haven of rest for quiet people." She took that as an omen, and after seeing the small number of tourists strolling the short main street, she parked and joined them. Small shops with beachwear, artists' studios, restaurants, only a couple of bars, a bookstore and several candy and ice cream shops. A place for families, not college kids on spring break.

The shops along the boardwalk were similar to those on the street. She sat on a bench and warmed herself in the sun, letting the quiet seep in. She nodded, stood up and walked until she found a 'help wanted' sign. She removed it from the door and entered the Taffy

Shoppe. Her instincts proved accurate; ten minutes later she had a job, a tip on a small apartment and a safe place to hide.

Joe left his car in the driveway and walked the couple short blocks to the town center. Morning sun sparkled off the crests of the tiny waves. He saw a cluster of women with baskets collecting shells and a man with a fishing pole. A few blankets dotted the beach. Where the boardwalk intersected Garfield Parkway, the main street, he turned right and glanced at the salt water taffy in the windows of the Shoppe on the corner. Moments later he pulled open the blue door of Bethany Beach Books.

He had made a deal with himself. He would give up being an angel. His fantasy of bringing justice to the world remained a lofty and noble goal, but had nearly killed him. His compromise was to keep his fantasies, but keep them in in books where they belonged, not in his actual life. The woman at the bookstore suggested Robert Jordan's "The Wheel of Time" series. "It's one of those perpetual fights between good and evil," she'd said. He'd devoured the first book. He paid her for the second, *The Great Hunt*, and brought it with him to the beach.

Joe's plan worked for an hour or so. He got into the book, it was comfortable on the beach chair he had found in the house, and the sun warmed him. Now the beach was filling up. Parents dragged wagons full of children, chairs and umbrellas onto the beach. Frisbees sailed around him, squeals of laughter punctuated the breeze. He closed the book and wondered where Lexan was. He checked the time on his cell. When he started to think of her, it was time for a drink.

Lexan had time for a run before starting her shift at the Taffy Shoppe. In the fifteen minutes it took her to reach the pier, the beach had changed from peacefully empty to rapidly filling. She kept to the town side and managed to dodge most of the blankets and people. After a quick shower she entered the Shoppe, wearing her pale blue uniform tee.

"Right on time, I see," Ted said. The man who had hired her had a comb-over and a bit of a paunch. Looking for someone reliable, he'd said, after she'd assured him her cast wouldn't get in her way. They left the other clerk, Susie, at the counter and went into the back room. "Couple of things to go over," he said as he held the curtain for her.

The taffy was made further back in the building. She could see machines and several paper-hatted workers through the smudged windows. The rest of the room was what she'd expected: shelves with different flavors of taffy, wrapping papers, a work table and a computer. What he told her was expected as well: pricing details, special offers, hours and office procedures. Pretty standard stuff except for the warning about the Bubble Gum flavor.

"If anybody asks about it, have them see me," he told her. "It's no big deal, but it's a family recipe, and we want to keep it secret."

"Your secret is safe with me, Ted." Lexan shot him a smart salute and he grinned.

"I think you'll do fine."

Susie proved to be a capable worker and good

teacher. After an hour or so Lex was filling boxes of taffy, explaining the flavors and recommending the best. She had no idea a little store like this could sell so much taffy. By the time her shift ended, shadows were creeping toward the water and she was tired.

A full day of human interactions had wired her up and she knew she'd never be able to sleep. It was either sit alone in a bar and drink, or have another run. She took the healthy choice and minutes later was pounding down the sand.

This time the running didn't free her mind, but directed it to Joe. She knew that leaving was the right thing to do. She'd already been hurt, and staying would hurt Joe, too. He didn't deserve it.

Joe tossed a tip onto the bar and slipped off the stool to the floor. He grabbed his book, and found the beach chair he'd left by the door. Abby held the door for him as she always did at the Mango Bar, and he winked at her as he always did. He kept his balance by holding onto the rail as he descended from the second floor deck.

He took a deep breath. Cool enough for a jacket, he thought, and increased his pace. Stomach full, pleasantly buzzed, he controlled his weaving and turned around the Taffy Shoppe onto the boardwalk. Idiots were still jogging on the beach, and parents were still trying to herd their children, but he didn't let it bother him. Soon he was nodding off in the porch rocker.

Several weeks passed. Joe knew he was drinking too much, but told himself he wasn't. He also told himself drinking was better than thinking about Lexan. There were fourteen books in the series he was reading, and he kept his stray thoughts on the Shadow and the Dragon Reborn and the One Power.

She fell into a rut working at the Taffy Shoppe and jogging. She did it deliberately to control her thinking. This was better than running away and she hoped it would work for her. She volunteered to work as many hours as she could and raised her fitness level.

They would have spent the rest of the summer like this if two things hadn't happened to Lexan. First, the prohibition of Bubble Gum taffy got to her. There were 52 flavors on the menu and she could see no earthly reason why she wasn't allowed to sell the 53rd. Ted sold the Bubble Gum and Susie did too, when Ted wasn't around. One night she decided to find out why.

She was working the late shift and would close up at 10:00 pm. She hadn't been trusted to work by herself the first month, but she'd made herself valuable and now was working alone. She put the 'Closed' sign in the window and stepped behind the curtain into the store room. The cooks were finished for the night and the factory floor dark. She pulled a box of Bubble Gum from the shelf and opened it.

It was a regular pound box of taffy. The small round pieces twisted into wax paper wrappers. She snorted a breath and poked around. Looked like every other box she'd opened. Someone rattled the handle on the front door and she jumped, spilling the box onto the floor. She rushed to the front, pulling the curtain behind her.

"We're closed!" she yelled to the two faces pressed against the glass. "Sorry!"

"Come on, we want some Bubble Gum!"

"Open at ten tomorrow." She checked the lock and turned off the light.

Too much of a coincidence, she thought as she made sure the curtain was drawn. Must be something here. She dropped down to the floor and looked at the strewn pieces of taffy.

She unwrapped one and bit into it. Tasted like bubble gum. Pink, like the gum in baseball cards. Sticky. She spat it into her hand and tossed it away. She felt the next dozen. Color the same, hardness the same. The next one squished. She unwrapped the paper and recoiled at the smell.

Dirty sox. Like the brownish powder she'd planned to kill her stepfather with. She wet a finger and tasted a tiny amount. Heroin. She re-wrapped it, re-filled the box, and carefully returned it to its spot on the shelf.

She would leave Bethany Beach tomorrow. She'd get her paycheck and leave before someone found the drugs and pulled her into the same thing she was running from. She checked the door from the outside and was taking a calming breath when the second thing happened: Joe was strolling down the boardwalk. She broke into a run.

Tonight Joe was in a booth at Bethany Blues. He rotated this place with Mango's and Baja Beach House, and chose seats on the deck or in a booth or at the bar to convince himself he wasn't drinking too much. He was

OK without her, almost OK anyway. Just one piece nagged at him. He usually got to that part of the conversation with himself after four beers or two Irish whiskies. He spun the large ice cube around the tumbler and set it down.

If Kimberly hadn't arrived and interrupted us, I'd be free, he told himself. I apologized to her, and she was about to open up to me. He took the last sip. Either way would have been fine. She coulda told me to go to hell and leave, and it would be over. She coulda said great, let's get together, I love you, and that woulda been great, too. Greater.

He waved the waitress to bring him the bill. But no, she never got to that point. I'm still waiting for her to say yes or no. He stepped carefully through the tables and retrieved his beach chair and book at the door.

That's no freaking way to live. Yes or no, in or out. He stumbled on the last step but caught himself and worked his way through the crowds of families to the boardwalk. Maybe I should call Jerry. I am drinking too much.

A pack of skateboarders clattered past, and he grabbed a bench to keep from falling down. He turned to yell at them and didn't see Lexan leaving the Taffy Shoppe.

Lexan ran away from him. Thoughts pounded through her head as her feet pounded the boardwalk--he's here--I won't hurt him anymore--heroin in the taffy--I have to leave. She ran past her apartment and only turned back when she couldn't run anymore. She stood in the shower until she stopped crying, then pulled out her suitcase and packed it.

She didn't sleep that night. She waited till 9:30, threw her belongings into the car and parked as close to the Shoppe as she could.

"You're not scheduled to work," Susie said. "You're on nights."

"I am, but something came up. Where's Ted?"

Susie nodded toward the curtain without looking up from her phone.

"Ted?"

The manager turned away from the shelves of taffy boxes. "Oh, Lexan, what can I do for you?"

"Is it possible to get my check early?"

The man frowned. "I usually pay after the bank closes. You know that."

"Something came up and--"

The bell over the door jangled. "For you, Ted," Susie called.

Ted looked past her. "Get out," he said.

"But my check--"

"At the start of your shift, Lexan, best I can do. Scoot."

Lexan squeezed past a heavy-set man in the doorway and out onto the boardwalk. She slumped down on a bench. The beach was filling up earlier now that summer had arrived. It would thin out for a couple hours around noon, than fill up again when the sun wasn't as hot.

She wondered if she could get by without the paycheck. She decided to empty her bank account so she could leave as soon as she got it. She closed the bank app on her phone. The heavy-set man was leaving the Shoppe. He took a step and collided with a kid on a bike and dropped his shopping bag. She passed him as he was cursing and grabbing for his things. He looked both ways, then carefully slid a box of Bubble Gum taffy into the paper bag.

She paused in a storefront, then followed him.

Joe stopped at the foot of the stairs to Bethany Beach Books and spoke to the man at the card table on the sidewalk. A local author trying to sell his book. Joe shook his head in sympathy then dodged two more skateboarders racing past. "Where are their parents?" the author asked.

"Not doing their jobs," Joe replied. "You take credit cards?"

"No, sorry."

Joe checked his wallet. "I'll be back when I have some cash." The author nodded sadly. Joe plunged through the stream of people trudging toward the beach, and stopped at the light where he could cross Garfield Parkway.

He heard the thump before he saw what happened. A man flopped to the pavement, a van screeched to a stop. Somebody with a shopping bag brushed Joe and stepped over the victim. Voices screamed from inside the van. The mass of people flowed around them or gawked from the sidewalk. The man tried to rise, but couldn't.

The driver of the van yelled out the window, "I had the right of way!"

A woman behind Joe cried, "Call 9-1-1!"

Joe crouched over the man in the crosswalk; sweat

beaded on his face and he coughed. "You all right?" The man clutched his left side and groaned.

"He's having a heart attack!"

"Give him some room."

Joe laid him flat. Blood ran from the back of his head.

The driver pounded the steering wheel, sirens wailed in the distance, the man stopped breathing.

No one else to help. Joe strained to remember his CPR. Something about ABC. Airway. He loosened the man's collar. The siren was nearer, but not here.

Legs pressed closer. Voices blurred to noise. The man's mouth gaped open. Joe fought back his panic.

Someone's knee grazed Joe's head. His vision sharpened. He pinched the man's nose and breathed into his mouth. Once. Twice. Nothing.

He put his palms on the man's sternum and pushed down, rapidly, ten times. No response.

He forced his fingers into the man's mouth. Airway clear. He breathed into the man again and checked his chest. No movement. He pumped the chest ten more times.

Joe didn't hear the sirens or the crowd. He didn't see the people closing in, only the man's pale face and blue lips. He raised up onto his haunches and forced his weight onto the man's chest. Ten more times.

Don't die! Joe pinched his nose and blew into his mouth. Nothing.

He leaned back. His arms burned. Bodies pushed closer, sirens screamed.

Two hands raised the man's chin and straightened

his neck. "Try it again."

Two more breaths. Hands on the sternum. Faster, two beats per second. His own breathing now tortured panting.

"Whoop whoop whoop whoop, stayin' alive!" Lexan's voice rose above the crowd. Someone sang along. Joe gaped at her. "Don't slow down, you're doing it."

Joe pushed to the beat of the song. Lexan bracketed the man's head in her hands.

The man coughed and pulled his head free. "Don't talk," Joe said and reached his hand to Lexan.

The Squad arrived and EMTs took their places. She helped him stand up and steered him to the ambulance. "Just to check you out," she said.

"I'm fine." He stumbled at the lip of the bright green unit, and she settled onto the floor next to him. He squeezed her hand.

"Pretty good work." She nodded at the dispersing crowd. The EMTs had loaded the man onto a gurney and were strapping him down. He was breathing into an oxygen mask.

"I thought he was going to die."

She put her arm around his shoulder. "We've had enough dying."

He sighed and leaned into her embrace. "More than enough."

CHAPTER FIFTY-TWO

A couple blocks up E. Main St. in Bexley, Ohio, Lance McCracken reached for his latte before realizing he hadn't bought a second cup. He remembered the taste and shook his head awake. He was excited at the prospect of dealing with the Governor's death-slash-suicide and shouldn't be nodding off. He re-focused his eyes and centered the car in the turn lane for Drexel Avenue.

The bald man and his partner watched the vehicle weave to a stop from a shaded parking space across the street. "Won't be long now."

"Long enough. Been watching him more than a year."

"Waiting for orders. You know how it works."

He faced the bald man. "Do you think GOTSOO knew how close he was to buying the farm?"

"Didn't have a clue." He peered at Lance's car. "Still doesn't. He thinks we work for him."

The other man gestured through the smeary windshield. "You know, I got to give the faggot credit. Didn't think he was smart enough to pull it off."

Lance's car lurched around the corner, careened across the sidewalk and slammed into the front of Graeter's Ice Cream. The bald man nodded. "He didn't pull it off."

His partner opened the car door. "No, but he made a good run at it. Covered his bases pretty well."

The RT leader followed. "Not well enough." Through the broken window, Lance's lifeless body slumped over the steering wheel. "You'd think a guy that uses poison would know enough to look for it."

"I have to say, Lieutenant Kramer, your office is really a dump." Agent Canfield gestured with his arm. "A dump in the fog. A foggy dump."

Kramer didn't quite smile. "But it's my dump."

"Last man standing." Canfield didn't smile either.

"That your official sit-rep?"

"I think the fog's a metaphor. Besides, now I'm re-assigned to Stradford, there are two of us."

"Three. Mangione assigned me a uniform."

Canfield raised his eyebrows. He had been taken off the narcotics team in Stradford and sent to Youngstown. After the Mayor's death, he was back. Kramer had avoided being fired by Mangione. Now another man was added to their team. Apparently Stradford was serious about the drug problem. "Is that a good thing?"

"We can use the help."

Canfield stared at the policeman. "We do need help."

"You're asking if we can trust him."

The BCI man nodded. "Who is he?"

"The Irish kid. Kennedy"

"You, me and the Mick. What could go wrong?"

Kramer leaned his elbows onto his desk. "Doesn't matter. We'll trust him unless or until."

Canfield completed the axiom in his head. 'Unless or until he screws us.'

"Thing of it is." Kramer waited for the younger man to look up. "We're back to day one. Better armed than before. You're here and maybe Kennedy. Our goal is the same."

"Follow the small fish to the big fish."

"And kill the big fish." Kramer smiled thinly. "Mayor Horvath is gone. The boys from the Hill are gone. The Russians are gone. A new gang will show up and off we go."

Canfield returned the grim smile. "Would be nice to know who's really on our side though, wouldn't it?"

"That would be nice," the Stradford detective said agreeably.

"Also be nice to know why everything got covered up so quickly. The blood is barely dry."

"That one I can answer, Agent Canfield." Kramer folded his hands on his desk blotter. "It's the Stradford way."

CHAPTER FIFTY-THREE

Joe inhaled a lungful of ocean air and cinnamon. He stretched and rolled over to snuggle her, but the bed was empty. Startled, he raised onto his elbow.

"Cathy's not there." Lexan stood naked in front of the balcony.

"What? 'Cathy'?"

"You called me Cathy." Lexan kept her arms around her waist and her back toward him. "It's not the first time."

"I, I'm sorry, Lex, I--" He threw his legs over the side of the bed.

She raised a hand. "No, don't."

His arms slumped to his knees. "Lexan."

She turned from the sliding door and pulled on her robe. "Actually, it makes things easier."

"I don't know what to say."

"There's nothing you can say. We were having sex and you called me by your dead wife's name. Again."

"I don't know why I did that."

"I do." He looked up. She jabbed a hand at her frizzy hair. "You still love her."

"I, do, no I--"

"You do love her, Joe, and you always will. That's what makes it so clear." She brushed past him and yanked open a dresser drawer.

"Can we talk about it?"

"Don't make this harder than it is." She rummaged in the drawer, her back toward him.

"It's not hard, it really isn't."

"What?" She spun around. "It's impossible, Joe."

"Don't say that."

"What am I supposed to do?" Her gray eyes flashed under her dark brows. "I'm not Cathy. I can't be Cathy."

"I don't want you to be Cathy."

"You still love her." She pulled out a bra and panties. "It's not a secret anymore."

"I tried to hide it, but yes, I think I'll always love her."

"That's supposed to make me feel better?" She snorted a breath.

Joe wanted to cup her face in his hands, but was afraid to approach her. "Cathy is dead, and that hurts. A part of her is still in my heart." His voice faltered. "But I love you, Lexan."

"Maybe you think you do, but there's no place for

me here." She clutched the underwear to her chest. "She's gone and you still love her. If I left, you wouldn't love me."

"Yes, I would."

"Bullshit!"

"Bullshit yourself," he said calmly. "You did leave me, and here I am."

The bathroom door slammed shut. He waited a second and followed her. Water was running in the shower. He took a breath and reached for the doorknob. It didn't turn.

Lexan didn't wait for the shower to heat up. She plunged into the freezing stream. It stung and she wanted to cry out but limited the sound to a gasp and a curse. *Does he really think he's an angel? Only an angel could love somebody who ran from him.*

She danced around in the cold water and rubbed feeling into her arms, the goose bumps prickling her fingers. *He didn't follow me here because he loved me. No way. That was a fluke. He doesn't love me.*

The water felt slightly warmer as she rubbed the washcloth over the long bones of her legs. When she ran the cloth over her shoulders, the scars stood out jagged and red against her blueish skin. *Joe can't love me because he doesn't know about me. If he did he'd run or puke.* She hurled the washcloth. It slapped the wall and held for a moment before sliding down. *Or worse; he'd pity me.*

Her tears ran as warm as the water. *Nobody who knows me, loves me. If my mother had loved me, she would have protected me. I let him hurt her and she let* him hurt me. She even denied it happened. Lexan covered her face with her hands and crumpled to the floor of the shower stall.

The water pelted down on her. Plumes of steam rose. My real father left me. My stepfather burnt me. Her muscles constricted. Her hands balled. Jagged blotches of red and black obstructed her vision. She twisted one way, then the other. She drew her legs to her chest and wrapped her arms around. Her fists guarded her face. "He raped me!" The words reverberated on the tile walls and fogged glass.

She heard the words she had screamed. Her vision cleared. Her breathing resumed. She released her fingers, her arms, her legs. She felt the now scalding water and saw how red her skin was. She pulled herself onto her knees away from the torrent.

I couldn't stop him. I didn't let him do it. I couldn't stop him. I tried, I did try. Her feet slid and she jammed her wrist into the wall. He did it to me. She grabbed the bar and levered herself to her feet.

I wish I had saved my mother. I wish I had saved myself. I sound like Joe. He wishes he'd saved Chelsea. He wishes he had killed Weigel and Kim. She adjusted the water and sighed. He says he loves me.

He wants to protect me. He fought for me. He wants to protect everybody, including me. She sluiced the shampoo from her hair and reached for the conditioner. He fights for people who need help. I love that about him. But I don't want him to fight my battles for me; I want him to fight alongside me.

He saved that guy today. She massaged the heavy

liquid through her curls. He didn't think of the risks, he didn't wait for help, he just stepped into the street and revived him.

She rinsed the last of the conditioner out of her hair and turned off the water. He said he loved me. He opened himself up, looked me in the eye and said, "I love you."

Joe looked at the ocean beyond the balcony. Voices reached up to him from the beach, faint and incoherent. A little more than a year since Cathy died. He hadn't sought Lexan out, yet here she was. Their clothes strewn on the floor, the bed rumpled. Here they were.

She burst from the bathroom. Her hair was damp and her face flushed. She stopped in front of him.

"Packing your bag?"

"Easier than carrying stuff in my hands." She dropped her underwear into the open suitcase.

He shook his head. "Where you going?"

"Home." She kept her eyes focused on his.

"Stradford?"

"I'm tired of this place. They're selling drugs with the salt water taffy."

"We, uh, have a few problems at home, too."

"I noticed." She pulled open a dresser drawer. But we're going home."

"We?"

"You and me." Her brows formed a question. "We're a couple, right?"

"I thought we were, we were, but you left, then--"

"Then what?" She hoped the twinkle in her eye wasn't too obvious.

Joe looked through the balcony to the ocean. Waves stubbornly advanced up the beach, oblivious to the sunlight sparkling on their crests and the ebbtide pulling them back. "You said I didn't love you."

"Oh, you love me all right. I just don't need you saving me anymore." She pulled pajamas from the drawer.

The tension drained from Joe's face. "That must have been some shower."

"What do you mean?"

"You went in there one person and came out another."

Lexan dropped the towel and put her hands on her hips. "You got a problem with that?"

He grinned. "Yeah, I do. I can't keep up."

"You're the romantic, do I have to spell it out for you?"

"Yes, please. I thought you were packing to leave."

"You are colossally dumb."

"I am, but what happened?"

"Two things." She snuggled into her negligee and nodded at the bed. "I felt loved."

Joe swallowed. "Except for me calling you Cathy."

Lexan held his eyes and waved that away. "Not important. I know you love me."

"I do." He smiled. "What's the other thing?"

"The guy we saved, remember? He was dead, now he's alive. We did that."

"Together. We did two loving things together."

She pushed the last of her doubt aside and moved her fingers to the wounds on her shoulders. "Can you love a girl with scars?"

"We all have scars, Lex." He wrapped himself around her.

She burrowed into his neck. "Joe, I want to tell you about my stepfather."

He held her closer. "You know my secret. Tell me yours when you're ready, or don't. I love you, Lexan. Either why."

She pulled back to see him. "No one--" she choked. He rubbed her back.

She held his face in her hands. Hers was puffy and red and wet. "Don't you want to know?"

"I do." He kissed her quickly. "But only if you want to tell me."

"No one ever--" Her lower lip quivered.

He rested his forehead on hers. "It can wait," he said softly. "You're worth it."

THE END

ABOUT THE AUTHOR

David Allen Edmonds has retired from the classroom, but teaching is not finished with him. *Indirect Objects* and its predecessor *Personal Pronouns*, are set in the fictional Stradford High School, as are his "Faculty Lounge Stories." He is currently exploring other settings and themes, including science fiction and romantic comedy. He lives in NE Ohio with his wife Marie Mirro Edmonds wishing the pandemic were over and they could hug their grandchildren. Visit him on Facebook, Twitter, Linked In and Goodreads or at www.davidallenedmonds.com

Reviews play an important role in publishing, especially for Indie Authors. Please leave an honest review of *Indirect Objects* at http://www.amazon.com/review/create-review?&asin=0998546631

BOOK CLUB DISCUSSION QUESTIONS

1. Why do you believe the author chose the title, *Indirect Objects*? Does it have any meaning other than the grammatical? How does it relate to the characters and plot?

2. There are several plotlines in this book. Are they complementary or do they detract from each other? Do they fit into an overall theme? Is the pace appropriate?

3. Consider the character of Joe's friend, Bob McCauley. What is his role in solving the mystery? Is he more than the comic relief? Is he jealous of Joe?

4. Several passages in the novel contain discussions about the roles of women and men. Are the women in *IO* strong enough to break through the 'glass ceiling'? Does the distribution of power motivate their behavior? Do the men or women use their sexuality for advantage?

5. Joe opens the book as the Avenging Angel, believing he can save Lexan and others. Does his attitude change? Can he save their relationship by saving her?

6. Does Joe convince Lexan to stay with him? Can he convince her to be vulnerable and trust him, or must she decide that for herself?

7. There are many murders in this book. Why do you think that is? What motivates the characters to kill? Do these deaths change anything?

8. Does *Indirect Objects* have a fitting conclusion? Are you satisfied at the end? Does it leave the reader wanting more? Will there be another book in the series?

9. Have you read the other book in this series, *Personal Pronouns*? How does this book compare? Is it necessary to have read the first, or is *Indirect Objects* a stand-alone work?

10. Does the cover add to the theme, the plot or the setting? Does the color evoke a response?

11. When Joe visits the book store in Bethany, he selects a volume in the "Wheel of Time" series by Robert Jordan. Is there a reason the author chose this book?

Made in the USA
Middletown, DE
10 October 2020